Excerpts from 666

I lost consciousness...I don't remember exactly what happened. There had been two stewardesses standing next to me; but when I awoke only one was there! I picked her up off the floor and she rushed to the pilot's cabin. When she came out she was ashen white...and put her hand to her mouth to hold a scream.

chapter 1

* * *

I felt a tap on my shoulders as I half knelt on the floor. I turned and saw a hand with a scepter...a scepter with six, sparkling stars... and I arose...and followed.

chapter 2

* * *

"...As much as I hate the word, we need an elective Dictatorship... a benevolent authority who will make the laws and see that they are enforced by military rule if necessary. It is our only hope for survival."

chapter 3

* * *

Rumor had it that the sophisticated cameras could photograph a man lighting a cigarette on a cloudy, rainy night from 100 miles high and could measure the growth of beard on his face.

chapter 4

* * *

"To put it bluntly, George, the one way to somehow resolve our population problems was to eliminate people—not bury them— disintegrate them. Miracle 1 did that for us. Special Bibles were printed..."

chapter 5

* * *

Faye looked so small and helpless as she lay on the hospital cart. The crisp white sheets were tucked around her. We followed an orderly as he pushed her down the long corridor towards the door marked NO ADMITTANCE. BIRTH CORRECTION PERSONNEL ONLY.

chapter 6

* * *

Just as Brother Bartholomew's car passed under the Arc de Triomphe a wild-eyed youth broke through the restraining barriers, a pistol in his hand. Those around him said he was hysterically shouting, "ANTICHRIST...ANTICHRIST!"

* * *

Above are some of the intriguing p̶ first 7 chapters of **666**. But you'll re̶ ing chapters that will keep you in s̶ page of the book!

Excerpts from **1000**

Abel Epstein quickly turned on all orbiting TV stations...The carnage of death that filled the screens was unbelievable...everywhere there appeared to be thousands of blind soldiers being trampled on by stampeding horses.   chapter 1

* * *

She knew what she must do. Tearing the buttons from Abel's shirt she yanked the money belt from around his waist...She flung the belt at the foot of the Throne...In an impassioned plea she cried: "He doesn't deserve to die..."   chapter 2

* * *

Faye was crying as Bill put his arms around her. That action of love triggered a violent outburst. "Get away from me, Bill! Look at you...holier than thou...I'm going to have your baby in seven months...but you're no longer my husband. You're a Resurrected Believer...and what am I...a peon on earth!"   chapter 3

* * *

Bodies looked like ours...but all physical defects gone!   chapter 4

* * *

He could offer Harry no hope. It was beyond that. All he could say was that Carole was judged at the Valley of Jehoshaphat...and while in the milling multitude of millions...Harry passed through the right gate, Carole was ushered through the left gate...escorted by a cordon of guards to Hades to await eternal punishment in the Lake of Fire.   chapter 5

* * *

Bart hushed the audience and stood next to Esther, his arm tightly around her waist...gently kissed her on the forehead and began his speech ..."I hope you are ready for another surprise. We were thinking of getting married in Jerusalem...but Phil Sutherland gave me an idea...the wedding will take place in MEGIDDO!"   chapter 6

* * *

"Do you want to lick the dust off the feet of the Jew? If you don't, then join us in our protest march to Jerusalem!"   chapter 7

* * *

Suddenly his thoughts came back to Sylvia. He had taken her for granted. If only he could hold her in his arms...just once...Suddenly he realized Hades had played a cruel trick on him. For not only now, but throughout eternity he would be plagued constantly with the torment of a MEMORY.   chapter 8

* * *

Above are some of the intriguing portions you will read in the book **1000**. But you'll read much more in this suspenseful novel on the Millennium Period...sequel to the best seller, **666**.

by Salem Kirban

Twenty-first Printing. . . . . April, 1981

Published by SALEM KIRBAN Inc., Kent Road, Huntingdon Valley, Penna. 19006. Copyright © 1970 by Salem Kirban. Printed in the United States of America.

Library of Congress Catalog Card No. 71-109942

ISBN 0-912582-05-7

DEDICATION

"...O Lord, thou art our father; we are the clay, and thou our potter; and we all are the work of thy hand."
(Isaiah 64:8)

The Master Potter, the Lord, often molds our lives by using individuals who help to shape us and our beliefs.

Consequently this book is dedicated to those who have had an important part in shaping my life.

To my mother, now with the Lord, whose quiet love and deep abiding faith in Christ started me seeking the Way of Life.

To my sister, Elsie, and my brother, Lafayette, who joined me in my new found salvation while a youngster at Montrose Bible Conference.

To the many dedicated speakers at Montrose Bible Conference, Montrose, Penna., who were faithful in the preaching of the Word of God.

To The Church of the Open Door (Philadelphia and Fort Washington) and its Pastors, from Dr. Merril T. MacPherson, Rev. Idwal Thomas, Rev. Jack Murray to Rev. Milton P. Achey and Rev. Richard S. Coons for fearlessly preaching the Word of God without compromise.

To Jim Boutilier, now with the Lord, whose untiring zeal for Christ was a tremendous inspiration to me.

To Mrs. Ruth MacPherson whose close walk with the Lord reflected through the years a shining testimony that made me a stronger Christian.

and to

To my dear wife, Mary, whose love and devotion is beyond all measure.

CONTENTS

WHY I WROTE THIS BOOK

It was Hughes Wagner who said,

> If a person is a socialist or a communist, I will know it in twenty-four hours; if he is a member of a labor union, I will know it within a few days; but if he is a member of a Christian church, it may be years before I will ever learn of it.

A majority of the scientific advances have been made in the last 50 years of human history. Man has reached the moon and now is setting his sights on other goals in space.

Yet man still has not learned to cope with his problems right here on earth.

In spite of our technological advances war is more prevalent, unrest is more apparent, moral decay has never been more shocking and famine is more widespread.

Never before in human history has there been a greater need for the Gospel of the saving grace of our Lord Jesus Christ.

And never before in human history has there been, comparatively speaking, less of an effort to reach the teeming billions with the Word of God.

While the Bible still remains the best seller there is a question on whether it is the best read.

One popular author recently stated, "There's more sex in — — — — — — [his current book] than in any of my other books, but paradoxically it's less noticeable. People are getting to take sex for granted."

This particular author is guaranteed $500,000 a year for his novels. Most of his novels are filled with sex in its rawest form and six of his books have sold a total of 70 MILLION COPIES! This is a sad reflection on the depraved conditions of today's world.

Yet in spite of this, missionary activity is slackening off for basically two reasons. Fields that were once open are now closed...there is a growing lack of interest among churches to stress the missionary ministry and the need for evangelism.

Many churches that once contended for the faith have now departed to what they believe are "greener" pastures. They have merged with the goliaths of churchdom...and are now preaching another gospel while excusing themselves with claims of "making the Gospel relevant to this day and age." They have watered down the message of man's sin and God's redemption and have replaced it with a social gospel that attempts to cure the ills of society... with a little sprinkle of Bible thrown in.

Tithes and offerings brought to the church are now being funneled into all types of recreational and social activity to "relate" to today's needs.

The music of the church has shifted from the holy hymns of adoration and praise to the howling hopping of the "new Christian beat" that breeds a surface conversion that many times dies out because of its implantation into stony ground.

It's the popular thing to belong to goliath churches of

today...to "tell it like it is"...to keep up with the times religiously.

In many circles the word FUNDAMENTALIST is sneered at, laughed at and held in contempt. And those churches who would hold true to the Word of God become suddenly unpopular. Satan becomes very active and their very existence is fraught with problems.

Yet in these End Times it will be this David that will emerge the victor as the Goliath of churchdom finds itself looking up from earth wondering where all those odd Fundamental Christians have suddenly disappeared.

They will have an explanation. Make no doubt about it! And gullible people worldwide will fall for their reasoning and follow their leading.

> "And for this cause God shall send them strong delusion, that they should believe a lie" (II Thessalonians 2:11).

And why did I write this book — 666?

While many people will not read the Scriptures or anything that has to do with church materials...most will read a novel...a novel built with suspense, photographs, intrigue ...and a novel that has to do with the FUTURE.

I hope that 666 has all of these elements but most of all it attempts to tell in novel form how events may occur during the Tribulation Period.

How important it is for us today as Christians to obey the admonition:

> "Let your light so shine before men, that they may see your good works, and glorify your Father which is in heaven." (Matthew 5:16)

For God tells us in II Corinthians 4:3, 4

> "...if our gospel be hid, it is hid to them that are lost. In whom the god of this world hath blinded the minds of them which believe not, lest the light of the glorious gospel of Christ, who is the image of God, should shine unto them."

Every born-again Christian should be an *active,* daily witness for his Lord and Saviour.

It is my hope that 666 may be used as a witness. Where many will not accept a tract...or perhaps they will accept a Bible, but not read it...they may gladly accept a novel...one that tells about TOMORROW.

And it is my prayer that in so accepting the novel 666, they will become convicted of their sin, realize their need of our Saviour, and accept Him as their Lord and soon coming King.

The novel 666 is not a pleasant book to read. It is alarming and filled with tragedy. Yet it leaves a Blessed Hope! And while the book vividly paints a frightening picture, the events of time may show that it is not even half as terrifying as the Scriptures themselves reveal.

It was Harold L. Lunquist who said, "They tried to stamp out the fire of God in Jerusalem, but they scattered the embers all over the world."

Now, more than ever before, the world and its pseudo-religionists will attempt to crush the faint burning embers underneath the heel of their social church.

May you and I burn brightly for God in order that the glow of our life might continue burning embers of redeeming light until that day arrives when the King of Light shall appear to claim His own.

Salem Kirban

Huntingdon Valley, Pennsylvania 19006
U.S.A.
January, 1970

ACKNOWLEDGMENTS

To Dr. Gary G. Cohen, Professor of Greek and New Testament at Biblical School of Theology, Hatfield, Pennsylvania, who carefully checked the final manuscript and supplied the Scripture references.

To Bob Krauss, artist, who skillfully designed the front cover and did finished art throughout the book.

To the following photographic sources who made their pictures available for use:

United Press International
Wide World Photos, Inc.
Time Magazine
Black Star
Yoichi R. Okamoto
Aluminum Company of America
NASA
The Matson Photo Service
Magnum Photos, Inc.
Life Magazine
Textron's Bell Aerosystems
National Observer
Joseph F. Morsello
H. Armstrong Roberts

Sovfoto
New York Times
Ewing Galloway
University of Akron
North American Rockwell
Camerapix Nairobi
The Bettmann Archive
American Museum of Natural History
General Telephone & Electronics
American Telephone & Telegraph Company

To The Church of the Open Door for allowing us the use of their sanctuary for photographing several scenes. And to models Sharon Boutilier and Jack Matthews.

To the Batsch Company for excellent craftsmanship in setting the type in this book.

To Dickinson Brothers for printing 666 with all possible speed and quality.

IN EXPLANATION

This book - **666** - is a novel. Therefore much of it is fiction. However, it is important to note that **very much** of it is also **FACT**.

Using the Scriptures as our basis...it is a **fact** that there will be Rapture (when born-again Christians meet Christ in the air in the "twinkling of an eye" 1 Corinthians 15:52, 1 Thessalonians 4:16, 17).

It is a **fact** that after this occurrence there will be at least a seven year period of great trials and tribulations.

This novel - **666** - revealingly takes many of today's little known discoveries and in story form shows how **antichrist** and his associates may apply them to achieve their own sinister goals. Such items as the picturephone, the ruby laser and the flying belt as well as other inventions already exist, although they have not yet always been perfected to the point we relate them in our novel. Where the story line corresponds with prophetic Scripture...actual Bible verses are given next to that paragraph.

What many people do not realize is that events of today are already paving the way for a world dictator! Christians should no longer express blind support. The days are critical and it is time Christians become concerned and active in what they believe. It's time for responsible patriotism. And there is a difference! Blind support allows the leaders of our nation to ban prayer in schools, release a floodgate of pornography and encourages censorship of press and television media.

On the next few pages are true reproductions of actual excerpts taken from the newspapers in 1969. Read them carefully. It may serve to awaken you regarding the End Times...and how close we are to the time when antichrist will be welcomed by the millions who will hail him as their hero and leader.

How important it is for Christians to be ready for the Second Coming of Christ as these days of the End Times approach!

> "Watch therefore, for ye know neither the day nor the hour wherein the Son of man cometh." (Matthew 25:13)

11

Surgeon Talks Of Preserving Human Brains

Beverly Hills, Calif. — (AP)— A neurosurgeon who reports he has kept more than 100 monkey brains. alive outside the skull for up to several days says human brains might be preserved some day and "trained" as computers.

Dr. Robert J. White of Case-Western Reserve University at Cleveland said he was able to communicate crudely with the isolated monkey brains through electrical signals.

Electrodes were implanted before the brains were removed, he said.
through the e
brain wave
ed.

White told
ed by Res
Blindness, I
"communica
brains thr
nerves left i
electronic in
the approp
serves visua
ions."

A WORLD OF 7 BILLION PREDICTED FOR 2000

Special to The New York Times

TUNIS, Nov. 8 — A wider use of all available contraceptives to meet the rapid increase in world population was urged this week at the meeting of the International Planned Parenthood Federation being held this year in Gammarth. The meeting started Wednesday and will continue through next week.

A report presented to a federation session said that "at today's rate of increase in world population, there will be four billion people by 1975, and nearly double, or seven billion

ople, by the year 2000." The present population of the world is estimated at 3.5 billion.

Federation members from 63 countries represented at the meeting not only urged wider use of contraceptives, but called for research into new ones and expansion of their distribution.

Mrs. Agnette Braestrup, a Danish pediatrician, was elected president of the federation, succeeding Lady Rama Rau of India, who had been its head for the last six years.

Limit Couples To 2 Children, Pauling Says

ATLANTIC CITY, Nov. 9. — Dr. Linus C. Pauling, two-time Nobel Prize winner, said Sunday said family size should be limited to two children to prevent overpopulation of the world.

Speaking at a news conference during the 88th annual conference of the Geological Society of America, he said this could be accomplished by voluntary abortion, sterilization, birth control and education.

Dr. Pauling said the world's population must be reduced to one billion from its present 3.5 billion and that the United States should keep its population under its present level of 200 million.

He said that man was changing his environment in ways that can affect his genetic makeup and said, "X rays and dental and medical work, television screens, air pollution and food additives can have effects not completely understood on the process of human inheritance.

"The changes we seem to be causing can only be harmful."

Surgeon's Report
Monkey Brains Kept Alive Outside Skull

BEVERLY HILLS, Calif., Nov. 9 (AP).—A neurosurgeon reported Sunday he had kept more than 100 monkey brains alive outside the skull up to several days.

He raised the possibility that human brains might be preserved as "biological computers."

Dr. Robert J. White of Case-Western Reserve Universty at Cleveland said he had been able to communicate crudely with the monkey brains by means of electrical signals sent through electrodes implanted before the brains were removed by surgery. The signals were followed by increased brain wave activity, as monitored by the electrodes.

Dr. Whit   a seminar

sponsored by Research to Prevent Blindness, Inc., that he also had sent electrical impulses to one of the monkey brains through eye and ear nerves left intact.

"I found that such an impulse traversed all the intricate intracerebral fiber pathways and arrived at the appropriate portion that serves visual or auditory retention of inherent electrical r
st ngly sugg   hat

THE PHILADELPHIA INQUIRER, MONDAY MORNING, NOVEMBER 10, 1969

Society Must Dictate Size of Families, Survival Study Warns

By PATRICIA McBROOM
Of The Inquirer Staff

The human race should work toward a zero rate of population growth by the end of the century if it is to have any chance at a decent life for all, according to the National Academy of Science.

Achieving this goal means that society will have to have a say in how many children a couple can have.

These are among the conclusions reached by the prestigious Academy after three years of study on man and the earth's resources.

In a document released Sunday, the Academy set down in broad scope steps that must be taken to help insure survival of the human race.

Prepared by an eight-man panel, the report covers food-production, mineral resources, marine resources, sources of future energy and, above all, pop-

ulation, projected over the next 100 years.

"Population control is the absolute primary essential without which all other efforts are nullified," the panel concluded.

World population is now 3.5 billion. At current levels of birth and death, the 30 billion mark would be reached in the next century, the report said in a preface to the report.

"Resources and, indeed, living space, near-starvation for the great 10 billion people.

Among the nations, only Hungary, Japan and Bulgaria have a birth rate low enough to stabilize the population. That rate is 14 births a year per 1000 people.

In the United States and elsewhere "the inadequate measur-

foreseeable sources of new food and manifold human problems that now pass for population control, the panel estimated, the items would intervene.

Ideally, the human population should be smaller than it is now, said the panel, but lacking achievement of the improbable goal, the Academy scientists concluded society should be halted "at a level of chronic ic near-starvation for the great ic near-starvation for the great

"that "serious dangers be-

majority and with massive imigration" to the less populated lands.

While this appears to be the earth's ultimate capacity, human populations probably will never reach that point, said the panel, because social destruc-

erably less than what has been projected by others.

But while food from the sea is an excellent source of protein, said the report, it is a poor source of calories. Only the land can supply this needed food.

The Panel estimated a future agricultural need of eight times the current production.

As for energy, the Academy scientists said nuclear energy must be developed as quickly as possible, and a breakthrough in atomic sciences is needed to supply the world with an inexhaustible source of uranium 235.

Uranium ore is now limited, which could severely restrict nuclear power in a few decades.

Petroleum liquids and natural gas used now for energy will be depleted in 50 to 65 years, said the panel.

There is little basis for assuming that many marine mineral and chemical resources are of large usable volume or that for many essential substances, there are any marine resources at all.

Among its conclusions, the panel placed priority on developing said breeder or fusion reactors to supply nuclear energy.

control at best eliminate only unwanted births," said the report.

To achieve real control will "require profound modification of current attitudes toward parenthood," said the panel.

"Ultimately this implies that the community and society as a whole, and not only the parents, must have a say about the number of children a couple may have."

The panel said that, contrary to popular belief, the oceans do not appear to harbor great mineral wealth.

City to Remove 'Eye in Sky' Crime Detector

OLEAN, N. Y., Dec. 26 (AP). — The police chief of this western New York city says an experimental crime surveillance system with cameras mounted on street lights worked "beautifully" during the day. But the system will be removed anyway.

Police Chief Michael Luty said the system has cut the number of burglaries in the business district where it is employed.

But William O. Smith, who won election as mayor after charging in his campaign that the system would be too expensive — up to $70,000 — calls it an "eye in the sky."

INVASION OF PRIVACY

He said its relentless, quiet surveillance smacks of an invasion of privacy.

Eight cameras are mounted on lighting poles in a three-block area of this Cataraugus County community of 22,000.

Noise Level Could Become Lethal If It Continues to Rise, Expert Says

Washington—(UPI)—The racket may not be killing you, On the other hand, maybe it is—slowly, insidiously.

The din that assaults our ears almost non-stop is shattering our tranquility and hurting our health.

Noise pollution is getting worse every year. Nothing very effective is being done about it. According to Sen. Mark O. Hatfield, (R-Ore), the United States is the noisiest of modern societies.

The consensus at an American Medical Association Congress in Chicago was "at noise is a ...

must be made aware that of-fensive noise can be controlled and must be made angry enough to do something about it."

Noise has been defined in many ways. It is unwanted sound, sound without value, un-restricted sound, sound that hurts, harms, distracts, de-stroys sleep, invades privacy, frightens, irritates or simply an-noys.

Dr. Vern O. Knudsen, chan-cellor emeritus of the University of California and a student of acoustics, the science of sound, says:

Council for Science and Tech-nology, a White House agency, notes that "growing numbers of researchers fear that the dan-gerous and hazardous effects of intense noise on human health are seriously underestimated."

There is no doubt that indus-trial din has inflicted loss of hearing on millions of workers. At least a million workers now living suffer from some degree of deafness. The federal coun-cil estimates that another 6 to 16 million are exposed to noise levels which many ruin their hearing in the future.

De... '',,s i ...

nology, a White House agency, vision sets, the endless ringing drivers, bulldozers, power saws, lawn mowers.

of dull music piped into eleva-tors or restaurants; the night shots but may only be back-squawking of auto horns.

pay the price. Other countries slation regulations in their building codes. These nations "'stria, I ... Bulgari-

triggered calamities.

Ailments which may have been caused or at least aggra-vated by noise include ulcers, diseases, allergies, and -mental illness, Foreign reports have been attributed sexual im-potency to high noise levels in factories.

Racket can drown out alarm signals or shouted warnings or verbal instructions vital to safe-ty.

Paul N. Borsky of the Colum-bia University School of Public Health, says that if a person " noise propagators ... 'oring .   eds

vision sets, the endless ringing of telephones; the din of the pile drivers, bulldozers, power saws, lawn mowers.

The conversation-killing sound of dull music piped into eleva-tors or restaurants; the night noises that sound like pistol shots but may only be back-fires; the round-the-clock squawking of auto horns.

Everybody says noise can be muffled—if we are willing to pay the price. Other countries have included national sound in-slation regulations in their building codes. These nations feels that t ...

Myriad Noises

We hear unmuffled scooters, "bikes sports cars 'rucks;

But more alarming than in-dustrial racket, because millions more persons are affected, is the steeply rising level of "com-munity noise" which affects everybody.

According to the federal coun-cil, old-fashioned dwellings of 40 to 50 years ago "were com-paratively quiet places in which to live." Thanks to modern con-struction techniques we have "some of the noisiest buildings in existence."

No Clean Air Found in U.S.

Pollution to Kill by '90, Scientists Say

SCOTIA, N. Y., Dec. 20 (AP).—The way some scien-tists see it, the choice will be simple. Wear a special breath-ing mask, or die from pollu-tion.

That's the prospect for life in the Northern Hemisphere by 1990 if the present pollution rate continues, according to scientists at the Atmospheric

and much plant life will be killed off.

—In 20 years, man will live in domed cities.

Even now, the scientists say, there is no more clean air left in the United States. A six-year search was con-ducted by members of the research center, which is

been increasing at a rate far greater than the air is able to cleanse itself.

The last vestiges of clean air the center noted in the United States was near Flag-staff, Ariz., but it disappear-ed six years ago when, Huls-trunk said, air pollution from the California coast reached

deadly for humans at 35,000 particles.

At the fatal point, Hulstrunk says, the only solution now apparent will be domed cities.

"We can put on a semi-spacesuit and roam around a deserted and dead country. The people will be inside and all living things outside will be dead Technology will have

Washington Merry-Go-Round
U. S. Trains Egyptians In Poison Gas Use

By JACK ANDERSON

Washington — Pentagon officials aren't advertising it, but the Army is instructing foreign specialists in chemical and biological welfare.

A total of 550 aliens from 36 nations—including Egypt, Yugoslavia and South Vietnam—have taken two-to-36-week courses at the Army's Chemical School at Ft. McClellan, Ala.

Although fewer than half-a-dozen Egyptians have learned about poison gas in the U.S., these key officers reportedly used their American know-how to help plan the poison gas attacks upon Yemen in 1967. Representatives of the International Red Cross verified that Egyptian pilots dropped canisters of poison gases from two Soviet-built MIG fighters and nine Ilyushin bombers over Ketaf, a remote Yemen community. Some 150 villagers gagged, coughed and bled to death.

The Egyptians, like other foreign specialists, supposedly were taught only "defense" against the hideous sprays and germs. As part of the courses at Ft. McClellan, however, they received expert instruction in the poisonous qualities of the gases, how these gases can be disseminated and which gases are most effective under various conditions.

Trained in Defense

The U.S. has trained Arab and Israeli officers alike to "defend" themselves against poison gas attacks from each other. In addition to the Egyptians, specialists from Iraq, Jordan, Lebanon and Saudi Arabia have attended the Army's Chemical School.

The only Communists who have been admitted into the secret chemical classes at Ft. McClellan are the Yugoslavs. However, close allies, such as the British, Australians and Canadians, have been given a deeper insight into our chemical and biological warfare technology at the super-secret Dugway Proving Grounds, Utah — site of nerve gas tests on animals.

Congressional incredulity over American storage of nerve gases abroad and the shipment of lethal gases inside the U.S. has now raised doubts about the training of foreign troops in gas and bacteriological lore. For the Pentagon has seeded the world with poison gas and germ warfare experts.

NEWSMEN RECEIVE VATICAN WARNING

Those Showing 'Incorrect' View Will Lose Rights

Special to The New York Times

ROME, Nov. 19 — The Vatican threatened today to withdraw accreditation from any correspondent deemed to have demonstrated an "incorrect attitude" toward the Pope, the Holy See or the Roman Catholic Church.

The threat was issued in an explanatory note accompanying forms sent to Rome correspondents to be completed for a new system of accreditation for coverage of activities of the Holy See.

Official Vatican sources sought to discount the significance of the warning. They asserted that they could not think of a single example of an "incorrect attitude" in Vatican dispatches in the last half-dozen years that would justify the withdrawal of accreditation.

Left clipping

The Evening Bulletin
PHILADELPHIA
Tuesday, July 8, 1969

28   B

America's Terrifying Arsenal

Germs Could Knock Out 60 Million In Single Raid by 10 Aircraft

Third of Several Articles

By COL. R. D. HEINL, Jr.
(Military Analyst)

Fort Detrick, Md.—(NANA)—
The world has lived uncomfortably with chemical warfare ever since the first German gas attack in April, 1915, but has so far been spared the ultimate horror of germ warfare.

Maintaining that state of affairs is the ultimate justification for the U. S. Army's biological laboratories here on the rolling green Maryland countryside.

Despite secrecy and security far lighter than that which surrounds our nuclear armaments, potential enemies of the United States, among the 15 other nations which have chemical and biological warfare (CBW) programs know that the American biological arsenal contains agents capable of inflicting as many million casualties as a thermonuclear attack.

Not All Germs Suitable

Not every germ or disease is suitable for military use. Basically, the scientists (like those here at Fort Detrick, look for

to 75 percent of unvaccinated victims), and Q-fever, a non-lethal incapacitant which brings on a week or more of high fever, chills, headache and muscle pains.

Four virus agents complete our biological inventory. These BW agents, Fort Detrick is heavily committed to defense against and safety precautions are in the rarely fatal; Rift Valley fever, likewise uncomfortable but not lethal; psittacosis (parrot fever) and Venezuelan equine encephalomyelitis.

also generally non-fatal and apparently well-suit-ed to incapacitate a hostile army or population.

Warning Device Sought

Besides the development of BW agents, Fort Detrick is developing a rapid, automatic, portable detection and warning device which would instantly register the presence of enemy BW agents in the atmosphere.

At present, Army scientists say, this is the laboratory's top priority.

Need for a warning device is underscored by the fact that the service gas mask provides as complete protection against biological attack as against chemicals. The high-quality filters of the mask will take out

any known BW agent.

Since air dissemination and ingestion through the respiratory tract are the unique means of transmitting military biological agents, a good chemical mask doubles against germ attack.

Production of the biological supplies developed at Fort Detrick takes place at Pine Bluff Arsenal, Ark. Originally a chemical warfare plant, Pine Bluff now devotes well over half its capacity to manufacturing BW

agents, loading them into shells, bombs and rockets, and storing our large reserve stocks of biological munitions in some 250 heavily-constructed "igloo" revetments throughout the base.

Underground Storage

To insure maximum safety, three floors of Pine Bluff's ten-story main producing and filling facility are sunk below ground. Safety is for obvious reasons a dominant theme in the BW program. The biological labora-

It was estimated in 1960 by a U. S. Army biological warfare expert, Maj. Gen. Marshall Stubbs, that ten aircraft, each dispensing 10,000 pounds of biological agents over the U. S. could kill or incapacitate 60 million people. Our enemies understand that such a situation could just as readily apply to Communist China or to Russia.

tories are maintained under negative air pressure. The work itself is done within front-tight biological safety cabinets by scientists or technicians using elbow-length surgical gloves fitted to airtight portholes.

Entrances have decontamination locks where germ-killing ultraviolet rays bathe persons entering and leaving.

All the sewage and exhaust air at Fort Detrick is heated-treated at temperatures guaranteed to kill biological agents.

The plumbing lines are welded; you can walk the laboratories without ever seeing a standard plumber's joint or elbow.

Next: Emotion Muddles Logic in Debate.

Right clipping

The Evening Bulletin
PHILADELPHIA
Friday, December 12, 1969

Hundreds Flee As Nerve Gas Leaks in West

Dugway Proving Ground, Utah — (AP) — Some deadly nerve gas leaked from a one-ton container to the earthen floor of a storage building yesterday and about 300 persons were removed from the area.

The Army said a team of specialists sprayed the ground with a chemical which rendered the agent, known as GB, harmless.

In March, 1968, 6,400 sheep were killed when nerve gas being used in an aerial test spray was blown into nearby Skull Valley.

Sen. Frank Moss (D-Utah) said the new spisode underlined "once again the continuing danger associated with storage and moving of chemical agents such as nerve gas."

Plug Is Damaged

Army officials at this test center initially refused to discuss the matter. Later they acknowledged that while "relocating a one-ton storage container of GB, a filling plug was accidentally damaged, resulting in a small leak."

Dr. Grant S. Winn, a state air ————— ————, estimated th-

THE NEW YORK TIMES, SUNDAY, SEPTEMBER 14, 1959

New Liberal Mood Is Found Among Fundamentalist Protestants

By EDWARD B. FISKE
Special to The New York Times

MINNEAPOLIS, Sept. 13 — Fundamentalist Protestants, generally regarded as the last major holdouts against ecumenical cooperation and the mixing of religion with social issues, have begun to modify their position on both counts.

Informed church leaders believe that the trend, if it continues, could produce one of the most major changes in American Protestantism since the bitter theological battles between liberals and conservatives in the early 20th century.

On the one hand, fundamentalists—or "conservative evangelicals," as most now prefer to be called—are moving toward liberal policies of openness and involvement in social issues like race, peace and poverty.

"They're beginning to come out of their shells," said the Rev. Oswald C. J. Hoffman, preacher on the "Lutheran Hour" radio program. "They realize that you can't withdraw into a kind of Protestant mo-

delegates from 93 Protestant denominations, was convened by a committee of laymen and clergymen headed by Dr. Hoffman, a Missouri Synod Lutheran. The Rev. Billy Graham, the evangelist, was honorary chairman and a major speaker.

The majority of the participants came from traditionally fundamentalist denominations, such as the Southern Baptist Convention. The rest represented the conservative wings of mainline bodies like the Episcopal Church.

The two groups were united in their acceptance of the traditional fundamentalist position on such doctrines as heaven and hell, the second coming of Christ, the literal existence of Adam and Eve and the divine inspiration of the Bible.

Such teachings were generally the norm in America Protestantism until the late 19th and early 20th centuries, when the conflict occurred between fundamentalists and the so-called modernists who challenged such ideas as the literal truth of Genesis.

New Groups, Not Expected

There is general agreement, however, that this new "evangelical ecumenism" will probably not lead to the creation of new organizations, such as a new conservative counterpart to the National Council of Churches or to widespread contacts beyond the conservative fold.

Delegates here have also generally agreed that the move toward many organized social action had been precipitated by the nation's ra-

mittee, expressed hope that the experience of working together on the 1973 evangelism effort would lead to cooperative efforts in other areas. "Evangelism is something all of us can agree on," he said. "It can be the spearhead."

Conservative leaders said that this emergence from the isolation of the past had been spurred by the success of Mr. Graham, who has drawn considerable attention to his evangelistic crusades and demonstrated that such cooperation could take place without compromising the specific doctrinal tenets of the various groups.

At some of his rallies he conducts "love-outs" and asks members of the congregation not only to make a "decision for Christ" but also to fill out a card committing themselves to a specific act of social involvement.

At his meeting here delegates responded warmly both to an appeal by a caucus of the 40 black delegates to work against racism in their churches and to an impassioned speech by the Rev. Tom Skinner, a black evangelist from Brooklyn.

Participants in the congress generally agreed that the move toward social action had been precipitated by the Rev. Alan G. Reuter, a young Presbyterian pastor from Richland, Wash. "They're asking whether it works. This means you have to be concerned with the humanity of Christ as well as with His divinity."

"new breed of evangelical is now emerging" is represented by the Rev. Leighton Ford, a 37-year-old Canadian evangelist who is a brother-in-law and heir-designate of Mr. Graham.

though mankind is sinful, the world was still created by God and thus must be good," said Dr. Hubbard, who is a Conservative Baptist and chairman of the Urban Coalition in Pasadena, Calif.

At the same time, even those who accept the need for social involvement have not worked out its full theological implications. "Some still regard social action as primarily a tactic for getting people to listen to the Gospel," said Dr. Hubbard.

Black participants also emphasized that the concern for social involvement was so new among evangelicals that it had yet to be shown whether it could be implemented by conservative local congregations.

Accompanying the new mood has been a movement away from traditional forms of individual piety, such as opposition to movies and card playing, that have characterized the fundamentalist position for decades.

"We need a new model of Christian piety," said Mr. Skinner. "The question is not whether to minister or not to minister. It's whether you are available to your fellow man."

CHRISTIANITY GOES MODERN

Affirmations Made Between Rock, Folk Music

By GEORGE W. CORNELL
Associated Press

NEW YORK — The hall is big and mostly dark, except for the garish, oscillating patterns of colored light flashing on the wide screens at either side and behind the throbbing clamor of the band.

Across the broad, dim interior, streaked with racing, phosphorescent beams, about 1,000 young people sit in little groups at white-topped tables, absorbed in the electric rock sounds and the shimmering psychedelic glow.

The the loud music stops, and a lean, thick-haired guitar player, in bright blue shirt and white pants, with a red kerchief at his neck, steps to the microphone and tells how a relationship with Christ got him off dope.

"It's a fantastic experience," he said. "Jesus gives you a way. He sticks with a man. He's for you, and once you tune in with him, you just keep wanting to know and love Him better."

Rock Reverberations

Bam, thump and strumming strings. Again, the amplified rock reverberations flood the room; the flowing chromatic lights trace phantom designs on the panels, and a shapely girl in a miniskirt steps up to song a ballad.

Each night after Graham's service in Madison Square Garden, where he is devoting special attention to young people, swarms of them migrate a block up the street to keep the mood jumping until midnight.

"It's a culture shock to most religious people," says Rev. John Guest, the wide-belted, wavy-haired young British Anglican priest who runs the program, and who looks and dresses like a swinger himself.

"Religion is generally regarded as something that belongs only in a staid, musty environment, but what we're saying here is that it fits into the secular world," he said. "It's a new scene."

Conversation About Religion

In between the rock and folk music, and the brief, simple affirmations of faith from the mi-

U. S. Is Fast Becoming Elective Dictatorship, Sen. Fulbright Says

WASHINGTON, June 19 (UPI).—Sen. J. William Fulbright (D., Ark.) said on Thursday the United States was well along the road toward "an elective dictatorship."

The chairman of the Senate Foreign Relations Committee opened debate on a controversial resolution asserting Congress' role in the making of foreign policy. It was expected to last through next week.

FOREIGN POLICY

Fulbright warned that the United States was "already a long way toward becoming an elective dictatorship, more or less complete over foreign policy and over those vast and expanding areas of our domestic life which in one way or another are related to or dependent upon the military establishment."

RESULT OF EMPIRE

If the nation continues its role of involvement and unilateral military action overseas, he said, "then the future can hold nothing for us except endless foreign exertions, chronic warfare, burgeoning expense and the proliferation of an already formidable military-industrial-labor-academic complex — in short the militarization of American life."

"If in short, America is to become an empire," Fulbright said, "there is very little chance that it can avoid becoming a virtual dictatorship as well."

The Evening Bulletin
PHILADELPHIA, Monday, December 22, 1969

Guillotine Is Still Legal In France; Used Sparingly

By RODNEY ANGOVE

Paris — (AP) — In a locked closet within Paris' Sante prison lies a collection of heavy beams and packing cases, a seven-foot wicker basket, a paillike large coal bucket, and a flat velvet-lined silverware box containing a polished trapezoidal blade with finely honed edge.

It is the famous French guillotine.

~~~~ have passed

No, Dr. Guillotine did not invent it. He merely promoted t in Parliment. No, he did not himself pass under its blade, although he did serve a brief prison term for political reasons.

The guillotine became famous in the revolutionary 1790s, but was being used as early as 1521, according to an engraving in the Nuernburg, Germany, museum.

It was the press that brought ~~~~ to public executions,

THE NEW YORK TIMES, FRIDAY, OCTOBER 31, 1969

20,000 Poison Bullets Made and Stockpiled by Army

By ROBERT M. SMITH
Special to The New York Times

WASHINGTON, Oct. 30—The Army has produced and stockpiled more than 20,000 poison bullets.

It is reliably reported that the bullets contain Botulinum —a toxin that produces an acute, highly fatal disease of the nervous system.

A secret memorandum prepared in 1966 by Chemical Corps officers for Secretary of the Army Stanley R. Resor said that thousands of the bullets had been produced and stockpiled at Pine Bluff Arsenal, in central Arkansas.

There is no evidence that the bullets have been used.

It is not known whether the United States is still producing the poison bullets. However, in recent private conversations with other Government officials, Defense Department personnel have indicated that the bullets are, at the least, still stockpiled.

Assassination Weapon

Officially, the Defense officials have shied from the questions of officials in other departments as to what the "special" weapons at Pine Bluff Arsenal are; they refer to them in only the most general terms.

Reliable sources say that the 1966 memo divided the poison bullets into two types—.38-calibre and "separable." It is not clear what "separable" means. The sources say the memo reported that considerably more than 10,000 bullets of each type were stored at the arsenal.

Knowledgeable sources indicate that the poison bullets could logically serve only one purpose: assassination. To kill an enemy leader with a poison bullet, it would be necessary to do no more than nick him; he would very likely die of botulism, the disease induced by the powerful toxin.

It is not clear whether the United States produced poison bullets before 1965. However, that is the first reference to the bullets that sources familiar with Army weaponry say they have seen.

The year 1965 was when the United States began to send large numbers of combat forces to Vietnam. In 1964, there were 23,300 American troops in Vietnam; in 1965, there were 184,300.

The Hague Convention of 1907—which the United States has signed—prohibits the use, but not the manufacture, of poison weapons. This injunction is repeated in the official Army guide to the rules governing warfare, Army Field Manual 27-10, "The Law of Land Warfare."

"It is especially forbidden," the manual points out, "to employ poison or poisoned weapons." At another point it notes: "It is especially forbidden to employ arms, projectiles or material calculated to cause unnecessary suffering."

The Pine Bluff Arsenal has both biological and chemical production facilities. In the biological area, five officers, four enlisted men and 323 civilians are engaged there in a $7-million-a-year operation centered in a 10-story tower.

The Army has described the biological plant at Pine Bluff as a "pre-production facility." It says that the arsenal produces biological agents to develop the technique and "hardware" necessary to mass-produce the germs if they are needed.

The operation, the Army says, also involves storing some of the germs and toxins (the dead but poisonous byproducts of bacteria) in refrigerated "igloos." The iglos, in the north and central portions of the arsenal, are reinforced concrete huts covered with two to three feet of dirt.

There are 273 igloos at the arsenal, plus 32 warehouses, 16 sheds and 72 concrete magazine, but it is not known how many of the igloos are used to store biological agents. Pine Bluffs also stores lethal chemical agents.

Presumably the poison bullets are stored in the concrete magazines.

Specific information on biological agents is secret. However, Representative Richard D. McCarthy, Democrat of upstate New York, an outspoken critic of American chemical and biological warfare policy, has said the disease bearing weapons the United States develops, tests and in some instances stockpiles would procuce — besides botulism — antarax, tularemin, Q-fever and Venezuelan equine encephalitis.

Another Army manual, Technical Manual 3-216, "Military Bilogy and Biological Agents," discusses the disease botulism in some detail.

The mnaual says that the mortality rate of botulism is 65 per cent in the United States. However, Americans contract the disease by eating contaminated and improperly cooked food. Presumably, the mortality rate would be higher if the toxin were introduced in a concentrated form and through a bullet wound.

The Amry manual says that the symptoms of the disease appear in 12 to 72 hours and that "antitoxin therapy is of doubtful value, particularly when large doses have been consumed." The disease is not contagious.

The manual also says that "through repeated purification procedures [the toxin] has been obtained in a crystalline form and is one of the most powerful toxins known."

"Botulism is an acute, highly fatal disease," the manual continues. "It is characterized by vomiting, constipation, thirst, general weakness, headache, fever, dizziness, double vision and dilation of the pupils. Paralysis is the usual cause of death."

The National Security Council is now in the final stages of a review of the United States' chemical-biological warfare policies. An interagency staff report has been prepared on chemical-biological warfare, and the report is currently being discussed by high officials of the Pentagon, State Department, Arms Control and Disarmament Agency and other agencies.

President Nixon plans to meet with the National Security Council in early November to consider the issue and to try to formulate a chemical-biological warfare policy.

Plea to Tax Churches Weighed by Top Court

Suit Cites Ban on Aid To Religion

VIRUS IS PROPOSED FOR A BIRTH CURB

DURHAM, N. H. (AP) — A University of New Hampshire botanist says that all women could be sterilized by an airborne virus, and those who wanted to have children could then receive an antidote.

Dr. Richard W. Schreiber says that the virus and antidote could be developed in three years at a cost of $5-million.

He said his system would require married couples to "make a human decision" to have a family, reversing the present approach that requires them to "work not to have children."

The antidote would be administered by injection and would be good for six months or less, he said.

Dr. Schreiber asserted that his system was justified by trends that show man is "fatally close to breeding himself out f existence."

WASHINGTON, Nov. 19 (AP). —The Supreme Court consideree Wednesday a plea that it reverse a practice as old as the nation and expose churches and synagogues to real estate taxes.

Edward J. Ennis, American Civil Liberties Union lawyer, presented the proposition that he said was "so obvious it is hard to expand upon"—that tax exemption is an aid to religion banned by the First Amendment.

BILL OF RIGHTS

Speaking for Frederick Walz, an almost recluse lawyer who owns a small lot on Staten Island, N.Y., the white-haired civil liberties lawyer said "the plain words, the first ten words of the Bill of Rights" make tax exemptions for property used entirely for religious purposes unconstitutional.

Only "the great political power of the religious organizations of this country," Ennis said, has permitted tax exemption in the face of the First Amendment's command that "Congress shall make no law respecting an establishment of religion."

VALUE OF RELIGION

But J. Lee Rankin, corporation counsel of New York City, argued in response that the tax exemptions are "recognition of the value of religion in sustaining this country."

Legislatures, he said, have the power to decide which groups shall pay taxes, and there is no constitutional reason why churches should be separated from other "charitable" organizations that are also exempted.

Rankin, a former U.S. solicitor general, contended that across-the-board t a x exemptions for all religious groups keeps government "neutral" in religious matters.

VALUE OF PROPERTY

Should the states be required to tax the churches, he said,

Explanation Of Terms Used In This Book

Antichrist

A name taken from I and II John. In Daniel he is referred to as the little horn and the vile person; In II Thessalonians as the Son of Perdition; and in Revelation as the Beast out of the sea.

Satan so completely possesses the man as to amount almost to an incarnation. Scriptures appear to indicate that he, as Judas Iscariot, will become indwelt by Satan.

Antichrist will oppose Christ, the saints, and the Jews. He will be first hailed as a Man of Peace and given unlimited power by the European countries, the United States and Israel. At his rise, Antichrist will be only a man, but with satanic power. His sudden, sensational rise as the saviour of a world threatened by destruction will mark the beginning of the Time of the End.

His later attempt to annihilate the Jews will bring about his defeat at Jerusalem by the return of Christ. All prophecy up to the return of Christ will be fulfilled in his day.

The False Prophet

Antichrist will be the political ruler who will work the works of Satan. *The False Prophet* will be the religious ruler who will undergird the work of the *Antichrist*. Both get their power from Satan.

The False Prophet never will attempt to promote himself. He will never become an object of worship. He will do the work of a prophet in that he directs

22

attention away from himself to one who he says has the right to be worshipped (the Antichrist).

The False Prophet will imitate many miracles of God. He will cause fire to come down from heaven imitating the miracles of Elijah in order to convince the nation Israel that he (The False Prophet) is the Elijah whom Malachi promised was yet to come! Having achieved this deception the False Prophet will declare that since this miracle (bringing fire from heaven) shows that he is Elijah . . . then, therefore, the Antichrist is truly Christ and should be worshipped.

He will also build a statue, and through some satanic miracle cause this statue (image) to talk and somehow come to life. When the people see this miracle they will fall down and worship the Antichrist believing him to be Christ.

Mark of the Beast

During the second half of the seven year Tribulation Period the Antichrist (who previously was setting himself up as a Man of Peace) will suddenly move against the Jews and all those who have accepted Christ as Saviour during the first 3½ years of this Period. In Revelation 13:16, 17 we read that ". . . he (False Prophet) causeth all, both small and great, rich and poor, free and bond, to receive some mark in their right hand, or in their foreheads: And that no man might buy or sell, save he that had the mark . . . "

Therefore those who refuse to submit to the authority of this system by having this mark (the Mark of the Beast), either starve to death slowly, or else are slain by the representatives of the government, who will treat as traitors all who refuse to accept this identifying mark.

Rapture

This refers to the time, prior to the start of the 7 year Tribulation Period, when believing Christians (both dead and alive) will "in the twinkling of an eye" rise up to meet Christ in the air.

" . . . if we believe that Jesus died and rose again, even so them also which sleep in Jesus will God bring with Him. For this we say unto you by the word of the Lord, that we which are alive and remain unto the coming of the Lord shall not precede them which are asleep.

For the Lord himself shall descend from Heaven with a shout . . . and the dead in Christ shall rise first: Then we which are alive and remain shall be caught up (RAPTURE) together with them in the clouds, to meet the Lord in the air: and so shall we ever be with the Lord" (I Thessalonians 4:14-17).

Second Coming of Christ

This is one of the most prominent doctrines in the Bible. In the New Testament alone it is referred to over 300 times. His First Coming was over 1900 years ago when He came on earth to save man from sin. The Second Coming is an event starting at the Rapture and comprehending four phases: *First,* at the Rapture Christ takes the believers out of this world to be with Him (I Thessalonians 4). *Second* Christ pours out His judgments on the world during the 7 year Tribulation Period. *Third,* Christ at the end of the 7 year Tribulation destroys the Antichrist and his wicked followers (Revelation 19). *Fourth,* Christ sets up His millennial Kingdom prophesied so often in the Old Testament.

IN EXPLANATION

1. "NOW IS THE DAY OF SALVATION" and no one should wait. The Bible does not encourage anyone to wait. Nevertheless, some disobediently do wait, and by God's grace get saved on the next day—or week—or year. This in no way detracts from God's command that all should turn to Him today. "Now is the Day of Salvation" (2 Corinthians 6:2), for the Scriptures make it clear that our life is like a vapor that vanishes away and for us tomorrow may never come (James 4:13-15).

2. A "Second Chance"? We deny that there is any "Second Chance" after death. Death, then the judgment. After Armageddon, at the Judgment of Matthew 25:31-46—when all the surviving people of the world (alive after the Tribulation) are gathered, there is no hint of a "second chance."

   At the Judgment of the Great White Throne, after the Millennium (Revelation 20), there is no Second Chance.

   However, after the Rapture (1 Thessalonians 4:13-18), those who are *not* taken up with Jesus are *still* alive on earth. They live into the awful Tribulation years—and many who live into this period will indeed turn to Christ (Revelation 7:13-14*).

   The vast majority of those who live past the Rapture will follow the Antichrist and *remain* lost (Revelation 13:7-8).

   Those, however, who do turn to Christ at this time will be saved (Revelation 7).

   No "Second Chance"—as long as you live you are still on that "First Chance."

*The Greek of Revelation 7:14 says that these have come out of "the Great Tribulation." Although not reflected in the King James Version translation, the definite article "the" is present in the Greek text.

When the Rapture of the believers occurs—this will usher in the seven years which are called the Tribulation.

In 2 Thessalonians 2:11 we read: "And for this cause God shall send them strong delusion, that they should believe a lie."

In this way, God will permit a person to rule on this earth who will promise and work miracles and wonders in his day.

This will be so convincing that people will think that he is a true world saviour and will actually be believing a lie.

Understanding the above, you will be better able to understand this book, which written in novel form, attempts to show what may occur when the saints of Christ rise.

Chapter 1

I Saw The Saints Rise

Bill and I had just finished covering the Presidential conventions. And it was with a sigh of relief that we boarded our flight in Chicago bound for the West Coast.

It seemed as though not a day passed without a major news event and my job as a reporter on the Los Angeles Times kept me running in circles.

There was always some cleric spouting words of peace and some "funny people" sitting on top of mountains waiting for the destruction of the world.

One thing I hoped for and that was that my wife would leave me alone and quit pestering me to attend church on Sunday. It was my only day of peace . . . and I needed a rest after those two political conventions.

As my eyes closed in a half sleep I could still hear her saying, "George, come on, get up out of bed and come to Church with the children and me." And I would just turn over and say, "Helen, leave me alone in peace, I see enough hypocrites throughout the week."

And she would always reply, "Alright, George, I'll leave you alone. There's a Bible by your bed and the bookmark's at I Corinthians chapter 15. Please read it and I'll see you at the Rapture."

That Helen could be a comic sometimes . . . I thought . . . half asleep . . . why is it every Sunday she had to hand me that same line . . . "I'll see you at the Rapture"? Did she really believe that stuff?

As our plane soared into the heavens and the sunlight came breaking through I glanced out over the fluffy white clouds below, stretched out in my seat, and while I slowly sipped a cocktail I mused to myself . . . Rapture . . . what a fairy tale. Why as a reporter I knew the world was getting better and better . . . new advances in technology . . . heart transplants an every day occurrence . . . our first rocket ships had landed on the moon and there was talk of a regular commuter service. It looked like Pan American would get the first scheduled airline flights. Why people were even living longer. At the medical convention I covered just a few days ago they had unveiled their first replacement bank of human parts. I remember viewing long cases of arms, legs, hearts, livers and kidneys. Doctors were talking about the success of their cancer replacement program . . . a program that made it possible to remove cancer ridden limbs and replace them with new ones from accident victims. And for the first time a serum for arresting cancer had proved 100% effective!

In my mind . . . there was no doubt about it. This old world was on the upswing. Why even people were living longer. And there was talk of discarding old bodies and having brain transplants. This was the 21st century—not the Middle Ages. That's why I couldn't understand Helen's old fashioned concepts about God. She was one of the few I knew and her type of church was on the way out. Most churches had kept up with the times. But Helen's old church keeps singing, "The Old Rugged Cross" as though they really believed it.

I remember someone once saying . . . "in unity there is strength." And this country was sure getting unified. Helen was horrified but I was happy when I covered the United Church Fellowship in Rome. It

I know thy works, that thou art neither cold nor hot: I would thou wert cold or hot. So then because thou art lukewarm, and neither cold nor hot, I will spue thee out of my mouth. (Revelation 3:15,16).

was an historic occasion. Two very important things happened. The Protestants finally acquiesed on some silly old notions they had held on to and united with the Catholic church. And that's the way it should be. They now call it the CHURCH OF THE WORLD. Their theme was "Heaven on Earth for the World." It was a marvelous banner and a real thrill to see all the Protestant denomination leaders and all the Catholic leaders join hands on the platform singing their newly written hymn as the congregation of over 5000 clergy joined in . . .

Praise God from whom all blessings flow
God's in His heaven on earth below
Let men unite, cast out all fears
For heaven is earth for endless years!

It was a catchy tune and set the pace for the entire convention . . . and that tune spread like wildfire all over the world. Even the President adopted it as the official United States hymn in the interest of world-wide harmony. It was a brilliant gesture on his part!

The second great thing that happened at the United Church Fellowship in Rome was the election of a new world leader. And in one of the major news events of the year . . . the Pope relinquished his position so a prominent statesman in the United States could be elected honorary leader of the CHURCH OF THE WORLD. Brother Barthomolew was a dark horse. He seemed to rise up from nowhere . . . and I can't describe it . . . it was like magnetism. He had resolved the Arab-Israeli conflict and gave the Jews peace. And it was he who had almost single handedly stopped the war in China. The United States had been fighting them for 5 years and it seemed like another Vietnam. Russia was just about ready to step in on the side of China. Brother Bartholomew secretly flew into China . . . and from what I heard miraculously cured Leader Chou from almost certain death. He walked unharmed through Shanghai. Some even said that he had given sight to the blind, hearing to the deaf and made crippled men walk straight.

And in the latter time of their Kingdom, when the transgressors are come to the full, a King of Fierce countenance, and understanding dark sentences, shall stand up. And his power shall be mighty, but not by his own power: and he shall destroy wonderfully, and shall prosper . . . (Daniel 8: 23,24).

China had never seen anything like it. And when he returned to the United States with a peace proposal in his hand—the Americans loved him—he could have asked for anything and got it!

And he did ask . . . and he did get it!

That's the only thing that bothers me. He seems so powerful . . . and yet as I've interviewed him . . . he seems so kind . . . so considerate . . . so dedicated to world peace which he says can only come about through a one world government.

Perhaps he may be right. Anyway he was kind enough to give me the exclusive story about his part in forming the Federated States of Europe and how he convinced our President to join the organization.

With that, the stewardess asked if I wanted another cocktail. I said no . . . which reminded me of dear old Helen again. To her drinking was a sin. How can it be a sin . . . I reminded her . . . when the cocktail lounge at the United Church Fellowship Building in Rome was filled with high clerics all drinking. And all she would say was . . . "You'll see, George . . . just you wait . . . they're tools of the Devil."

How ridiculous I thought . . . but why argue with my wife.

It was then . . . as I was half daydreaming . . . that Bill asked me a funny question . . .

"George, do you believe in flying saucers?"

"In this modern day and age, Bill, do you still believe those fairy tales?"

Then we which are alive and remain shall be caught up together with them in the clouds, to meet the Lord in the air: and so shall we ever be with the Lord. (I Thessalonians 4:17).

"Well, not really, but I've never seen the heavens look so funny. Look way over there at that unusual formation of clouds."

"Bill, why don't you take a drink . . . maybe you'll see some more clouds!"

With that I left him to his cloud watching and I went back to my half-dozing day dreaming.

Brother Bartholomew was a man of action. And the people loved him. Our war with China, which he stopped, had seen over 250,000 of our prime young men killed in action. Oh . . . we killed over 2 million Chinese . . . but that seemed like a drop in the bucket.

So it was a real tribute to him and the United States when he was elected Honorary Leader of the CHURCH OF THE WORLD. The people were grateful. And the President in deference to his abilities had summoned us to the White House to make an announcement "of great import to the peace of the world."

I'll never forget that announcement as over 1000 reporters stood on the White House lawn on a warm, sunny day. The President was all smiles. Next to him was Brother Bartholomew. TV cameras were everywhere. This was the first time the WORLD NETWORK OF TELEVISION was telecasting. This was a new network that Brother Bartholomew had brought about. It was his belief that if all news media could be controlled to send out GOOD, then *evil* would not prevail and the world would understand each other and get better and better.

Now, why hadn't I thought of that idea? So far the Federated States of Europe had joined the WORLD NETWORK as well as the United States, Canada and South America.

And now the President was speaking:

> Ladies and Gentlemen . . . all of you know how hard I have worked for world peace. But there comes one far better than I who has achieved that which I thought would never be possible. The Bible tells us that faith can remove mountains. And with us today is one who I firmly believe is God's man for this hour—a Saint on earth—Brother Bartholomew. Through his good works he has demonstrated that he truly can remove mountains. I am happy to announce to you today that Brother Bartholomew has convinced both Russia and China to join the WORLD NETWORK of television and to work for mutual understanding of all nations. Because of his work in China in ending their war and because I feel that the leaders of the world tomorrow will be leaders in God's church I am directing to be built within the year a new 50 story WORLD CHURCH HEADQUAR-TERS building in the heart of Washington, D.C. on the Capitol grounds.

This was the most sensational news of the year! And the reporters scampered to their phones!

This convinced me that the world was getting better and better every day. I was going to really give it to Helen . . . tell her all about this fantastic new

And for this cause God shall send them strong delusion, that they should believe a lie. (2 Thessalonians 2:11).

development . . . about world leaders finally recognizing God and asking a holy man to be the leader of the country . . . for the world. This was really heaven on earth . . . and I was witnessing it.

But I knew it—that day I rushed home to tell Helen the news first hand—you would think she would have been thrilled. Instead she just sat down on the couch and cried and kept repeating to me, "George, you just don't understand, you just don't understand. This is the beginning of the END!"

And I must confess, I didn't understand. How could anyone understand her and her Bible . . . especially Revelation with its trumpets and seals and horsemen . . . what a fairy tale!

How glad I was to be in on all this momentous news as it was happening — great advances in medicine, a cure for cancer, a united world church, a world leader appointed right from the United States and now a world church headquarters right in Washington, D.C.

Brother Bartholomew had confided to a few of us what his next project was and it seemed unbelievable . . . for no one thought that the Jews in Israel would ever find peace. They were constantly harrassed by enemies all around them. Russia threatened to bring their massive armies down and even their horsemen and swallow them up. It was like the perils of Egypt all over again. But over the doorway to Brother Bartholomew's office was something that was symbolic of his whole leadership.

WORLD PEACE IS HEAVEN . . .
WHERE PEACE ABIDES
HEAVEN IS THERE ALSO

The turmoil of Israel was threatening world peace. And the Presidential conventions conveyed this element of unrest. It seemed that there was no suitable candidate in either party. Both parties appeared deadlocked.

Vote after vote was taken but no standard bearer was chosen. And then I remembered that grand old white haired man stand up at the Republican convention and given a standing ovation. He was one of the former leaders of the Presbyterian Church who was instrumental in bringing his church into the CHURCH OF THE WORLD at the Rome meetings.

"Gentlemen," he said, "It is evident that when man proposes, God disposes. I have watched man after man propose a leader for your party and for the Democratic party . . . and man has not succeeded.

May I be so bold to suggest that now God should have his way. Let's have a new UNITED CONVENTION of Democrats and Republicans and let's give God a chance. I move that we so do, and elect Brother Bartholomew as our DUAL representative as PRESIDENT of the United States and HONORARY HEAD of THE CHURCH OF THE WORLD!"

I'll never forget that day. The delegates went wild with excitement. And I was amazed as I watched them join hands and circle the auditorium singing ". . . let men unite, cast out all fears . . . for heaven is earth for endless years." And now that convention was over. Brother Bartholomew was elected unanimously. And I was going home. I almost missed the plane. These new supersonic jets carry 1000 people but I was the last one to get a seat. I was happy I had made the late afternoon flight. I would be home shortly. And I had a lot to tell Helen!

Just then Bill shouted excitedly, "George look out that window . . . I tell you that's not just a cloud. I've never seen the sky so funny looking. It's as though it was opening up . . . George IT IS OPENING UP . . . PEELING BACK LIKE A SCROLL . . . George what's happening?"

And there shall be signs in the sun, and in the moon, and in the stars; and upon the earth distress of nations, with perplexity; the sea and the waves roaring. (Luke 21:25)

He was shouting now . . . and I felt embarrassed. But I looked around and everyone in the plane was standing up and pointing with excitement.

And then it happened . . . Almost like a twinkling of an eye.

In a moment, in the twinkling of an eye . . . the dead shall be changed. (I Corinthians 15:52).

It seemed like the plane got much lighter . . . turned abruptly and went into a dive from 80,000 feet high.

I lost consciousness . . . I don't remember exactly what happened. There had been two stewardesses standing next to me; but when I awoke only one was there!

Then shall two be in the field; the one shall be taken, and the other left. Two women shall be grinding at the mill; the one shall be taken, and the other left. (Matthew 24: 40,41).

I picked her up off the floor and she rushed to the pilot's cabin. When she came out she was ashen white . . . and put her hand to her mouth to hold a scream.

Just then the intercom came on and we heard a voice . . .

"Ladies and Gentlemen . . . something rather unusual has happened. We are not sure what . . . but please be calm . . . everything is under control. Our pilot has vanished . . . perhaps some mysterious celestial illness. This caused the abrupt dive . . . but your co-pilot now has full control of the aircraft. Please keep your seatbelts fastened."

Why should that make the stewardess shout with fear . . . I wondered . . . and then I looked around me and she pointed with trembling hands . . .

"LOOK . . .," she screamed, "HALF OF THE PASSENGERS ARE MISSING!"

I'll never forget the chills that ran up and down my spine. HALF OF THE PASSENGERS ARE MISSING. It wasn't half . . . but it looked as though 100 or so just disappeared. And I turned to tell Bill.

BUT BILL WASN'T THERE!

And suddenly it came to me.

I WAS HERE!

When we landed, I rushed to my car. Crowds were collecting at the airport because many flights had been cancelled due to crew members not reporting for duty. I got on to the clogged highway . . . clogged with driverless cars . . . was the world going crazy? It seemed as if a multitude of sleepy drivers had all at once decided to stop no matter where they were. Most had pulled to the side of the road; but nowhere were any of these drivers to be seen. A train was halfway across a highway!

I just had to get home. Tears poured down my cheeks . . . and a cold sweat engulfed me.

I drove up the drive. Thank God, Helen's car was still there. She was home.

I rushed in the door and shouted, Honey I'm home . . . are you alright?"

No answer.

Again I shouted, "Helen, where are you? I'm home! Where are the children?"

No answer.

Frantically, I ran through every room shouting, "Helen, Helen!"

And my own voice came echoing back through the empty halls!

And then a voice of the past seemed to echo in my mind . . . "Alright, George, I'll leave you alone. There's a Bible by your bed and the bookmark's at I Corinthians, chapter 15. Please read it and I'll see you at the Rapture."

For the Lord Himself shall descend from heaven with a shout, with the voice of the archangel, and with the trump of God: and the dead in Christ shall rise first: Then we which are alive and remain shall be caught up together with them in the clouds, to meet the Lord in the air: and so shall we ever be with the Lord. (I Thessalonians 4: 16,17).

"THE RAPTURE! That's it! This is the RAPTURE!

And my Helen and my children are gone!"

Quickly I ran into the bedroom and there it was—the Bible was still on the bedstand. I hurriedly opened it at the place of the bookmark.

Hurry, read, hurry, read. I must hurry. Why can't I read? The tears were flowing down my face. My eyes were so filled that the print seemed blurred . . . but I had to read what it said. Time was so precious. Why didn't I read this book before . . . when there was so much time. Why? Why?

Finally my eyes focused through the tears . . . and I read . . . I Corinthians 15:52,53.

"Behold, I show you a mystery; We shall not all sleep, but we shall be changed.

In a moment, in the twinkling of an eye, at the last trump; for the trumpet shall sound, and the dead

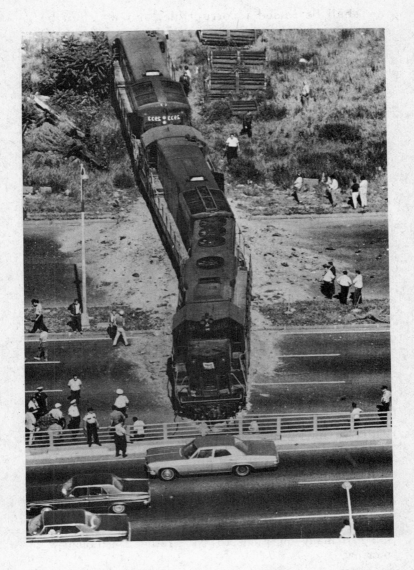

I got on to the clogged highway...clogged with driverless cars...was the world going crazy?...A train was halfway across a highway!

shall be raised incorruptible, and we shall be changed . . . . "

It must be true! It must be true! Everything Helen said must be true! That Bible . . . that talk about accepting Jesus Christ as personal Saviour . . . that talk of Christ dying on the cross for our sins . . . to give us eternal life . . . that talk of the Tribulation period. ALL OF IT MUST BE TRUE! I was hysterical, sobbing, kissing the picture of Helen. Then the phone rang!

That jangled, harsh ring jarred me from my hysteria. With a crying voice I answered it . . .

"Hello," I said.

"Hello, is this George?"

"Yes."

"George, this is Tom Malone at WORLD NETWORK TELEVISION. Brother Bartholomew has called a news conference for tomorrow in CHURCH OF THE WORLD Headquarters in Washington. He has some important peace moves to discuss and also will explain this weird disappearance of some heretics. I want you to be there to cover the story for us."

"OK, Tom I'll be there. Goodbye."

And with a sigh of relief, I hung up.

The world was getting better and better. This so called Rapture must be a hoax. Why did I let myself get excited? This was God's way of punishing those who did not unite in a world church—that's why Helen disappeared and her following.

WHERE PEACE ABIDES . . .
HEAVEN IS THERE ALSO!   Revelation
                                        Chapter 17

World peace was just around the corner.

I had many questions to ask Brother Bartholomew tomorrow.

But Brother Bartholomew would have the answers!

And that's all that mattered!   2 Thessalonians 2:1-12

Chapter 2

The Great Reassurance

The last rays of sunlight were painting a fantasy of beauty as they hit the earth.

But as I drove to the airport those rays revealed the ugliness of the world...and the sudden shock of the recent disaster. I passed a car still aflame and a woman in apparent distress running for her life.

Was this all a bad dream? Would I awaken and find that everything was back to normal?

When I arrived at the airport I was soon brought face to face with the reality of it all. People were running around in a state of confusion. It was impossible to park in the airport parking lot so I swung my car to the side of the road and walked to the main entrance of the terminal.

As I entered the terminal I could hear the public address system blaring over and over again the news. It's funny how politely they couch their words as though today's disaster was just a temporary inconvenience.

I passed a car still aflame and a woman in apparent distress running for her life.

MAY WE HAVE YOUR ATTENTION, PLEASE! BECAUSE OF CURRENT CONDITIONS, ALL FLIGHTS ARE TEMPORARILY CANCELLED. NEW SCHEDULES WILL BE POSTED JUST AS QUICKLY AS POSSIBLE. PLEASE RETURN TO YOUR HOMES AND TUNE IN TO YOUR EMERGENCY RADIO FREQUENCY BAND FOR FURTHER INFORMATION.

I groaned when I heard the words, "ALL FLIGHTS ARE TEMPORARILY CANCELLED." But then I heard my name being called.

GEORGE OMEGA PLEASE REPORT TO AMERICAN AIRLINES TICKET COUNTER

Quickly I pushed my way through the crowd. The sea of faces seemed hostile to me as if to say, "Who was I...someone special?"

Hopefully, and yet in my heart I knew there was no hope, I looked for Helen, my wife, and my two children, Sue and Tommy.

But all the faces were strange to me...and quite dejectedly I finally reached the ticket counter.

"Hello, my name's Omega. You called me on the intercom."

"Yes, Mr. Omega, we had a call from Washington to clear you for immediate passage. Right from the top man...Brother Bartholomew himself. You must be pretty important. Anyway, the plane is on the runway. Take ramp 6. It's a special emergency flight."

"Fine. Thanks a lot," I replied, "but how will I know which plane?"

"Can't miss it, Mr. Omega, just look for the number on the tail. It's number 666!"

For some reason, I don't know why...but a chill went up and down my spine. What was it that disturbed me? There was something odd about that number but somehow I just couldn't place it. Was my imagination playing tricks on me? It had been a long hard day...so I chalked it up to overstrain and hurried towards the gate.

As the jet soared into the heavens I could see the patchwork of destruction down below. It was as though someone had tipped a stack of dominoes...as we used to do when we were kids. Everything seemed in a state of confusion. Turnpikes were clogged with autos that seemed to merge together into one welded mass. Nothing moved. What little farm land there was appeared overrun with cars trying to reach their destination.

The sun was slipping slowly over the horizon now and the shades of darkness seemed to carry a message of impending doom.

I was never one for extra sensory perception...but somehow I felt like I was standing at the brink of a large chasm... and I was to have a front row seat in history's holocaust of horrors.

The words of the ticket agent echoed through my mind... "You must be pretty important...just look for the number on the tail. It's number 666."

Funny, I never considered myself important. How I became projected into a place of prominence was because I happened to be at the right place at the right time.

It was on a trip to the Middle East. I wasn't a religious person but my wife had begged me to take her and the children to Jerusalem.

I dreaded the trip but I decided to combine business with pleasure. I left my wife and Sue and Tommy in Jerusalem while I flew to Bagdad to check up on some startling news reports...reports about a man who was performing miracles and who, they said, had no father.

Upon returning to Jerusalem I could tell that my wife was unhappy and I asked her why.

"George," she replied, "somehow the face of this nation has changed...changed so drastically that I'm afraid the Rapture might occur any minute...and you still have not accepted Christ as your personal Saviour. George, please, complete our family circle."

Little Sue gripped my hand and Tommy just looked down at his feet. I knew Tommy only did that when he was about to cry. Plaintively Sue looked up and said, "Please, daddy, please take my Jesus."

If ever I was close to making a decision for this Christ... it was then. But revealing news I had uncovered in Bagdad cast more doubts on Helen's religion...as far as I was concerned.

"Look, Helen, I appreciate your concern and the kids, too. But I've just discovered some things that change the whole picture. Just be patient. By the way, what makes you think this Rapture is so close?"

Helen looked at me with tears in her eyes as she told how the face of the Holy Land had drastically changed. The once quiet hills of Judea were now covered with ugly concrete apartment houses hastily erected to make homes for the flood of Jews. Bethlehem was a thriving industrial town belching smoke from automobile and ammunition factories. Smog covered the once familiar scene of the Shepherd's field where the angel of the Lord came and said,"...behold, I bring you good tidings of great joy...." The kibbutz at Ein Gev was working at what seemed insurmountable odds to rid the Sea of Galilee of industrial pollutants that had killed the once famous "St. Peter's fish."

Then Helen leaned on my shoulder and sobbed, "George, even the Garden Tomb has disappeared. And do you know what's in its place? A big super 8 lane highway that starts at Tel Aviv, goes through Jerusalem and ends at Haifa. All that's left is a little marker on the side of the road that says, 'Here once was a Tomb where some Christians believed their Christ was buried.'"

A jolting air pocket awakened me from my sleep of memory. How I wish I could relive those days with Helen in Jerusalem. But it was too late. Soon I would again meet Brother Bartholomew. I had confidence in him. Many had asked me what he looked like. To me he looks like a prophet. In him there is no hypocrisy, and his followers love him. Tall, well shaped, his hair is not too long, just long enough to portray that fatherly appeal...that appeal of confidence. His eyes are bright blue, crystal clear. I have seen him laugh. I have seen him weep. And to me his extraordinary attractiveness and divine perfections surpass the children of men in every sense. He is most eloquent. And if there was such a thing as divine...this man Brother Bartholomew is divine!

The landing in Washington was uneventful...that is, until I stepped out and seemed swarmed over by a bunch of reporters and photographers. How odd, I remember thinking, why me? I am a reporter. Why would anyone want my picture?

One of my photographer friends caught my eye, "Hey, George, look this way. I need a good shot for my paper."

"What's the big event, fellas?" I'm not important. Is this a joke?"

With that Tom Malone grabbed my arm. He was an important cog in the WORLD NETWORK TELEVISION conglomerate.

"Tom, what gives and why all this publicity?"

"I'm sorry, George, you weren't informed earlier...and I can't tell you yet, but Brother Bartholomew has some big plans for you...that's why you're in the spotlight. Right now we have to rush to the TV station. BB is having a nationwide ON THE AIR press conference."

"BB, who is that?"

"BB...that's our short nickname for BROTHER BAR- THOLOMEW...but don't ever use it in his presence. It offends him. With his plans he will have to be some sort of god!"

THE PRESS CONFERENCE

The TV studio was huge. In fact it was the biggest one in the world. There were 6 tiers of cushioned seats curved in a semi-circle so everyone had a front row view of the speaker. This intimate arrangement seated 666 people. The first rows were reserved for Brother Bartholomew's cabinet and a select number of reporters and photographers. Special micro- phones were worn at the lapel of each reporter. The room was entirely dark...except for one spotlight that focused on Brother Bartholomew.

As I entered the studio I sensed the quiet, reverent hush. The thick carpeted rugs cushioned my footsteps. An usher led me to the front row and he quickly adjusted a micro- phone to my lapel. A glint of recognition seemed to come from the face of Brother Bartholomew.

Suddenly the red ON THE AIR sign blinked away the darkness and the announcer broke the silence while a world listened.

LADIES AND GENTLEMEN, THE PRESIDENT OF THE UNITED STATES

As though he had the situation well under control Brother Bartholomew started speaking. I had often said that if bullets were flying all around him and if his boat were sinking, Brother Bartholomew could speak one word and the bullets would cease...he could take one step and walk on water. There was something special about this man...something that demanded respect and inspired confidence. His voice broke my thoughts...

GOOD EVENING AMERICA and the WORLD! This is a night to remember.
To some it may be a night of confusion,
             a night of disaster
             .a night of despair
But it is none of these.
No this night,
       Tonight
    IS A NIGHT OF DESTINY
And because I want you to know all of the facts I have decided against a prepared text. Instead I have selected 6 of America's best reporters to question me on today's events...events known by some as RAPTURE...but which were indeed phenomena easily explained.

The announcer then said, "Thank you, Mr. President. Our first question is from George Omega."

I was shocked. No one had prepared me for this. This certainly was going to be unrehearsed. What would I ask? Certainly I couldn't jeopardize my career now. My remarks would be seen by hundreds of millions across the world. Hesitatingly I stood up and in my mind I framed a question, then spoke: "Sir, all of us must agree that something most unusual happened today. People have just seemed to disappear. My wife..." I couldn't go on. My voice choked up. Brother Bartholomew intervened and broke the embarrassing silence:

> *Friends,* I told you this would be unrehearsed. George Omega is a trusted advisor to me. I value his guidance. What he is trying to say is that in this rapture occurrence his wife and two children have disappeared. I have already instituted a search for them. It would seem the Darts of Satan would attempt anything to undermine the quest for peace...even to strike at a wife and two tender little children. But, George, rest at ease, we will not fail.

It was as though Brother Bartholomew was making a holy command. His voice had a reassuring ring as he proceeded to answer my question.

> Friends of the World. Yes, even BROTHERS OF THE WORLD, for in this time of need, all of us must be BROTHERS. It would seem from time immemorial people have been telling us the sky is falling. But has it fallen yet? Of course not. Remember in June 1969 when the San Francisco CHRONICLE reported that a planet was about to hit the earth. That was 31 years ago. Did it occur? Of course not. And in December 1943 Edgar Cayce predicted Atlantis would rise again. Has anyone seen Atlantis?

The audience laughed.

> Cayce said Japan would go into the sea; New York City would disappear. But these events have not

occurred! We must emulate Alexander the Great. An eclipse of the sun occurred just as Alexander was preparing to engage in a major battle. The event spread panic among his troops. Alexander was a man of courage. To him the eclipse was not an omen of doom but a benediction of blessing. He inspired his army to go on. The next day he won a smashing victory over his enemies. I ask you this one question...if this so-called RAPTURE occurred, why are our outstanding clergy still here? Bishop Arthur has just arrived from Europe. Brother Arthur, please stand up and tell us what you have discussed with me.

Bishop Arthur stood up. I had heard about him, but had never met this man who Brother Bartholomew respected. I understood he was a cleric who came from France. Some

Beware of false prophets, which come to you in sheep's clothing, but inwardly they are ravening wolves. (Matthew 7:15).

referred to him as the progressive cleric. He had a godly appearance, seemed humble, yet had piercing eyes that commanded attention.

Thank you Brother Bartholomew. May I first say the world has always had its "Chicken Littles" to cackle and crow about the sky falling down on our heads.

But may I remind you of I Corinthians 10:13 which tells us: "There hath no temptation taken you but such as is common to man: but God is faithful, who will not suffer you to be tempted above that ye are able; but will with the temptation also make a way to escape, that ye may be able to bear it."

And the next verse, my friends, is most important! "Wherefore, my dearly beloved, flee from idolatry."

The audience was spellbound as Bishop Arthur continued:

The event you witnessed today which some call the RAPTURE is simply a temptation. But God is telling us here that He is faithful and He will make a way to escape. We are also told that those who believed this heretical doctrine of the RAPTURE are idolators. Why the word RAPTURE does not even appear in Scripture. And I have quoted these verses from the beloved original King James Version of the Bible. This is not a new version, my friends. Putting aside faith, would it not seem strange to you that if there were such an event as the RAPTURE, that we clergy who are closest to God and have the mind of God would STILL BE HERE ON EARTH? The fact is WE ARE HERE. And every outstanding clergyman is *here*. WE HAVE NOT DISAPPEARED. The disappearance of many seems to be a biological secret that we cannot at this moment yet explain. But in due time, it will be revealed. But this much I can tell you, God has allowed these events to occur for a purpose. RIGHT NOW, those of you who have a Bible, turn to Revelation 1:7. It reads:

Behold, he cometh with clouds and every eye shall see Him.

There is no doubt we are living in a day of clouds. And right now every eye, through the scientific miracle of our TV space stations, is witnessing a most momentous event.

QUICKLY NOW, read verse 16:

And he had in his right hand seven stars...

And his countenance was as the sun shineth in his strength.

LOOK NOW AT BROTHER BARTHOLOMEW. LOOK AT HIS RIGHT HAND!

There was an audible gasp in that huge auditorium. All eyes focused at the spiral of light that shone on Brother Bartholomew. Slowly a smile came across his face. No one had noticed it before. But in his right hand was a shining gold septer. And emblazoned in diamonds was a cluster of stars.

The air was electric.

Slowly Brother Bartholomew arose and waved the scepter as if to impart a blessing on the audience. The reflecting light from the diamonds seemed to cast a halo around his head.

I am come in my Father's name, and ye receive me not: if another shall come in his own name, him ye will receive. (John 5:43).

And somehow I knew no further explanation of today's event was needed. We were standing in the presence of God's messenger.

The silence was broken by the click of heels as the smartly dressed U.S. Marine Band snapped to attention and broke into the martial strains of HAIL TO THE CHIEF.

It had been a hard day. Emotionally I was wrung out and drip dried. Bed was a welcome sight and soon the day's events faded into slumberland.

I awoke to the sound of church bells. It must be Sunday. For once I planned to attend the National Cathedral in Washington. After breakfast I hopped a cab and within a few minutes was at this imposing entrance.

A guard stopped me.

"May I have your ticket, please?"

"Ticket for what?" I asked.

"I'm sorry, sir, you may not understand," he replied. "National Cathedral, as is the case with many churches, is now a museum of living history. Six months ago Brother Bartholomew proposed this wonderful opportunity at the suggestion of Bishop Arthur."

Then it all came back to me. Of course, how could I be so forgetful? I purchased a ticket and entered.

There were many displays, some enclosed in glass, other set in a scenic panorama. They captured history and events as they were in 1969 and 1970. This was now the year 2000 and the last 30 years had seen some very radical changes. That's why Bishop Arthur thought it wise to use the mostly empty churches for a worthwhile cause.

A crowd was gathered in the area the National Cathedral pulpit once stood. I later learned this one exhibit was among the most popular. For it was an exhibit of something that now was almost non-existent.

It is called THE LIVING TREE exhibit. It is one of the last remaining trees in the world. It looks rather small and frail and leaves have an autumn appearance. In the background a painted mural of a forest shows the visitor how the tree once looked in its natural environment before the pollution disaster that almost wiped out all vegetation from the earth.

A wise scientist, seeing the handwriting on the wall, had carefully placed this tree in a germ and pollution-free environment for posterity.

Suddenly my heart leaped forward!

Could I believe my eyes?

Was it all a dream? The rapture couldn't have occurred. There looking at the LIVING TREE was Helen...there was little Sue and Tommy. I was sure it was them.

Tears welled up in my eyes. I cried out...HELEN, HELEN ...but I was so overcome, only an awkward sound came out. SUE...TOMMY...YOU'RE HERE! THANK GOD YOU'RE SAFE.

Quickly I pushed my way through the crowd. The puzzled looks on their faces didn't disturb me. Suddenly the path was wide open. They were still looking at the LIVING TREE.

HELEN! SUE! TOM! I shouted.

The family turned.

And to me it seemed like the bottom of the world collapsed as I dropped my head in unbelief.

For the faces I saw were not Helen, not Sue, not Tom. The silhouettes were close resemblances. But these were people I did not know.

I felt a tap on my shoulders as I half knelt on the floor. I turned and saw a hand with a scepter...a scepter with six, sparkling stars...and I arose...and followed.

Was it all a dream? The rapture couldn't have occurred. There looking at the LIVING TREE was Helen...there was little Sue and Tommy. I was sure it was them.

Chapter 3

The Sinister Plot

Brother Bartholomew was a man of compassion. He understood my grief and disappointment at the Living Tree exhibit.

Half in tears my voice cracked as I said to him, "Sir, I don't know how I can go on!"

"I understand, George," he replied softly, "it reminds me of the philosophical clock which spent great time meditating upon its future. It reasoned that it had to tick twice each second, 120 times each minute or 7200 times every hour - in 24 hours, 172,800 ticks. This meant 63,072,000 times every year, calculated the clock. And in ten years it would have to tick 630,720,000 times! At this point it collapsed from nervous exhaustion. But when it revived, it saw in a moment of insight that all it had to do was *one tick at a time.* So it began, and now, after a hundred years, it is still a respected grandfather clock. What I'm trying to say is this, George, there are perilous times ahead . . . but we must live one minute at a time meeting each challenge as it presents itself. Otherwise this country and the world will be lost."

The next day Brother Bartholomew summoned me to his office at the White House. I could tell there was something on his mind as I hesitatingly sat down. He seemed in deep thought and I was afraid to disturb him.

My inner fears were quickly dispelled. I looked up at Brother Bartholomew and smiled. I knew then that everything would turn out all right. The next day Brother Bartholomew summoned me to his office at the White House. I could tell there was something on his mind as I hesitatingly sat down. He seemed in deep thought and I was afraid to disturb him.

"George," he began, "I need a trusted advisor, one who can be my right arm, one who has had some touch with the Rapture problem and yet one in whom I can place complete confidence. George, I want you to be that man."

I was stunned. Me, an ordinary reporter. Why had Brother Bartholomew taken a sudden liking to me and thrust me into the place of prominence. What would this mean?

"Sir, I don't quite understand, why me?"

"Good question, George. You haven't tasted leadership. There are too many leaders in my Government with big ambitions. I need a down-to-earth individual to become my Presidential advisor. I've watched you ever since you first interviewed me in the Middle East. And somehow, I knew one day I would be relying on your assistance. I have big plans, George, very big plans . . . plans that may seem fantastic to you now. But I want you to be a part of these plans. All I can tell you now . . . is one day the whole world will know Brother Bartholomew. And humbly I want to serve my Father in Heaven."

This was what impressed me about Brother Bartholomew . . . and yet somewhat confused me . . . his constant reference to God as though he had a holy calling. And yet I must admit, it was because of this that I replied, "Yes, Mr. President, I will accept."

"Good, I knew you would."

With that he rang a buzzer and Tom Malone entered. He was no longer a television executive. Malone was now Presidential Secretary and quite efficient. While rather tall I noticed his head always dipped slightly forward. It gave him a rather apologetic appearance. It also made him not quite as tall as Brother Bartholomew. In the days to come Tom and I were to become fast friends. It would be a mistake that I would regret.

"Tom," Brother Bartholomew instructed, "summon the Mayors to my office tomorrow for an open press conference . . . all of them . . . New York City, Miami, Philadelphia, Los Angeles and Chicago . . . and, oh yes, Dallas. I want to brief George on the state of the Union as well as make public the problems we face."

Brother Bartholomew gave frequent press conferences. In private he told me that the public must always be informed on every step. It was what he called, "communication." After all, he reasoned, an informed public will accept all types of news if they know about it. It was a good way to keep down revolts and problem areas. BB must have taken a course in psychology for he understood people . . . knew how to agree yet disagree, how to quell factions and make them the best of friends. It was this type of leadership that projected him so quickly to the Presidency.

The United States was now made up of six cities. I remember the history books of the 1970's. I called it the Golden Era. Hardly any problems, a few rebellious youth, age of the mini-skirt, a small war they called the War in Vietnam, and many, many hundreds of important cities. But now with the population explosion . . . only six cities were left. What once were Indianapolis and Fort Wayne, Dayton, St. Louis and Minneapolis were now called CHICAGO. City after city had been merged into this Midwest conglomerate. The countryside was gone. These small towns were now suburbs of CHICAGO. PHILADELPHIA had swallowed up Harrisburg, Pittsburgh, Scranton and Williamsport. NEW YORK CITY extended as far north as Portland, Maine. LOS ANGELES went as far east as Denver. One patch of farm land remained. The state of Kansas was declared farm area. Topeka and Wichita were leveled to make the complete state a farm oasis. The rest of the United States was basically the six major cities.

Brother Bartholomew summoned in a group of reporters, and announced to them my appointment as his Presidential Advisor. From then on the world about me seemed to change. I was greeted everywhere with a hallowed respect. It was as though I was an advisor to god. A few reservations about this new appointment crept into my mind, but each time I would hastily dismiss them as fantasy. This was a new age and I had complete confidence in Brother Bartholomew.

The meeting the next day brought me closer to the problems of the day. As the TV cameras focused in on the meeting of city mayors the striking voice of Brother Bartholomew caught my attention.

My fellow citizens and honored mayors. We are facing a crisis in our cities today . . . a crisis of which each citizen must be aware. This informal meeting of mayors, I hope, will bring you current on these problems and what you and I can do about it. It was Sir Julian Huxley who said in 1969 that the 1980's would be a perilous time. It is now the year 2000 and it is very evident he knew what he was talking about. It took initially thousands of years to reach the first billion human beings by 1700, only 130 more years to add the second billion by 1830, 30 years to add the third billion by 1960, 15 years to add the fourth billion in 1975. And now in the year 2000 our population is almost 7 billion. To be exact 6 billion, 6 hundred and 66 thousand.

Therefore, I have asked my Presidential Advisor, George Omega, to brief you on two recent edicts we have recommended to Congress. This will be a good way for you to meet the new man in my cabinet in whom I place utmost confidence. . . George Omega.

"Thank you, Mr. President. Honorable mayors and citizens of the United States. Here are the two new laws to take effect upon confirmation by Congress:

1. TRANSPORTATION BILL
   This bill seeks to solve both   And he shall...think to change
                                      times and laws.... (Daniel 7:25).

the air pollution and transportation crisis that plagues our country. The bill recommends the abolishment of all automobiles over the next two years. Automobiles will be used after that only by members of local and national government.

2. BIRTH COUPONS
The rapid rise of population has made voluntary birth control ineffective. Passage of a bill is recommended to control births, issuing birth coupons to a limited number of eligible, healthy young adults.

These are the first of many bills Brother Bartholomew will introduce to Congress this year. Thank you, Mr. President."

And with that, I sat down, somewhat horrified at what I had read. I had not seen the script earlier. It was thrust into my hands just moments before we went on the air. While these were Brother Bartholomew's recommendations, the entire nation was looking at me. I was the one who announced the edicts. I had a lurking suspicion that it would be I who would soon become the unpopular one.

Television news was most important in these chaotic days. NBC alone was budgeting over $5 million per week for news coverage. Live color signals via satellite was costing $25,000 for the first ten minutes and $1000 for each additional minute . . . and this was reaching every city in Europe. Film crews were earning $2000 per week.

Brother Bartholomew arose and addressed the assembly of mayors. He called on the mayor of New York to present his report. The mayor, a handsome and quiet young man had the air of efficiency as he described the almost impossible conditions of his city.

"Mr. President, some still think of New York as a Dream City, but I believe a more appropriate word would be "nightmare." Three-fourths of our population is on welfare. We haven't seen the sun in weeks! New York City belches into the air 10,200 tons of sulphur dioxide, 1200 tons of dirt and 28,000 tons of carbon monoxide daily. Robberies have increased to such a proportion we have assigned civilians in each block as patrolmen with power of arrest. They also may act as jury and judge. It is our only way to combat this age of lawlessness. Our sewage plant has backed up to the point of a health disaster. Over 1300 million gallons of raw waste

This know also, that in the last days perilous times shall come. For men shall be lovers of their own selves, covetous, boasters, proud, blasphemers, disobedient to parents, unthankful, unholy.
Without natural affection, truce-breakers, false accusers, incontinent, fierce, despisers of those that are good.
Traitors, heady, highminded lovers of pleasure more than lovers of God. (2 Timothy 3:1-4).

still pour every day into surrounding rivers and ocean. And there are over 20 million cars in New York! New York is a disaster area, Mr. President. I am afraid the next step is the Titanic lifeboats scene — every man for himself. Everybody is trying to get into their lifeboat to survive. It's everyone for himself. May I suggest a pure democracy or republic cannot work in this day and age. As much as I hate the word, we need an elective Dictatorship...a benevolent authority who will make the laws and see that they are enforced by military rule if necessary. It is our only hope for survival."

And with that the mayor of New York sat down. For a moment there was silence. All of us knew conditions were getting out of hand. Ever since a Vice President's speech 30 years ago in November, 1969, when it was implied that television media needed some type of governmental control . . . the populace was more open to acceptance of wider federal regulations. And Congress, embroiled in political favortism, simply could not act fast enough to meet the crisis of the day. Certainly something had to be done, and done quickly. Everyone knew what had to be done. But none had the courage to say it. Now it was said — so everyone not only in the United States but in all the world could hear. America was on the road to a dictatorship . . . a benign dictatorship. It was her only hope of survival. America was no longer unsinkable. Like the Titanic, it was approaching the iceberg of disaster. It must act now before an unruly population in a rush to save themselves catapult an entire nation into a chaotic revolt from which it would never recover.

As the other mayors droned on with their reports, all similar in their brink of disaster content, my mind wandered. What was this world coming to?

Could it possibly be true that we were saying goodbye to a free elective system? There seemed no other way to turn. Funny, how America grew so fast technologically, turned a virgin farmland into ugly, gasping industrial complexes . . . something like a cancerous growth that soon revolted spreading disaster wherever its tentacles reached. The 1976 World's Fair had as its theme AMERICA, LAND OF FREEDOM AND PROGRESS. And now, just 24 years later, both of these facts were to become just a bad dream. I remember my parents telling me how proud they were to sing "America The Beautiful." There were no more "fields of amber grain" nor "purple mountain majesties." The early riots of young people in the late 1960's had triggered a nation of irresponsibility. Then some thought it shocking that youth should dictate to teachers, have freedom in love and sex without marriage. Their freedom came but it became a hollow victory for they lost purpose in life and never found the utopia for which they were seeking. The sex filth I view today openly on the streets, in specially built communion booths in churches — they call it the communion of love — was simply too shocking for me to think further upon.

Now it seemed we had made full circle. Like the decline and fall of the Roman Empire we were going to be swallowed up in our own wickedness . . . unless a saviour came along. Somehow I feel, Brother Bartholomew is that saviour. How privileged I am to serve him.

The meeting was drawing to a close and the Mayor of Los Angeles was making a proposal.

"Mr. President, all of us are aware of how critical a problem our nation faces. Such a problem calls for drastic steps to be taken immediately. As mayors we have individually met with leaders in our constituency and collectively we agree that an elective dictatorship is urgent right now . . . if we are to exist. Ancient Rome elected a dictator in times of extreme urgency. It is with this same thought in mind that our mayors have been unanimous in asking that you be entrusted by Congress with dictatorial powers, subject of course, to recall by a majority vote of the 6 mayors. And to this end we have forwarded such a bill to Congress."

No one apparently was surprised. The inevitable had come. There was no other way. There just had to be a strong man if we were to survive.

And I stood upon the sand of the sea, and saw a beast rise up.... (Revelation 13:1).

Brother Bartholomew then stood up. Everyone had confidence in him. Every problem he tackled in the past he had accomplished and resolved excellently. True, not everyone could be satisfied but recent polls placed his popularity at a high 76% . . . much higher than any other President enjoyed under less chaotic circumstances. I am sure he realized this as he spoke.

Let me first say that I indeed am gratified by the confidence you have placed in me . . . and also very humbled . . . for I am a new citizen to your country.

My Middle East origins and birth were most unique and now I can see the reason for them. For this simple upbringing away from the clutter of humanity has, I believe, prepared me for my mission on earth. I do believe that I do indeed follow God's will, and under God nothing is impossible.

Suddenly the door burst open. A flushed Tom Malone rushed in with a paper in his hand, quickly mounted the podium and handed it to Brother Bartholomew. Brother Bartholomew quickly glanced at the sheet and retaining his composure continued: "I have just been handed a memo from Senator Mason who is in Congress which is now in joint session. He has advised me that Russian troops are moving in the direction of Israel. He has also assured me that Congress will quickly approve the TOTAL POWERS LAW for the Presidency."

The audience was bristling with whispers. What many had feared was already beginning to happen. Russia would no longer wait for Israel. And now powers greater than the Gulf of Tonkin resolution were about to be granted to the President of the United States. But there was no other way.

And thou shalt come up against my people of Israel, as a cloud to cover the land; it shall be in the latter days, and I will bring thee against my land, that the heathen may know me, when I shall be sanctified in thee, O Gog, before their eyes. (Ezekiel 38:16).

Brother Bartholomew spoke again: Gentlemen, after this meeting I will be ordering my Presidential Advisor, George Omega to fly to Russia with a plan for peace.

Brother Bartholomew, with steel-like composure and firmness during a crisis, continued:

But now I have another proposal which will help resolve the problems confronting our population which, despite the present emergency, I might as well announce now as planned. As wonderful as our computers are, our rising population makes it difficult to record each individual by a name plus a Social

Security number, a Medicare number, a Birth
Guarantee number and a Food allotment number. I
am therefore recommending to Congress that each individual be assigned one number. That one number
will be carried by him through life. By this one number identification system we will save billions of
dollars, be better able to control crime, offenders of
our population and food laws. At first this may seem
drastic and harsh. . .

But you have appointed me because I have resolved the problems of our day. And this is the only
way to reach the road of sensibility and peace. I am
most confident Congress will pass favorably on this
recommendation and on others that I will issue upon
receiving the TOTAL POWERS confirmation from
your elected officials. Thank you.

It was all over and I rushed over to congratulate Brother
Bartholomew, as did all the Mayors and important government officials.

Then, quite worn out, I headed for my office for a little
relaxation before lunch. On my desk was a package. It was
tied with string and falling apart. Suddenly my heart leaped.
That handwriting. I recognized it instantly. It was Helen's.
She was alive!

But then I saw the postmark . . . it was dated before that
dreadful Rapture date. It seemed as though this box had
followed me around the country and months later it had been
at last finally delivered to me here in Washington.

Quickly I tore it open. Crumpled newspapers were used
as packing. Funny, they were very old newspapers from a
little town called Tunkhannock, Pennsylvania. There was a
column titled "From our Early Files" and bits of news as
they occurred in 1908 and 1928.

1908
Rev. Wolcott, of Mehoopany, has organized a
Bible class of about 20 men. They meet in the
classroom of the M.E. Church.

Funny, how memories come back. Bible classes hadn't
been held anywhere since 1975. The religious leaders felt this
was a restriction of individual freedoms. The early 70's were
filled with so many new versions of the Bible that soon they
lost their impact on the people. It became unpopular to even
have a Bible. Church leaders admonished their congregations
to be more concerned about the social conditions of today
than the fairy tales of yesterday. I glanced back down at the
paper.

> 1928
> Several cars went through town Tuesday
> morning, occupied by members of the
> Roosevelt Highway Association going to Erie.
> The leading car was driven by a woman
> smoking a cigarette.

So that's when it all started . . . the growth of the automobile to where now it was a curse and a threat to human
existence. And if those people thought a girl smoking a
cigarette was an oddity those day, they should have lived
today. This was the age of unisex. And somehow I was uncomfortable in it. Little did I dream two years ago that Birth
Coupons would become a reality but rampant sex without
marriage had overpopulated the world much quicker than
biologists had earlier predicted. Cigarettes had long ago
been abolished by law but the law looked favorably on a
new item which resembled a cigarette but placed the user
into a highly euphoric condition. Some Senators had argued
however, that even though this was a drug, it was beneficial
in this age of crowding and over population to have at least
half of the population in a placid, half drugged attitude. As
bad as the situation was it was the most acceptable way to
somewhat quell what could become an insurmountable
problem.

After throwing out what seemed like a boxful of paper
suddenly I spotted at the very bottom a little black book.
Instantly I knew what it was and quickly I glanced around
the room to see that no one was looking. I reached in to lift

it out . . . but then I remembered . . . all trusted advisors are also watched by a trusted TV spy system. Each room had hidden monitors. But I knew where mine was simply becuase it was in need of minor repairs. A slight beeping sound was being emitted . . . a sound normally too soft to hear. But one day soon after the Living Tree episode when I thought that I had found Helen I had knelt down at my desk to pray. No sooner had I knelt when Brother Bartholomew called me in and suggested that prayer would best be answered by faith in his ability to solve not only the problems of the world but my personal problems as well.

How did he know I was praying, I wondered. When I returned to my office I was determined to find out. And I did. The small television monitor was part of a plaque that read PRAYER CHANGES THINGS.

Quickly I grabbed the box which Helen had sent. I walked out of the office and rushed to my apartment. In the privacy of a small closet I tenderly lifted the black book. It was more than a book. It was a Bible purposely very small so it could be hidden. For they had long ago become a rarity. I knew I must at all costs hold on to it and read it. Yet I knew that doing so might later cost me my life. I had full confidence in Brother Bartholomew but somehow I felt he must not know of my find.

On the way back to the office I stopped for a quick bite of lunch. Even this had changed. No more thick, juicy steaks or corned beef sandwiches like my father had been fond of. Scarcity of land made it impossible to graze cattle and the population explosion had placed all meat at a premium. Hardly anyone could afford it at $600 a pound . . . for this represented to most a week's wages. Besides the substitute foods weren't too bad once you got used to them. Science had developed new foods from unexpected sources in the race against starvation. Worms, toads, termites and grasshoppers are now made to look and taste like ham. Special spinning processes take crude oil, mix it with bacteria to develop protein cakes. Protein cakes are chicken, steak and ham

flavored. For lunch I settled on the special of the day . . .
ham protein cake with french fried grasshoppers and a cup of
coffee.

As I entered the office, Tom Malone stopped me.

"George, Brother Bartholomew would like to see you on
that Russian announcement. And when you're through there,
stop in to my office for a briefing."

With my schedule so hectic there was little time to think
about Helen and my two children. And it appeared that my
schedule would become even busier in the near future.

Quickly I stepped into Brother Bartholomew's office. He
was looking out the window but as though he knew I was
coming he said, "Hello, George, did you have a nice lunch?"

"Yes sir, thank you . . . Tom Malone said that you wanted
to see me about the Russian situation."

"That's right, George, sit down."

And with that he left the window and sat behind his desk.
On his desk was a plaque. It appeared like mine but as I
looked at it . . . it was different for it read THINGS CHANGE
PRAYER. He saw me look at it and spoke before I could ask.

"THINGS do change prayer, George. For we must be doers
not only hearers. Do you recall James 1:22. It goes like this:
'Be ye doers of the word, and not hearers only.' It's in your
Bible, George, the one you took home with you at lunch and
opened in your closet. You see, George, I know, but don't
be fearful, everyone should read God's Word. The trouble is
that not many can read it with understanding. I believe if
my people will pray, then things will change. And as their
leader I have the power over THINGS which will CHANGE
PRAYER into rejoicing."

I was stunned. How did he know I had a Bible? I must be
more careful in the future. Well, anyway, he couldn't read
my thoughts . . . or could he?

"Enough preaching, George, I really called you in to confirm to you that I am sending you to Moscow and to the other

capitals of Europe. Premier Alexi Bazenoff is getting itchy feet over Israel and I have a personal message that may surprise him. I want you to carry that message. I've alerted Air Force One to fly you."

"Very well sir, I can go immediately. I can stop by Tom Malone's office for the briefing."

"Very good, George, but won't you want to say goodbye to Faye before you leave?"

My face turned ashen. My knees felt as though they would buckle from underneath me. Faye! How did he know? In fact in my anguish over Helen and Tommy and Sue, I had forgotten about Faye. Faye, my daughter by a previous marriage, had not been one for religious formalism. My first wife had died in a plane crash. Faye was in her teens at the time. When this tragedy occurred she went to New York to complete her studies, and then she married Bill Sanders, a rising young executive. Helen had often talked to her and to Bill about Christ but they shrugged it off with, "We'll enjoy life now . . . there's plenty of time."

Brother Bartholomew was speaking again, "Yes, George, I know about Faye and about Bill. They're safe in New York. We've located them. Why not go into Tom's office and talk to them on the Picturephone."

Quickly I ran to Tom's office. It seemed prophetical that Tom had already known, for he was dialing New York for me. Suddenly a picture came on the tube. It was Faye picking up the phone in her apartment and as I picked up the phone she saw me and in joy filled with tears she shouted: "Daddy, oh, daddy, it's so good to hear from you! Where's Mom?"

She always called Helen, Mom, because she loved her even though she wasn't her real mother. Faye said that Helen had certain spiritual qualities about her that she wished she could attain.

As best I could I explained the Rapture incident, and that since then I couldn't locate Mom or little Sue or Tommy. The conversation ended after 15 minutes with a promise we would get together for a reunion the minute I came back from Russia.

I was walking on Cloud Nine as I hung up the receiver.

I felt I was a part of life again. Not everything was gone. I still had Faye and Bill. The link had not been broken.

But as Tom Malone briefed me on my Moscow mission somehow deep within me dwelt a feeling that I was to become an instrument in a sinister plot. If I had known then what I now know I could hardly have kept on living. But the die had been cast. And I was part of the mold.

Chapter 4

Flight To Moscow

Tom Malone was to accompany me to Russia, whether as an aide or an informer, I did not know. But I was prepared for any event and decided that caution on my part was the better part of valor.

We arrived at the airport a little ahead of schedule so Tom and I sat down for a cup of coffee. For lack of desire to say much I commented, "Flight operations have certainly changed in the last 30 years, haven't they."

"Quite so, George. When I was a boy in the early 70's we were all thrilled about the 747. My parents called it a new air age. I can remember it held up to 490 passengers and was three-fourths of a football field in length. Its average cruising speed was 625 miles an hour. It was a bargain at $20 million each. And the amazing things were those tractors which wheeled them from the terminal to the runway. They were $125,000 each."

"Funny thing, Tom," I replied, "I was just thinking about my grandparents . . . they just wouldn't believe the world

"...There was grandmom and grandpop looking at the moon."

if they saw it today. Back home I had an old charcoal picture a friend of theirs made on their honeymoon. There was grandmom and grandpop looking at the moon . . . so much in love. It took them 7 days to cross the Atlantic. Now it takes just 2 hours, 20 minutes! Somehow I feel they packed a lot more living into their life, simple as it was. Maybe that's what made life so rich, so meaningful. They had a reason for living . . . and they enjoyed every minute of it."

"George, it was Dorion who said, 'The love of the past is often but hatred of the present.' Could it be that these times disturb you? I recall a story my father told me. One night three horsemen were riding across an Eastern desert. As they crossed the dry bed of a river, a voice called, 'Halt!' They did so and the voice continued telling them to dismount, pick up some pebbles and put them in their pockets. Then the voice said, 'You have done as I commanded. Tomorrow at sun-up you will be both glad and sorry.'"

"Mystified, they rode on, as directed. At sunrise, they reached into their pockets and found that the pebbles were diamonds, rubies and other precious stones. Then they thought of the warning, and they were both glad and sorry — glad they had taken some, sorry they had not taken more."

"George, you are living in an enlightened age. Pick up all the pebbles you can now . . . for somehow I have a feeling that this opportunity won't be knocking too long."

I didn't know what to make of Tom. Sometimes he was like a philosophical patronizing father.

A military officer notified us our flight was ready. Quickly we boarded the Boeing SST. This was the President's own plane built to fly 2000 miles per hour. This luxury craft had special offices and extra roominess so that it only carried 50 passengers. All types of electronic gear, special cameras and exotic equipment were aboard. Some referred to it as the Spy in the Sky. Rumor had it that the sophisticated cameras could photograph a man lighting a cigarette on a cloudy, rainy night from 100 miles high and could measure the growth of beard on his face.

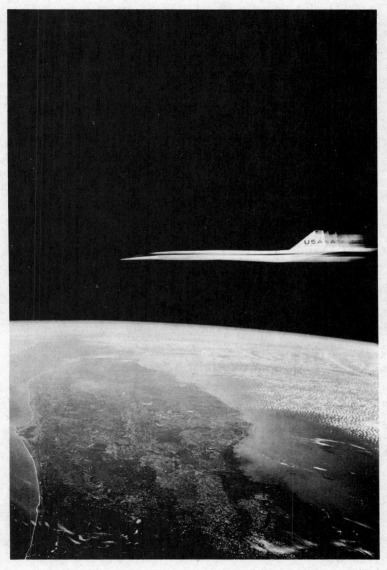

This was the President's own plane built to fly 2000 miles per hour ...we had reached 60,000 feet.

Tom quickly settled down for the flight by ordering a cocktail. Many times I would have done the same thing. But since the Rapture occurrence, perhaps I had become somewhat religious. When Tom offered me a drink, I declined. As Tom stretched wearily back into the seat, took a few sips, I could feel one of his little lectures coming on.

"You know, George, there's a rule of thumb in transportation that every time you cut travel time in half you double the volume of traffic between two points. This was true thousands of years ago after man first caught a horse and rode him. And its true now. No wonder Brother Bartholomew had to abolish cars from the scene. We were being overrun by them. This is no longer a 24 hour world. It's a 12 hour world. That's it, George, a 12 hour world! Man is now able to fly to any major airport in the world in just 12 hours — just half a day. Think of it."

With that the "droop snoot" nose of our SST eased up and locked into position. Within minutes we had reached an altitude of 60,000 feet. This was 25,000 feet higher than the commercial jets of the early 70's. At 60,000 feet additional engines — more powerful than the engines of the Queen Elizabeth II ocean liner — sent the craft forward at mach 2.2 speed.

Tom took me up to the cabin to look at the controls. I noticed one dial suddenly flashing a red warning signal. The plane nosed down into a sharp dive. It was like dropping suddenly in an elevator. I felt sick, lost my balance and slid half way back to the tail. Tom accompanied me, cocktail and all. It was a silly, yet frightening sight. Shaking and wet with perspiration I made my way back to my seat. Tom filled me in on the details.

"Sorry, George, I should have known. You see at 60,000 feet or higher solar radiation and solar flares become a real hazard to planes. That flashing light warned us that our radiation meter had encountered dangerous conditions. That's why it was necessary to swoop down to 40,000 feet."

Time had certainly been shortened. Just 2 hours 20 minutes to London and just 45 minutes more to Moscow. I fell asleep and the next nudge I felt was Tom telling me to freshen up and shave. We would be landing in Moscow in 10 minutes.

Tom briefed me on protocol. Said our guide would be Tamara. She would make sure we said hello to the right people in government, and pronounced their names correctly.

When we arrived at the deplaning ramp instead of a welcoming committee it looked like a funeral. Black crepe hung over the terminal entrance. I could see that the delegation of officials awaiting us all had black armbands. Alexi Bazenoff did not seem to be in the delegation. This was most unusual.

We came down the ramp, shook hands with all the dignitaries and then proceeded to the microphone stand that was awaiting us. Brother Bartholomew had already provided me with the script to read at this welcoming ceremony.

Fellow Brothers,

In less than 3 hours I have flown from America to Russia. This feat alone must make us brothers.

Brother Bartholomew has asked me to come to Russia to convey his deep wishes for cooperation. The United States has long had a policy of co-existence. But this Administration has now adopted the policy of cooperation. We are with you in your plans, as well as in your aspirations. Our sincere hope is that our discussions with your leaders might prove fruitful for world peace. Thank you.

There was polite clapping and we entered the waiting limousines. Tamara introduced herself. She was a solidly built, determined-looking Russian of 35, daughter of the director of a large Moscow factory. Quite jokingly I said, "I didn't know our arrival would have a funeral welcome."

Quite apologetically she replied, "How foolish of me. You couldn't have known. It happened so quickly. Some of our best men including Premier Bazenoff's son were captured by the Israeli army, tortured and their bodies thrown into the Dead Sea. Our whole nation is up in arms. I'm afraid there's going to be a war. Plans are being made to erect in the Bell Tower of Ivan the Great the enormous Tsar Kolokol, the King of Bells.

...well-drilled soldiers marched past the coffins.

We entered Red Square. The vast cobblestoned rectangle was echoing to the stamp of thousands of feet as well-drilled soldiers marched past the coffins. The familiar Kremlin wall runs the entire length of Red Square and its twenty towers give credence to the banner which says GLORY TO THE PEOPLE — THE BUILDERS.

Tamara reminded us that Russia is not a state, but a world. And within its borders, the Soviet Union — offers a breathtaking geographical sweep being the globe's largest unbroken land mass under a single flag.

Noting our ignorance of their country Tamara suggested that we have an orientation lunch together. Our meeting with Premier Bazenoff was not until 3 so we agreed.

Tom was much impressed with Russia. Apparently he knew some things I didn't know. I got the feeling that Russia was not really our friend and that Brother Bartholomew had a plan in mind . . . a plan to once and for all dismiss this threat to the United States. I was soon to find out.

Tamara told us more of her country.

"From its western extreme near Kaliningrad, the U.S.S.R. stretches some 6000 miles eastward to Bering Strait. There are 149 separate languages spoken by peoples of U.S.S.R. And our country covers 8,650,000 square miles. Moscow alone has 20 million residents!"

"What about Siberia?" I interrupted.

"Siberia is a gold mine of wealth. With Russia's recent discovery of weather control, Siberia is now the bread basket of our nation. You probably remember a time when temperatures were as cold as -96° Fahrenheit but that's a thing of the past. There are still trees here in Siberia! You don't find this true in America, do you? And Russians are better fed than most Americans. When is the last time you had real roast beef? Tonight you will feast on roast beef Stroganof. We Russians have harnessed the sun giving Siberia an even 70° climate year round. It has been a life saver during these difficult days. In the days of your President Eisenhower you sent Mr. Nixon to this country. Your country erected a $3,600,000 exhibit in Sokolniki Park to show us how America lived. But your technology has outraced your common sense. And now Russia is better fed, better clothed and the size of our population while a problem is not as great as yours. You see years ago our State limited the number of children born in each community. We saw what was coming."

I was forced to reluctantly nod affirmatively . . . and as I did Tamara's winning smile brought back memories of Helen. I reached to touch her hand. Somehow she knew and understood the anguish that was mine.

Tamera left us at a guest room in the stately Kremlin halls. We had an hour before our meeting with Dr. Ivan A. Kapitsa, Dean of Soviet physicists. It was Kapitsa who Brother Bartholomew told us believed in the ultimate convergence of the Soviet and American systems of government. And BB was anxious that we sound him out. Perhaps, he had told us, Russia would merge with the United States. If there is any thinking on these lines, let's grab the initiative.

"...Plans are being made to erect in the Bell Tower of Ivan the Great the enormous Tsar Kolokol, the King of Bells."

Tom seemed to think otherwise. As though he knew it from memory he began to rattle off the Kremlin record of Broken Pacts, as he called them.

". . . George, their pact breaking continued through the end of World War II, and through the partitioning of Berlin. The Reds waited until we defeated Japan before conveniently entering the war, then painlessly extracted $1 billion in industrial equipment from Manchuria. They broke every agreement with President Eisenhower; fooled President Johnson. In every war in Vietnam, Laos, and Cuba the Soviet government supplied four-fifths of all of the explosives and 80 percent of all the bullets and mines. President Nixon's Non-Proliferation Treaty was broken by the Reds within one year. And Humphrey and President Ted Kennedy had no better luck. And that was in the 70's. Since then Russia has grabbed up not only Sweden, Finland and Norway but also France."

Tom was right. Something had to be done. Somehow I felt Brother Bartholomew would do it.

A knock on our door signaled us that the time for the big

The long tables of official delegates amazed us. Several hundred dignitaries must have been there. And at each place stood bottles of Russia's best wine and vodka.

meeting had arrived. Tamara led us to St. George's Hall in the Great Kremlin Palace. Inside the hall itself, a huge chandelier illuminated the white marble wall plaques which celebrated the knights who had won fame and honor in the Czarist army. And in the center, of course, there was the usual huge painting of Lenin.

Premier Alexi Bazenoff, wreathed in smiles, quickly came over and gave us the familiar Russian kiss. The long tables of official delegates amazed us. Several hundred dignitaries must have been there. And at each place stood bottles of Russia's best wine and vodka.

We sat down and the proceedings began. Premier Bazenoff spoke first.

"May I first welcome our brothers from America. This is both a happy and a sad occasion. Happy because we are together seeking a common meeting ground with the United States. Sad, because the sinister Jews have slain many of our youth in the prime of their life . . . one of them being my only son."

He choked somewhat as he continued. "Throughout the world their are 88 countries with communist influence, over 1 billion active communist members. This is a rich heritage. To them and to you, we make this toast."

As one, everyone stood and toasted Premier Bazenoff. A hand tapped me on the shoulder. I turned. It was Dr. Kapitsa.

After the introductions Tom and I, taking him aside, peppered him with questions.

"Dr. Kapitsa, why do you believe America and Soviet systems of government will converge?" I asked.

"It's inevitable, Mr. Omega, because only through such a convergence can the two great powers avoid a fatal clash. Look at your government now. It is becoming more dictatorial while ours is becoming more democratic. Your folly in the ABM system made this quite evident. For each anti-ballistic-missile you employed, we too, increased the number of our missiles. We must unite for survival."

Brother Bartholomew had given Tom Malone a sealed envelope before we departed for Russia. Now Tom handed it to me. It was titled simply MESSAGE TO MOSCOW. Premier Bazenoff called for silence and asked me to step to the podium. I had no idea what I was going to say. Tom instructed me that as Brother Bartholomew's representative I was only to read his message.

> Premier Bazenoff, Members of the Politburo,
> Citizens of the World. The United States
> mourns with you the passing of some of your
> nation's youth.
>
> It recognizes that these are desperate days,
> days that call for immediate corrective action.
> For unless the fire of controversy is quickly
> put out, there will be no world tomorrow.
>
> In your quest for freedom the United States
> stands with you. Your actions will be our
> actions. We support Israel's right to exist
> but we condemn her expansionist policies.
>
> This is one world and together, hands across
> the sea, we join with you as brother to brother.
>
> Brother Bartholomew

The words came out but I was shocked at what I was reading. How did Brother Bartholomew know that these Russians would be killed even before it happened? And why this reverse stand supporting Russia against Israel?

The Russians were delighted. The applause was loud and long. Something was happening, right under my nose, but for the life of me, I couldn't put my finger on it.

Late that night we walked through Red Square. Newsboys were hawking the news . . . front page headlines declaring how Israel had tortured Russian soldiers, dumped their bodies in the Dead Sea . . . how America announced it would stand behind Russia.

Tom urged me to hurry back with him to the Palace. It was time to retire for tomorrow would be a long day. I had so many questions but Tom ignored them . . . he seemed intent on reaching our room.

As soon as we entered, he quickly closed the door, pulled up his shirt sleeve to disclose what I thought was a wrist radio. He quickly adjusted some dials, pulled out two ear-phones and told me to listen.

I heard voices . . . but they were in Russian. He quickly pulled a wire from his tie-clasp. Seeing my puzzled look he explained that the tie clasp was a Translating Unit — the wrist radio, a transmitting unit. The voice of Bazenoff was now coming through clearly but not in Russian. It was in English.

"Lenin could have never thought of this plan. Even the Americans were fooled. My son got too close to a Chinese border. The fool. He was always too ambitious anyway, and getting democratic. It's better he's dead."

"Brother Bazenoff, how did you arrange for the bodies in the Dead Sea?"

"There were no bodies found in the Dead Sea. It was all a hoax to give us an excuse to march on Israel, gain U.S. support. There are no bodies in those coffins. The coffins are filled with wax life-like dummies.

"But what about your son," an aide inquired?

"The Chinese did good work on my son, used his body as a pin cushion. That's the picture that appeared in the papers. But his body has been sent to the Rejuvenation Laboratory. We are working on a new discovery . . . a discovery that will bring my son back to life."

The shock of these words must have had a humorous effect on Tom. He switched off the Wrist Radio and burst into laughter. I was stunned. The United States had been fooled and here all Tom could do was laugh.

Was I in a dream world? Could this be true? "Tom," I half shouted, "what's this all about?"

Tom became serious and shocked me all the more. "George, when you've worked for Brother Bartholomew as long as I have, you will come to understand that nothing will surprise him. First, Brother Bartholomew has a most sophisticated spy system, an electronic network that apprises him of every move of the Soviet Union. Just as our Wrist Radio picked up their conversation from a few hundred feet away . . .

Washington Control can pick up conversations thousands of miles away, ferret out the inconsequential, and retain the data of significance. It's a memory bank that surpasses anything in your parent's time. Remember the telephone of your father's day. It had 752 parts. These new electronic systems operate on as few as six parts."

"You mean Brother Bartholomew knew about this plot even before it happened?" "Yes, George, he not only knew about it, in his own way he helped plan it. For years Russia has been aiding Egypt and Syria, supplying them with arms. They were a source of constant irritation to Israel. Brother Bartholomew knew something would break . . . he just wants it to break in his favor. And it will. How, I can't say, but it will."

"But why would he assure Russia of the U.S. support in its problem with Israel?" I asked.

"Let's put it this way," Tom replied, "to calculate the number of moves possible in a game of chess, you would have to start with the figure one followed by 50 zeros. Then you take the number 10 and multiply it by itself that many times. Brother Bartholomew figures . . . why let the Russians be the leader in a chess game that has so many alternative moves. So he makes the first move—supports Russia against Israel. And I predict for Russia it will be the last move!"

I must admit I didn't understand, but then I had a lot to learn and tomorrow would be another long day.

In Russia one could still see the stars in the sky. The air pollutants had not dealt their mask of death in this strange land. My eyelids closed in drowsiness. Somewhere I seemed to hear little Sue. She was kneeling by her bed. My mind wandered to two years ago. I had come home late and tired, tip-toed upstairs, heard her praying, saying, "Dear Lord, please bring Daddy with us at the Rapture . . . if it be thy will. And if not, dear Lord, please give Daddy wisdom and grace when the bad days come. Then, mommy says we'll meet him near Heze . . . Heze . . . something or other tunnel . . . please dear Lord."

Funny how at the brink of sleep how such memories come back. Hezekiah's Tunnel. It was at that tunnel entrance in Jerusalem that Helen cried. She didn't know why but she said somehow this tunnel would have a special meaning to all of us. She insisted right there that we all kneel and pray. I had never knelt before with my family. But her tears reached me . . . and for her sake, I knelt. Soon Sue's hand clasped mine. My small son Tom reached over for my other hand while Helen said a simple prayer. I can't remember all of it but I do remember her small, believing voice saying, "Please dear Lord, if not at the Rapture, make us a family again at Hezekiah's tunnel."

That seemed so long ago. The still night was broken by the tolling of a bell. Was it the enormous Tsar Kolokol, the King of Bells? I did not know. I only knew I was falling asleep . . . asleep in the Kremlin.

Chapter 5

Cloud of Death

Upon returning to Washington Tom Malone and I gave a report on conditions as we saw them in Russia. Brother Bartholomew was very attentive although somehow I got the feeling that he knew exactly what had happened even before we told him.

I could tell he was preoccupied. He got up from behind his desk, slowly walked over to us, pulled up a chair and sat down. Whenever he did this in the past it was always to let us in on some momentous decision.

The world was moving too fast for me and I didn't know whether or not I could stand any more surprises.

He spoke.

"This world has too many religions. That's one of our underlying problems. Do you realize that each of the seven days in the week is designated as the Sabbath by various nationalities and religions. *Monday* is the Greek Sabbath, *Tuesday* the Persian, *Wednesday* the Assyrian, *Thursday* the Egyptian, *Friday* the Turkish, *Saturday* the Jewish and

Sunday the Christian. The population explosion is so critical that there is no longer room for so many diverse thoughts. Something must be done about it."

"Sir, isn't that a bit old fashioned in thinking?" Tom asked.

"Tom, rejecting things because they are old fashioned would rule out the sun and the moon. Let's look at today's world. Thirty years ago who would have dreamed we could reach London in a couple hours by commercial aircraft? Next year jets will make this time seem long — by flying from Chicago to Tokyo in a half hour. We've been able to climate control our cities although we haven't licked the pollution problem. Russia has solved the weather problem in Siberia, and she has floated icebergs down to irrigate the reclaimed land. Pinhead-sized microcircuit radios in stereo are small enough to be inserted in a person's ears. Our laser beams can crumble a mountain in seconds. And while this is restricted information, you and I know this to be possible."

"What are you trying to tell us, sir?" I asked.

"Just this, George, I say we already have inventions enough. Our bathrooms are more luxurious than those of ancient Rome. We jet around the world faster than Caesar could march from Pompeii to Rome. But our basic instincts and thinking processes have ...seal the book, even to the time of the end: many shall run to and fro, and knowledge shall be increased. (Daniel 12:4) not improved. Let us get down to the basics. To change the world we must first change ourselves. Five million patents have been issued by the U.S. Patent Office. But has this helped our world? NO! Everywhere you turn someone is espousing a new religion. Not even the Pope was good enough for the Catholics. They couldn't accept his infallibility. The fundamentalist Protestants have disappeared. And the watered down Protestants have merged with the watered down Catholics into a watered down new religion...a United World Church."

"What does the Bible say about these times?" I asked rather boldly?

"Glad you asked, George. Take a look at your Bible. It's in your coat pocket...inside coat pocket."

Brother Bartholomew must have noticed the surprised look on my face. It had been so long ago that I hid it in a specially made pocket on the inner lining of my coat I had almost forgotten about it. Rather sheepishly I pulled it out.

"Now turn to Psalm 9:17 and read it."

I read it aloud.
> "The wicked shall be turned into hell,
> and all the nations that forget God."

"Do you believe that, George?"

"Well, uh, yes, yes sir, I do, don't I?"

"Of course you do, George. Don't be so fearful. Remember, I trust you or I would not have appointed you to be my Presidential Advisor. The Bible is true...*every word of it.* And never forget that. Many, of course, err in their interpretation of it. That's why it was banned from all except for those whom our country felt would be wise in discernment."

His words rang in my ear...don't be so fearful. Here was a good time to ask him why those churches called Fundamentalist were wrecked, why some still lie in shambles from the destruction caused by Church Renewal mobs.

"The explanation is rather simple, George. It was Max Muller who said 'All truth is safe and nothing else is safe; and he who keeps back the truth, withholds it from men, from motives of expediency, is either a coward or a criminal or both.'"

Tom Malone sat there not saying a word. I wondered just how much he knew about Brother Bartholomew.

Brother Bartholomew continued. "Those which you term Fundamentalists were really heretics who were throwing not only this country but the world into chaos. The Lord knows this world is chaotic enough without a group of people

For the time will come when they will not endure sound doctrine; but after their own lusts shall they heap to themselves teachers, having itching ears. (2 Timothy 4:3)

screaming the world is coming to an end...and filling people's minds with silly tales about a rapture. Anyone who has read the Bible knows Matthew 22:29 states, '...Ye do err, not knowing the Scriptures nor the power of God.'"

"But how do you explain the book of Revelation and that verse about catching up together in the clouds?" I asked rather boldly.

With that Tom interjected, "George, I think we better go. Brother Bartholomew is very busy and has an important meeting coming up."

"No, wait," Brother Bartholomew insisted, "let me put George's mind at ease. First, George, let's make this clear. The Bible is the word of God. There is no doubt in my mind about it. But Fundamentalists were teaching that the book of Revelation was to be interpreted literally."

"Now some of it is literal, some of it is symbolic. Those who can discern the Scriptures know the difference. The Fundamentalists didn't. Take Revelation 9:7-10. Remember it tells about the Fifth Trumpet judgment. Now who ever heard of locusts that looked like horses, wearing crowns of gold, with faces as men, hair of women and teeth as lions and tails like scorpions? Can you imagine interpreting this literally?"

"Well, it does sound a little off beam, sir," I replied.

"Now about that catching away verse. That's found in I Thessalonians 4:16, 17. I can quote it from memory. There's hardly a verse in the Scriptures that I don't know. It goes like this:

> For the Lord himself shall descend from Heaven
> with a shout, with the voice of the archangel,
> and with the trump of God: and the dead in
> Christ shall rise first:
>
> Then we which are alive and remain shall be caught
> up together with them in the clouds, to meet the
> Lord in the air: and so shall we ever be with the
> Lord.

Foolish Fundamentalists termed this the 'Rapture.' It is

no such thing. First, have you or have I seen the Lord descend from Heaven? Of course not. His time has not yet come. But the time is coming. Do you think for one moment that the Lord would allow Christ to finish His work before the judgments that are to come are completed? No, his spirit and his body are with us right now. Soon, George, you will know that Christ indeed does live. But the time for that is not now."

"But, sir, about the disappearance of so many people?"

"George, what I am now about to tell you, you won't believe. It is too fantastic for you to believe...but it is true. Our population throughout the world was getting far out of hand. Religious factions and fanatics were adding to the problems. Something had to be done. I attended a secret meeting in Basel, Switzerland with heads of state and prominent scientists. There a special powder was revealed to us. It is called Miracle 1. When properly mixed with a printing ink, it generates particles of sub-microscopic molecular size. This reaction is called a Quark. And when touched by the human finger, that body heat sets a series of reactions in motion. In short, Miracle 1, in one second disintegrates the body that has come in contact with this powerful powder."

"I don't understand sir."

"To put it bluntly, George, the one way to somehow resolve our population problems was to eliminate people — not bury them — disintegrate them. Miracle 1 did that for us. Special Bibles were printed. I Thessalonians 4:16, 17 were printed in a different ink, an ink mixed with Miracle 1 powder. These Bibles were distributed to all Fundamentalist churches and to all individuals who wanted them.

> But evil men and seducers shall wax worse and worse, deceiving, and being deceived. (2 Timothy 3:13)

The United World Church issued a memo to all churches asking them not to preach from I Thessalonians, chapter 4. You know the rest. The persistent Fundamentalists did...the very next Sunday. And as their fingers brushed past verses 16 and 17...POOF...they were gone!"

"Incredible!" I exclaimed!

With that, Tom spoke up. "Sir there are two problems at hand. The Mayor of New York City is giving us difficulty on the Birth Coupon system and the Transportation Bill..."

Brother Bartholomew interrupted, walked over to the side of his desk, flipped a switch. A wall opened. Down came a security control panel with a TV screen. A light blinked and a picture appeared on the screen. In fact there were four screens...each transmitting a different picture. Brother Bartholomew punched the NEW YORK key. The pictures

changed. On Screen 1 crowds appeared filling New York streets. The screen showed hundreds of people waving their fists in demonstration of their protest of BB's actions. On Screen 2 was Mayor Bill Marcon talking to someone in his office. Brother Bartholomew turned up the sound control. Marcon's voice came out loud and embarrassingly clear.

"Bartholomew has to go. BB is too big for his boots.

My people won't stand for this banishment of all automobiles. And Birth Coupons take away their individual freedom."

Another voice in the Mayor's room came on....

"You're right, Bill. BB is too much of a dictator. If we let him get away with it, he'll think he's God. Listen, I have a plan..."

With that Brother Bartholomew turned the set off. I got the impression he knew of their plan even before they planned it.

Tom cleared his throat and spoke again. "As I was saying sir, you know the problem in New York, and the meeting coming up in a few minutes at the United World Church headquarters. Seems some of the ministers are getting cold feet. Starting to take the Bible literally. Seem to think your recent pronouncements on that Birth Coupon and the turning of some churches into museums are a little too much."

"We'll take care of that, Tom, let's go!"

And with that Brother Bartholomew motioned towards the door and we walked out.

This had been some revelation to me. Was I understanding the Bible more clearly? I had heard scuttlebut about Miracle 1. No one knew it by that name. There was reference to a powerful powder, however. Perhaps I had pegged Brother Bartholomew all wrong. The closer I got to him the more he seemed like someone from outer space...someone who knew what the problems were even before they began. Could he be sent by Satan? No, there was too much love in his heart. His constant reference to the Scripture impressed me. Could be he was an angel sent from God? If I only knew the Scriptures better, I thought. And then again, maybe I'm doing too much thinking. BB knows the way. I'll just follow him.

The platform of the United World Church auditorium was crowded. All of the important clergy vied for a seat near Brother Bartholomew. As President he was also automatically head of the United World Church. Tom Malone had quite a problem making sure no clergy was offended. While the denominations had merged, it seemed the best way was to have the leading head of the old Methodist Church, the old United Presbyterian Church, the old Episcopal Church and the Pope's representative from the old Catholic Church... all sit together in a semi-circle with Brother Bartholomew in the middle. The Convocation on Church Union had indeed been very effective in bringing the churches into one unified body.

Bishop Arthur, about whom I had almost forgotten, stood up and addressed the assembly. He was giving a short history of the progress of the church in the last thirty years.

In the last thirty years the churches have made great strides. Some of us have all but forgotten the great service rendered to us by those termed "new evangelicals" in the early 70's. They solved the word problems that plagued our growth. Through their initiative they eliminated the word *"saved,"* substituted for it a much better word, *"estranged." "Born again"* was changed to an *"encounter with God."*

"Salvation" and *"new birth"* became *"commitment."* And to these pioneers of church union we shall be eternally grateful, because their small first step has made ours so much easier.

Those words struck a chord of remembrance in my mind. I could remember Helen as she was housecleaning singing, "Jesus Saves, Jesus Saves." Was Bishop Arthur's remarks really one of progress? I wondered.

The Bishop continued.

We are called here because there are some who are concerned with the apparent deterioration of the church. Let us remember Christ's admonition to us:

"Ye are all the children of light, and the children of the day: we are not of the night, nor of darkness."

"Yes, Bishop Arthur," Brother Bartholomew interrupted.

"But the next verse in I Thessalonians 5:5 and 6 is important, too. It is this:

> "Therefore let us not sleep, as do others; but let us watch and be sober."

Thank you, Brother Bartholomew. You are so right. Our council at the United World Church feels that as children of light more of our churches should be opened now that the heretics have disappeared. Our people need spiritual comfort and recreation that is geared to their needs. That is why we have called you to address us.

With that the audience as one arose and started clapping wildly.

Brother Bartholomew acknowledged the applause and began to speak.

> May we open with a word of prayer, please.
>
> Almighty Father, in whom we place our faith and trust, we humbly come before you as a nation in need of spiritual guidance, a nation broken and contrite, whose commitment is to thee and thee alone.
>
> Bring us that voice from heaven assuring us that promise of Revelation 21:3, "Behold, the tabernacle of God is with men..." Make this earth a new earth, pure and clean.
>
> And to thee we give all the honor and all the glory, Amen.

It was as though the audience was hypnotized. You could hear a pin drop. The silence was as if God was standing in their presence.

Brother Bartholomew continued.

> I have been deeply concerned about the needs of the church. My offices gave you wholehearted support in the destruction of those churches that nearly singlehandedly caused chaos in our nation

through their false doctrines. We must guard against any such thing reoccuring. And I know that it will not. Our churches must be big. They must meet the social needs of their respective communities. Too long have we endured the teaching of those who were more concerned with sin and less concerned with social welfare. If the church is to survive, and it will, it must be, as Jesus was, concerned about the social welfare of its peoples.

Fundamentalists taught the miracle of the loaves and fishes. It was no miracle. The productive use of oxygen and CO_2 through modern farming have given us such bounties of food from a few loaves which far surpass that so-called miracle of Matthew 14:15-21! Five loaves and two fishes fed 5000 then. Since man has ventured into space we can now pack more into the area occupied by five loaves and two fishes than would feed—not 5000—but 15,000 people!

Is the Bible wrong? No the Bible is not wrong. But those who interpret it wrongly are wrong! I say the miracle is not the miracle of making five loaves and two fishes multiply. But rather the miracle is that Christ was concerned about the SOCIAL WELFARE OF THE PEOPLE. And THIS IS THE MESSAGE AND MINISTRY THAT OUR CHURCH MUST RELATE TO TODAY!

The round of applause was deafening. It would have gone on indefinitely, but Brother Bartholomew held up his hand and continued.

Congress has given me elective decision powers. I am making a decision right now. It will take effect immediately. I am appointing Bishop Arthur as my Presidential Consultant on Religion. Hear him. His words are wise. He has proven his faithfulness and concern...concern for the church and for the people.

Furthermore, at his suggestion, I have directed Congress to appropriate funds...whatever funds are necessary...to reconvert every church in America to its primary ministry of meeting the social needs of our time. Bishop Arthur will apprise you of our plan, aptly called PLAN ADVANCE. Thank you and God bless you.

With that the audience stood up and sang the theme hymn of the church. I remember first hearing it at the United Church Fellowship in Rome.

Praise God from whom all blessings flow
God's in His heaven on earth below
Let men unite, cast out all fears
For heaven is earth for endless years!

Bishop Arthur took the podium and addressed the audience.

Thank you Brother Bartholomew for your kind remarks. I am both humbled and honored to accept such a position of responsibility as Consultant on Religion. My life will be devoted to your cause of peace and justice. Now to the business at hand. Brother Bartholomew has asked me to convey to you briefly PLAN ADVANCE. It is a plan I am sure all of you will approve. Quite simply it is three-fold.

1. Recreational facilities of all churches will be expanded. Government money will be available to assure every church of adequate facilities to meet the social needs of our people.

   Every church will be assured of an olympic size swimming pool, a baseball and basketball diamond and tennis courts.

2. We must follow Paul's admonition in I Corinthians 8:22 "...that I might by all means save some." Our constitutions must be changed, our barriers made less stringent. Churches are encouraged to employ psychedelic lights or whatever worldly fad that they might attract those not in the church

> Love not the world, neither the things that are in the world. If any man love the world, the love of the Father is not in Him. (1 John 2:15)

body. We have organized special teams of "Christian rock" groups to conduct concerts in every church in the nation. We are of the world, we must be with the world if we expect them to come to our world.

3. The church must become more relevant to today's problems. We have adopted successfully in our churches God's direction of complete sexual freedom. We must also be ready to adopt his condoning of mass destruction of life. We cannot cope with present population growth. As a church we must accept and approve certain actions that will wipe out millions of those degenerates who would ruin us all. This is as God has willed. For the survival of all some will have to be eliminated. May I remind you of Lamentations 4:9, "they that be slain with the sword are better than they that be slain with hunger...."

Thank you for your attentiveness. The ushers will give you complete details on PLAN ADVANCE. You may get them on the way out. Let us close in prayer.

I ran out ahead of the crowd anxious to get back to the office. It was going to be a long day.

Tom Malone met me in the hall. He looked as though he had seen a ghost.

Tom, who was so reserved...shook? I couldn't believe it. Whatever this news was, it would be earth shaking.

"What's up, Tom? You're rushing around like a cloud of dust!"

"Have to run, George, but something big is about to happen!"

"WHAT?" I shouted. "Tell me, Tom, please!"

"BB put the finger on New York. They're due for a Dust Cloud Crystal Drop."

"Tom, I don't understand, what's a Dust Cloud Crystal Drop? And what's so drastic about that?"

"George, several years ago scientists discovered that a

river of red dust flows on the trade winds across the South
Atlantic and into the Caribbean area. Tropical meteorologists
found this cosmic dust forms a belt around the earth.
BOMEX, that's short for Barbados Oceanographic and
Meteorological Experiment believed that this dust triggered
hurricanes. That was in the 70's. Now our scientists know not
only that dust clouds exist, more important, they know how
to harness them, send them where they want, seed them with
whatever they want...and how to control them from space
platforms high above the earth. Yet they can pinpoint their
direction to within a few feet...and dispense their lethal
ability by the flick of one switch.

What I'm trying to say is this, George. Mayor Marcon of
New York is giving BB problems. And besides that the
population problem up there is getting out of hand. Some
people want more than their six feet of personal living space.
Others are tired of living 200 floors up and sharing their 9 x
15 apartment with two other families."

"But didn't Bill Marcon himself say in his speech '...we
need an elective Dictatorship...a benevolent authority'?"

"Yes, he did, George. But politics makes for strange bed-
fellows. And Marcon has some aspirations of unseating BB
and taking the Presidency himself. That's why BB carefully
primed Bishop Arthur on Lamentations 4:9 and his statements, '...we must accept and approve certain actions that
will wipe out millions. ...For the survival of all some will
have to be eliminated!' BB leaves for Cape Kennedy tomorrow
for a space flight above New York. He will personally trigger
MIRACLE 1. It will be injected into a dust cloud. Roving
satellites will gently waft the cloud over New York, encircling
it with air to prevent it from seeping elsewhere. Within a
twinkling of an eye—the people of New York will cease to
exist. Miracle 1 will have disintegrated them. Then BB flicks
another switch, neutralizes Miracle 1's potency. Presto it
becomes just another cloud!"

I was shocked beyond words. Tom started to walk down
the hall. I ran after him.

"My God, Tom, Faye and Bill are in New York. Tom, what will I do. You've got to help me!"

"*...Roving satellites will gently waft the cloud over New York...*"

For the first time in his life, as far as I can remember, Tom's eyes reflected a bit of sympathy, some small understanding for my grief. His wife and children were still alive. He went home to them every night. Thus he could understand the grief that was mine. With Faye and Bill gone, I would have nothing. And with nothing...no hope...I would be of little value to BB. Tom knew he had to do something... and do it quick.

"Look George, quick, get up to New York. I'll tell BB I've sent you up to get a last minute report on conditions."

"But, let me call Faye and Bill before I catch the flight."

"Impossible, George, time is short. All flights to New York have been cancelled. I couldn't even clear Air Force 1 to go into New York today. The ACV's are still running, though. It's your only chance. And while you dash to the docks, I'll be alerting Faye and Bill to be ready."

Tom was right. No time to waste. And the ACV's would be the only way now. How thankful I was that in the early 1980's the Air Cushion Vehicle became an efficient means of sea transportation. Each ACV now carried 800 passengers and 75 cars. They skimmed over the water on a cushion of air. Their cruising speed was 200 miles per hour. I would make New York within the hour from Washington. It was now 3:30 in the afternoon. Tom told me the last return ACV from New York would be tonight at 11:15.

Faye rushed into my arms at the dock in New York. Both she and Bill were waiting for me. It was the first time in a long time that I had seen Faye cry. She had been a highly sophisticated girl. But the events of the last few days had changed all that. Bill was bewildered. Tom had told them I was coming, that it was important they come back with me. He couldn't tell them anything more. And I couldn't either. Somehow I felt Brother Bartholomew knew my every step. And I knew that I might as well keep silent on the fate that was to befall New York — for no one would believe me anyway.

The ACV ride back to Washington was uneventful. Faye unburdened her heart to me. Tears welled in her eyes as she recalled the last Thanksgiving Day that Helen and Sue and Tommy were alive. Helen always went out of her way to witness her faith to Faye. And Faye resented having religion pushed on her. That Thanksgiving, Helen bought an extra large turkey, and some extra foods, foods she knew Faye liked. The turkey was a special protein mixture, molded to look like a turkey, injected with flavorings that were almost as succulent as the old fashion bird-type turkey. We sat around the table. Helen asked us to bow our heads and give thanks. I can still hear Helen's voice,

"Dear Lord,
We are thankful for thy blessings on our
home, for the good food thou hast placed
before us...."

It was then Faye, pushed back her chair, her face flush she shouted at all of us, but particularly Helen.

"Good food! What good food? Thankful for blessings? You have the nerve to thank God for this trash? If God were God would he let us starve and eat junk they call food that's made from crude oil? Would he let us overpopulate so greatly that we live in horrible square cubes two and three hundred stories high? Where is God...if there is a God? You stupid fools. How long will you keep up this masquerade of holiness?"

And with that she stamped out of the house and out of our lives. That was the last I heard of her until Brother Bartholomew revealed her location to me.

As Faye recalled this incident, she started to cry. The silent swoosh of the ACV over the waters was broken by her uncontrollable sobs. "I'm sorry, Daddy, so awfully sorry, Daddy. If Mother were only here. If only she knew how sorry I am. She was so good."

I put my arm around Bill and held Faye tightly. As her head lay on my shoulder and her damp blonde curls brushed by my face, I said, "Don't cry, Faye, I know you're sorry. And somehow, I feel Helen knows you're sorry. We must be brave. There's a strange world ahead. We've got to search the Scriptures. Somewhere there must be a clue."

We arrived in Washington. Faye insisted that we search out the old Bible church where she went to Sunday School. I knew what she would find but I didn't have the heart to tell her.

The government car met us at the dock. I told the driver that I wanted to investigate a church for possible renovations under BB PLAN ADVANCE.

When we arrived at the church, I whispered to Bill to take Faye in alone. I explained that I would follow.

It was quiet. But in my mind the strains of little children singing seemed to echo back and forth....

> Jesus wants me for a sunbeam,
> > a sunbeam,
> > a sunbeam,
> Jesus wants me for a sunbeam
> To shine for Him each day.

My thoughts were interrupted by sobbing from within. Quickly I dashed inside the weather-worn church. The interior was in shambles...chairs broken, hymnbooks thrown on the floor. It was as though a tornado had swept through the place. This was one of the churches earmarked for destruction because of its teachings. And Bishop Arthur and his group had certainly done an efficient job.

Faye and Bill were kneeling at the communion table. Faye was praying. I only caught the last few phrases.

> "Dear God, thy will be done over this life to be.
> And thank you, God.
> > Amen."

"Life to be? What life to be, Faye?" I asked fearfully.

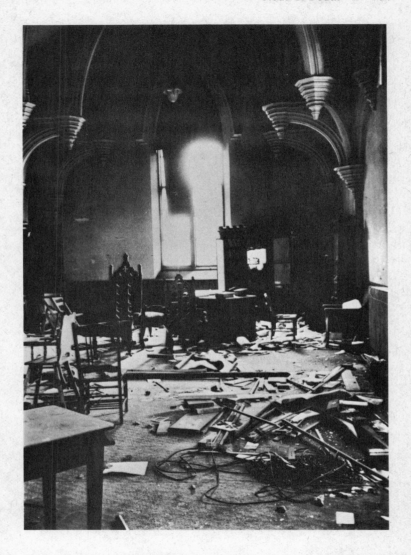

The interior was in shambles...chairs broken, hymnbooks thrown on the floor....This was one of the churches earmarked for destruction because of its teachings. And Bishop Arthur and his group had certainly done an efficient job.

Tenderly she looked up at Bill. Bill hugged her tightly, softly kissed her on the forehead.

"Dad, we're going to have a baby."

My heart sank. I should have been joyful. Faye had no Birth Coupon. I knew what would happen. And for the first time in what seemed ages...I knelt in prayer...and I cried!

For, behold, the days are coming, in the which they shall say, Blessed are the barren, and the wombs that never bare... (Luke 23:29)

Chapter 6

Invasion from the North

Faye looked so small and helpless as she lay on the hospital cart. The crisp white sheets were tucked around her. We followed an orderly as he pushed her down the long corridor towards the door marked NO ADMITTANCE. BIRTH CORRECTION PERSONNEL ONLY.

Bill was on the verge of tears. Never have I found it so difficult to retain my composure. But I had to, for Faye's sake.

That day I had returned to Presidential quarters, Brother Bartholomew outlined every step I had taken. Said he was sorry Faye was pregnant...pregnant without a Birth Coupon.

And while he had compassion and understanding he was firm in that he could make no exception. It would cause problems. Birth Coupons were rarely issued anymore. Those who had no coupons were forbidden to conceive and give birth. If they did, it was mandatory they enter the hospital immediately, and report to the Birth Correction Center.

It broke my heart to tell Faye. But I had no other choice. I would have to sacrifice a new life so that I could keep Faye and Bill. It was the only way.

We reached the doors. Bill gently kissed Faye. Faye gripped my hand as if to say, "Pray, daddy, pray real hard."

And then she was gone. Only the swinging of the doors broke the silence. Faye screamed...and then I knew the reality of the thing had hit her. And I cursed toward God! Even as I did, I knew it was wrong. The only prayer I knew was the Lord's Prayer and softly my lips formed a plea...

"...lead us not into temptation, but deliver us
from evil: For thine is the kingdom, and the power,
and the glory, for ever. Amen."

Inside the operating room, Faye lay still, her eyes closed. Her scream came when an intern had injected her with sodium pentothal and she knew that soon her baby would be taken from her. It was all done very efficiently and quickly. The hall was lined with 15 other women, all in a state of semi-consciousness, all without Birth Coupons. In the early 1970's the President had requested that people limit their families. That didn't work. Now Birth Coupons imposed severe restrictions to control population growth. Everyone in government and in religious circles approved. There simply was no other way out of the dilemma.

The doctor pulled the small IBM card from the chart holder above Faye's head. The card read

FAYE SANDERS
Age 27
Father: George Omega
Assigned Number: 061 23 481 2

The mysterious punched holes in the IBM card would tell the doctor what to do. Quickly he took the card, slipped it into a sophisticated electronic machine. The card zipped through several channels. Lights blinked on and off. The card dropped down into a tray. Into another tray dropped a vial and out the side came a strip of instructions. They were crisp, impersonal. No time for bedside manners. There was a job to do and the hallway was lined with similar cases. The doctor read the instruction slip.

FAYE SANDERS
Drug 666X

The doctor knew what to do. Quickly he picked up the vial, inserted it into a thigh injection needle. In a moment it was over. No need for anesthesia. The sodium pentothal was just to induce a light sleep and to calm down a hysterical woman until it was all over. Then it would be too late. 666 was the code number for Birth Eradication. X was the designation for the additional drug compound that prevented all future conception. Not everyone who entered the Birth Correction unit received the X compound. But most did. Many, in fact, wanted it.

When Faye awakened back in her room both Bill and I were at her side. We could not pray here. The ward was filled with fifty women. Each was allowed one hour of recuperation before being sent home. And the carts were being wheeled back and forth with a distressing regularity. When the dizziness passed, Faye got dressed, and we went home.

Faye looked like a defeated woman. There seemed nothing more for her to live for. Soon the drugs would work, quickly, painlessly. The life within her ceased to be.

I could care less about the consequences as I rushed into Brother Bartholomew's office. Once and for all I was going to tell him what I thought about his plans and edicts. I owed it to Faye. No longer could I control my inner feelings.

I opened the door, rushed into his office and stopped in my tracks both shocked and surprised. Temporary scaffold-

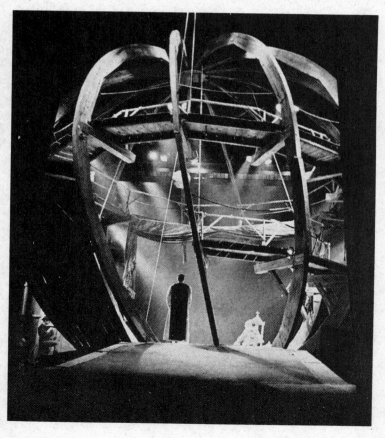

ing was up. There, with his back turned towards me was Brother Bartholomew. But not in a business suit as I had always seen him...now he was in a robe with a bright red cape. And with rapt admiration he was viewing a pure white ivory carved throne. For a moment I thought I was stepping into the very presence of God.

He turned, beckoned for me to come up the slightly inclined ramp.

My face flushed with anger as I shouted, "YOU KILLED HER! YOU KILLED HER! YOUR LAWS HAVE KILLED FAYE'S BABY AND HER HOPE FOR LIVING. WHY DON'T YOU KILL ME?"

He said nothing. He gently held my arm and led me to the side of the room...as though such business was too holy for this spot. He pressed a button on the wall. A television screen eased out. On the screen were three people. Helen, little Sue and Tommy. They were crying and Helen was speaking...

"George, darling, I know it's hard to understand.
Please do everything Brother Bartholomew says.
He loves you George. Soon he will be annointed of God."

I stared in disbelief. I rushed to the screen. The light slowly flickered into darkness and the sound kept echoing from the wall...

"He loves you, George. He loves you, George.
He loves you, George."

And the last soft, fading words I heard were...

"Soon he will be annointed of God."

Was I going out of my mind? It must be a trick. Was this in the Bible?

Brother Bartholomew put his arms around my shoulders and spoke: "George, there are many things we do not understand. I don't understand why God is going to place His mantle of service on me. But I accept it. George, pull out your Bible and let's together read II Timothy 4:5-7.

I took the Bible from my pocket. But my mist-filled eyes could not find Timothy. And even if my eyes were clear I wouldn't have known if Timothy was in the Old or New Testament. Brother Bartholomew quickly leafed past Colossians and Thessalonians and his finger rested on the verses in Timothy. Haltingly I read with him the verses he directed...

> "But watch thou in all things, endure afflictions, do the work of an evangelist, make full proof of thy ministry.
>
> For I am now ready to be offered, and the time of my departure is at hand.
>
> I have fought a good fight, I have finished my course, I have kept the faith...."

"George, don't you think God is an all-knowing God. You weren't much of a Christian before. Your wife was the testimony in your home. How important it is for us now to endure afflictions and to prove ourselves. That's what Paul is saying. None of us know how much longer we have on earth. The problems we face today are monumental compared to 1970 or 1980. But at the end of our course, we must be able to say as Paul, 'I have kept the faith.' Helen would want it that way. And, George, I need you."

I looked up at Brother Bartholomew. He was right. I must get this hatred from my heart. Truly he was sent from God. I again looked forward to working with him to save the world.

The silence was broken by the incessant buzzing of the HOT LINE Picturephone. Brother Bartholomew walked over to it, picked up the receiver. The screen brightened. And there on the picture tube was the Premier of Israel.

Shalom Ben-Mayer had only recently been elected Prime Minister of Israel. A soldier and statesman, he was well respected in his country. I recalled the time I interviewed him right before he won the election. "Do Jews accept Jesus as the son of God?" I asked.

"One God has created us," he replied. "We all have one father. A Christian cannot say exactly the same thing...But we do not accept Jesus as the son of God because we do not think that God has a son...It is the most humane of all religions...the Jewish religion. Our Bible does not begin with the Gospels. Our Bible does not even begin with Abraham being the first Jew. It begins with the first human pair... They were neither Jews, nor Christians, nor Moslems. They were neither white, nor black, nor yellow. We don't know what they were. But all human beings were created in the image of God. This is the essence of our religion."

Seeing from my face that this explanation wasn't really enough, he cleared his throat and continued.

"We have our books of the Torah—you call it the Law. In the third book you call it Leviticus—it is said you should love your fellow man like yourself...In my view, my humble view, Christianity was created by St. Paul, not Jesus. Jesus was a Jew like other Jews. The Jewish religion is not the same as the Christian or any other religion. It is...a nation."

I then asked, "Do you believe that in the continuing development of Israel there is a conscious effort to change the people's character, to have an Israeli character different than that of Jews elsewhere?"

Ben-Mayer had looked at me with a smile on his face and replied, "It must not be an Israeli character, but a real Jewish character, which is one which the Bible said we must have. It was said by Moshe. You call him Moses. His name to us is Moshe. What Moshe said some 3300 years ago is true today as it was then. He said, 'You are a few among peoples, and therefore you must be...'" Ben-Mayer paused, then continued, "Because I can't find an expression in English which is correct, I must say it in Hebrew. 'Am segula.' It means your quality must be much higher than your quantity. You should be spiritually better than any other people in the world. A Jew here may be fanatically religious, or he might be an atheist. I don't go to a synagogue. Yet I am not an atheist. I am convinced that there is one supreme thing—

whether you call it God or any other name it doesn't matter...." And with that the interview had ended.

That was 3 years ago. Now the HOT LINE PICTURE-PHONE shown brightly with Shalom Ben-Mayer's face. Usually smiling, Ben-Mayer's face was drawn and concerned. The Hot Line is only used for emergencies. I could tell this was just that.

"Mr. President," Ben-Mayer was saying, "Intelligence has informed us that Russia is on the move again. Forces from Germany, Poland, Yugoslavia, Iran, Turkey and other Arab states have men and tanks mobilized on all fronts for a great pincer move into our territory. Tanks have massed the full length of Turkey, like an army of horses, ready to devour us the minute the signal is given. We urgently need your help right now."

Brother Bartholomew was calm as he flipped the switch to talk. It was as though he knew every step before it happened.

"Brother Ben-Mayer, I know the situation looks desperate. But here's what I want you to do. Tonight, go on your national television hook-up. Announce that I will arrive tomorrow in Jerusalem to give a special message to the Jewish people right on the Mount of Olives. Announce that I will perform a spectacular feat that

Even him, whose coming is after the working of Satan with all power and signs and lying wonders. (2 Thessalonians 2:9)

will show to the world that the sacred land of the Jews must remain in their sovereignty. Have as many of your people as possible fill the Kidron Valley to watch us. I will speak at 12 noon. Will the sun be shining?"

Shalom Ben-Mayer turned to an aide, checked the weather, then said, "Yes, Mr. President, there will not be a cloud in the sky tomorrow."

"Good," Brother Bartholomew replied. "Set the stage for something really big!"

With that the picture faded and Brother Bartholomew

turned to me promising, "George, you are going to see God's power in action tomorrow."

With that he led me down the hall to a room marked CONFIDENTIAL TOP CLEARANCE PERSONNEL ONLY. BB rang the buzzer. We were admitted. The room seemed unpretentious. Except for one corner. There stood a small cabinet with thirty 3" x 8" file drawers, each with a special combination lock...each labeled in what appeared to be a hieroglyphic code.

Brother Bartholomew pointed to the drawer with 3 rows of strange lettering.

ylwqqazy∤wqℾaya∀ïaⱨⱨyoỷyⱦʒ×ỉⱨⱦ
ⱨỷ∀×ⱦoỷaℍ⒐ℾⱳⱵⱶⱶqⱷℍⱶⱷℾℙ⁊ℍℷⱨⱳⱥⱶⱶℷ
ⱷⱷ⅋⋞∤yⱦⱶⱶqℍℷⱳquoℷⱷowℙℷⱶⱶgℷⱦⱶℷⱳℷoⱶⱷ

"Are you sure you want this, sir?" the scientist asked. "We have tested this under laboratory conditions but it may prove more powerful than any of us can anticipate."

"Quite all right," BB replied, "This will be a good opportunity to test its effectiveness under actual conditions."

"You need a full sun and accurate aim, sir."

"Yes," Brother Bartholomew assured the scientist, "I've taken all these things into consideration."

With that the scientist twisted the dial at what seemed an innumerable number of times. The lock clicked open. He pulled out the drawer, and then he set it down on an examining table cushioned in a plush layer of white dense foam rubber.

I was amazed at what I saw. It looked like an ordinary ring...a gold banded ring with a pitch black onyx face and a sparkling center diamond.

"Why, that's only a ring," I exclaimed!

"You mean it looks like a ring," Brother Bartholomew replied. "But under the right conditions it captures the energies of the sun over its black surface, generates unbelievable energy and channels it through the diamond sending-device to become a devestating laser beam of destruction. Properly used it can crumble a building in seconds. The laser was first discovered in the early 1960's. The perfected instrument you now see was only made operational last month, right here in this laboratory."

Diagram of Brother Bartholomew's
RUBY LASER RING

1 Light from sun excites chromium atoms in rod.

2 Resulting photons are reflected from end to end.

RUBY ROD   FLASH TUBE   LASER BEAM

MIRROR

POWER

COOLING SYSTEM

PARTIALLY TRANSPARENT MIRROR

3 Photons build up in number until they are emitted as a pulse of intense red light.

Would wonders ever cease? This seemed impossible!

The scientist who perfected this laser ring went on to explain: "Many years ago a beam from what we call a ruby laser was aimed at the moon, 240,000 miles away. It reached the lunar surface a second later. Working at this speed this laser ring works as follows: When the sun hits the diamond the chromium atoms under the onyx surface turn into an excited state. These excited atoms then generate energy millions of times more powerful than a similar surface area on the sun. Within one minute this destructive power is released into a laser ray through the diamond channel. It will destroy anything in its path. Whoever uses this ring must hold his hand high at 12 noon to absorb the sun's rays and within a minute point the ring exactly at the target in question. There is no room for error."

Brother Bartholomew took the ring and placed it on a finger on his right hand. Then Brother Bartholomew showed

New York City...instant tragedy had struck here. Fringe area casualties did not disintegrate but were killed...and the world had already forgotten.

RUBY LASER RING'S DESTRUCTIVE CAPACITY DRAMATICALLY SHOWN
IN SERIES OF 8 PHOTOGRAPHS EACH TAKEN ONE SECOND APART

(2) A puff of smoke appears.

(4) The right section collapses.

(1) The test building shown intact.

(3) The Ring's powerful rays begin their work.

(5) Laser Ray's destructive force at its peak.

(6) Entire building begins to disintegrate.

(7) After 7 seconds...a puff of smoke.

(8) Building disappears...as if never there!

us a series of photographs which revealed the awesome destructiveness of the ruby laser. The scientist then covered the onyx surface with a protective cover. Time was now too precious to take Air Force 1 to Israel. In the early 1990's aerospace craft were made capable of landing at ordinary jet airports. These vehicles were part rocket, part orbiting spacecraft and part airplane. Development was begun way back in 1970 under the then President Nixon's Space Task Group. These Space Shuttles, as they were called, stood 225 feet high, weighed 1.5 million pounds and are capable of carrying 25,000 pounds of cargo and passengers. It would take us to Jerusalem in a little under one-half hour.

I had never ridden in a space craft before. But the take-off was unusually smooth. It seemed no different than an ordinary jet. BB was anxious for me to go on this flight with him to see how earth looked hundreds of miles up. Within a minute he pointed down toward our floor windows. I noticed nothing but brown masses of earth. He pushed a button marked SIDE DIMENSIONAL. What seemed like a special glass suddenly slid through the paneled window. It was a tremendously clear and sharp magnification. I could see what appeared to be a countryside. Articles of clothing were strewn everywhere, and young people were searching and picking up bits and pieces.

"That was New York City," Brother Bartholomew explained. Funny, I thought, instant tragedy had struck here, and the world had already forgotten. Even I had forgotten.

Twenty minutes later the space shuttle paused over Israel. Down below I saw the entire Holy Land. It was a magnificent sight. I could see that BB was getting excited. It were as though he was coming home.

Our space craft came to a smooth landing at Jerusalem Airport. Brother Bartholomew quickly changed clothes, slipped on his robe and bright red cape, checked his Laser ring, and motioned to the steward to open the door. I remembered the old Bible pictures in my mother's Bible. He reminded me so much of Jesus. It was as though Christ himself were returning to the Mount of Olives, but not on a donkey, in a modern Year 2000 space craft. Incredible, I thought!

As he stepped down the flight of stairs the Israeli Army Band struck up HAIL TO THE CHIEF. Brother Bartholomew looked up at the sun. It was shining brightly. Not a cloud in the sky.

Shalom Ben-Mayer saw his upward glance and seemed to convey that he knew everything would be all right. The limousine quickly whisked us through the streets of Jerusalem up the winding road to the Mount of Olives. The streets were packed with people. They must have been twenty deep. Only a narrow aisle permitted our car to pass.

As we reached the top of the Mount of Olives I gasped in amazement. Literally every spot of land was covered with people...from the Mount of Olives down the hill to the Kidron Valley, up the other side of the hill to the walls of the Inner City. An aide told me that never before in history had so many people assembled in one place. He estimated that five million people filled the valley and surrounding areas.

I shivered with fear as suddenly I thought...suppose BB's ring is aimed just slightly off course. Millions would die and he would be massacred for his action.

Shalom Ben-Mayer approached the podium specially erected for the occasion. A hush fell over the valley. He spoke.

> For 4000 years Jews have lived in Palestine. The Six Days' War in June, 1967 brought the return of the whole city of Jerusalem to Israel for the first time since A.D. 130-132 during the Bar Kochba rebellion against the Romans. Here Abraham prepared to sacrifice his son Isaac. Here rose the City of David. Here Solomon built his temple in the days of Israel's glory. Here the Queen of Sheba's caravan—a "very great train" of camels bearing "spices and very much gold, and precious stones"—made its soft-footed way into Solomon's resplendent capital.

> Jerusalem knew the heavy tread of conquerors: Nebuchadnezzar, who carried its populace off to Babylon....

As Ben-Mayer continued his introduction I looked out over this vast expanse of people. Pharaohs and emperors, sultans and kings all vied through the ages for these hills of Judea.

Ben-Mayer was finishing his speech.

> Forces from the North since the early 1960's have been seeking to devour us. They have agitated our Arab neighbors, have led them to believe we are their enemy. For years we have fought little wars, skirmishes. But now these evil forces are massed at our borders...massed waiting for the signal to march on Jerusalem. I say they will not conquer Jerusalem. For no matter how large their armies, no matter how big their arms, no matter

how great their leaders, God is on our side and He will prevail. This Goliath will be slain. For they may have their Goliath. But we, the proud nation of Israel, we have our DAVID!

Never before had I heard such a fiery speech. The response was like a roaring thunder, creeping up the valley until it became a deafening roar that seemed to shake the very earth beneath us. Five million Jews all shouting in unison...

WE HAVE OUR DAVID
WE HAVE OUR DAVID
WE HAVE OUR DAVID

BROTHER BARTHOLOMEW stood up, held up his hands. Slowly the crowd quieted, sat down on the verdant ground. He spoke.

My brothers and sisters in the Lord. Since the days of Pharaoh your people have suffered. Ramesses II, who for 67 years ruled Egypt, made the lives of the children of Israel bitter with bondage. Yet from ancient papyri found back in his day...comes a school teacher's message that applies well to those who would seek to invade this beloved country. For years Russia has been the poison whose venom has touched every country surrounding Israel. She has spewed her hate at every opportunity. When your great leaders talked, she would not listen. Let's read the proverb an ancient Egyptian penned thousands of years ago. It reads like this:

The ear of the boy is on his back, and he listens when he is beaten.

This Promised Land once and for all must teach the intruder his lesson. If he will not listen with the ears on his head, America will stand with you in making sure he listens with the ear on his back. For Russia will be beaten. The United States will form ranks with Israel to bring eternal peace to this sacred land.

The Al Aksa Mosque fire in 1969 was the first step used by Russia to camouflage its dastardly intents. It was then that the Saudi Arabia King called for a holy war with his statement, "We Moslems should call for a day not far away when we will all meet in Jerusalem to save our holy places and our holy land and achieve either victory or death in martyrdom."

Look behind you, 34 acres in the heart of your city. Yet it is not yours. On it is Al Aksa Mosque and the Dome of the Rock Mosque. In all Jerusalem they still remain the focal point of every eye...the bone in the chicken's throat. And right here God will declare his judgment.

I looked up at the sun. It was almost overhead now. I looked at Brother Bartholomew. Unnoticed by anyone I saw Brother Bartholomew quickly slip the protective cap from the laser ring.

In A.D. 73, he went on, the Jewish people sacrified their very lives at Masada. No more will Jews be asked to suffer another Masada. God has given me a special annointing...many years ago in this Holy Land...an annointing that some day I would save His people. Today is that day. Today your nation can once again build your Temple on the site which has been denied you. Today the 34-acre compound dominated by the Dome of the Rock...today that holy ground so precious to every Jew...today that will be yours....

With that Brother Bartholomew raised his right hand high into the sky. The sun was directly overhead. The rays of sunlight seemed to focus on the diamond channel in the center of the onyx ring. To me it seemed that some extraordinary power was surging through his body. When would he take down his arm and point it as the Mosque area. One minute must certainly be up. It seemed like minutes had dragged by. Not a word was said. I am sure the people thought Brother Bartholomew was offering a prayer to God. He looked like Moses...like a prophet of old. Then, slowly, almost unperceptibly, his arm slowly lowered, the fingers on his ring hand curved slowly. The arm stopped.

Like a bolt of lightning there was a rapid flash but no

thunder—just a deadening WOOSH! I looked quickly at that familiar golden dome upon the Dome of the Rock mosque. Then...my eyes darted back and forth...before my very eyes, and the eyes of everyone there...it had VANISHED!

The people went wild. They jumped to their feet screaming "MESSIAH, MESSIAH, MESSIAH!" Hordes of them were climbing up backs until they formed ladders over the Inner City wall. When they reached the hallowed spot they kissed the ground.

I am come in my Father's name, and ye receive me not: if another shall come in his own name, him ye will receive. (John 5:43)

Shalom Ben-Mayer was elated. He kissed Brother Bartholomew with the kiss of welcome and led him to the waiting limousine. I entered with him.

The car had just started when the red light flashed on the mobile Picturephone. BB picked up the phone, flipped the video screen switch. An Israeli General appeared. He was standing outside a kibbutz on a hill overlooking a Jordanian valley.

He spoke sharply and quickly. "Mr. Prime Minister. THE RUSSIANS ARE COMING!"

And the word of the Lord came unto me, saying,

Son of man, set thy face against Gog, the land of Magog, the chief prince of Mesheck and Tubal, and prophesy against him,

After many days thou shalt be visited: in the latter years thou shalt come into the land that is brought back from the sword, and is gathered out of many people, against the mountains of Israel, which have been always waste: but it is brought forth out of the nations, and they shall dwell safely all of them. (Ezekiel 38:1, 2, 8)

Chapter 7

Triumph and Tragedy

Alexi Bazenoff was more than an armchair general. As Premier of Russia he offered the country new energies and direction. His grandfather Nikita Koschenov, unknown to many, had been in his younger days a Bible scholar. His sudden downfall in the 1960's was to lead to a misguided purpose. For in his day after day of inactivity he would carefully school little Alexi in the ways of man and the tactics of war.

One of Koschenov's favorite portions of the Bible was in Ezekiel. Disheartened because his personal ambitions were thwarted, he wanted to lead Russia on to new heights through his grandson. Alexi Bazenoff, he was sure, was destined for greatness.

Sitting by the hearth with the fire crackling through the logs, Nikita would open up a well-worn Bible, one his mother gave him.

"Alexi, read this," he urged. In halting childish tones Alexi read:

"And thou shalt say, I will go up to the land of the unwalled villages; I will go to them that are at rest, that dwell safely, all of them dwelling without walls, and having neither bars nor gates.

...In that day when my people of Israel dwelleth safely, shall thou not know it?"

"Good, Alexi, Good, read on. This next verse, Ezekiel 38:15, is very important!"

Alexi continued:

"And thou shalt come from thy place out of the north parts, thou, and many people with thee, all of them riding upon horses, a great company, and a mighty army."

"Now read verse 16, Alexi, read verse 16!"

"And thou shalt come up against my people of Israel, as a cloud to cover the land..."

"That's enough, Alexi, now listen to me. I am a very old man but I see my destiny for tomorrow in you. Someday you will be great. And I want you to remember what I say. Someday the Russian forces will be as a cloud so big and so great that they will cover the land of Israel. The wealth of the Dead Sea is without estimate. You will have for an inheritance all that is now Israel. Look at her, dwelling without walls, arrogant, gobbling up more and more land...land that could be better put to use by our beloved country."

And thou shalt say, I will go up to the land of unwalled villages; I will go to them that are at rest, that dwell safely, all of them dwelling without walls, and having neither bars nor gates,

To take a spoil, and to take a prey; to turn thine hand upon the desolate places that are now inhabited, and upon the people that are gathered out of the nations, which have gotten cattle and goods, that dwell in the midst of the land. (Ezekiel 38:11, 12)

"But why horses, Pop Pop? I want to shoot them down with atom bombs and big tanks."

"Listen, Alexi, that's exactly what they would expect and prepare for. You could almost spit over Israel. And one bomb would kill everyone, Russians and Jews. There is no God; but this Bible was written by someone with a clever mind. What could be more deadly than an entire army of galloping horses, winding in and out of the valleys, the roads, and the forests which the Jews so foolishly planted after the Six Day War? They would have to fight us singlehandedly. And there would be more of us than of them. What I wouldn't give to live in that day, Alexi. But alas, I am old. But I will live through you. You must remember this, Alexi. You will lead an army as a cloud to cover the land...all of them riding upon horses."

That had been 30 years ago but Alexi Bazenoff never forgot that conversation. Pop Pop Koschenov had long been dead...but his words were to live on in the plans Bazenoff had laid before his field staff that night.

Bazenoff inherited his grandfather's Bible and he made an exhaustive study of horses and the part they played in warfare. He read in I Chronicles 18:4 where David took from the Philistines a thousand chariots and seven thousand horsemen and their horses.

And he knew Job 39:19-25 by heart, and that night encamped at Maras at the southern portion of Turkey, he recited it to his elite group of generals under a moonlit tent:

> "Hast thou given the horse strength?
> Hast thou clothed his neck with thunder?
> Canst thou make him afraid as a grasshopper?
> The glory of his nostrils is terrible.
> He paweth in the valley and rejoiceth in his strength:
>
> He goeth on to meet the armed man.
> He mocketh at fear, and is not affrighted;
> Neither turneth he back from the sword.
>
> The quiver rattleth against him,
> The glittering spear and the shield.
> He swalloweth the ground with fierceness and rage;
> Neither believeth he that it is the sound of the
> trumpet. He saith among the trumpets, Ha, ha; and he
> smelleth the battle afar off,
> The thunder of the captains and the shouting."

Bazenoff reveled in the fact how well he knew Jewish history. They were now so filled with modern modes of transportation, the horse was almost unknown to them. He knew that early in the Israel-

Deuteronomy 17:16
1 Kings 4:26

ites' history that the king was prohibited by Mosaic law from multiplying horses to himself. And while Solomon had ignored this law, yet now horses were only a zoo animal in Israel.

The Russian horses combined Arab and English breeding. They stood over 17 hands, weighed a ton and could pull 27 times their own weight.

Morning came, cool, bright, and glorious. The Turkish Government had sent a guard of honor to meet Premier Bazenoff. Premier Bazenoff knew a little of the language and greeted the guard with, "Merhaba."

"Sağol, sağol," the guard replied.

Turkey was a very hospitable country. Sagol was the greeting meaning long life.

Turkey began her conquest of Asia Minor in the fourteenth century A.D. Then in 1453 Constantinople and the Eastern Roman Empire at last fell at the Turkoman onslaught. In 1516-17, in the reign of Sultan Salim I, the Turkish army captured Palestine. Turkey's seizure of the Mecca and Medina, Islam's holiest cities, earned for the Turkish Sultan the title of Caliph, head of the believers in the Islamic religion.

When Palestine fell to the British in World War I, Turkey longed for the day when this land would again be in her grasp. So, when the opportunity presented itself now in the 1990's, an unholy alliance was formed with Russia, Iran, Iraq and other countries to once and for all wipe the Jews from the face of the earth.

It was because of this desire that Turkey's leaders per- mitted Premier Alexi Bazenoff to use their country as a step-

ping off point for their impending great invasion of Israel...
an invasion of mounted horsemen.

It was late May. Summer was beginning. The air was dry.
The skies were clear and only in the coastal areas was there
any evidence of water when the nights brought refreshing
dew. During the day the temperature would soar over 100°F
and at night suddenly drop to 30° F.

The Esdraelon-Jezreel Valley is the largest valley in Israel
and its plains were the scenes of many bitter battles.

Brother Bartholomew and Prime Minister Shalom Ben-
Mayer were now comfortably seated in a specially con-
structed tower observation post atop the Mount of Olives.
Brother Bartholomew had rid-
den up the gradually sloping
mount only an hour before. He
had exited from a special car
and he was invited to climb the
hill astride a white horse which
had been readied for the occasion. The throngs nearby
cheered and Brother Bartholomew waved sternly but cor-
dially. I followed with Ben-Mayer behind and on foot. The
crowds obviously looked upon him as a saviour arriving at
the crucial hour. Now from their vantage point atop the
tower they could with binoculars see Tiberias and Nazareth
70 miles to the north. Special television monitors mounted
on roving space satellites were also focused on the northern
border of Israel.

> And I saw, and behold a white
> horse: and he that sat on him had
> a bow; and a crown was given
> unto him: and he went forth
> conquering, and to conquer.
> (Revelation 6:2)

A row of screens faced both men. Brother Bartholomew
was talking. "Tune in Tiberias and angle the screen north."

Some dials turned...soon a picture was coming in to focus
on Screen 2. There appeared to be nothing but a cloud of
dust.

"That's only dust," commented Ben-Mayer.

"Is it important?" Brother Bartholomew questioned.

"Not only important, my dear brother, but very dangerous.
That dust you see is the dust of galloping horses. Turn the

space camera east to west. Now, look at the expanse of dust. It runs the whole gamut of the country. There must be one million horses or perhaps even more!"

"Horses?" Ben-Mayer said in derision. "Those stupid Russians are still fighting a Dark Ages war. Our military arms with nuclear heads will wipe them out in minutes. I'll alert the Generals to begin firing."

"Hold it, Shalom, it is you who are the fool, not they. For, for every thousand horses you kill, they will replace them with two thousand and your indiscriminate nuclear arms will kill more of your people than theirs and horribly contaminate the land...and they know it!"

"What shall we do?" Ben-Mayer shouted in distress.

"Nothing," Brother Bartholomew calmly replied, "Just let them come!"

"Are you mad...just let them come?...surely you must have a plan." With that, the Communications sergeant handed me a report off the picturephone teletype. This new teletype pictorially reported what it saw, combining it with commentary from the general in that specific field.

I handed it to Brother Bartholomew. He read, "The main force has left Maras, they are passing near Damascus." He turned to me and ordered, "George, get me Washington on the picturephone. Get me Science Strategy Division."

I pushed the necessary buttons. Abel Epstein appeared. He was such a mild-mannered man on the surface, it somewhat belied his tremendous intelligence. The laser ring was his discovery as were a few other highly sophisticated methods of destruction. His father was a Jew. His mother a Christian. But Abel was an atheist who believed in nothing, nothing except Brother Bartholomew's power to save the world. And for this he worked day and night to give BB that superior power.

"Abel, looks like an unusual invasion here. The nuclear detonation equipment won't work. Estimate millions of Russians on horseback already near Damascus. What do you suggest?"

"Kill or maim, sir?"

"We can't kill them all, they'd clutter up the countryside. Just stop them...turn them back."

"That rules out CBW sir. That's fatal in 30 seconds and a shift of the wind could prove disastrous. VX would kill them and would react again after six hours. That would get most of the bodies out, sir."

"No," Brother Bartholomew shouted.

"What about Q fever?"

"Epstein, have you lost your senses? You know that six ounces of the Q fever virus would be enough to wipe out 28 million people!" "Not this new mixture, sir, it's a watered down version, mixed with smallpox, typhus and encephalitis."

"Fine, Epstein, but mix in a little of that nerve gas that throws the enemy into a state of confusion, affects their thinking powers. Will three ounces be enough?"

"Yes sir. It will be ready in ten minutes."

"Good," BB replied, "We have no time to waste. Send it over by special Rocket messenger. Land on the Mount of Olives. We must have it here within the hour."

The screen faded.

I punched Screen 3 to get a later battle strategy report for BB. "The horses are near Capernaum at the northern end of the Sea of Galilee and are headed towards Mt. Tabor, sir."

Alexi Bazenoff rode his horse like a king. A most unusual horse it was. A mutation in cross-breeding had made it a fiery red in color. It was the only blood red horse ever bred. Leading his army through the desert paths he held up his banner to hail another army of horses coming from Jordan to join forces.

A cloud to cover the land, he mused as he looked around him. The dust of the horses had cast an ominous cloud over all the land. Pop Pop Nikita had been right. He was to be a man of destiny. A saviour!

> Thou shalt ascend and come like a storm, thou shalt be like a cloud to cover the land, thou, and all thy bands, and many people with thee. (Ezekiel 38:9)

Alexi Bazenoff knew his history well. Palestine had been the homeland of Arabs for 2000 years. Zionism, the political movement designed to create a Jewish state, was the catalyst that pitted Arab against Jew. Russian policy was to help fan this conflict...fan it to the advantage of the U.S.S.R. Charges and counter-charges arose. The 1967 Six Day War had been a bitter blow for the Russians. Bazenoff was a boy then, but he remembered Nikita telling him of the toll. 15,000 Arabs killed. Only 679 Israeli casualties. $700 million in new Soviet military equipment captured by the Israelis. From that encounter Bazenoff had formulated his own military principle: namely, if you are going to fight a war, fight it— quickly, fiercely, totally, aiming for nothing less than complete victory at the earliest possible moment.

To bolster his hatred for the Jew his grandfather had pointed out President Truman's statement in his memoirs:

"My efforts to persuade the British to relax
immigration restrictions in Palestine might
have fallen on more receptive ears if it had
not been for the increasing acts of terrorism...
committed [by Jews] in Palestine...

I do not think I ever had as much pressure and
propaganda aimed at the White House as I had
in this instance. The persistence of a few of
the extreme Zionist leaders—actuated by political
motives and engaging in political threats—
disturbed and annoyed me..."

With these thoughts in his mind Bazenoff felt sure of his gamble that the United States would not rush in to rescue the Jew. The thunder of hoofs behind him assured him he was leading an avalanche of power...power no one could stop!

Back in Washington Faye and Bill were trying to collect their thoughts. They huddled in the little bedroom in George's apartment. The room, about the size of a large closet afforded Faye and Bill the privacy they so much needed at this time.

Faye was heartsick. She still had not gotten over the shock

of the last few days since her hospital experience. George had warned them about the PRAYER CHANGES THINGS plaque on the wall.

That's why they huddled in the bedroom and as though they were commiting a criminal offense they furtively pulled out George's Bible from beneath the mattress.

Faye spoke first.

"Bill, I don't remember much Scripture. I never listened to that religious stuff. Now I see things so much more clearer, but some of these passages I still don't understand. Bill, I am sure now there is such a thing as the Rapture. I'm sure Helen and the kids were caught up in it. And I remember once a preacher speaking about a Great Tribulation and Israel. Then I recall, he said that Russia would in those days come marching down on Israel. Bill, we've got to begin to memorize the book of Revelation today. I don't know how long we will have this Bible."

> For then shall be great tribulation, such as was not since the beginning of the world to this time, no, nor ever shall be. (Matthew 24:21)
>
> Alas! for that day is great, so that none is like it: it is even the time of Jacob's trouble, but he shall be saved out of it. (Jeremiah 30:7)

"Faye," Bill replied, "I know you're upset and I agree something is happening but I'm sure it can all be explained. There's peace in the Middle East. The Jews have never had more freedom. You must be wrong."

A thud on the door brought them to their feet. Faye quickly slipped the Bible under the mattress. Bill went to the door, opened it, just as the newsboy was walking down the hall. Bill picked up the newspaper. His face turned pale. Faye ran to him, looked at the headlines. She fainted.

RUSSIAN HORSEMEN INVADE ISRAEL

Bazenoff's band of horsemen would not be stopped. They were rounding the east side of Galilee. The historian Josephus Flavius, writing in the first century A.D. had related, "For the men of Galilee were warriors from a tender age and great in numbers at all times; their hearts were never ruled by fear, nor did this land ever lack men ready to bear arms."

But northern Galilee with elevations of 3-4000 feet offered a rapid descension for the hordes of Russians. Brave as they were the Israeli forces were no match. The cloud of dust engulfed them and moved on...like a giant steamroller crushing a mustard seed. The Jews had faith but the Russians had power.

The horsemen had traveled over 300 miles since they left the rendevous point of Maras in Turkey. And the million or more horsemen, from their very first mile of the journey had kicked up clouds of dust. Now, some 300 miles later the blue sky had turned to a blanket of dull brown. Everywhere you looked the thick choking dust penetrated the nostrils, blinded the eyes and the flying grit had ground to a halt many an Israeli tank and piece of mobile equipment.

From his observation post on the Mount of Olives Brother Bartholomew was noting this new development as he talked to Shalom Ben-Mayer. "This dust storm is something I hadn't anticipated. It can cause atmospheric hazards and upset nature's delicate balance. Anything can happen now."

The light on Picturephone 4 was blinking. BB flipped on the switch. It was the Mt. Tabor command post but the dust all but obliterated the picture. BB pushed the Atmospheric Clear-ing Device. Almost all of the haze disappeared. You could see the horsemen approaching the foot of the 1843 foot Mt. Tabor. The rider on the Red Horse was clearly visible.

And there went out another horse that was red: and power was given to him that sat thereon to take peace from the earth, and that they should kill one another: and there was given unto him a great sword. (Revelation 6:4)

"Give me a rundown on Tabor, George."

I pushed the computer search buttons. A screen lit up with the Tabor data.

MOUNT TABOR

Limestone mountain in Galilee,
5 miles east of Nazareth. Isolated.
Scene of Gideon's defeat of Midianite

camel raiders. From Tabor's summit
one looks down on the Plain of Esdraelon.
Nearby river Kishon known to reach flood stage.
Height 1443 feet. Based upon a plain 400 feet
above sea level. Summit 1843 feet above sea level.

Ben-Mayer and BB were not paying attention to my comments. They stared intently at the action on Picturephone 4. Suddenly the screen clouded up again. BB angrily punched the ACD button...but this time the clearing device was not operative. Later we learned the dust had become so thick even the ACD could not penetrate it.

Air view of Mt. Tabor relayed on Picturephone 4.

Picturephone 4 screen was now almost black. Suddenly a brilliant flash of light surged across the screen! For a minute the whole area at Mount Tabor was exposed in raw, brilliant light...light so blinding even over the picturephone that for a moment I couldn't see. A long, rolling thunder could be heard in the far-off plains. It was like standing behind the pins in a bowling alley. First the roll of the ball. The sound builds up and within moments an awful, ear-splitting crash that shook the very mountain from which BB and Ben-Mayer viewed the battle.

Above the din BB was shouting to Ben-Mayer: "There's been an earthquake!" We looked at the screen. Mt. Tabor had split in half. Fire was erupting! What appeared like molten lava was rushing down its sides lapping up men and horses in its wake. From the black clouds above a space ship came hurtling to the ground. I recognized it as ours. It exploded in a fiery flame.

"My God!," BB exclaimed. "The space ship carrying Q fever is down!" The noise on the roof was deafening. "What's that?" BB shouted. "Hailstones, sir, as big as grapefruit." Ben-Mayer turned white. "Hailstones in Israel in 100° heat? Have the gods turned on us?"

With that he slipped to his knees, his head and hands facing heavenward. "Oh God of Jacob, hear us, help us, save us! Thou art one God. There is no other." With that he buried his head in his hands and wept unashamedly. Brother Bartholomew looked at him. I could see disdain and disgust form on his face.

Quickly he turned to the screen. Above the confusion Premier Alexi Bazenoff was still on his Red Horse, urging on what remained of his army of horses. The speaker on Picturephone 4 picked up his voice. In Russian he was shouting

ON TO JERUSALEM
ON TO JERUSALEM
ON TO....

Just then his voice trailed. From the heavens came a bolt of lightning making a direct strike on Bazenoff. There was no telling him from the fallen red horse and the ever widening pool of blood that eddied where he once had commanded. Bazenoff was dead!

The minute the surrounding horsemen saw this, they fled in confusion. A puff of smoke emerged from the fallen space ship. As it passed through the ranks of horsemen they suddenly become disoriented, confused, beginning fiercely to fight each other.

BB pushed the CLOSE-UP button on the Picturephone. The scene he saw was not a pleasant one for tender stomachs. Sores erupting over the skin of the Russian soldiers; running, open sores that generated welts of puffed up flesh. The hot sun combined with the unquenchable fires made the flesh burn. The crazed horses were trampling on man and beast. The crazed army was pitted man against man, dying on their brother's sword, becoming victims to their brother's bullets.

> And it shall come to pass at the same time when Gog shall come against the land of Israel, saith the Lord God, that my fury shall come up in my face.
>
> For in my jealousy and in the fire of my wrath have I spoken, Surely in that day there shall be a great shaking in the land of Israel;
>
> So that the fishes of the sea, and the fowls of the heaven, and the beasts of the field, and all creeping things that creep upon the earth, and all the man that are upon the face of the earth, shall shake at my presence, and the mountains shall be thrown down, and the steep places shall fall, and every wall shall fall to the ground.
>
> And I will call for a sword against him throughout all my mountains, saith the Lord God: every man's sword shall be against his brother.
>
> And I will plead against him with pestilence and with blood; and I will rain upon him, and upon his bands, and upon the many people that are with him, an overflowing rain, and great hailstones, fire, and brimstone. (Ezekiel 38:18-22)

Just a few miles away...the Israeli army was kneeling in prayer. The intense heat and fire of the battle did not touch them. The heavens had opened and flooded the Israeli position with a violent, blessed rain.

The battle was over. The Lord had given His remnant people, the Jews, the victory. No matter what Brother Bartholomew said about the wonders of his Science Strategy Division, this was not a battle won by man. It was a battle won by God.

The Shofar horn sounded. And the Jews rushed to the Western Wall to go offer their grateful prayers. This was a day of rejoicing for them. Almost all of these Jews were attributing this victory to God. One young Israeli soldier—who told me that he had only a day ago become a Christian, a Christian-Jew—told me that Christ

Thus will I magnify myself, and sanctify myself; and I will be known in the eyes of many nations, and they shall know that I am the Lord. (Ezekiel 38:23)

was the one who had intervened. I had no time to listen, BB was leaving.

Brother Bartholomew said goodbye to Ben-Mayer and promised that he personally would financially sponsor the building of the new Temple on the former site of the Moslem Dome of the Rock. It was going to be, BB assured the Prime Minister, the most magnificent structure in this part of the world.

BB and I boarded the Presidential plane at the Jerusalem airport. The pilot walked back to BB's inner office and handed him a communique. The Common Market states were praising BB's feats in Israel. They urged him to stop immediately in Brussels, Belgium for a most important meeting. The die was cast. BB instructed the pilot to fly to Brussels.

It seemed like every newsman in the world was covering

Common Market Headquarters Building, Brussels, Belgium.

this Brussels event. I met many of my old friends there. Tom Malone, BB's Presidential Secretary, was there also.

"That was some coup BB pulled in Israel," Tom remarked. I added in a half lament, "You'll never believe the destruction. I have never seen such carnage in my entire life. Bodies, blood everywhere. It will probably take a month to bury everyone."

"You must be kidding," Tom replied, "practically the whole Russian army was killed. Israeli officials estimate it will take seven months just to bury the dead. They'll be shoved into one valley. Tourists will know it as the Valley of Russia's Host. The pictures we got back here make the battlefield look like a scene from a Middle Age history book. Bows, arrows, shields, spears everywhere. Crude weaponry but highly sophisticated with nuclear explosives for close-up fighting. Some say it will take seven years to burn the stuff."

> And it shall come to pass in that day, that I will give unto Gog a place there of graves in Israel, the valley of the passengers on the east of the sea: and it shall stop the noses of the passengers: and there shall they bury Gog and all his multitude: and they shall call it The valley of Hamon-gog.
> And seven months shall the house of Israel be burying of them, that they may cleanse the land. (Ezekiel 39:11-12)
> And they that dwell in the cities of Israel shall go forth, and shall set on fire and burn the weapons, both the shields and the bucklers, the bows and the arrows, and the handstaves, and the spears, and they shall burn them with fire seven years. (Ezekiel 39:9)

The long table of delegates was impressive. Heads of every participating state were present from the King of England to the Prime Minister of Sweden. Even a delegate from the United States had been invited in anticipation of its union with the European bloc. England's King was taking an active role in politics now. Quite a switch from the 1970's.

The Table of Power, as I called it, was a circular affair with a slight extension coming out one side. Along this table were ten chairs. The eleventh chair was at the end of the extension. It commanded the view of all ten delegates.

The following countries were represented:
     England

France
West Germany
Italy
Canada
Belgium
Norway
Sweden
Finland

The smaller European countries had long ago merged into France and Belgium. With Russia out of the picture, France was once again a free nation. The newly seated United States delegate was in the tenth chair.

The King of England was speaking: "...The armies of the North have been defeated through the brilliant maneuvers of Brother Bartholomew. But while the problems of the North have been solved, at least temporarily, our security is threatened by the forces of the Orient. In today's complex world another war could destroy man himself and make this earth uninhabitable. As spokesman for these ten countries of Europe and America we realize that we must now be as one under one head, under one government, under one leadership. In private meetings already held, each government has unanimously commissioned me, Mr. President, to invite the United States into our Federation—a Federation hereafter to be known as the United States of Europe. Your United States representative, John Marsh, is already seated in your nation's newly set up chair. And we ask you, Brother Bartholomew to be our Leader and President of this newly organized Federation."

With that the delegates of all ten nations stood up. Everyone in the vast rotunda stood up, clapping and looking at Brother Bartholomew. I sensed a look of triumph on his face... yet a triumph that was masked in a godly humility.

And the ten horns out of this kingdom are ten kings that shall arise: and another shall rise after them; and he shall be diverse from the first, and he shall subdue three kings. (Daniel 7:24)

The King of England motioned to the chair at the head of

the table. Brother Bartholomew approached it...sat down. The King removed the Crown of England from his head, knelt slightly, arose and then gently placed the crown on Brother Bartholomew's head.

The audience was hushed into silence. The King was speaking. "Ladies and Gentlemen, The PRESIDENT of the UNITED STATES OF EUROPE."

France was chosen for the Victory Parade...a parade that would convince the world of the solidarity of this new alliance of countries. It had borne the brunt of many wars and this gesture was one to bolster its tarnished pride. The great parade would pass through the famous Arc de Triomphe, the monument commemorating Napoleon's victories, completed in 1836. At the center is the tomb of France's Unknown Soldier, guarded by an eternal flame. The Arc, situated on the Place de l'Étoile (Star Place) is so called because 12 avenues radiate from it. Paris, the City of Light, was to be host to the world's most brilliant light—Brother Bartholomew.

It was a clear day. The sun accented sparkles of beauty as streaks of light played on the highly polished rifles carried by the armies of Europe. Never had so large an assembly of combined military might been witnessed.

The crowds were unbelievable. The crush of the crowds was tremendous. Viewing tiers four stories high had been erected to accommodate all the people who wanted to see the miles-long parade.

In the front limousine, standing up waving, was Brother Bartholomew. In each of the ten cars behind him rode the delegates of the other United States of Europe. THEN...

Just as Brother Bartholomew's car passed under the Arc de Triomphe, a wild-eyed youth broke through the restraining barriers, a pistol in his hand. Those around him said he was hysterically shouting, "ANTI-CHRIST, ANTI-CHRIST!"

A shot rang out. I was walking by the side of the lead car. I looked up at Brother Bartholomew. Blood was pouring from his temple. In a moment his lifeless body had crumpled to the floor of the car.

There was much shouting and confusion. A doctor ran to the car.

"Oh no!" I shouted. "Oh, no...no...it can't be...."

I knew it before he spoke.

"I'm afraid," he said, "Brother Bartholomew is DEAD!"

Chapter 8

Secret Flight to Babylon

The world was stunned.

Brother Bartholomew dead? It was true! Tom Malone quickly got on the intercontinental picturephone to Bishop Arthur. As the second highest officer in the government Bishop Arthur would automatically succeed to the Presidency. His appointment as the President's Consultant on Religion had assured him of this advancement. And as President of the United States he was now also President of the United States of Europe.

The free world looked to him. Times were desperate. And Bishop Arthur had to pull the world out of the fire.

Tom was speaking, "Sir, what shall we do with Brother Bartholomew's body?"

"Where is the wound?"

"In the temple, sir. The bullet is in the brain."

"Keep the body cold," Bishop Arthur replied. "This must be done at all costs. Dr. Curter will fly to Paris within the hour to prepare the body for the deep freeze. He'll bring a cryo-capsule with him."

In the morgue the still, lifeless body of Brother Bartholomew seemed godly even in death. A surgeon from the Rejuvenation Division of the President's experimental health department was already working.

This Division was rather new. Most people did not know it existed. Only the President's close aides were aware of the purpose of the RD department. The doctor worked skillfully and without wasted motion, carefully removing the spent bullet and cosmetically stitching the wound in BB's temple.

As he finished, Dr. Curter walked in. Behind him two men were wheeling the cryo-capsule.

From Dr. Curter's briefcase came foil sheets in roll form. Brother Bartholomew's body was sprayed with a special solution. From a pocket in his case Dr. Curter pulled out a plastic hood. It was placed over BB's head. There was an opening at one end...like the nozzle on a tire tube. Dr. Curter screwed a metal capsule on to it, pulled a release switch. Liquid swished into the plastic hood, enveloped Brother Bartholomew's face. Then the slow process of enveloping the

The body was carefully placed in cryo-capsule.

entire body in foil began. The body was then lifted, and carefully placed in the now very cold cryo-capsule.

Everything went like clockwork...as though it had all been planned beforehand. And somehow I sensed that it had.

The gold market had collapsed. The financial stability of the entire world was jeopardized. What little gold that was left was kept behind sturdy protective bars in an underground, secret room. But it gave the international business world no hope. Money was worthless. Governments could not control their own people. The population of each country was out of hand.

The ominous cloud of dust generated by drying and treeless regions had in recent years triggered disaster around the world. Much of the United States had not seen the sun for months. Only 25% of the sun's rays were filtering through. Now with the recent dust storm in the Middle East caused by a million galloping horses this was cut down even more. The now aggravated usual dust blanket over the cities created a form of carbon-dioxide pollution. It kept sunlight from hitting the ground. Blanketing the cities in the middle of summer, the weather was freezing. A simple virus, that in the past could have been shaken off with a few aspirin, now meant death in many cases. Burial was out of the question. There was no room for those 1970 niceties. Bodies were carted to disposal centers, treated to remove harmful bacteria, ground into special protein cakes. To me at first it sounded gruesome. Soon everyone accepted it. It was the only real meat anyone knew. And it made it possible for each one of us to exist just a little bit better off.

Bishop Arthur had alerted the international television network to be ready for his emergency Presidential address to the United States of Europe.

I knew that the transition had been made when I saw an aide slip a red mantle over the Bishop's shoulders.

Bodies were carted to disposal centers, ground into special protein cakes.

The address began.

Fellow citizens of the United States of Europe, brothers of the world. This is a solemn occasion. This is a sad occasion. Yet I accept this new office with a degree of humbleness and responsibility.

The events of the last few days have shocked all of us. Brother Bartholomew has given his life for us all. He died while serving us. Oh what love! He has also, in this case, given his life especially for the Jew. He and he alone stopped the hordes of Russian horsemen from swallowing up the little state of Israel. Not content to direct activities from Washington, this great soul without regard for his own safety, personally directed the battle from the Mount of Olives. And for this zeal and dedication what was his reward? The Jews, even Prime Minister Shalom Ben-Mayer rushed to the Western Wall thanking God for their victory. But it was not God who had promised to rebuild their Temple. Brother Bartholomew promised this. And the Temple will be built! How sad that as Brother Bartholomew humbly took part in the Victory Parade his yet young life was to be cut down by an assassin's bullet—the bullet, ladies and gentlemen, fired by a fanatical Jew! Their so-called Messiah, Jesus Christ, who they have yet to acknowledge, was crucified only between two thieves. Brother Bartholomew, however, in the prime of his youth, 33 1/2 short years, gave his life between millions of adoring followers.

But I promise this, while no one has seen or heard since of this fabled Christ who supposedly rose again... you will see...you will hear BROTHER BARTHOLO-MEW...for he WILL YET RISE AGAIN! RISE TO BE THE SAVIOUR OF THIS SICK AND DYING WORLD!

The papers that day emblazoned the news:

BROTHER BARTHOLOMEW TO RISE AGAIN
Bishop Arthur Blames Jews For Growing Famine

In school I remember reading about the 1969-1970 famine in Biafra. I can still remember being appalled at those photos of starving children. The death of some 3 million Ibos seemed a great tragedy.

...lo a black horse; and he that sat on him had a pair of balances in his hand. And I heard a voice in the midst of the four beasts say, A measure of wheat for a penny... (Revelation 6:5, 6)

But the world today was experiencing far greater tragedy. Food was never very plentiful, but because I was in the inner circle I managed to obtain artificial orange juice and a protein cake for breakfast, a spaghetti-like crude-oil concoction for lunch and a slice of DC protein meat at night. The Disposal Center protein meat, while only 8 ounces, was a life saver.

Now my food allotment had been reduced to the artificial orange juice and half a protein cake for breakfast...no lunch... the other half of the protein cake for dinner. Once a week, 6 ounces of DC protein meat.

Faye and Bill had the same fare. But somehow we made out. We knew we had to endure. More and more we delved into the Scriptures. And more and more we were discovering a hope worth living for. Our only fear was that Bishop Arthur's new rage against God might spell our doom.

Tom Malone and I were becoming very loyal friends. I couldn't tell him to his face, but somehow I felt he wanted the same hope of living that Faye, Bill and I possessed. But Tom had to be careful and I didn't want to place him on the spot.

I was afraid that out of his fight for mere existence, he would then have to terminate our friendship.

The whole country was a death camp. Tom filled me in on the reports that were coming in on the Picturephone. He was always careful to talk to me in a private office which not even BB seemed to have known about. This office had no PRAYER CHANGES THINGS spy plaque.

"George," he said, "I am sure we are on the brink of disaster. Refugees from all over the world are swarming to

America. Our one protein cake a day is heaven to them. What **And there shall be famines and pestilences...(Matthew 24:7)** meager possessions they have they carry on their heads. The sight of the children is pitiful. Wrinkled faces, haunted staring eyes, the utter apathy of aged men and women. In many cases I have seen the skin stretched so tight that every rib, hip and shoulder bone protruded. When they are given a protein cake the food won't stay in them. Mostly they are dying of diarrhea and malaria, a vicious strain our doctors can't control. When they die there's hardly any flesh left... so they can't even be put in the DC units. George, we are entrapped in a cruel web of circumstances. There is no way out."

"Tom, can't people be sensible about this? Stay where they are until a solution is worked out?"

"People will fight their own grandmother to live, George. Yesterday, walking through those muddy pools we call streets a girl accidentally dropped just a small piece of her protein cake. You would have thought that the inferno had broken loose. Immediately a band of girls were grovelling in the mud to claim the food. Two of them didn't come up alive."

"Tom, I remember reading predictions years ago about a day when there would be wholesale famine...but I didn't believe it."

"I have an old newspaper clipping here, George. It's yellowed with age. Sunday, July 6, 1969, Philadelphia Sunday Bulletin. Let me read these paragraphs my father had circled:

> A child born today, (that's 1969)
> living on into his seventies would know a world
> of 15 billion. His grandson would share the
> planet with 60 billion.
>
> In 6 1/2 centuries there would be one human being
> standing on every square foot of land on earth.

I feel fortunate to have a 12 foot square room all to myself."

"Tom, give me the facts straight, how critical is this famine?" "Far more critical than any of us can imagine. Even Bishop Arthur doesn't comprehend its magnitude. Health experts already are agreeing that at least one-fourth of the population of the world will be dead within the year!"

And when he had opened the fourth seal, I heard the voice of the fourth beast say, Come and see.

And I looked, and behold a pale horse: and his name that sat on him was Death, and Hell followed with him. And power was given unto them over the fourth part of the earth, to kill with a sword, and with hunger, and with death, and with the beasts of the earth. (Revelation 6:7, 8)

I was shocked beyond words. I slipped to my knees, right in front of Tom and uttered a simple prayer...

> Dear God, if we ever needed you, we need you
> now. Watch over Faye and Bill and Tom and
> me. Give us the crumbs from the Master's table
> to sustain us until the answer comes. Thank
> you Jesus.

Tom wiped the corner of his eye and walked out.

I ran all the way home to tell Faye and Bill the bad news that had just been revealed to me. I was surprised how calmly they accepted it. In the last few days their faith had grown stronger. Faye beckoned me to sit on the stool near the bed. She pulled out the well-worn Bible from beneath the mattress...then spoke.

"Dad, Bill and I have found some wonderful comfort in the Scriptures and today both of us discovered Psalm 91. Bill, you read the words we underlined."

In a soft voice, Bill read:

> He that dwelleth in the secret place of
> the most High shall abide under the shadow
> of the Almighty....
>
> Thou shalt not be afraid for the terror by
> night; nor for the arrow that flieth by day...
>
> A thousand shall fall at thy side, and ten
> thousand at thy right hand; but it shall not
> come nigh thee.

I, George Omega spoke, "Isn't it odd how things come back to us now that we have re-discovered God's Word. As Bill was reading from the Psalms I remember the Bible story that was taught to me in Sunday School about Elijah...how he multiplied that handful of meal. Faye, look up Elijah in the Proper Names Index in the back of the Bible."

Quickly she turned to the index.

"Here it is, Elijah raises the widow's son. I Kings 17...and here's another reference about Elijah taken up by a chariot of fire. II Kings 2."

"Read that I Kings reference first," Bill urged.

She turned the pages and read:

> And she said [the widow], As the Lord thy God
> liveth, I have not a cake, but an handful of meal
> in a barrel, and a little oil in a cruse: and
> behold, I am gathering two sticks, that I may go
> in and dress it for me and my son, that we may
> eat it, and die.
>
> And Elijah said unto her, Fear not; go and do as
> thou hast said: but make me thereof a little cake
> first, and bring it unto me, and after make for

thee and for thy son....

For thus saith the Lord God of Israel, The barrel
of meal shall not waste, neither shall the cruse
of oil fail, until the day that the Lord sendeth
rain upon the earth.

"God's promises are wonderful," I responded. "And I've
noticed something here that slipped me in the past. Here the
widow had but one meal left between her and death and yet
she shared that meal with God's prophet...and because of
her faithfulness God multiplied the little that she had.

You know, Faye and Bill, I realize that this proposal may
seem most unusual. But starting tonight let's share our
protein cake with God...he will be our unseen guest and
King."

Tears welled up in Faye's eyes. She put her arms around
my neck and hugged me as she exclaimed, "Oh, Dad I love
you so much."

For a moment she sat quietly, just dabbing her eyes with
her handkerchief. "Oh, I almost forgot," she exclaimed, "II
Kings 2, that's when Elijah rode a chariot to heaven. He did
not die. He was translated. Here it is...verse 11...

And it came to pass, as they still went on
[that's Elijah and Elisha], and talked, that,
behold, there appeared a chariot of fire,
and horses of fire, and parted them both asunder;
and Elijah went up by a whirlwind into heaven.

Isn't that wonderful, Bill?"

"Seems almost too fantastic to be true," Bill replied. "If
Elijah didn't die, whatever happened to him? How I wish
that all of us could right now ride in a chariot of fire right
up to heaven. It would be an answer to prayer."

I added, "Come to think of it Bill, somewhere in Revelation
there's reference to two witnesses. Somehow I wonder if we
might get to meet Elijah. I remember at one of Helen's
prayer circles overhearing the women talking about the day
Elijah and Moses would come back to earth. I wasn't inter-

ested then. I wish I had listened more closely."

"Well, I know one thing," Bill added, "I certainly would hate to be a Jew today. Bishop Arthur, in fact most of the world, has built up a real hatred

Alas! for that day is great, so that none is like it: it is even the time of Jacob's trouble, but he shall be saved out of it. (Jeremiah 30:7)

for the problems they have caused all of us. But in my heart I can't condemn them. None of us is without sin...and the Jews are God's chosen...

After a while the subject changed. Faye inquired of me, "Dad, how did Brother Bartholomew ever reach such a high pinnacle of power?"

"Well, basically the people put him there," I replied. "The previous Presidents were spending taxpayer's money in areas which the people believed to be very foolish. Take the mid-1960's of President Johnson's era. $89,000 was awarded the University of Texas to study the sea breeze. The Department of Agriculture spent five years revising pickle standards in order to describe the difference between curved and crooked pickles. A grant of $33,101 was given to the Israel Institute of Applied Social Research to study a 'test of husband-wife relationship.' Among the $1 billion allocated in one year by the Food for Freedom program was a grant to study the behavior of elephants in Ceylon. And all this while a world was slowly starving."

"Then to top it off, the 1968 Presidential election set the trend for expensive politicking. Total bills then for all offices reached over 250 million dollars. Presidential timber to have any chance for success needed two things...a good advertising agency and $25 million dollars. The first they could do without...the second was a necessity. After several elections like this, people said it's time for a change. That's when Brother Bartholomew came into the picture. He had temporarily settled the Arab-Israeli cold war, eased the China picture and the Pope had made him honorary leader of the Church of the World."

"Where did he come from, dad?" Faye questioned.

"Faye, that's it!" I exclaimed. "I had never given that much thought. Oh yes, I interviewed him once in the Mideast before he came to America. That's when he began to like me. But I never researched his origins. They seem to be somewhere in Iraq. Was it Baghdad or Babylon? Say I remember that at the time there were some strange rumors about his birth and early life—almost like Christ's angelic announced birth. Faye, you've hit the nail on the head! I'm going to fly to Iraq tomorrow and get to the bottom of this. Tom will find some excuse to send me. I can depend on him."

When I arrived at Tom Malone's office he was busy poring over the latest Picturephone reports on world conditions. Disgustingly he flipped a sheet in my direction.

"Here, look at this," he said.

Young people using brooms and insecticide were trying to knock down the doors of a religious library in Rome. The insecticide was to symbolically disinfect the poison the clergy had spread about Brother Bartholomew.

I put the report down and put my hand on Tom's shoulder. "Tom," I said, "I've got to go to Iraq. Get me clearance, please to get the next space shuttle to the Mideast. Send me on an investigative mission...give any excuse."

Tom could see the earnestness of my face. And I knew he would make all the arrangements.

I took a slower shuttle to Iraq because I wanted some time to catch up on research on the country. Tom had slipped an old history book into my attache case. It filled me in on the facts.

Rumor had it that Brother Bartholomew came from Babylon. This was just a small town about 65 miles south of Baghdad in Iraq.

Ancient Babylon was once the rich and powerful capital of a civilization that almost created astronomy, added richly to the progress of medicine, and which taught the Greeks the rudiments of physics and philosophy.

Young people were trying to knock down the doors.

When Nebuchadrezzar II took over the second Babylonian kingdom he spent the tolls of his trade and the taxes of his people in beautifying his capital. "Is not this the great Babylon that I built?" he had asked.

Babylon a mysterious word! I always had known that the word *Babel* in the Hebrew meant "confusion." My further

> Therefore is the name of it called Babel; because the Lord did there confound the language of all the earth...(Genesis 11:9)

research, however, revealed that *Babylon* also meant the *Gate of God*. Nebuchadrezzar, as other ancient kings, was not very humble. For all the bricks archeologists recovered from the site of the original Babylon bear the proud inscription: "I am Nebuchadrezzar, King of Babylon."

Just north of the Tower of Babel were the famous Hanging Gardens, which the Greeks included among the Seven Wonders of the World.

What would I find in this little town of Babylon? I did not know. The space shuttle landed in Baghdad. The streets were bustling with people. They were rushing to the city square.

I asked why but no one seemed to respond. Quickly I followed the crowd. Soon I was to see the reason for all the excitement. There in the square were scaffolds. And uncontrollingly jerking back and forth were the spasmodic bodies of Jews...stars of David painted on their foreheads.

> And at that time shall Michael stand up, the great prince which standeth for the children of thy people: and there shall be a time of trouble, such as never was since there was a nation even to that same time: and at that time thy people shall be delivered, every one that shall be found written in the book. (Daniel 12:1)

I turned my head and walked away.

The purge had already begun.

I managed to get an official car to drive me to Babylon. We passed Al Mahmudiyah and Al Musayyib. Knife-edged mountains of shifting sand scallop the barren countryside. The plains suffer extreme heat and strong northeasterly

Uncontrollingly jerking back and forth were the spasmodic bodies of Jews hanging in the city square.

winds. Arabs comprise about 75 per cent of the population of Iraq. The largest minority (15 per cent of the people) is the fiercely independent, nomadic Kurds.

I started a conversation with my driver-guide. I knew he could be of inestimable help to me. Tahir Arif had a kind face. I was sure he would be cooperative.

"Tahir, you know we all mourn the loss of Brother Bartholomew. It is my understanding that Iraq is his homeland and that Babylon is his birth place."

"Honored sir," Tahir replied, "I hear only rumors that a great one was born in Babylon some 33 years ago. But no one seems to know the facts. It's as if they are hiding something. Please sir, I want no trouble."

"No trouble, Tahir, I assure you. I come representing the United States of Europe."

With that Tahir appeared to tense up even more. As we drove into Babylon I began to interrogate him again. In answer to my question he replied..."Sir, some say that the one you call Brother Bartholomew had no father. His mother swears to this day it is so. But, sir...I am only telling you what *they* say. I want no trouble."

"One who I call Brother Bartholomew? What do you mean one who I call 'Brother Bartholomew,' Tahir? Don't people in Babylon know him as such?"

It was amazing. I as a reporter had been so sloppy in my early reporting days. I had accepted the fact that this was his name; I had never investigated his origins closely.

Tahir Arif stopped the car in front of a very small make-shift house. We got out, went to the door of this rock-hewn dwelling. Inside was a surprisingly beautiful Persian faced woman of about 50. She beckoned us to sit down. Tahir acted as my interpreter. He explained why I journeyed here.

I interrupted. "What is your name?"

Through the interpreter she replied. Tahir turned to me and said, "In our language you would not understand the name. In English you say it; Mary.'"

"Was Brother Bartholomew her son and if so, who is his father?"

As the interpreter asked her my question I could see her get highly excited. She waved her arms as she spoke.

She says, "My son have no father. My son miraculously born. No father. Over there. Over there!"

For false Christs and false prophets shall rise, and shall shew signs and wonders, to seduce, if it were possible, even the elect. (Mark 13:22)

I looked in the direction she was pointing. It was a manger! "What is his name," I asked.

The interpreter repeated the question in her language.

The reply confused him.

He asked her again.

She repeated slowly gesturing with her fingers and pointing to a well-worn calendar as she spoke.

He understood.

She says, "My son was born in June, the 6th of June at 6 o'clock in the evening. He was born without father. So I cannot name him after father. June is 6th month. Day is 6. Time is

Here is wisdom. Let him that hath understanding count the number of the beast: for it is the number of a man; and his number is Six hundred three score and six. (Revelation 13:18)

6. His birth is miraculous. I give him no man name. He is above sinful man's name. I give him number name. No one has number name but my son. You are the first one I tell this to. His real name is Six hundred sixty-six!"

I shuddered. Could it be true? Born in a manger. Miraculous birth. No name but a number. And the number 666? Quickly I thanked the woman and beckoned for Tahir to drive me back to Baghdad.

Upon my arrival back in Washington, Bishop Arthur called me into his office. To me it looked more like a throne room. I could see he was angry. He had discovered the real reason I flew to Iraq. He warned me that I would be dealt with harshly as would Faye and Bill if my loyalty to his service bordered on disunity.

I assured him this was not the case. I was merely following through in investigative reporting procedures to help him in resolving Brother Bartholomew's death.

Faye and Bill were overjoyed that I had returned home safely. In the short time that I was away conditions had become even more critical. Food allotments were cut down further. There was talk of more drastic action: elimination of the weak, the elderly over 55 and those not useful for the progress of society.

I was in a stupor as I quickly told Faye and Bill in our little bedroom corner what I had learned in Babylon. All the pieces were now fitting together. We could see it clearly. Faye had been doing some intensive studying of Revelation and Daniel. Bill would read some verses, then they would tell each other what they thought they meant. After much repeating, soon the truth of the verses became plain. Much time had been spent on their knees, pleading and pleading to God for wisdom. "Dad," Faye cried, "God must be answering our prayers for the Scriptures are becoming clear to me now."

With that came a knock on the door. As though it was well rehearsed, Faye quickly slipped the Bible underneath the mattress. I walked to the door. Bill sat down in the tiny living room.

"Open up, George, it's me, Tom."

I opened the door.

"George, I just had to see you as fast as possible. I have some bad news. Bishop Arthur is going to make a strange pronouncement tomorrow in his telecast. In commemoration of Brother Bartholomew everyone must honor him as God. This homage must be so indicated by a mark either in the right hand or on the forehead."

And he causeth all, both small and great, rich and poor, free and bond, to receive a mark in their right hand, or in their foreheads. (Revelation 13:16)

"What kind of mark," I exclaimed?

"The mark of 666!"

Chapter 9

Startling Pronouncement

Bishop Arthur insisted that I fly to China with him. I felt he was beginning to doubt my loyalty and wanted to make sure of my every movement. I had to be careful, not for my sake only, but for Faye and Bill.

Bishop Arthur had promised that Brother Bartholomew would rise again. I was hoping his promise would not come true for I felt that anything Bishop Arthur had a hand in would not be for the good. And yet I longed to see Brother Bartholomew again. He had been so kind to me and in spite of my findings in Babylon I felt that perhaps he might have the answer.

But I couldn't reconcile Brother Bartholomew with the Scriptures. In fact the more I studied the Scriptures the more I doubted. If it were not for Faye, I am afraid I would have become more confused and simply thrown in the sponge.

It was apparent to me that Bishop Arthur never glorified himself. But he was like a catalyst, generating respect and then directing praise and homage to Brother Bartholomew.

And I beheld another beast coming up out of the earth; and he had two horns like a lamb, and he spake as a dragon.

And he exerciseth all the power of the first beast before him, and causeth the earth and them which dwell therein to worship the first beast...(Revelation 13:11, 12)

But Brother Bartholomew was dead. Or was he? Of course, he was! I had seen his lifeless body with my own eyes. I had seen Dr. Curter wrap his body in a protective foil. Come to think of it, in all that hysteria of that day I don't remember any burial. The last I heard was that his body lay in a special room in the Rejuvenation Division of Capitol Hospital.

Bishop Arthur could have taken the fast one-half hour shuttle to Peking, but he later decided to take the slower 2 hour flight. The rapid change of time zones always gave him a severe headache. Dr. Curter had made sure that I was loaded down with anti-disorientation capsules. One day, shortly after Brother Bartholomew had died, Dr. Curter confided to me that with one slight change this powdered substance could become a lethal disorientation mix. When spread by spray such a mix would affect the nervous system, make one confused, disoriented, and ready to follow any command or directive.

Our space ship took off. Bishop Arthur patted me on the head like one would do to a good little boy.

"George," he said, "Things are moving very smoothly. I have a few surprises in store for you, in fact for the world. This quick trip to China should unlock the final door to my plan. By the way, did you catch my speech yesterday in my worldwide address?"

"No, I didn't sir, I was..."

"No need to tell me, George, I know exactly what you were doing. Our Central Intelligence knows every step you take. Not that we don't trust you. It's simply a matter of maintaining your loyalty Our CI division is very efficient...no botched up mess like that Green Beret episode in the late 1960's or the My Lai massacre in Quang Ngai Province that we once discussed. We have checks and double checks. Since the 60's our people have accepted very well the fact that their government has a right to lie...and does lie."

"You mean your statement about Brother Bartholomew rising again is a lie, sir?"

"No, George, that will become a reality."

And with that he punched a button on the work table in front of him. A television screen emerged.

"There, George, thought you'd like to see an excerpt of yesterday's address."

As the picture came into focus, I could see the Capitol Building. Everywhere I looked there were people, raising their hands in a victory salute.

...and in closing may I say this. At no time has this administration questioned the loyalty of its peoples. But we

And the ten horns which thou sawest are ten kings, which have received no kingdom as yet; but receive power as kings one hour with the beast. (Revelation 17:12)

are no longer a nation. We are many nations merged into one...ten nations all giving their allegiance to the new unit of power...the unit called The United States of Europe.

In these days of distress and famine, we must not be discouraged. We must lift up our eyes. We must become the Master of our Ship. Those who would betray this sacred trust can no longer hide under the cloak of respectability.

I have declared, in honor and in homage of our late Brother Bartholomew, each citizen shall from now on bear proudly the mark 666. For convenience of our ladies, it may be placed either in the right hand or on the forehead.

What greater way is there to show respect and loyalty than by this external evidence of our pride in being a responsible citizen of the world?

Those who refuse to bear this mark will automatically show their disloyalty to each of us

And he causeth all, both small and great, rich and poor, free and bond, to receive a mark in their right hand, or in their foreheads:

And that no man might buy or sell, save he that had the mark, or the name of the beast, or the number of his name. (Revelation 13: 16-17)

and to the honored soul of Brother Bartholomew.

It would not be right for them to pluck the morsels of bread from faithful families whose children may die for lack of nourishment.

The already restricted allocations of food must not be wasted on those who will not make a sacrifice of love and obedience.

No one may buy or sell without this mark. Such a decision needs time. A grace period of 30 days, starting today will be allowed. At the end of that 30 days, everyone must bear the mark of 666.

Remember, we have nothing to fear but fear itself. Let us lift our hearts to God and give thanks, for God told us in His Word, *'in everything give thanks.'*

May our faithfulness bring an Elijah, an Elijah who will take our barrel of meal and cruse of oil and multiply this finite substance dedicated to God..."

Now I knew Bishop Arthur was aware of my every step. Elijah! Faye and Bill and I had just discussed this miracle ourselves. Life seemed so unreal.

The screen went blank and the unit returned to its original position.

As we prepared to land in China I could see the venerable Great Wall. Built 22 centuries ago as a defense against invaders, the wall still was a wonder of the world. Serpent-like, it winds from east to west across more than 1500 miles of China.

Leader Chou, Chairman of the Chinese Communist Party greeted us quite warmly. We drove to the Gate of Supreme Harmony, a magnificent structure of typical chinese architecture. Chou told us that here the first Manchu emperor took his throne in 1644. The Gate of Heavenly Peace provided the entrance to the Imperial Palaces.

I wasn't sure why Bishop Arthur was coming to China but I knew, as I smelled the aroma coming from the palace kitchen, that here was one of the last places on earth where food, real food, still existed. But only on very special occasions could even Leader Chou enjoy such a feast. Once or twice a year, the vaults would be open where these frozen delicacies were stored. A bowing Chinesewaiter told me that most of the delicacies were put in those vaults 25 years ago in 1975 when Chinese leaders became aware of emerging famine symptoms.

Chinese, standing in line, were shoving and pushing hoping to retrieve just a scrap of left-over food.

The large round table was extremely glossy from a million rubbings. In Chinese letters burnished in gold and lacquered red were the words Hou Te Fu — meaning "Unbounded Virtue and Happiness."

I had never seen so much real food in over twenty years. While my taste buds had become accustomed to the protein cakes I knew it would not take long for them to relish food that was not artificially made.

The first course brought what Leader Chou considered his favorite, "Fire pot eggs" — a fluffy souffle with thinly sliced lily bulbs suspended in its golden interior. Bear claws were also on the menu, but I never got around to trying them.

The main course was duck. It was a thing of beauty. First thin crisp slices of skin, dipped in sauce and wrapped with a small spring onion in a thin unleavened pancake, then the juicy meat, finally a fragrant soup.

The meal was topped with a dessert called Peking Dust. I could see Bishop Arthur's mouth water when this was mentioned. It was a puree of chestnuts, slathered with whipped cream and dotted with preserved fruit.

Imagine not having eaten real food in twenty years and then suddenly feasting on this table. Of the billions of people on earth, I was part of a very select few...eating real food. What a privilege! And yet I felt guilty. After the first burst of enthusiasm my heart sank. For I could see Faye and Bill, kneeling at the bed in our apartment, carefully breaking half a protein cake into two quarters...then each gently breaking the quarter into an eighth...setting aside one tenth as a tithe for Jesus in a little offering box we had made...slowly eating what remained...and then giving thanks to the Lord.

Right now they had so little. I had so much. Yet I was unhappy. I was sure they were rejoicing at their precious banquet and praising God.

After the meal both Bishop Arthur and I excused ourselves, walked quickly to the restroom. The meal had been too much for us. Like starving men we had eaten ravenously. Our stomachs could not contain such wholesome fare. As I bent over the washbasin I realized that real food had lost its meaning to me. No longer would I desire it. Such a lesson was preparing me for the months ahead.

Chinese, standing in line, were shoving and pushing hoping to retrieve just a scrap of left-over food.

Bishop Arthur was anxious to make sure the Chinese were sympathetic with the aims of the United States of Europe. Previous frequent border clashes with Russia had come almost to a standstill since Russia's defeat in Israel. And Bishop Arthur was fearful that this Asian Giant would start flexing her muscles in our direction. He seemed to fear this especially now because of BB's being assassinated and not on the scene to control things.

China's influence had grown in the last twenty years. She had swallowed up Japan, India, Pakistan, Vietnam, Laos, Thailand, all the little islands, Taiwan, and the Philippines. Finally even Australia was now yielding.

Leader Chou assured Bishop Arthur that the nations would live at peace. Each country, he said, had too many internal problems to solve. And Chou had remembered America's sincere humbleness in the late 1970's when she recognized China and shared her nuclear advances with China. Leader Chou had respected Brother Bartholomew and thus he had invited Bishop Arthur to make this trip to discuss the possible rejuvenation of this great man through the administration of the Chinese miracle-drug herbs. Both China and the United States of Europe were working for many years to bring a dead man back to life. Both were so near to the solution, yet so very far away.

Chinese Herb Doctors were still plying their trade in spite of what Americans called advance medical techniques. China had 24,000 pharmacies, 8700 licensed herbal doctors.

Leader Chou snapped his fingers. A door opened. An elderly gentlemen with the traditional long grey-white beard entered.

"This," leader Chou proudly introduced, "is Dr. Wu Hai-feng. Were it not for him I would have been dead long ago."

Bishop Arthur spoke: "Dr. Hai-feng, I am sure you have read of the modern advances which we have made in medicine. Do you feel your herbal remedies are better than our most recent discoveries?"

"Begging humble pardon, Great One," Dr. Hai-feng replied, "but the very fact that you are here is evidence enough that perhaps we have something you are seeking."

Bishop Arthur blushed. "Yes, Dr. Hai-feng, Brother Bartholomew is dead. A bullet through the brain. Dr. Curter of our Rejuvenation Division has developed a formula that should bring him back to life. But there is a missing link. For a brief second the body comes to life, the eyelids flutter...and then total collapse...dead again." Bishop Arthur then asked, "Why don't you use our Western techniques?"

"Easy to explain, Great One," Dr. Hai-feng continued, "We shun such so-called advanced Western practices as X-rays and blood tests. Chinese medicine is 5000 years old. Chinese herb medicine cures your disease fundamentally, even if it takes time. Western medicine — it cures quickly, but the disease may come back. Your ingredient brings life... but the disease...death...comes back. In this case...very quickly."

Bishop Arthur queried: "But the body is a most complex instrument, one must have a knowledge of the inter-actions of muscle, nerve and blood vessels. Am I not correct?"

"Not so, Great One. Herbs control the balance of yin and yang, the opposing forces that dwell in every person. Yin is passive and dark; yang is active and light. When a person has a cold, the yang dominates. Therefore I prescribe a herb to redress the balance of yin and yang."

"But there is more to the science than that," Dr. Hai-feng continued, "Traditional Chinese medicine says the body is composed of five elements — wood, fire, earth metal and air — and each of these elements has yin and yang. In a complicated illness, the balance of yin and yang in the five elements varies. That's why treatment varies from person to person. Because of the greatness of such a one as Brother Bartholomew and what we here in Asia hear of his supernatural birth, treatment of yin and yang may prove most difficult."

As I listened I wondered silently, "Was Dr. Hai-feng speaking of yin and yang to keep the Chinese discoveries secret—or did he believe this?"

With that Dr. Wu Hai-feng placed a flask on the table. In it were what appeared to be brown and green slushes bubbling. He explained that this was a herb mixture which included chin pu hun, a pulverized twig called ma huang and a few other exotic names which I could not remember.

"Leader Chou," Dr. Hai-feng continued, "has told me in detail of your mission. Perhaps our old customs of medicine combined with yours may bring back Brother Bartholomew. One catalytic ingredient — Formula 6 — is still missing to make this flask potent. Years ago Leader Chou had it flown to the moon and deposited in a crevice called China Crevice. There in underground vaults it is held. Place one cubic centimeter of Formula 6 in with this flask. Complete instructions are in this envelope. Give it to Dr. Curter. We wish you success."

I had never been to the moon. This was to be a real adventure. Leader Chou had made his spacecraft available for our use. Our own space craft was to rendevous above the moon and wait for us.

At the airfield the space craft prepared for lift-off. I had never seen such a vehicle. We were advised that it was a utility aircraft, a flying, crawling vehicle for lunar exploration. It looked like two large tubes connected with two center posts. Each of the tubes had landing gear resembling wheels ordinarily seen on tanks. On lift-off these tractor-type wheels receded into the spacecraft.

As we approached the moon Bishop Arthur pushed a button that revealed the floor viewing screen. There below us was Tranquility Base...the original landing sight of man on the moon back in July, 1969 some 31 years ago.

"We've made much progress since then, George," Bishop Arthur commented. That landing site is now an international shrine. The bubble enclosure makes it habitable. Millions of people since 1981 have taken the Earth-Moon shuttle to view this accomplishment. The first 240,000 mile journey was a big project then. Apollo-Saturn V which launched those first space men was 363 feet tall, the height of a 36-story building. Since then we modified the height and weight through miniaturization of materials and use of nuclear energy."

"Wasn't it one of our astronauts that said after that first landing, 'I've always believed that nothing is impossible and now I'm convinced of it.'"

"That's right," Bishop Arthur replied. "And it was the President at the time who replied, 'This is the greatest week in the history of the world since the Creation.' You have a Bible, George. It's a King James Version...rather outdated... but our new Revised Standard Version spells this feat out quite clearly in Genesis 11:6...

> And the Lord said, "Behold, they are one people,
> and they have all one language; And this is
> only the beginning of what they will do and
> nothing that they propose to do will now be
> impossible for them.

"That's why, George, Man is the Master of his fate. The Jews recognized this when they forced back the Arabs in that Six Day War. Many said it was God...the Jews were returning to Israel. Others were much wiser, however. It was their might, their energies. Now they have softened. I fear they are returning to that imposter God of the Bible. You will see, George, Man will bring Brother Bartholomew back to life. It will be a miracle. I promise that you will see this with your very eyes."

The grayish-tan surface of the moon came into focus as we prepared to land. It reminded me of the Sahara desert. A fine grain dust covered the surface. When we walked on it, it had the cohesiveness of wet beach sand. Every step we took left footprints. But our footprints were hard to distinguish. So many people had walked here that one footprint simply was superimposed upon another. The area we were walking on was restricted territory. Originally the then United States had hoped that the moon would be a neutral territory. The U.S. had thus made an agreement with Russia. But as with all agreements with Russia, this too was broken.

And once it was broken, the other nations rushed in to claim their territories on the moon.

What was commonly called by us "The Chinese Crevice" was located near the 2-mile-deep, 56-mile-wide Crater Copernicus, whose flat but rubble-strewn floor was broken by a chain of 1,000-foot high hills.

A Chinese astronaut was lowered by crane down into the crevice. We were told that at its base was an underground vault, guarded with special electronic spy-gear to prevent others from entering. China's top classified secrets were kept here.

Within a few minutes the astronaut returned to our space ship. In his hand was a vial. It was labeled, "Formula 6."

The talk in Washington was all about The Mark 666. How would it be administered? Was it a large mark? Women buzzed about the cosmetic significance. Most women were inclined to have their mark placed on their hand. Some felt it would show a greater sense of loyalty to have the mark on the forehead where all could see. Rumor had it that those with the mark on their forehead would be allocated a greater ratio of food, receive the better jobs. Earth's population had grown so out of control and resources were so limited that those who were able to find jobs were restricted to only two hours per week. It was the only way to somehow, ineffective as it seemed, spread the work opportunity. Many learned the trick of not notifying an employer that their brother or sister had died. The unemployed in the family would then take on that two hours of work as though nothing had occurred. Strange alliances among employees kept such shady dealings, for the most part, secret.

Faye, prior to the announcement of The Mark, had already been reduced to the one hour per week work category. Bill could find no work...not even in the disposal centers.

Bill walked in the apartment that night discouraged. Over 6000 people had lined up that day at the disposal center... eager to apply for the one job opening that had been posted. Bodies were coming in at a faster rate...thus the opening.

Faye could see the disappointment on his face.

"Bill, come over here honey. I know how you feel. Life today seemed hopeless for me, too. The girls at work were all talking about The Mark. I said nothing. I sensed that they knew I could not wear the brand. At the end of my work hour my supervisor came over. He said my work privilege had been cancelled. We'll starve to death with no protein cakes... but we must not lose our faith in God."

"I know Faye," said Bill, "my mother used to tell me it's darkest right before the dawn."

Bill then sat down on the floor in the bedroom next to Faye. They looked out the window. Of course they could not see the stars. The murky haze of thick brown dust clouded the view.

"Bill, let's pretend this is our little honeymoon cottage. The fireplace is over there. You've just put a log on the fire. The wood is crackling a sweet song of peace and contentment. Outside the snow is gently falling blanketing the tiny shoots of grass and the tall stately trees in a brand new white winter coat. And you and I are alone together. The night is still. Not a sound. And we're all alone with our dreams. Up above the stars are twinkling a canopy of light. And the baby stars nestle in the velvety blanket of midnight blue."

Bill dreamily responded, "Then, Faye, the moon will majestically make its way across the Heavens and the stars will play tag happily following. Watch, I'll find the big dipper for you!"

"No you won't, Bill, honey. I'll find it first. And look there's Pleiades. Oh, how I remember how much fun we used to have in naming those six sisters."

And with that tears formed in Faye's eyes. Her sobbing broke Bill's heart.

"Oh, Bill, Bill, Bill, why does life have to be this way? What has happened to the simple freedoms of life? Why has man's advances cursed man's living? Why did I turn my back on God for so many years? Helen, little Sue and Tommy. They're in Heaven now enjoying the blessings of God. But we're here on this miserable, sophisticated, progressive, godless, everything-goes earth. Bill, I have faith. I believe God...but I can't go on. I can't go on. I can't go on!"

Bill was crying.

"Faye, just lean your head on my shoulder...remember that honeymoon cottage now. Careful, honey, your tears will put the fire out. Then I'll have to go out and get some more dry logs. And it's awfully cold outside. Remember Faye, that night we watched the sun rise. It was very dark. Then just a slight hint of red peaked across the horizon. A little hue of yellow. A few impatient streaks fanned out. The dark sky became a mirror reflecting that precious light, bringing a lighter cast over the earth. Soon just the tip of that bright red sun appeared. The velvety shadows began to disappear. The warmth of the sun began to fill our room. Soon the darkness vanished...vanished so quickly that it seemed it had never appeared. Faye, right now the dark sky is above us day and night. But beyond it, waiting for God's holy signal is the sun, God's Son. We've read the Book of Revelation and

> For then shall be great tribulation, such as was not since the beginning of the world to this time, no, nor ever shall be. (Matthew 24:21)

Daniel together. We have seen the signs God has told us... the Great Tribulation, the last half of Daniel's Seventieth Week, is about to come. It will be dark, Faye, very dark. But it's in God's timetable. And we should be rejoicing...for beyond this brief time of Tribulation the sun will bring back to the world its love, its warmth.

And Faye, when you and I look back, basking under His light in the New Heavens and New Earth, why it will be as though the darkness of Satan never

> And when these things begin to come to pass, then look up, and lift up your heads; for your redemption draweth nigh. (Luke 21: 28)

appeared. God in speaking about His nation Israel, told us in Isaiah 48:10:

> Behold, I have refind thee, but not with silver;
> I have chosen thee in the furnace of affliction.

And that is our promise too. Then in II Corinthians 4:17...

> For our light affliction, which is but for a moment, worketh for us a far more exceeding and eternal weight of glory.

Faye, you're smiling now."

His head bent down to hers.

Their tears mingled as they kissed, tenderly, not in passion, but in understanding.

Faye jumped up...like a little girl with a toy.

"Bill, I've a little surprise for you...and for daddy."

The sound of a key was heard at the door. It was George. "Daddy," Faye shouted, "you came just in time." Then realizing she was in the room with the PRAYER CHANGES THINGS plaque, she whispered in George's ear to come to the bedroom.

George entered, shook Bill's hand, and then sat down wearily on the floor. Quickly he briefed them on his trip to China and to the Moon. His face betrayed his emotions. He was afraid something drastic would happen soon.

"But let's not talk about me, what's the surprise?" Bill questioned.

Faye held a compact, small rectangular box in her hand. "It's that pocket record player you and mom gave me one Christmas, Daddy," Faye replied. "And remember that little plastic record mom's church used to pass out on visitation nights. I still have the one she gave to me. It was one of the

few things I threw in the overnight bag that night we fled New York. And I had forgotten about it until just a few moments before Bill came home from job hunting. Let me put the record on and play it. I have never yet played it so it will be a surprise to all of us."

Faye hurridly placed the record on the spindle. Flipped the ON switch. Nothing happened.

Disappointment shone on her face.

George picked up the record player...then spoke. "Faye, this won't play. The batteries have long since lost their power. I remember Helen giving that to you over three years ago. The batteries are dead. How cruel can life be to us?"

Bill's face lit up. "Wait a minute. I wasn't a Boy Scout for nothing. As a kid I remember how we made record players play. I'll just put my finger on the turntable and turn it around manually at the speed where the record makes sense." And with that he started the turntable spinning. At first it sounded like a Model T Ford being cranked up with all sorts of sounds emanating from the machine.

Then when Bill found the right speed, he maintained it and words of a song sung in a beautiful contralto voice filled the little room....

> It's not the first mile
> that's so important;
> It's the last mile
> when day is done.
>
> Then you'll see Jesus
> in all His Splendor;
> And He will have for you
> the Crown you've won.

Over and over again they played it like little children. Then George spoke. "You know, I had forgotten it until now but I can remember Grandmother singing to me while she put me to sleep. In her rocking chair besides the bed...she would sing the hymn 'Blessed Quietness' over and over again. She sang it so often, I could repeat it by heart — all five verses."

And with that he broke into song...

> Joys are flowing like a river
> Since the Comforter has come
> He abides with us forever
> Makes the trusting heart His home.
> Blessed quietness, holy quietness

What assurance in my soul!
On the stormy sea, He speaks peace to me,
How the billows cease to roll!

Bill spoke. I could tell his heart was touched. "George, Faye, I have had perhaps greater opportunity to study God's Word because I have had no job. And it just dawned on me. We've been talking about God...about how we know He will care for us, how we understand His prophecies. But I can't recall that any of us have ever asked Christ to come into our hearts...accept Him as our personal Saviour. John 6:37 tells us that

...him that cometh to me I will in no wise cast out.

and John 6:47 says

Verily, verily I say unto you, He that believeth
on me hath everlasting life.

And Romans 10:9

That if thou shalt confess with thy mouth
the Lord Jesus, and shalt believe in thine
heart that God hath raised him from the
dead, thou shalt be saved."

"How true, how very true, we have forgotten the most important thing of all," Faye replied. Let's right now make a pact with ourselves and with God. Let's kneel and hold hands and pray asking Christ to come into our hearts. Dad, you've heard mother pray so many times. You lead...please."

George, Faye and Bill knelt in the tiny room, each holding the other's hands. George began:

"Dear Lord, we don't know the right words
to say. In fact we don't understand much of
thy Word. But Helen told me there's a verse
about 'Lean not to thy own understanding.' And
we don't understand.

But I know this and so does Faye and Bill.
We are sinners. Lost sinners. The world
has gone mad...and we're headed straight
for Judgment and Hell.

> Lord Jesus, we want to right now confess
> our sins. I want to confess my sins. I
> believe you died and rose again from the
> dead. I know that I cannot save myself.
>
> Save me dear Jesus according to the promise
> in your Word. I want Christ to come into
> my heart, be my Saviour and my Lord.
>> Amen"

Bill continued the prayer...

> "Precious Lord, we claim Romans 10:9
> as a promise for our lives, for my life.
> I, too, want Christ to come into my
> heart right now."

Then Faye prayed...

> "Thank you Lord for keeping us together
> as a family. Thank you for Helen's
> testimony to us. Thank you for dying
> on the cross of Calvary for my sins
> and the sins of the world.
>
> Save me now, Lord. Forgive me for turning
> my back on you. Save me and keep me.
> Make our reunion with Helen and Sue and
> Tommy soon, dear Lord.
>
> I, too, accept Christ as my Saviour and
> my Lord.
>
>> Amen"

As Faye finished a loud buzzer sounded. It came from the wall near their heads. Startled the trio stood up quickly.

"What's that, Dad?" Faye asked.

"Sounds like its coming from behind the drapery," George replied. Quickly he pulled back the drapery.

There like a symbol of death hung a plaque. On it the words

PRAYER CHANGES THINGS

A voice then spoke from the very plaque itself. It was the voice of Bishop Arthur.

"George, you have betrayed me. And more important you have betrayed the soul of Brother Bartholomew. You and your daughter and your son-in-law will pay for this decision you made to your God. Then let's see if He can save you. The first payment will be in blood...the day after tomorrow. Bill will be the first to meet the convincer. And what a most appropriate place we have for that spectacle to occur! The day after tomorrow Bill will die. He will die by guillotine!"

And when he had opened the fifth seal, I saw under the altar the souls of them that were slain for the word of God, and for the testimony which they held. (Revelation 6:9)

...and I saw the souls of them that were beheaded for the witness of Jesus...(Revelation 20:4)

Chapter 10

Search for Safety

Dr. Curter was pleased with his progress.

"Those Chinese are clever, Bishop Arthur, their age-old medicine appears to be the missing link we desperately needed. I believe we are going to have success."

Bishop Arthur smiled. His diabolical plan must succeed. Brother Bartholomew must be brought back to life.

The damage to the nerve cells of the brain worried Dr. Curter. His remarks conveyed this fear: "I feel sure of success in restoring life, Bishop Arthur, but we have no way of telling what mind will evolve...a genius, an evil or benevolent mind, or a mentally slow person."

Bishop Arthur interrupted, "Don't even suggest such a thing, you idiot."

"Now, now, Bishop," reassured Dr. Curter, "we mean no disrespect to Brother Bartholomew. We are just evaluating the situation realistically. You see the 10 billion nerve cells of the brain make a bumpy knot of gray and white matter inside the skull. The brain is an integrated unit. I'm particularly worried about the cerebral cortex. This is the brain's most elaborate center, where voluntary actions are initiated. It has been called 'the seat of all which is exclusively human in the mind,' for here decisions are made, higher thought processes occur, and memories are stored."

"What about brain transplant?" Bishop Arthur queried.

"I don't think it's indicated here, sir," Dr. Curter continued. "And besides it is Brother Bartholomew's head — not his body—that we want to bring back. Besides, while medical science has advanced we haven't perfected the technique yet. Complete head transplant is no problem. In the early 1960's we were transplanting heads on dogs. And here's how advanced we have become..."

With that Dr. Curter pressed a button, a door slid open from the wall. There in a glass viewing enclosure was a dog... but not an ordinary dog. This one had a human head!

Momentarily even Bishop Arthur was shocked. He stepped back and motioned with his hand to Dr. Curter to close the viewing door.

"A head transplant would be out of the question. We must maintain the same head, the same features Brother Bartholomew had before he was shot," Bishop Arthur now affirmed.

"For the most part," Dr. Curter continued, "the brain controls the 600-odd muscles of the body. And damage to the brain may affect the 60,000 miles of tubing which carried blood to every part of the body. But in this particular case it's the nerve cells that worry us. Nerve cells in the brain alone use up as much as 20 per cent of all the oxygen available in the adult body, for they are working at a frantic speed 24 hours a day. Sleeping does not, as some would believe, give the brain much of a rest. Quite aside from maintaining breathing and the rate of heartbeat, the brain may function during these sleep periods to try to search out answers to particularly difficult problems and to reconsider experiences of the day that were flowing in too fast to be dealt with carefully at the time. Normally, during the course of every 24 hours, we lose some neurons. They wear out and die. Fortunately great numbers would have to die to produce any noticeable effect, but the small losses inevitably accumulate. Once a neuron is destroyed—it is destroyed. No new nerve cell will ever take its place; a year-old baby has all the neurons it will ever have. If we can find the answer to this we can slow down mental old age, eliminate senility."

"Enough of these medical explanations, Dr. Curter, what are you trying to tell me?" Bishop Arthur asked impatiently.

"Just this, sir, with the special solutions we injected into Brother Bartholomew's body and his prompt placement into the cyro-capsule...we were able to forestall complete death and deterioration and place him in what medical science might term a death-sleep. During this death-sleep the brain still remains active...just as active as when you and I sleep. But with no physical activity, brain activity increases, and in this case the neurons may or may not die. Once brought back to life we have no way of knowing the direction Brother Bartholomew will go. Will this intense brain activity explode into a man-created monster who may kill half the world with plans which, in his pre-dead condition, would have never occurred to him? And the neurons...will they be effected in some way so they direct him to evil? It could even be that he may upon awakening see himself as a god!"

"Stop, stop," interjected Bishop Arthur. "I should have had you replaced..."

* * * * *

The heads of state from all over the world were invited. It was to be the most historic occasion the world had ever witnessed. Even greater than man's landing on the moon.

Looking at the new structure from the air, it resembled a cross. In physical beauty it was stupendous. Pure white marble steps led up to the main entrance. This was the building Bishop Arthur had talked so much about. The building to house a memorial for BROTHER BARTHOLOMEW. Three stately columns were on each side of the entrance door. On these columns were recorded the accomplishments of Brother Bartholomew.

Six large oval screens appeared over the building's door. A special black light made the area between the pillars and the building wall completely dark — so as you looked at the structure from the front you were met by a mass of darkness broken by the light emitting from the open door. Then there was in color, the six television-like screens portraying activities and events that Brother Bartholomew took part in before his assassination. One screen would light up at a time and as the picture of Brother Bartholomew walked across the panorama of screens his voice filled the square. Similar television screens were mounted throughout the city of Washington and were awaiting the press of a button that would make all of them relay stations showing Brother Bartholomew. They were as plentiful as street lights. Plans were made to install them throughout the United States of Europe. Wherever you looked one would see Brother Bartholomew.

What was not known at this time was that these relay video-lights had a dual purpose. They could not only send pictures over the screen but act as a very effective spy system to weed out dissenters. No one noticed the receiving units located at the bottom of each screen.

Bishop Arthur insisted that I and Faye and Bill accompany him to the ribbon-cutting ceremonies.

A special elevator brought the dignitaries and Bishop Arthur to the main floor. We were made to walk up what seemed endless steps. There were six landings before one reached the main floor. On each set of landings were 66 steps. I know because I counted them!

Upon entering the long hall it was difficult at first for us to see. Darkness seemed to envelop us until our eyes became used to the conditions. An usher with a small flashlight guided us to our seats. We were ushered right to the very front.

It seemed like a church, yet the front appeared devoid of anything. A long black drape from ceiling to floor blocked the area where a pulpit normally would have stood many years ago.

Bishop Arthur was now talking...

> Friends of the world. How significant it is that leaders from every country of the world have gathered here...gathered for one purpose only...that singular purpose of paying homage to the greatest of men...so great we in honor refer to him as god-like.

> I will not take the time to recount even his recent exploits: His single-handed victory over Russia and his bringing of peace to the land of Israel.

> The video-lamps installed on every street corner in the western world will convey that message far better than I.

> Today I press two buttons. One to light these video messengers of God's will...the other to light both the outside and the inside of this building, illuminating forever the name of this hallowed structure.

He pressed the first button. A large screen above lit up showing a panorama of the city of Washington, and in the darkness little dots of light formed. The video screens were telling their message.

Then the large screen disappeared.

He pressed the next button. On each side of the wall, as though they appeared from nothing, words glowed in a brilliant gold:

BROTHER BARTHOLOMEW
THE SON OF GOD

Then as quickly as they appeared, they disappeared.

Bill, Faye and I stared in horror and in disbelief. We held each other's hands tightly as a way of giving each of us inner strength.

In the very dim light I glanced at Bishop Arthur. Something big was about to happen. I knew not what. But his face no longer resembled that of a Bishop of the Lord. Somehow, in my heart, I knew him to be a Prophet of Satan himself. And whatever his surprise, it would be Satanically inspired.

Suddenly the lights went out. The long hall was pitch black. I could tell that even the honored delegates were ill at ease.

Slowly a pale light played on the velvet-like drape in the front of the vast structure. It was not a flood light, but more like a spot light that only lit one small portion at a time.

It started at the very bottom. It looked like a rough-hewn piece of wood. As the light went up it appeared that this was a vertical standing piece of wood...then some feet appeared... a spike piercing them. You could see what seemed to be real blood gushing down the black velvet in rivulets of stain. Then legs, a body. Suddenly a cross piece of wood appeared. The light played on one hand. Then went out. Then played on the other hand.

Both hands were pierced with a spike and from those hands blood oozed.

It was all clear now. It was a cross. The cross of Calvary. But why would this godless man display the Cross of Christ?

Then it became all too clear. The light in a burst of dramatic drum roll shone on the face. Faye sobbed.

The face was not the face of Christ. It was the face of Brother Bartholomew!

It was all too clear now...too sickening clear! The apostasy of the early days in the 1930's, 1960's, 1970's had borne its fruit. First it was the liberal churches. Then it was the evangelicals watering down the Gospel with their introduction of the beat Gospel music...the Christian Rock groups...the relevant Christianity that played down the prophetic Word of God...stressed only the need for social concern. Now I saw how subtly the forces of evil had worked to turn the zealousness of the Church away from winning souls towards a more material, business-like type of Christianity.

The wine of apostasy had been emptied fully. And Faye,

Bill and I were to inherit its bitter dregs.

Bishop Arthur continued:

> Brother Bartholomew sacrificed his life so that we might have life. He bore his cross to make our burdens lighter.
>
> This painting was suggested by the Bishop-delegates at the last United World Church Union. What a fitting memorial from such an auspicious religious body. To them we owe our deepfelt gratitude.
>
> The fabled Christ of the Scriptures of the New Testament has not met our needs...has not saved the world. God is still on the Throne. He has sent his son. My own discovery of scrolls near the Dead Sea shed light on this revelation. There is no evidence that the Christ of the heretical New Testament rose from the Dead. Not even the records of Josephus can confirm this. And if he rose...I ask you this... WHERE IS HE? Our scientists in their might have built spacecraft. We have searched the heavens. We have scoured Venus and Mars. Inch by inch we combed the moon. It was obvious that this Christ was not walking with us on earth. And our astronauts have not located him walking even in the heavens!

So called Christians have quoted John 14:2,3

> "In my Father's house are many mansions: if it were not so, I would have told you. I go to prepare a place for you.
>
> And if I go and prepare a place for you, I will come again, and receive you unto myself; that where I am, there ye may be also."
>
> But the scrolls that I have found near Mezad-Zohar at the Dead Sea reflect a picture that will revolutionize the world.

With a flick of the wrist, Bishop Arthur unrolled a long scroll, obviously a duplicate of what he claimed was an original. Tom Malone had told me some ancient bits of hide

were photographed and printed into scroll form for this
occasion. He had believed them to have been made into reproductions of some of the missing Dead Sea Scrolls.

Bishop Arthur continued:

> This scroll contains the complete book of BAR-
> THOLOMEW, a book which previous church his-
> torians have chosen to ignore.

> Let me read you verse 6 of chapter 66.

> "If I should die, I will come again and prepare
> a place for you, a place for you on earth.

> And those who would seal their devotion with
> a mark shall live again in newness of life. Old
> things shall pass away...behold all things shall
> become new.

> Beware of false prophets and continue in
> steadfastness until my soon coming again."

> Let us now pause in silence to meditate upon these
> words.

With this again the lights in the building went out. A
minute passed in complete darkness. Not a sound. It seemed
like an eternity. At first the silence was broken by hushed
whispers. Then silence.

Then as if on cue, what appeared to be a roll of thunder shattered the silence. A bolt of lightening in a blinding flash rent the veil-like drape in two.

> And, behold, the veil of the temple was rent in twain from the top to the bottom; and the earth did quake, and the rocks rent. (Matthew 27:51)

The audience gasped. Behind the drape stood a life-like
statue of Brother Bartholomew in gleaming gold. The way
the lightening had struck seemed almost Elijah-like.

Bishop Arthur went on to describe the statue...that it was 90 feet or 60 cubits high and 9 feet or 6 cubits wide. con-structed from elements found in

> Nebuchadnezzar the king made an image of gold, whose height was threescore cubits, and the breadth thereof six cubits: he set it up in the plain of Dura, in the province of Babylon. (Daniel 3:1)

the Dead Sea.

Then he continued:

"What you are viewing is more than a statue of refined gold. For it is symbolic of life...the life of Brother Bartholomew." And then raising his voice, he shouted:

"Brother Bartholomew will you LIVE AGAIN?"

Slowly the mouth of the statue started to move. The lips opened ever so slightly, the cheekbones rose, the eyes appeared to twinkle, the tongue came slightly forward.

SUDDENLY THE VERY STATUE WAS SPEAKING! It was Brother Bartholomew's voice!

YES, I WILL LIVE AGAIN.

I AM HE THAT LIVETH, AND WAS DEAD; AND BE-HOLD, I AM ALIVE FOR EVERMORE, Amen; AND HAVE THE KEYS OF HELL AND DEATH. [Revelation 1:18]

And he had power to give life unto the image of the beast, that the image of the beast should both speak...(Revelation 13:15)

There was a stirring in the audience yet no one moved. Photographers suddenly leaped from all parts of the hall and lit the room with the flashing bulbs.

Suddenly the room darkened. From high on the ceiling a youthful sound of angelic-like voices came. First the chord of an organ...the words seemed so familiar...

Hallelujah! Hallelujah!
Hallelujah! Hallelujah!
....
And He shall reign for ever and ever
....
King of Kings and Lord of Lords....

Now I remembered.

It was the Hallelujah Chorus!

Then a spotlight was directed to the ceiling. It seemed as

though a platform broke through the ceiling...and it now was descending. Soon a man's figure was apparent standing on what appeared to be nothing. It must have been a square block of glass.

The light shone on his face. The audience gasped as one voice

IT'S BROTHER BARTHOLOMEW!

Women fainted. Faye collapsed in Bill's arms. Photographers were fighting for space to get a picture.

He descended slowly and came to a stop on top of a podium I had not noticed before.

A woman's shriek pierced the hall...

HE'S ALIVE! HE'S ALIVE!

Bishop Bartholomew was alive. He had come back from the dead! Bishop Arthur had performed a real miracle. This man, Brother Bartholomew, could hold the world in his hands now. They would follow him like lost sheep!

And I saw one of his heads as it were wounded to death; and his deadly wound was healed: and all the world wondered after the beast. (Revelation 13:3)

Then a strange thing happened.

Slowly Bishop Arthur approached Brother Bartholomew... looked up at him...then knelt down as though he were a knight paying homage to a king.

Brother Bartholomew smiled benevolently at Bishop Arthur, then extended his arm as if in blessing...then spoke.

"Well done, thou good and faithful servant:
thou hast been faithful over a few things,
I will make thee ruler over many things."

Then Brother Bartholomew turned to the audience and spoke:

I have risen again and my ministry is to build my kingdom here on earth...for all those

Let no man deceive you by any means: for that day shall not come, except there come a falling away first, and that man of sin be revealed, the son of perdition;

deemed faithful...who bear my Mark...and by so doing die again, bury their selfish pride... and rise to walk with me in newness of life.

Who opposeth and exalteth himself above all that is called God, or that is worshipped; so that he as God sitteth in the temple of God, shewing himself that he is God. (2 Thessalonians 2:3-4)

I am a God of love but I hate sin. Tomorrow the punishment of sin will be shown throughout the world. One will die. I have spoken.

Then, looking at Bishop Arthur he continued:

For your faithfulness, I pronounce you Prophet Arthur...for you have been a worthy prophet of the Messiah.

The Marking Stations were doing a land-office business. After the news had been published of the MIRACLE of the Shrine...it seemed that everyone was convinced Brother Bar-

And he exerciseth all the power of the first beast before him, and causeth the earth and them which dwell therein to worship the first beast, whose deadly wound was healed. (Revelation 13:12)

tholomew was God. Marking Deputies worked throughout the night applying the identification numbers 666 on foreheads and right hands. The deputies were quite surprised that most people wanted the marking on their forehead. They felt this a greater show of loyalty. Very few asked for the mark on their right hand.

Police stations and schools served as Marking Stations as did Churches. With the population growth schools had long been closed. I recall, the first day that schools closed, seeing the pathetic picture of a teen-age girl coming to school and finding it empty. It did not happen overnight. In the late 60's and early 1970's riots and demands by students were very effective. They soon had the courses they wanted...lovemaking, bar tending, mystic meditations, sex and family re-education. Soon the system had degenerated to such a state that, combined with the over-populated masses, school closing was made mandatory. Schools now became living quarters. As many as 30 families lived in each classroom.

I recall seeing a teen-age girl coming to school and finding it empty.

The Marking Stations were quite efficient, Tom Malone had told me. Everyone was now a number anyway. A small IBM-like card which resembled a credit card had various holes punched in different positions. It became your identification number throughout life. Upon entering a Marking Station you indicated where you wanted the Mark 666 placed and whether you wished a cosmetically branded or a bold visually branded number. A cosmetically branded number was applied by laser-beam and appeared invisible. However, as one walked on the streets and passed the video-lamposts, a special ultra violet light emitted from the base of the video unit made the invisible number very visible. Wherever one walked other "check lights" would verify whether the citizen was loyal and bore the Mark 666.

And yet, surprisingly, most everyone wanted a visual 666 and most chose red as their color preference. This was applied by an instant-heat radio beam branding iron. To them it became both a beauty mark and a mark of sacrificial loyalty as it involved some pain at the moment of application.

For application of The Mark, the laser or the branding iron method could be selected. The branding iron method further combined its flash heat with application of a red flourescent dye. There was the pain but it soon departed. Scar tissue in a few weeks made the Mark impression irreversible. No plastic surgery could conceivably correct it should one change his or her mind.

Again, most chose the branding iron method.

It was necessary to keep perfectly still. A slight movement could cause the Mark of the instant-heat radio beam to miss its mark and blind the citizen for life. Therefore recipients were asked to lay on a special stretcher. A mild sedative was administered. Hundreds of stretchers lined the halls and spilled out onto the street. The line moved fast. Out the rear of the building those who had received the Mark were dismissed. A mirror at the back door was installed so they could view their new badge of identification.

Children were given a light anesthesia, and strapped down tightly to the stretcher. From our apartment Faye, Bill and I could hear the muffled screams of what appeared to be an endless stream of children—bewildered, frightened...suddenly drowning into the soft anesthesia of sleep.

Only one stretcher moved into the Marking Room at a time. The Identification Badge of each individual was removed from the card holder at the foot of the stretcher. The Badge was run through a computer. The identity was automatically transmitted to Central Intelligence and the so numbered person became an acknowledged disciple. While this was being done, the patient's head was carefully positioned in a firm, but cushioned brace. Above was a bright light and a plate about 2" x 4" which automatically molded itself to the curvature of each individual forehead. It was as though one's head was looking up at the stamping mechanism of a printing press.

Most patients were relatively calm. But under these circumstances even the loyal would develop doubts. But not for long. As they looked up at the branding iron...they failed to notice the quick spray of an air needle on their leg. Within a second they were asleep...dead to the activity that surrounded them.

Everything worked like clockwork. A button was pushed. Quickly the branding iron came down, molded itself around the forehead. Another button was pushed...a special red dye came coursing downward through a transparent plastic tube that terminated at the head of the branding mechanism.

There was a short burst of steam as instant heat met dye and iron met forehead. Then it was all over. The branding iron returned to its original position. The stretcher was whisked out through the swinging doors.

Another air needle was sprayed — this time on the arm. The patient instantly awakened as though nothing had happened. The injection not only awakened him but erased the memory of the last hour. It was a relatively new medical discovery called the Sleep and Memory Fader.

The patient climbed to his feet, was given a pill to swallow, then directed to the door. It was then and only then that reality hit him full blast. On his forehead, still slightly puffed, was emblazoned in brilliant red his mark of identity and loyalty...

666

George knew he must do something to save Bill. He persuaded Tom to give them passes for flight to Asia. George was surprised how quickly and anxiously Tom consented.

George's Dad had fought in Vietnam and before his death, had many times recounted how cleverly the Viet Cong built underground hide-aways, stocked with food and ammunition. He remembers his dad saying that the discovery he had made of one such unit made it very evident that the enemy could hole-away for years unnoticed.

Little foilage was left in Vietnam now, but George remembered one incident of an underground home that dad said was never destroyed. Some GI's used it at the end of the war. It was located not too far from Saigon at Xuan-loc.

After three days of searching Faye and Bill discovered the air vents that were hidden in the bushes...but these vents were too small for one to enter. It was then that George remembered that sometimes these underground quarters were entered by a pond passageway. Soon they found the pond,

And to the woman were given two wings of a great eagle, that she might fly into the wilderness, into her place, where she is nourished for a time, and times, and half a time, from the face of the serpent.

And the earth helped the woman, and the earth opened her mouth, and swallowed up the flood which the dragon cast out of his mouth. (Revelation 12: 14, 16)

swam underwater towards the shore and after passing under earth for about five feet finally hit an air pocket. Then there was a mound of earth walled with a passageway that brought them entrance into their underground hide-away. Besides the small supply of man-made food provisions which they had managed to collect, they had only brought one thing with them...their Bible. It was to serve them well through the long weary days and nights. Here they also fortunately found real food, old C-ration cans abandoned over 30 years ago.

Air vents hidden in bushes

Secondary escape under fireplace in village house

Pond

Siphon   Arms dump   Supply dump

One night as they were praying a song formed on George's lips. And as he began singing, Faye and Bill joined in....

It will be worth it all
When we see Jesus
Life's trials will seem so small
When we see Him.

One glimpse of His dear face
All sorrows will erase
So bravely run the race
Till we see Christ!

That night if Helen and Sue and Tom were looking down from Heaven they must have surely been rejoicing. I wonder if the Lord Jesus Christ wasn't gently whispering to them? Just a short while longer and their song would become a glorious reality.

Suddenly their worshipping was broken by the sound of heavy equipment moving down a road somewhere above their bunker. The sound of one vehicle breaking rank was apparent as the sound of its motors came clearer. Then it appeared to stop directly overhead above their underground hideaway. Voices could be heard.

George held his finger to his mouth to warn Faye and Bill to keep still and quiet.

Then a penetrating sound and a WHOOSH as though a vacuum bottle had been opened. The entire dirt ceiling above them was suddenly sucked up as though someone had cut out a neat little circle.

A floodlight cruelly exposed their hideaway.

Faye, Bill and George stood up, temporarily blinded by the sudden light. But there's was no mistaking the voices.

One was that of Brother Bartholomew speaking:

"Congratulations, you did a fine job of discovering them."

The other voice replied,

Then shall they deliver you up to be afflicted, and shall kill you: and ye shall be hated of all nations for my name's sake.

And then shall many be offended, and shall betray one another, and shall hate one another. Matthew 24:9-10.

"I knew they were there, sir. Since they refuse to bear The Mark. I wanted to be the first to expose theo , sir."

Blindfolded, we could have spotted that voice with ease. No longer our friend, we had been betrayed by a Judas. For the voice was the voice of TOM MALONE!

Chapter 11

The Shocking Spectacle

Brother Bartholomew had Faye, Bill and I returned to Washington. We were quite surprised that we were allowed to return to our apartment. Brother Bartholomew warned us there was no use trying to escape. Dr. Curter had implanted micro-detector units into the muscle of our arm. We were told Central Intelligence had us tuned in. These detector units would relay our every move...but not only that, our every thought. With some pride Dr. Curter told us of his devious discovery that enabled BB to partially read one's mind. Our brain waves would register on a computer-indicator which would monitor us. It would show when we were tense and when we were relaxing; when we were thinking hard and when we were passively listening and learning. Now even our thoughts were no longer private.

One day left for living for Bill. And BB had allowed us to have a picture phone in our room, much as one would give a sumptious meal to a person ready for execution. We could tune in on any part of the world and as BB put it, "See how my influence has spread over the entire earth."

Before Tom's betrayal of us he had told me of strange happenings in Jerusalem. Two men had appeared as though from nowhere and were going through the land like the old time preachers of judgment of the 1800's and early 1900's.

Laughingly Tom had called them the "modern-day Dwight L. Moody and Billy Sunday."

But then his face took on a troubled look as he told me how these two men were seeing flocks of Jews becoming converted to their message. He had said that there was talk of these two performing miracles, even striking some down to their death simply by a vocal command.

> And I will give power unto my two witnesses, and they shall prophecy a thousand two hundred and threescore days (1260 days), clothed in sackcloth.
> And if any man will hurt them, fire proceedeth out of their mouth, and devoureth their enemies: and if any man will hurt them, he must in this manner be killed (Revelation 11:3, 5)

I picked up the picture phone, dialed Jerusalem, a direct dial that tied me in with local television lines. Faye, Bill and I crowded around the screen. There suddenly were two men, near the Damascus Gate. They wore harsh appearing sackcloth garments. They were surrounded by people. Voices were shouting..."IT'S MOSES and ELIJAH!"

An announcer appeared on the screen...

"Ladies and gentlemen,
recent disturbances in Jerusalem have
caught the attention of Brother Bartholomew.
He is sending Prophet Arthur to inspect the
area and make his recommendations.

Jews are flocking to the Temple given by
Brother Bartholomew to offer thanks to God."

The earth suddenly shook. The screen darkened. There was a low, long rumble. Bill and Faye looked out the window. Faye screamed...

"Look, Dad, it's like a long row of dominoes falling. One building after another is falling. Earth is splitting open. Whole buildings are disappearing. Dad, it seems like it's headed this way!"

Not since the San Francisco earthquake of April 18, 1906 had such devastation been seen.

The first quick burst of disaster was soon over...but the low, continuing rumble was a constant reminder that more was to come.

...and earthquakes in divers places. (Matthew 24:7)

Brother Bartholomew nervously fidgeted in his office. He called in Tom Malone.

"Malone, what's the latest report on these earthquakes?"

"The San Francisco suburb of Los Angeles has been completely devastated, sir. Much of it has disappeared. The entire city of Los Angeles shows danger of sinking. Dallas reports dangerous crevices with some chasms dropping as much as 1000 or more feet. Other reports from around the country are the same. In fact Europe, Asia and the Middle East report similar earth disturbances."

"Malone, we've got to move our headquarters temporarily. Earthquakes, disturbances in the sun, meteor showers, cloud formations such as have never been seen...and this infernal rumbling is still continuing! We're bound to have another quake, perhaps more deadly. What's the safest place you know?"

And I beheld when he had opened the sixth seal, and, lo, there was a great earthquake; and the sun became black as sackcloth of hair, and the moon became as blood;
And the stars of heaven fell unto the earth, even as a fig tree casteth her untimely figs, when she is shaken of a mighty wind. (Revelation 6:12-13)

Malone thought for a moment. His eye lit up as though he had made a discovery. Then he spoke: "My grandfather, sir, was a member of the Church of Jesus Christ of Latter-Day Saints. They were known as Mormons. I understand they kept perpetual storage vaults deep within a granite mountain in what was then called Utah. Salt Lake City, I believe."

Brother Bartholomew pushed some Memory Bank buttons behind his desk. In front of him a card slowly emerged from a slot in his desk. He read it:

GRANITE MOUNTAIN RECORDS VAULT

Little Cottonwood Canyon
25 miles from Salt Lake City

Average temperature 58° F
Electrostatic air filters
Protective Vault Door — 14 tons
Inner Protective Doors — 9 tons
Natural water supply provides 8000 gallons a day
700 feet below surface

He turned to Tom Malone, then spoke: "Malone, alert Air Force 1. We're flying to Little Cottonwood Canyon in two days."

Meanwhile Faye and Bill and George were praying, hoping against hope, that somehow God would rescue them from what seemed certain death.

There was no food to eat. Their protein cake allotment had been cut off. Hunger pangs began to become evident. One guard, however, had left on a chair some oil base purple grapes. Faye picked them up and spoke, as though something had suddenly occurred to her.

"Dad, Bill, we've never done it before. But we should. Let's together take communion, just as the Lord Jesus Christ did before He went to the cross."

Bill questioned: "How can we take communion? We have no bread. We have nothing to eat. All we have is a little water and these few grapes."

"That's it, Bill," Faye replied, "we DO have bread. Don't you remember how each day as we broke our protein cakes, how we placed a portion away in this drawer as the Lord's share?"

Pulling out the drawer she exclaimed, "Look! It's still here.""But if its the Lord's, we can't eat it." George reminded.

"But Dad, today I was reading the 12th chapter of Matthew and how David when he was hungry ate the shewbread, holy bread. We will be eating only a portion to represent the body of Christ and drink just a little purple grape water to represent his saving blood shed for us."

George nodded his agreement and smiled, "Reminds me of that verse in Ecclesiates 11:1 which I memorized just a few days ago. Funny, how, in the midst of hunger we each day set aside a portion of our protein cake to the Lord and now in the midst of need that verse becomes a reality...

Cast thy bread upon the waters:
for thou shalt find it after many days.

George broke one protein cake into three small pieces. With heads bowed they placed it on their lips and prayed. Then George give Faye and Bill each a teaspoon of the juice. And with them he drank the precious drops and prayed. Faye's joyous voice began to sing...to sing a song I never realized she knew. It was such an old hymn. I could remember my grandparents singing it in church. The entire congregation, after communion, without the benefit of any musical instruments would sing their praise in glorious harmony... Faye began this very song and soon all three of us were singing.

From ev'ry stormy wind that blows
From ev'ry swelling tide of woes
There is a calm, a sure retreat:
'Tis found beneath the mercy-seat.

Ah! wither could we flee for aid,
When tempted, desolate, dismayed;
Or how the hosts of hell defeat,
Had suff'ring saints no mercy-seat.

After their communion, George turned on the picture phone to see if he could once again get Jerusalem. The rumbling had eased up a bit and the picture was once again coming on clear. The camera was showing areas of destruction. Prophet Arthur had diverted his space craft to Petra. The reporter was announcing that many high-ranking officials had fled to the natural mountainous refuge of Petra...many were hiding in the rocks and caves near the Dead Sea.

> And said to the mountains and rocks, Fall on us, and hide us from the face of him that sitteth on the throne, and from the wrath of the Lamb:
> For the great day of his wrath is come; and who shall be able to stand? (Revelation 6:16-17)

It was as though an eclipse had occurred, the announcer reported. The sun had turned black, the moon blood-red. Meteors began to fall.

Then he continued:

"The surprising thing is that in the midst of all this havoc and destruction many Jews were like Daniels in the fiery furnace. They were not touched... not a hair was singed, and not a bone broken.

From all over the world Jews have been flocking to Jerusalem. They bear a strange seal on their foreheads...not the customary Mark of 666 that is beginning to appear all over the world.

We have 12 representatives with us at this telecasting studio. They have agreed to brief us on their mission."

With that the announcer turned to one who appeared to

be the spokesman: "Sir, our on-location television cameras have been photographing the catastrophes as they occurred —the earthquakes, the fires, and in each case where masses of people have disappeared or been crushed to death...those with this seal on their forehead seem to have some guardian angel over them...they come through unscratched."

"Yes, sir, that is true. The living God, the Lord Jesus Christ, has annointed us from above to become witnesses for Him in these last days of tribulation. From each of the 12 tribes of Israel 12,000 Jews have been elected to bear His seal and bear a testimony to all that Christ is coming again. Working with our two prophets, the modern Moses and Elijah, we are ministering throughout the world. Already many thousands, yes even great multitudes from every nation, kindred and tongue are coming to Christ, their Saviour, their Risen Lord, their soon coming King."

> Saying, Hurt not the earth, neither the sea, nor the trees, till we have sealed the servants of our God in their foreheads.
> And I heard the number of them which were sealed: and there were sealed an hundred and forty and four thousand of all the tribes of the children of Israel. (Revelation 7:3-4)

> ...These are they which came out of great tribulation, and have washed their robes, and made them white in the blood of the Lamb. (Revelation 7:14)

The low-pitched rumbling increased...the picture phone screen went black. The earth shook violently as though it were heaving its last breath. George, Bill and Faye placed their hands on the Bible, held it firmly, bowed their heads and prayed.

And outside the terrifying screams of men, women and children penetrated the still air as they stumbled down what seemed to be bottomless chasms of judgment.

Just as quickly as it came...the earthquake ceased. Outside the window George could see dust and smoke rising everywhere. Silence prevailed. It seemed as though the whole earth was one big funeral pyre...for as far as the eye could see not an inkling of movement could be detected.

Never had the trio experienced such quietness. Deadly silence. Just deadly silence.

Slowly the darkened sky gave evidence that dawn was coming.

There was a knock at the door.

George opened it.

There stood their Judas...Tom Malone.

He was rather apologetic.

"George, I'm sorry, but when it comes down to brass tacks, my loyalty must be to Brother Bartholomew. I've come because I have bad news that could be good news. In a few minutes the guards will come to take Bill to the Guillotine site. Brother Bartholomew has asked me to come and talk to you. He promises that if Faye will accept The Mark—not the cosmetic invisible Mark but the visual-branded Mark of 666...he will be merciful and spare Bill from the guillotine."

For a moment Faye, Bill and George stood in silence. Then Faye shouted, "I will, I will. If it will save Bill, I'll give my life!" Bill pulled Faye closely to him, "No, darling, never. If it's my time to die it means that it will be that much quicker that I will meet my Lord and Saviour. I know your love for me, darling, but your taking that mark would be like kneeling in obedience to antichrist. It's a trick. He will kill me anyway. He and his world government are a Beast!"

> And I stood upon the sand of the sea, and saw a beast rise up out of the sea...(Revelation 13:1)

"No," Tom replied, "Brother Bartholomew will keep his word."

Just then six guards entered. Two positioned themselves at Bill's sides and held his arms, one stood behind him, another in front of him. Two more led the way. They jerked him away so quickly he had no time to kiss Faye goodbye. He turned as he was let down the long hall, his voice echoing against the sides of the wall...

"Faye, don't take the Mark...Faye, don't take the Mark!
Faye, don't take the Mark!"

Faye was crying hysterically. George held her firmly in his arms. His arms slackened as he broke out in uncontrollable sobbing.

The glass cubicle was mounted on a high pole thirty feet in the air. Its base was only two feet square...allowing little room for movement. Imprisoned inside was Bill. Execution was set for twelve noon. It was now 8:30 in the morning. Already crowds were forming. Special tiered seats had been erected to accommodate those who were fortunate enough to receive special passes. All could look up in the sky and see the glass cubicle. The crowd was getting frantic. Bill looked down in both disgust and horror. It seemed like a bad dream...a nightmare. Down there wherever he looked...upturned faces, sneering, scoffing, all bearing the brilliant red 666 on their foreheads. "What has happened to humanity?" he thought. "Have they all turned into a pack of wild animals?"

Bill felt calm in spite of his trials. Now he knew what dying grace meant. For his heart was at peace. Soon he would have victory...complete victory.

Tom ushered George and Faye down to the waiting limousine. Faye was already reconciled to the fact that in spite of Bill's pleading she would accept The Mark. In her heart, she thought to herself, her alliegance will always be to God. Christ was her Saviour and Lord. He always would be. This outward mark would, in her mind, stand only as her symbol of contempt for antichrist and his sin. George had whispered a plan...a plan of escape to Jerusalem. All three would go. The last thing George had told her was:

"Faye, the ones they call Moses and Elijah will save us!"

As they entered the limousine, Faye stepped back in astonishment. In the back seat waiting for them was Brother Bartholomew. He motioned for them to enter.

"Well, what is your decision? "Brother Bartholomew questioned, "as if I didn't know already." With that he broke into a laugh.

Faye spoke, "You're a son of the devil. Enjoy yourself now while you can for the day will soon come when God's judgment will be poured out against you. Then we'll see who has the last laugh!"

"So you think your God will save you? What a fairy story. Who arose from the dead...your Jesus? Of course not. But with your own eyes you witnessed my resurrection."

He thrust his hands in George's face. "Here," he continued, look at my hands. What do you see?"

George looked on in shock, but said nothing.

"What do you see? you fool. Speak!" Brother Bartholomew commanded.

"Nailprints, sir."

Faye spoke, quietly and firmly,

"II Thessalonians 2:11
And for this cause God shall send them strong
delusion, that they should believe a lie..."

Brother Bartholomew was visibly angered. "Don't quote your fabled Scriptures to me. What is your decision? Right now your husband is imprisoned in a glass cubicle at the execution site. Shall I give the command to proceed with the execution?"

"No," Faye replied, "I will accept The Mark."

Faye and I fully expected to be taken to the Marking Station. But the car approached a huge crowd of thousands. Above the crowd could be seen a tall pole. Atop the pole, a glass cubicle. And in the cubicle, a man.

Faye's heart sank as she caught a glimpse of Bill. George tried to give her reassuring comfort by putting his arm around her.

The crowd parted to make way for the limousine. There in front of them was a sight that looked as though it had come out of the Middle Ages...there in its grisly horror was the guillotine. Much more polished and refined than those of antiquity, this one had a special electronic triggering device, and a large numerical counter that registered each time the heavy-bladed knife went swishing to its mark.

At the base, where the knife came to a halt, was a transparent box. A liquid swirled about in it...like a washing machine display in a store that had a cutaway transparent section to make visible the swishing action. When the head was severed, it would drop into this purification tank, jet streams would wash blood and dust away...it then would move up a conveyor that would diabolically project it into a display stand the same height as the glass cubicle. It was to be a dramatically staged gesture to show the people that the penalty had been paid.

The heavy blade slid easily between the two grooved posts. Up and down, up and down, the executioner was testing his equipment to see that all was in order.

This was to be the first execution by guillotine. The numerical counter was turned to 0.

The car drove slowly passed the guillotine site. Faye had thought the execution was scheduled in a public square. But as she looked up she saw a cross...then a steeple. How cruel, she thought. The execution site was on the front lawn of a church...a church that once was a center for the preaching of the Gospel. Because of its testimony, this church had been wrecked inside.

"What blasphemy!" George exclaimed.

"Why are you taking us here?" Faye demanded. "This is not the Marking Center."

"You are a very special person," Brother Bartholomew chuckled. "And for very special people we have a most unusual Marking Center."

They entered the church parking lot. Guards met them at the door. George and Faye were ushered up the long aisle. The familiar picture of Christ knocking at the door had been changed. Brother Bartholomew's face was substituted.

As they came to the pulpit area, two husky guards stood at each side of the communion table. On the table in a special unit lay the Instant Heat Branding Iron. Special portable equipment was plugged in. A transparent tube from a unit on the floor was surging red flourescent dye to the branding head. The mold on the die was clearly visible....666.

Brother Bartholomew quickly motioned to two guards. They grabbed Faye...dragged her to the communion table...the branding iron released a small whisp of smoke.

Faye looked at the front of the communion table. The carved inscription read:

THIS DO IN REMEMBRANCE OF ME

Then, as though she received an extra measure of faith... she stopped dead in her tracks, looked directly into the eyes of Brother Bartholomew. Her own reflection seemed to come back. She could see the guards dragging Bill down the hall. She could hear the voice of Bill calling back: "FAYE, DON'T TAKE THE MARK; FAYE, DON'T TAKE THE MARK."

With determination she spoke, "I will not take The Mark. 'Fear not them which kill the body, but are not able to kill the soul: but rather fear him which is able to destroy both soul and body in hell.' This is my testimony from Matthew 10:28. And it is the testimony of Bill and my father. Do what you may...but I will not take The Mark!"

Brother Bartholomew was enraged. Tom Malone pleaded with her, assuring her that no harm would come to Bill if she accepted The Mark.

...If any man worship the beast and his image, and receive his mark in his forehead, or in his hand,
The same shall drink of the wine of the wrath of God...(Revelation 14: 9-10)

Faye remained firm.

With that Brother Bartholomew quickly motioned to the guards. They grabbed Faye by each arm, dragged her to the communion table. Two guards forcibly held her back, pressing it down against the table. Another held her hair, forcing her chin on the table, her face looking upward.

Brother Bartholomew directed Tom Malone to activate the branding unit. The limp tube of dye stiffened. The branding iron released a small whisp of smoke.

George tried to rush forward. Two burly guards held him back. "ANTICHRIST! ANTICHRIST!" George shouted. "YOU DIABOLICAL DEVIL. Is there no mercy in your heart? Give me The Mark. Let me take The Mark in place of Faye!"

Faye squirmed, kicked, but to no avail. The guards held all

the tighter. Above her The Mark slowly came closer. The moist red numbers glistened with crackling heat. It was all a bad dream, she thought. Yes, a bad dream. I'll wake up and find I was dreaming. But those ugly numbers came closer. She screamed. That's all she remembered.

The next sound she heard was Brother Bartholomew laughing. He directed Tom Malone to bring a mirror.

"Now Holy Queen," Brother Bartholomew shouted, "look at your beauty mark! Kneel and pay homage to your God!"

She turned her back on him, her head drooped in despair as George put his arm around her and together they prayed for strength.

Tom Malone rushed over, tears in his eyes. "Don't feel bad George and Faye. I know it's a shock to both of you. But you've saved Bill, and that's what's important."

"Malone, you foolish one," Brother Bartholomew reprimanded. "Did you think for one minute that Bill would escape the guillotine? Why you are more foolish than these two. Dr. Curter, come over here."

Dr. Curter walked over carrying a little black box.

"You seem to forget, Dr. Curter has implanted micro-detector units in all of you," Brother Bartholomew reminded. When your nervous tension goes above a certain level the micro detector begins to record your every movement and whisper."

"Play a portion of the recording from Faye's unit, Dr. Curter."

Dr. Curter flipped a switch, turned a dial...from this black magic box what were Faye's whispered thoughts suddenly came forth.

My allegiance will always be to God.
Christ is my Saviour and Lord.
He always will be.

The ones who are being called
Moses and Elijah will save us.

The recording stopped. Tom Malone now joined the ranks of the saddened and shocked.

They walked out of the church stunned, Bill, who had already been removed from the glass cubicle, was standing head bowed at the base of the guillotine.

The guards quickly placed Faye and George on a special hoist, and squeezed them into the small cubicle above the hysterical mob. Faye and George looked down. On the front row sat all those whom Brother Bartholomew considered his distinguished and faithful clergy. On every forehead was The Mark—666.

Faye was sobbing hysterically. The confines were so tight the whole unit shook with each sob.

His hands tied behind him, Bill was led up the six steps to the guillotine. Prophet Arthur was reading the death sentence:

> Bill Sanders, being of sound body and mind,
> refused to bear The Mark of our God and our
> King either on his forehead or on his right hand.
> In accordance with the laws of the New Earth
> death shall be awarded by guillotine. May
> Brother Bartholomew have mercy on your soul.

With that, a guard assisted Bill in kneeling at the guillotine. His head was placed in the molded receiving block. The top semi-circle restraining block was clamped down. His head was secure.

As though to say, don't mourn for me Faye...his pleading eyes looked upward at the two forms in the glass cubicle.

The executioner's hand went up to the electronic release switch.

Faye screamed.

SWOOSH!

The severed head of Bill dropped in the swirling bath.

The maddened crowd surged forward. The pressing weight bent the pole on which the cubicle was suspended.

...and I saw the souls of them that were beheaded for the witness of Jesus, and for the word of God, and which had not worshipped the beast, neither his image, neither had received his mark upon their foreheads, or in their hands, and they lived and reigned with Christ a thousand years. (Revelation 20:4)

Suddenly the pole snapped.
The cubicle came hurtling down on the crowd!

Chapter 12

The Strange Destroyer

George and Faye were momentarily stunned as they lay on the ground. The glass cubicle had shattered as it fell. The mobs in their frenzy to reach the guillotine all but ignored the two.

George quickly lifted Faye up to avoid being trampled upon. The glass cubicle apparently had been made from safety-breaking glass which shattered upon impact into tiny safe round-edged smooth bits. Had it been the old time glass of the 1960's they would have surely been severely cut or killed on the jagged pieces.

Just as they came to their feet, Tom Malone was by their side. Without trying to explain he grabbed George's arm and motioned for George and Faye to follow him.

Somehow I felt it was for our own safety and we obeyed without hesitation. Tom urged us to run while the interest of the crowd was still on the guillotine scene and on Bill's now beheaded body.

About two hundred yards down the main highway he diverted us down a small country road to a waiting compact car.

We jumped in. It was a Press car. Press cars had special driving privileges since the Press was controlled by Brother Bartholomew. Tom Malone knew this.

"What's happening?" George asked.

"No time to talk now, George, wait till we get to the dock."

Since only government officials had cars and most of them were at the execution site...the roads were almost empty.

Arriving at the airport, Tom advised the control tower that we had been cleared for take-off to New York harbor. The city of New York had long since been destroyed...but the harbor was already an active port again.

Within a matter of five minutes we were landing at the port airstrip. Faye and I both turned to Tom and almost in one voice asked, "WHY?"

Tom spoke, half apologetically. "At first I had been a fool ...a sincere fool...who was so sincere, sincerely wrong. My allegiance had been to Brother Bartholomew. I was sure he would solve all the world problems. This would call for drastic action. In the last three years he accomplished so much. He brought peace to Israel. He built them the Temple which for two thousand years they sought after. Major conflicts have ended. But at that Temple scene I realized that the face of Brother Bartholomew was not one of God...it seemed like one of the devil reborn. But I was afraid...secretly I accepted The Mark—but made from a special fade-out dye... I was afraid...And Bill..." Tom's head dropped. For the first time I saw Tom actually weep. Quickly he regained his composure.

"When they killed Bill, I knew I had to stand up and be counted for Christ. This fade-out Mark on my forehead may have for a time identified me with Brother Bartholomew...but inside...in my heart, I now know I am a child of God. I don't know what the future holds for me...for my acceptance of Christ now may be too late. I am still a marked man in more ways than one."

Faye cautioned, "You were at the beginning deceived just

as we were...you didn't know."

George spoke up: "Tom, Faye, we can't go on talking like this. Don't you realize we have micro-detector units implanted in us. Brother Bartholomew's men will be here in minutes."

Tom smiled and spoke: "No they won't, George."

With that he reached into his pocket, pulled out a small pill box. He held it gingerly as if its contents were the most precious things on earth. Four tiny red pills.

"Here," Tom urged, "quickly swallow one of these pills." Without asking they followed Tom's initiative and each swallowed a pill. "Now what was that all about?" Faye asked.

Tom replied. "For some time now I have become very close to Dr. Curter. He may be a diabolical man...but he's a man with a heavy burden of guilt on his heart. There are two faces to him. He must under all conditions show complete loyalty to Brother Bartholomew. But one day in his weaker moments he confessed to me his doubts. He deeply admires you, Faye, and George. He knew Bill would be killed regardless of your acceptance of The Mark. That's when he unloaded his inner feelings on me. Somehow he had compassion on me. He gave me these four red pills. Since we three have each taken one, there's only one left now. But just as Dr. Curter cleverly used his medical and scientific knowledge to bring back Brother Bartholomew from the dead...to create the sinister micro-detector units that read both thought impulses and relay location...he also developed an antidote that renders powerless the micro-detector unit."

"That antidote was the red pill each of us just swallowed. And now, from this port, as far as BB is concerned, we could be heading to anywhere in the world. He won't find us."

Faye, joy on her face, reached up and gently kissed Tom on the cheek. "Tom, you're simply wonderful. I thought you were a Judas...but God has provided a way...and used you as a channel."

Tom blushed and then became serious again.

"Let's get to the dock quick. We're going to board one of the new inventions that Brother Bartholomew has instituted to help answer the problem of the population explosion."

At the dock we boarded a small AVC water-surface transfer ship. Suddenly, over the horizon we saw a most unusual sight. Two ships, as if at anchor in the middle of the ocean. Between them an odd-looking object...very, very large. A

circular steel dome-like building with a funnel projecting from the center.

"That," Tom told us, "is a Sea House."

"But does it just stay there?" Faye questioned.

Tom replied, "Normally it stays anchored in one position. You are only looking at the roof of the Sea House. It extends down to the ocean floor once it is anchored at its final location. Until then, the bottom telescopes up to within 50 feet of the surface of the water. This particular Sea House is destined for use in the Mediterranean Sea, just off the coast of Cyprus."

"Are we going to board it now?" George asked.

"Yes, George. It's our safest way to escape. Brother Bartholomew may have all the other modes of transportation covered in search for us. He will least expect that we will board an empty Sea House."

"But what about the crew? Surely they will suspect something and turn us in," Faye said fearfully.

"Normally yes," Tom replied, "but this is a most unusual crew. Everyone is a Jew for these are Israeli ships. The Sea House is a gift from our government to theirs...probably the last gift they will ever receive from BB."

Now it was all clear. We settled back for the uneventful ten day cruise.

Brother Bartholomew was in a rage. Nothing Prophet Arthur could do seemed to calm him down. The console in front of him was blinking lights...but the message wasn't getting through.

He flipped a switch...an intercom. "Dr. Curter, come into my office immediately."

Within a few moments Dr. Curter appeared. He thrust his hands into his long white coat so Brother Bartholomew would not see that he was visibly shaken.

"Curter," Brother Bartholomew bellowed, "I punched every button on this console and still cannot locate Faye, George or Tom Malone. What's gone wrong? When I find them I'll have a triple guillotine execution. The people will go wild! What's wrong with this unit?"

Dr. Curter walked over to it, pretended he was trying to make some adjustment...pushed a few buttons...the machine buzzed defiantly indicating that the Locate Numbers and Thought Numbers were not operative.

He turned to Brother Bartholomew, "I'm sorry sir, I don't know what is going wrong."

Prophet Arthur chimed in, "Have you pushed the right identification numbers? Perhaps we have the wrong numbers?"

"No Arthur," Brother Bartholomew said, "here they are right here." He held up the identification cards:

FAYE SANDERS	777 02 583 11
GEORGE OMEGA	777 11 624 38
TOM MALONE	777 32 395 00

"Strange," Prophet Arthur thought out loud, "each one begins with 777!"

The Sea House trip was quite smooth despite the bulky bottom. The accompanying host ships anchored the Sea House at Lido di Ostia, about 25 miles from Rome. There they were to pick up a group of people that witnessing Jews had led to Christ. It was an unscheduled stop...one which would not have gone unnoticed if Brother Bartholomew hadn't been so pre-occupied with finding Faye and George.

Faye accompanied Tom into Rome as both of their Marks looked genuine. George could not go, for without the Mark it might prove rather dangerous. Faye had never been to Rome and Tom briefly showed her what was now considered the most fabulous city in the world. It was the center of trade. Activity among the merchants was so voluminous that Lido di Ostia had become a major seaport. Gold, silver, pearls, the finest in fabrics...all this and more made Rome a world center for business. Noted for its wines, its convivialty, it was like a magnet attracting trade from around the world. When Brother Bartholomew was first installed as President of the United States of Europe one of the congratulatory telegrams he treasured most was signed...

...Alas, alas that great city, that was clothed in fine linen, and purple, and scarlet, and decked with gold, and precious stones, and pearls!

The merchandise of gold, and silver, and precious stones, and of pearls, and fine linen, and purple, and silk, and scarlet, and all thyine (perfumed) wood, and all manner vessels of ivory, and all manner vessels of most precious wood, and of brass, and iron, and marble,

And cinnamon, and odours (perfumes), and ointments, and frankincense, and wine, and oil, and fine flour, and wheat, and beasts, and sheep, and horses, and chariots, and slaves, and souls of men. (Revelation 18:16, 12, 13)

And here is the mind which hath wisdom. The seven heads are seven mountains, on which the woman sitteth. (Revelation 17:9)

Best wishes from the City of the Seven Hills.

Rome, a city of two faces: One reflecting its past history, the other glassy skyscrapers that towered over medieval palaces. Powerful floodlights illuminated centuries-old cathedrals while loud speakers blared rock tunes amid Renaissance treasures.

The Colosseum, symbol of ancient Rome, still attracted a constant stream of modern-day visitors. Dedicated A.D. 80 by Emperor Titus, the amphitheater witnessed 200 years of bloody games, games in which many Christians may have been brutally martyred while thousands cheered.

Now the sound of hammers was being heard again. As Faye peeked in between the columns she asked Tom, "What's that going up in the center of the Colosseum?"

"Faye, apparently they are following Bishop Bartholomew's plans to the letter. They are erecting six guillotines in each of three locations...in the center of the Colosseum floor and on the two sides...almost like a circus with a center ring and two side rings. Six...six and six."

Tom went on to give Faye a background of Rome...a background he knew well for Brother Bartholomew, who had expressed a great interest in this city, urged Tom to do as much research as possible on it and give him a report.

"Rome, once an imperial capital and still a focus for worldwide religious loyalties, has been a tourist attraction for over 2000 years. Tourism ranks high among industries earning foreign money. In the first 7 months of 1969 almost 3 million outsiders swarmed into Rome as tourists. That was small. This year, 2000, almost 50 million have come in a comparable time period. There are many ways the leaders of Rome make money. As an example, for many years Michelangelo's masterpiece statue of Moses stood in the Church of San Pietro in Vincoli. The statue was shrouded in shadows. But by inserting a coin in a nearby coin machine and electric bulb would light permitting the photographer-tourist 30 seconds to snap his picture."

Tom Malone continued: "Every summer night the Roman Forum revives the drama of Caesar's triumphant return from Gaul and Mark Antony's funeral oration."

"But what about Vatican City?" Faye questioned.

"One of the most magnificant sites is St. Peter's Square," Tom continued. "The Basilica of St. Peter utilized the genius of Italy's finest artist-architects — Bramante, Raphael and Michelangelo."

"Tell me about the Pope," Faye urged.

"Faye, until recent years the Pope had executive as well as legislative and judiciary powers. He could be judged by no man. There was no appeal from his decisions. Besides being the ultimate word, speaking infallibly on religious matters, he could also:

1. Approve or sanction or supress religious orders
2. Grant indulgences
3. Beautify or canonize saints
4. Appoint bishops
5. Erect, administer, alter or suppress bishoprics
6. Assign an auxiliary bishop for one who is incapacitated
7. Found and legislate for papal universities
8. Issue liturgical books

and a host of other powers."

"How much does the Vatican own?"

"No one really knows, Faye. But Brother Bartholomew has shown a keen interest in this. It is known that they own one of the largest corporations in the world that deals in mining, metallurgical products, fertilizers, and pharmaceuticals as well as electric power. While not owning outright, it controls 70 per cent of Italy's artificial and synthetic textile fibers. One fully owned Vatican company with capital into the millions controls gas companies in at least 36 Italian cities. They are heavily involved in banking and own and control hundreds of banks. A large number of insurance companies are Vatican owned. As early as 1970 it was estimated that one-third of Rome was owned by the Holy See. Estimates of wealth are in the billions."

"Incredible," Faye remarked.

"Yes it is, but one must remember that even in the 1960's the then Protestant arm of the church was also very much in big business...the real estate business, as an example. They had invested $80 billion in real estate, mostly in Church structures...structures that were used less than 1% of the time. No wonder BB turned them into museums and living quarters. They placed money in apartment buildings, electronics firms, shopping centers, plastic companies, and even in a girdle company! All this, when their time and attention should have gone to preaching Christ and reaching the seeking men with the message of eternal life."

"There's been quite a change since then," Faye commented.

"Quite a change. Slowly the Pope lost respect. Even Catholics questioned his authority. This paved the way for Protestants to effect a merger into one great religion just a few years ago. Leadership in the UNITED WORLD CHURCH changes every 4 years by election now.

The present Pope is a pretty shrewd man, too. And I am of the impression that BB is a little on edge about this whole situation."

Back in Washington Brother Bartholomew was more than edgy...he was furious. Not only could he not locate the "troublesome trio" as he called them, but he sensed that the United World Church was taking on too much power. It had once been fanatically loyal to him; they both in a sense had helped each other — Brother Bartholomew and the United World Church — to rise in power. Now, however, the World Church was becoming too independent!

So he carried me away in the spirit into the wilderness: and I saw a woman (World Church) sit upon a scarlet coloured beast (Antichrist), full of names of blasphemy, having seven heads and ten horns. (Revelation 17:3)

He summoned Prophet Arthur into his office. Prophet

Arthur, once a dissident religionist, had been thrust into office with surprising rapidity. Brother Bartholomew was very fond of Prophet Arthur. He served him faithfully without question. He never directed glory to himself...always gave the glory to Brother Bartholomew. BB never forgot this humbleness on Prophet Arthur's part. And he was to be amply rewarded.

"Prophet Arthur, it's time we make our next move. I have great plans for both you and me. This United States of Europe is only but a fourth of the world. The whole world must be placed under our wise dominion. And you will have a part in my glories. Tonight we fly to Rome. Tomorrow I will install you as permanent leader of the United World Church. The others will be banished for, shall we call it, 'lack of dedication to the cause?'"

After some further talk, BB continued, "...Good idea. You clean up the mess in Rome. Proclaim me as the one and true God. Install my pictures and statues in place of Jesus or Mary where these appear. Use the guillotine as frequently as necessary to keep the populace in line. Make a spectacle of each occasion right in the Colosseum. There are three rows of 6. Have the trip levers go off in sequence. For a change, let a little child push the electronic release button. Stage the whole thing like a big Hollywood production."

"If necessary, offer an extra ration of water. Only have it spiked with Dr. Curter's new mind-influencing drug...the drug that lulls the senses, makes people obey one central voice."

Prophet Arthur beamed. "Fantastic sir, with the lack of any rainfall the past 3 years they'll rush to drink that extra water ration like flies around honey."

"As good as done, Arthur. Let's get ready to go. I'll drop you off at Rome, see that you are officially installed, then fly to Jerusalem. I have a most unusual job to accomplish there. One I will most certainly relish!"

George was relieved when Faye and Tom returned to the Sea House accompanied by a group of believers.

"Am I glad to see you. I've been getting worried. Picture phone reports indicate that Prophet Arthur and Brother Bartholomew will be flying tonight to Rome. Nothing was said of the purpose of their mission. I was afraid that they may have found our hiding place."

The Captain of the Sea House spoke: "Your brave testimony for Christ has meant a great deal to us. When our time comes, we will also suffer gladly, for Christ has promised to gather us under his wings like a hen gathereth her chickens. But

> O Jerusalem, Jerusalem, thou that killest the prophets, and stonest them which are sent unto thee, how often would I have gathered thy children together, even as a hen gathereth her chickens under her wings, and ye would not! (Matthew 23:37)

right now, it's time for quick action. Each Sea House is equipped with a small shuttle heliojet. Doesn't fly very fast; only 700 miles per hour but it can land anywhere because it lands vertically. Nuclear powered, too, so your available fuel should last quite some time. Tom, you know how to fly these. Take ours and take Faye and George with you. Don't tell us where you are going. That way our thought processes will not reveal your location. But you must leave within the hour."

We thanked the captain for his courtesies to us, boarded the heliojet, and took off. Down below the Sea House looked like a bobbing ball...but it was a happy first step in an escape that would hold terrifying moments for all of us.

Tom first intended to fly straight to Jerusalem. All of us wanted to go there to see the two prophets who were being called Moses and Elijah. We had heard they were clothed in sackcloth. That didn't matter to us. We just wanted to touch the hem of their garment. Somehow we dreamed that in so doing we might be translated like Elijah in a chariot of fire— directly to Heaven to see our loved ones again.

But our hopes were soon crushed.

Tom looked at his water-coolant indicator, then shook his head. While there was sufficient fuel, the water level was low. The 3 years of no rain made water very precious. Someone had siphoned off most of the water...just to survive.

"What are we going to do?" Faye cried.

"How long will this thing stay up?" George asked.

"Not too long, George, but long enough to get us to a land area. Let me check out my flight map. Looks like we have about two hours of flying time in water-coolant left. We could go about 1400 miles. But we're not going to find much water in Jerusalem."

"Let me see that map," George asked.

Tom handed him the flight map.

George rested his hand on his chin as if in deep thought. Suddenly it came to him. "I have the answer, Tom!"

"What is it?" Faye exclaimed.

"Remember in late 1969 when some scientists announced they thought they had discovered the remains of Noah's Ark? It was buried deep in a frozen lake near the ice-capped summit of Mount Ararat."

"Where is Mount Ararat?" Faye chimed in.

"Mount Ararat is the high northern twin-peaked cap of an entire elevated range. This range—once called Mount Ararat—the Bible says was the resting place of Noah's Ark after the Flood is in the eastern part of Turkey," George replied. "And they found pieces of timber preserved by ice. I recall reading that pieces of timber were showing near the surface of the ice pack. And underneath this spot was reported to be a small lake covered by an ice and debris cap, varying in thickness from 20 to 30 feet. Ararat is 16,946 high. There must be some small flat surface near there where we can land."

"But I don't get it," Tom queried, "what are we going to do, build another ark? Is there going to be another flood?"

"No, Tom," George smiled. "Let's land our heliojet there. People have forgotten about this spot. And yet it probably is one of the few places in the Middle East where a fresh water supply still exists. You can replenish your water-coolant tank and we can take off again. That same water may help us survive in the days ahead. Who knows?"

It was an excellent idea. And after refueling at Mount Ararat we took off again.

From the air we could see that Jerusalem was covered with a mass of people. They seemed to converge around the Temple area. Tom directed the heliojet to land in the vicinity of nearby Bethlehem. The town was almost empty. Everyone was in Jerusalem. He was able to store the heliojet in one of the many large caves of this region.

The cool water of Mount Ararat had refreshed us. We took long drinks while there and stored sufficient water in our heliojet. We were going to need it.

George wanted so much to go with Tom and Faye into Jerusalem. He, however, had no Mark and Tom was afraid he would be discovered. While many in Jerusalem did not bear The Mark, it was risky. George had another idea.

"There's a tent down there," he said pointing down near a ravine. "See if you can buy some native dress. Get an abayeh and that headcloth that's worn like a turban. It will cover my forehead and help avoid suspicion."

Soon all three were dressed like natives of the country. They melted into the crowd at Jerusalem. Tom remarked how the woman who sold them the clothes looked strangely familiar, but the remark was soon forgotten. By shoving and pushing they were able to make their way near the entrance of the Temple. Tom explained to George and Faye that the Temple was considered most holy by the Jews. The High priest only entered its holiest chamber the Day of Atonement. The Temple was built as closely as possible to look like Solomon's Temple. Long and narrow, the entrance was at one end, the Holy of Holies at the other. Fifteen broad steps led up to the entrance. Two landings in the flight provided dramatic space for ceremonial processions of singers. To enter the priests passed through tall, narrow cypress doors carved with symbolic cherubim, palm trees and open flowers inlaid with gold.

The Temple layout comprised three elements: (a) the Ulam, vestible porch from which the priest walked into (b) the main chamber, called the Hekal, or Holy Place and (c) the Debir, the innermost Holy of Holies or Oracle, the special abode of the Lord. Here in Solomon's Temple in times past rested the Ark of the Covenant. Here is where dwelt the invisible presence of the Lord.

It was the Day of Atonement. There on the steps walking ahead of the priest was Brother Bartholomew. A man in front of him was carrying a small statue, a statue of Brother Bartholomew. The priestly procession walked into the Temple. We were later told that Brother Bartholomew went into the Holy of Holies, and revealed himself to the High Priest as the one containing the very Spirit of very God returned to earth in flesh to save his people.

> Let no man deceive you by any means: for that day shall not come, except there come a falling away first, and that man of sin be revealed, the son of perdition;
> Who opposeth and exalteth himself above all that is called God, or that is worshipped; so that he as God sitteth in the temple of God, shewing himself that he is God. (2 Thessalonians 3-4)

In a short time, the priest, his aides and Brother Bartholomew emerged. The priest approached the bank of microphones at the top of the Temple steps. He spoke:

"Children of the Lord. For years, yea, many thousands of years, we have been waiting for our Messiah.

Today is the Day of Atonement. Today is the day we can have complete communion with God.

For today our Messiah has returned. Brother Bartholomew is our Messiah...."

Brother Bartholomew was smiling, bowing to the multitude. Everything was going as he had planned.

Then suddenly the High

> When ye therefore shall see the abomination of desolation, spoken of by Daniel the prophet, stand in the holy place,
> Then let them which be in Judea flee into the mountains. (Matthew 24:15-16)

Priest paused, then spoke rapidly, shrieking as he spoke:

> "THIS IS NOT YOUR MESSIAH. HE IS AN
> IMPOSTER. HE IS NOT GOD. HE HAS DESE-
> CRATED THE TEMPLE OF THE MOST HIGH.
> HIS BLAMPHEMOUS STATUE NOW STANDS
> OVER THE ARK OF THE COVENANT IN THE
> HOLY OF HOLIES. OBEY HIM NOT. FLEE
> FOR YOUR LIVES!"

That's the furtherest he went in his warning.

For Brother Bartholomew held up his hand. Within a twinkling of an eye, the High Priest simply disappeared, disintegrated.

Brother Bartholomew patted his ruby laser ring, replaced the protective cap, went to the stirring multitude, assured them that he and he alone was their God...and ended with:

> Before your very eyes you have seen that the hand
> of the Lord has spoken. His judgment is swift.

Suddenly the skies opened. The dull, grey, air polluted skies seemed to part in one vast explosion that seemed to split the heavens. It was like being in semi-darkness for three years and then have a brilliant light shine on your face. The sudden heat of the sun was terrifying.

The first angel sounded, and there followed hail and fire mingled with blood, and they were cast upon the earth: and the third part of trees was burnt up, and all green grass was burnt up. (Revelation 8:7)

Grass, browned by lack of rain, suddenly crackled into flames all around us. Hail came down. A large fleet of jumbo jets overhead were crumbling, disintegrating with the forces of wind and hail. It seemed as though hail mixed with the blood of thousands of air passengers was falling all over us. It was a ghastly sight.

Then a pause.

Suddenly from the sky a huge red object looked as though it was hurtling straight for the earth.

The people were shouting...

IT'S EROS! IT'S EROS!

"What's Eros?" I shouted to George.

"Faye, Eros was discovered in 1969. It's a brick shaped chunk of debris. At that time it was about 15 miles by 5 miles in size. It last passed earth in 1975...about 17 million miles away. From the looks of it, apparently it has picked up other debris and has changed its orbit. It looks as though it will strike earth itself," George shouted.

"How prophetic," Tom yelled so we could hear him. "Eros, the god of love that sent the United States down the sewer of servitude to sin and Satan!! What a cruel hoax. From this angle it looks like Eros' main force will strike the United States itself!"

> And the second angel sounded, and as it were a great mountain burning with fire was cast into the sea: and the third part of the sea became blood. (Revelation 8:8)

Brother Bartholomew was whisked to his new headquarters atop the Mount of Olives. From this command post he listened to reports filtering in from around the world. Chaos was king. The news everywhere was bad. His picture phone consoles showed nothing but devastation, death, confusion.

Prophet Arthur had flown to Headquarters immediately on hearing the news of the Eros meteor.

"What's the report from Oceanography?" Brother Bartholomew asked Prophet Arthur.

"Not too good, sir. Early reports show one-third of all of our ships have been destroyed, estimates are that one-third of all the fish have been killed and the seas are rapidly having much of their surface covered with blood."

> And the third part of the creatures which were in the sea, and had life, died; and the third part of the ships were destroyed. (Revelation 8:9)

Just then an aide interrupted their conversation shouting, "Sir, another giant meteor has been sighted. It is falling toward earth in flaming fire because of the atmospheric friction generated as it passes through our air...Meteorology

Department has just informed us that its density is..."

Brother Bartholomew quickly flipped the HORIZON switch. An oval screen lit up and a view of the earth could be seen from a hovering satellite. A flaming star, large, brilliantly red, was streaking down through the atmosphere towards earth.

"Can it be Icarus?" Prophet Arthur cried out in terror.

"I don't know...but it's bound to hit earth. We're on a collision course!"

As it hit the atmosphere of earth, the flaming tail intensified in brillance...suddenly a blinding flash filled the screen.

Oceanography was back on the picturephone reporting. "Sir, quick checks around the world have indicated that about one-third of all the available water, rivers, seas, springs.... are POISONED. Apparently that meteor hit an underground water source that reaches many of the tributaries. Some people have already died from drinking the stuff. A few before they gasped their last breath complained about the extreme bitterness, sir."

> And the third angel sounded, and there fell a great star from heaven, burning as it were a lamp, and it fell upon the third part of the rivers, and upon the fountains of waters.
> And the name of the star is called Wormwood: and the third part of the waters became wormwood: and many men died of the waters, because they were made bitter. (Revelation 8:10-11)

"Prophet Arthur," Brother Bartholomew commanded, "get my heliojet. I'll show the people who is Lord. If we don't do something they'll be in a state of uncontrollable panic. To the Underground Complex!"

Just then a long roll of thunder shook the earth. In an odd occurrence the sun, moon and stars were visible. But even more strange a third of each surface was darkened on the sun and moon and suddenly even the flickering stars dimmed.

> And the fourth angel sounded, and the third part of the sun was smitten, and the third part of the moon, and the third part of the stars; so as the third part of them was darkened, and the day shone not for a third part of it, and the night likewise. (Revelation 8:12)

The panic had started. This latest phenomenon had triggered the population into an uncontrollable madness.

The heliojet arrived at the Underground Complex location. From outward appearances it seemed like the flat scrub plains of a typical Judean desert. But it wasn't. A small shed stood at one side. It was surrounded by guards. For many days people had speculated why guards would stand around a small shed in the middle of nowhere. They were soon to find out.

Brother Bartholomew entered the shed. A special elevator whisked him down deep within the earth. Satisfied with what he saw, he returned to the surface.

"They are ready, Prophet Arthur. Stand back."

In the small shack was a small panel on the wall. A series of switches and locks appeared when the door was removed. Brother Bartholomew pulled a series of switches in sequence, and then he inserted one key. Prophet Arthur inserted the other key...turned it to the left. Brother Bartholomew turned his key to the right...Suddenly a red light lit above Brother Bartholomew's key. On it were the words ABADDON IGNITION. Quickly he pressed the red button.

There was a slow steady roar, a roar as though it were coming from the very depths of the earth. Suddenly the earth in front of them began to rise, like two portions of a drawbridge, leaving a large gaping hole in the center. A blast of acrid black smoke funneled its way out the hole, cast a pale of death over the countryside.

And the fifth angel sounded, and I saw a star fall from heaven unto the earth: and to him was given the key of the bottomless pit.

And he opened the bottomless pit; and there arose a smoke out of the pit, as the smoke of a great furnace; and the sun and the air were darkened by reason of the smoke of the pit. (Revelation 9:1-2)

Faye, Tom and George had just reached a small knoll overlooking the area just as the smoke cloud rose.

And there came out of the smoke locusts upon the earth: and unto them was given power, as the scorpions of the earth have power. (Revelation 9:3)

Tom shouted. "Look, in the

From the depths of the earth flying men suddenly appeared!

smoke clouds. It looks like thousands...even millions of flying men."

The roar of jet noises was almost deafening.

"Flying men?...Tom. How can man fly without a plane?"

"That's it, George. It's a relatively new discovery, the jet belt. Look, they're covered with a special armor to protect them against projectiles...or against flying bits of meteorities. That gold dome on their heads is their directional device. Brother Bartholomew can automatically change their course, zero them in on any target he wishes."

> And the shapes of the locusts were like unto horses prepared unto battle; and on their heads were as it were crowns like gold, and their faces were as the faces of men. (Revelation 9:7)

"What's that long tail-like effect that flutters behind them?" Faye asked yelling in Tom's ear?

"It's a special virus spray. The liquid is stored in that long tubular section on their back. A switch on the jet belt works the release lever and it dispenses a fine spray over a 150 square yard area. BB calls them ABADDON...that's Hebrew for THE DESTROYER."

> And they had tails like unto scorpions, and there were stings in their tails: and their power was to hurt men five months.
> And they had a king over them, which is the angel of the bottomless pit, whose name in the Hebrew tongue is Abaddon, but in the Greek tongue hath his name Apollyon. (Revelation 9:10-11)

"Does it kill?" Faye asked.

"No, but it would be better if it did...just to end the suffering. Two years ago I saw it tested on some prisoners. It was an awful sight.

The spray feels like a vicious sting...like the sting of a scorpion and the pain lasts for months. After a few weeks, people try to kill themselves... the pain is so unbearable.

They were so close to the take-off point that the army of

> And to them it was given that they should not kill them, but that they should be tormented five months: and their torment was as the torment of a scorpion, when he striketh a man.
> And in those days shall men seek death, and shall not find it; and shall desire to die, and death shall flee from them. (Revelation 9:5-6)

flying men flew over them... headed for Jerusalem.

As they passed overhead George shouted, "They look almost like a plague...a plague of LOCUSTS!"

"Hurry," Tom motioned, "let's get to that heliojet before it's too late." Tom spoke as we ran, "That woman who sold us the clothes. I can't get it out of my mind how familiar she looked...and yet I can't recall ever seeing her."

"Maybe your mind is playing tricks on you, Tom," George suggested. "I don't know, George, there was something evil, something sinister. I just can't put my finger on it. We better be careful...just in case. Let me approach the heliojet first. You and Faye stay about 500 yards behind."

Tom walked on ahead. Coming over the crest of a slight hill he ran towards the heliojet. Not too far away the tent, where he had purchased the clothes, seemed still and quiet.

Faye and George lay behind a clump of bushes watching Tom's every move, waiting for him to signal the OK.

Suddenly out of the tent emerged a man and that woman. She pointed to Tom and shouted...

"He's the man! He's the man that came in that flying machine." For a moment, Tom stopped, dazed, then made a dash for the heliojet. Brother Bartholomew laughed derisively...held up his hand, removed the cover from his ring...the ruby laser beam did its work swiftly, like the cruel snap of a whip.

In a moment, Tom, the heliojet and the cave had disappeared! They disintegrated into scattered dust that in a few seconds settled back down upon the quiet Judean desert.

Faye and George were shocked. They dare not move. They could see Brother Bartholomew bend down and kiss the woman on the cheek. In the dead stillness they could hear his voice.

"You have been wonderful...just wonderful...my dear mother. Poof...there went Tom Malone, there goes George Omega, there goes Faye Sanders and their escape heliojet. Thank you, mother. Thank you."

Chapter 13

The Sound of Death

Leader Chou was getting impatient. Moves by Brother Bartholomew disturbed him. With Brother Bartholomew moving into the Middle East, Leader Chou was sure the next target would be Asia.

As Chairman of the Chinese Communist Party Leader Chou felt a responsibility to his country. And he and his leaders believed that the Middle East belonged to them, and not only the Middle East but all of Africa.

It was amazing the striking resemblance of Leader Chou to the earlier Chinese leader Chairman Mao. Mao had long since died but his goals had been expanded.

China's military might had increased. She had perfected nuclear weaponry. At last the long road to leadership had been accomplished. China was recognized as a power to be feared. Up to now relations with the United States of Europe had been half-way cordial...at least each allowed the other to exist. But that relationship was soon to cease. For Leader Chou had his own worldly ambitions.

From the sights and sounds that filled the night, a visitor may have thought it was a Chinese New Year's celebration.

Blazing lights outlined the buildings around Peking's vast Tien An Men Square and poles on the street corners were laced with strings of multicolored bulbs. Hundreds of thousands of chanting citizens pressed towards the already jammed square, raising great clouds of dust over the center of the city. Everywhere were 30-foot-high papier-mache busts of Leader Chou. Loudspeakers, drums, cymbals and gongs produced a never-ending, nerve-shattering cacophony of sound.

The festivities had been ordered to celebrate the announcement of a historic major political event.

Suddenly, with a flurry of trumpets, Leader Chou stepped to the microphones and addressed the people:

Workers for Tomorrow,

It was our late leader Chairman Mao who said, "The outstanding thing about China's people is that they are poor and blank. On a blank sheet of paper, free from any mark, the freshest and most beautiful characters can be written."

The East wind now prevails over the West. Our country will never again be an insulted nation.

Tomorrow our armies begin the March of Victory. And with us to march as Brothers and allies will be our Russian neighbors who have suffered greatly.

Like Antiochus IV Epiphanes we will march wherever the River Euphrates runs its course. But where Antiochus failed, we will not fail. We will conquer all of Asia, we will conquer the Middle East, we will conquer Africa.

Tomorrow 200 MILLION warriors will march. We will not be stopped until the whole world kneels at our feet. We will be victorious.

The ovation was spontaneous and tremendous as the citizens raised their familiar Red Book and shouted...VICTORY, VICTORY, VICTORY!

Saying to the sixth angel which had the trumpet, Loose the four angels which are bound in the great river Euphrates...And the number of the army of the horsemen were two hundred thousand thousand (200 million): and I heard the number of them. (Revelation 9: 14, 16)

The plan was clear. Euphrates, the longest river of southwest Asia was to be the focal point of conquest. It follows a circuitous course of 1780 miles beginning at two headstreams in Turkey, passes near Babylon, merges with the Tigris River and together they empty into the Persian Gulf.

Leader Chou met with Russian leaders to map out the conquest that would begin the next day. He pointed to a map of the world as he directed the plan of attack:

Most of the Chinese and Russian forces will follow the flow of The Euphrates down through Turkey and head towards Jerusalem.

Another group of our forces will move down into Greece, cross the Mediterranean into Libya and come across the continent, and up to meet us at Jerusalem into a pincer movement.

Russia's previous defeat had made her weak and conciliatory. China controlled her territory and this control made it quite convenient to swarm directly south to the Holy Land.

It was a route somewhat planned after the exploits of Antiochus IV. Leader Chou had read his adventures of conquest with interest. One thing both had in common. Both had a hatred for the Jews. When Antiochus IV was expelled from Egypt by Popilius (168 B.C.) the news reached Jerusalem in the form of a report that he had been killed. The rejoicing Jews deposed his appointees, massacred the leaders of his party and cleansed the Temple of what they felt to be pagan abominations.

Antiochus, not dead, and convinced that the Jews had obstructed his victory for African conquest, marched to Jerusalem, slaughtered Jews of either sex by the thousands, desecrated and looted the Temple and commanded the Temple be rededicated as a shrine to Zeus. He forbade the keeping of the Sabbath, and made circumcision a capital crime. Every Jew who refused to eat pork was to be jailed or killed and the Holy Book was to be burned.

Leader Chou was determined that his reign of destruction would far outshine that of his idol, Antiochus. Leader Chou well knew the devastating power of his arsenal of destruction.

Like a surging flood the march began. Across the Mediterranean Sea millions of Chinese made their way on specially constructed space shuttles that carried 2000 troops at a time. Landing at Tripoli in Libya in early dawn they caught the populace by surprise.

Traveling on individual tracked motorcycles and wearing bullet proof vests and modern gas masks the invaders appeared to be a type of horror horsemen from the Middle Ages. Short snub-nosed nuclear

And this I saw the horses in the vision, and them that sat on them, having breastplates of fire, and of jacinth, and brimstone: and the heads of the horses were as the heads of lions: and out of their mouths issued fire and smoke and brimstone. (Revelation 9:17)

rifles laid down a lethal spray of death wherever resistance appeared. These new weapons were very effective, being able to kill anything ahead in a path from 5 feet fanning out to 100 feet in width in an area one mile long. Soon the Chinese Army was rampaging far south in Africa, and in Kenya killing that country's leader. It had made a half circle route and was now inching north to the Sudan.

The Sudan with 12 million blacks and 18 million Arabs savagely fought the invader in Juba, in Wau and at Malakai. Using bullets filled with Anya'Nya, a slow but fatal poison made by grinding the dried head of the cobra into a fine powder, they successfully killed many Chinese in the forward advance columns. But for every one that fell there seemed to be a thousand to replace him. It was an impossible fight. The White Nile became filled with the blood of the Sudanese.

Nothing would stop them now. They continued past the Sudan and up into Egypt.

From the North, the upper half of the pincer movement of the Chinese-Russian army crossed the Black Sea, crossed Turkey and was headed down through Syria.

In their path, both on land and in the air, their nuclear striking force left a wake of dead almost impossible to imagine. Two nuclear strikes had almost wiped out all of Europe. Most of Africa was reeling under the blow of the Chinese heel of death.

By these three was the third part of men killed, by the fire, and by the smoke, and by the brimstone (flaming sulphur), which issued out of their mouths. (Revelation 9:18)

Most of the 200 million army had come through these earlier conflicts unscathed. Now the real kill awaited them... Jerusalem...Brother Bartholomew and Prophet Arthur... then Leader Chou would be ruler of all the earth!

Brother Bartholomew was pacing the floor in his hideaway headquarters on the Mount of Olives.

The news reports were bad. The Chinese were no longer

Soon the Chinese Army was rampaging far south in Africa, and in Kenya killing that country's leader.

It was an impossible flight. The White Nile became filled with the blood of the Sudanese.

Dr. Curter's
SOUND SYNDROME
Decibels Chart

A decibel is an arbitrary unit based on the faintest sound that a man can hear. The scale is logarithmic, so that an increase of 10 db means a tenfold increase in sound intensity; a 20 db rise a hundredfold increase, and 30 db a thousandfold increase.

Since 1950 the noise level in the United States alone has doubled every ten years.

DECIBEL SCALE

140	**JET PLANE** 100 ft. away
130	**PNEUMATIC RIVETER**
120	**ROCK MUSIC WITH AMPLIFIERS** 4 to 6 ft. away One trillion times greater than least audible sound Human pain threshold
110	
107	**POWER MOWER**
100	**NOISY KITCHEN**
	SUBWAY inside
90	
85	**CITY TRAFFIC** inside car
80	Hearing damage occurs if noise prolonged
70	**FORTISSIMO SINGER** 3 ft. away
60	**ORDINARY CONVERSATION**

meeting with any resistance. Something had to be done and done quickly.

He called in Dr. Curter.

"Curter, look at those video screens. Everywhere the Chinese are like a horde of ants, overrunning everything... dead everywhere. We've got to come up with a plan that will stop them dead in their tracks."

Curter thought for a moment. Then spoke. "I have a plan, sir. It's been worked in experimentation only. But it may be the answer. We can inflict them with the SOUND SYNDROME."

"The sound WHAT?" Brother Bartholomew questioned.

"Sound Syndrome, sir. Since the early 1960's man has been concerned with the increasing noise level. We measure noise by decibels. A decibel is an arbitrary unit based on the faintest sound that a man can hear. As an example the rustle of leaves has a decibel rating of 20. Conversational speech a decibel rating of 60. Now at the decibel range of 85, if it is prolonged, hearing damage can occur. A Jet airliner 500 feet overhead has a decibel rating of 115. And coincidentally, rock music with amplifiers is rated at 120 decibels which is also the noise level of human pain threshold."

"What are you trying to tell me, Curter?"

"Just this, noise above 120 decibels, controlled noise, can be deadly. Since 1950 the noise level in the United States alone has doubled every ten years. Noise can work on humans two ways. One, of course, is to cause deafness."

"But the second effect of noise upon humans is psychological. Excessive exposure to noise constricts the arteries, increases the heartbeat, dilates the pupils of the eye. In tests on animals we found that continued excessive noise made them turn against each other, eat their young and eventually die of heart failure."

"But how can we use this against the Chinese without killing our own people?" Brother Bartholomew questioned.

"There will be some sacrifice, sir. Noise is not selective. But if we act now our Noise Amplifiers can be directed from space platforms in the direction of Syria and Turkey and in the south, towards Egypt and Ethiopia...in other words, we can still reach them before their troops intermingle with ours in the Jerusalem region."

"Excellent idea, Curter, at the same time we'll kill off some of our excess population. Solve two problems at one time. Advise the Noise Amplifier Division to proceed immediately with the plan."

The rapidly advancing Chinese never knew what hit them. At first the slowly developing shrill sound had them looking around wondering where the noise was coming from. They could not locate the source. Soon they became irritated with one another. After a few hours, fights erupted, their nuclear guns were aimed at their own ranks and they became disoriented and confused.

Leader Chou, from his palace in Peking, watched the progress of the war on his video screen. It was not a pleasant sight. Suddenly his marauding army was falling to pieces... but from what? The enemy was no where in sight. In fact innocent bystanders were dropping over like flies as well.

Piles of human flesh marked the trail of the marching Chinese Army. For a while some existed by covering their ears. But the deep penetrating noise level rose to higher decibel ratings and soon even this protection was pierced by the deadly sound.

Leader Chou hurridly called Brother Bartholomew via Picturephone. "Good to hear from you Leader Chou," Brother Bartholomew answered. "If you will surrender I will advise our Noise Amplifier Division to cease operation."

Leader Chou quickly conceded.

"Good," Brother Bartholomew continued, "you have made a wise decision. Besides we should not be fighting each other. A greater war lies ahead, one that will take our combined efforts to wipe out those who think God still exists...those who fail to honor me as the world leader...as the God of this world."

The war had been won. Brother Bartholomew, more sure of himself than ever before, ordered more statues of himself, statues in gold, brass and stone to be placed in every major city in the world. And wherever these statues appeared, people flocked to worship them.

Both Faye and George were covered with bruises and scratches. They had not yet gotten over the fact that their friend Tom Malone was dead— disintegrated right before their eyes. Yet while they mourned

And I heard a voice from heaven saying unto me, Write, Blessed are the dead which die in the Lord from henceforth: Yea, saith the Spirit, that they may rest from their labours; and their works do follow them. (Revelation 14:13)

his death they praised God that his soul was now safe in heaven with Christ. And as George said, "Not a slow chariot ride like Elijah...but in a blinding flash."

Slowly and dejectedly they walked together down a lonely path that at one time was a road.

"Where are we, Dad?" Faye questioned.

"I'm not sure, Honey, but I believe a little past the village of Emmaus. We should be about seven miles from Jerusalem."

Suddenly, as if from nowhere, they heard the footsteps of two strangers behind them. Fearfully they turned and looked. It was too late to run. And even if they could, they did not have the strength.

"Don't be afraid of us," one man called out. "We are your friends."

"Who are you?" Faye asked.

"If we told you, would it matter? You have been walking this road long. You look weary, thirsty. Have you journeyed from afar?"

"You would never believe us if we told you," George replied. "It seems too impossible to be true. We have not had a drink of water for what seems to be ages. No protein cakes...

nothing. We have just about given up hope."

"Where are you going?" the other man inquired.

"We are headed for Jerusalem," Faye answered. "We want to see the two prophets who are called by many Moses and Elijah. Somehow we hope that by our touching their garment, we might be saved from any more tribulation."

"I see the Mark on your forehead," the stranger replied, looking at Faye. Faye quickly sobbed, "But...oh...they forced it upon me. I screamed...I didn't want it...."

"You have gone through much tribulation," one of the two men responded.

The other one spoke. "I am afraid your journey is in vain. The two prophets or witnesses of which you speak were killed by Brother Bartholomew. For 3½ days their bodies lay exposed in the streets of Jerusalem. Many mourned, but far more people spat on them, sneered, and then went into the Temple to worship the idol of Brother Bartholomew."

And when they shall have finished their testimony, the beast that ascendeth out of the bottomless pit shall make war against them, and shall overcome them, and kill them.

And they of the people and kindreds and tongues and nations shall see their dead bodies three days and an half, and shall not suffer their dead bodies to be put in graves. (Revelation 11:7, 9)

"Then what happened?" George questioned.

The stranger spoke. "The two witnesses disappeared. Some say they ascended to heaven."

The other stranger continued, "While your journey to reach the prophets may not be successful, we can tell you where you will find a stream of pure, crystal water...a place where you will be safe from your persecutors."

And after three days and an half the spirit of life from God entered into them, and they stood upon their feet: and great fear fell upon them which saw them.

And they heard a great voice from heaven saying unto them, Come up hither. And they ascended up to heaven in a cloud; and their enemies beheld them. (Revelation 11:11-12)

"Where, where?" Faye anxiously cried.

"Hezekiah's Tunnel."

And with that the two strangers suddenly stepped behind some rocks and disappeared.

Faye and George looked at each other in astonishment... then collecting their thoughts, both exclaimed together: "MOSES and ELIJAH?"

Could it have been...that the two called Moses and Elijah before ascending from the streets of Jerusalem to heaven paused just briefly on the Emmaus road??? They didn't know. But both Faye and George stopped to praise God and give thanks.

Hezekiah's Tunnel. George had heard of it before. Helen in her tour of Jerusalem had mentioned it...but George had only listened half-heartedly as then he was not interested in Bible history. How he wished he had been more attentive.

"There's only one way to find out where this tunnel is, Faye...and that's to go into the city of Jerusalem, find some faithful Jews who do not bear the Mark. Perhaps, they may have old books which reveal the location of Hezekiah's Tunnel. Maybe a Hasidic Jew?"

"What's a Hasidic Jew?" Faye inquired.

"They are the very orthodox Jews, often disliked by the conservative and liberal Jew...but in past ages they have been learned men, doing much reading. They may provide the clue. And yet we must be careful."

Brother Bartholomew was facing unexpected problems. The recent war with China had resulted in the death of 1/3rd of mankind in the Afro-Asian world. This helped ease the population crisis but the use of nuclear weapons had affected the genes of many women. The next generation would be pitifully sick it was feared.

He presented the problem to Dr. Curter.

Dr. Curter as always had an answer.

"Sir," he explained, "in 1968 experiments began on a way of making babies outside of natural means. Since then we have made great strides and can now determine what IQ we want in a child, whether we want a boy or girl, whether we want all Einsteins or automatons that will follow every order. We call it Cloning."

"CLONING? That's an odd name. What does it mean?" Brother Bartholomew inquired.

"Cloning is the most bizarre development to come along in the field of biology to date. Cloning will make it possible to duplicate any type of man or beast. And each WILL BE A PRECISE DUPLICATE, A CARBON COPY OF THE ORIGINAL."

"Fantastic!" Brother Bartholomew gasped as his mind began thinking of ways he could use such a discovery for his own devious means. "Tell me more."

"Well, if one Einstein could lay down the whole foundation of modern-day physics, what might a dozen Einsteins — or 1,000 — either together or individually accomplish? Cloning can make it possible for a man to achieve in some sense immortality. For as soon as he dies, his family can simply make a whole new copy of him."

"Why the word CLONING?" Brother Bartholomew asked.

"Cloning is a word which comes from a Greek root meaning 'cutting' and is sometimes defined as 'asexual propagation.' This simply means reproduction-without-sex or, put another way, reproduction-without-fertilization."

"What are you saying, Dr. Curter?" interruped Prophet Arthur who had been standing quietly by.

"Just this, sir. We now can produce children of any specific intelligence pattern, boy or girl, to lead or to follow, from long-dead parents, or even from only one parent."

Brother Bartholomew spoke. "Well done, Dr. Curter. You have the problem well in hand." He paused, quickly scribbled some notes on a piece of paper and handed them to Dr. Curter, saying: "Here are my specifications, get that Cloning department working. Money is no object. I'll appropriate whatever is necessary. I want followers, not leaders, and see if you can make them immune from nuclear radiation. And oh, by the way, Curter, I'm giving you a heliojet. My compliments for your fine work."

Suddenly the ground shook. The long, low rumble was a familiar one. They had heard it before. It was an earthquake.

As George and Faye were walking into Jerusalem they were met by thousands of shouting, screaming people fleeing the city, running towards the mountains.

Those who ran all bore The Mark 666. Their faces shone with fear. Boils and sores had erupted on their faces and hands. The Mark 666 seemed to stand out in puffiness, oozing a sickly white pus that streaked their face.

George stopped one man, asked him why he was running.

And the first went, and poured out his vial upon the earth; and there fell a noisome and grievous sore upon the men which had the mark of the beast, and upon them which worshipped his image. (Revelation 16:2)

And the second angel poured out his vial upon the sea; and it became as the blood of a dead man: and every living soul died in the sea. (Revelation 16:3)

"Earthquake in Jerusalem. We have been told that even the ocean has turned to a sea of blood. Everything is dying. The rivers and springs are turning to blood. We are fleeing to the mountains. Come, it is our only hope!"

Each will be a PRECISE DUPLICATE, a CARBON COPY of the Original. We can make 1000 Ministers identical and patterned to obey Prophet Arthur."

"Thank you, friend, but we're headed for Jerusalem!"

"Don't go to Jerusalem," the old man pleaded. "Already there are 7000 dead there lying in the streets!"

And the same hour was there a great earthquake, and the tenth part of the city fell, and in the earthquake were slain of men seven thousand: and the remnant were affrighted, and gave glory to the God of heaven. (Revelation 11:13)

George and Faye continued walking towards Jerusalem on the old Nablus Road. They had seen too much to turn back now. Soon, George remarked, they should reach the Jericho Road bordering the inner city wall.

For the first time in a long time Faye seemed calm and relaxed as she spoke. "Dad, when did religion start falling apart? I mean when did people start turning away from Christ and developing their own theology?"

"That's a hard question to answer, Faye," George replied. "Some say it started in the late 1800's and in the early 1900's. Perhaps the most marked change occurred way back in 1968-69 almost coinciding with the then famous campus revolts. Students were seeking what they called a new religion, one that was mystical, symbolic. One Roman Catholic theologian of that day said,

'Almost everybody tends to think of religion as an institutional structure. That's really not true. What's really religious is an ultimate view of self and community and doesn't necessarily have anything to do with God.'

Another Professor of religion at a well-known college said,

'I call drug-induced experiences, as well as the whole ethos built around drugs in the youth counter-culture, religious.'

Some well-meaning but misdirected people tried to bring Christ down to the level of the people instead of lifting the level of the people up to the standards of Christ. Part of a musical work I remember had phrases such as this running through it,

'Cause this is real, man. This Person died for me.'
And Wham!!!! That really rocks me!!!!

Then there were the Rock Communions, and the flaunting of sex in the church. Fundamentalists became unpopular. There was more social concern and less soul concern. Slowly but surely, it watered down to a watered down religion...a religion that eventually paved the way for Brother Bartholomew. After all they had experienced everything else. Their appetites had become jaded. Life had lost its kicks. And that's when we entered into the scene. And, Faye, Honey, that's why you and I are walking down this road... searching for tomorrow, a tomorrow when Christ rules the world as King of Kings and Lord of Lords...a tomorrow where every man and woman is safe lying beneath his own vine and fig tree. How much grief you and I could have eliminated if only we had accepted Christ before the Rapture took place!"

"*If*, Dad, *if only*. How often I've heard it said, 'experience may be a good teacher, but some people never graduate from kindergarten.' I guess that's me."

George and Faye reached the end of Nablus road. It dead-ended into the Jericho Road.

"Which way shall we turn, Dad, right or left?"

George looked both ways. The high walls of the city were an impressive sight. Somehow the earthquakes had not affected them. Then George remembered the tour with Helen. He looked to the left and pointed. Look up there!"

"I don't see anything," Faye replied.

"Look closely, Faye, in the rock. Those indentations that resemble a face. That's Golgotha! The Skull. The place of our Lord's crucifixion."

"Then the Garden Tomb must not be far away," Faye replied, hopefully. "It isn't, Faye. It's close by and so is Gethsemane...the place where Jesus prayed before he was crucified."

"Dad, I have a wonderful idea. Somehow I feel right now

we should go to Gethsemane and pray. God will be there. He will answer our prayers. I've never been to Gethsemane, Dad. Take me there now."

"Praise God, Faye, a wonderful plan...both of us praying in the Garden of Gethsemane, just as Christ did some 2000 years ago. The power of Christ's love has not diminished. How I love that verse...

> 'That I may know him, and the POWER of
> His resurrection, and the fellowship of
> His sufferings, being made conformable
> unto His death.'

That's Philippians 3:10 and then in verse 14 it continues...

> 'I press toward the mark for the prize of
> the high calling of God in Christ Jesus.'

You know, Faye, that's exactly what we're doing, pressing toward the mark...."

Faye and George opened the gate of the old churchyard. And there, there was Gethsemane. Somehow grass was still growing here, the gnarled olive trees still stood as they have through the centuries. The flowers were blooming as if this tiny garden stood still through the ages while the rest of the world deteriorated in sin.

It was dusk, the shades of night were rapidly falling. At the other end of the Garden they saw a movement. A man had been standing, and now he knelt as if to pray.

Faye and George knelt to pray near him.

Suddenly the man stood up. It was hard to see him in the darkness for he wore a cloak around his head and his robe reached to the ground.

He came nearer, touched both of us on the shoulder as we knelt. We turned.

"Faye and George, I thought that if I waited long enough I might find you here at this silly shrine. Brother Bartholomew will be most elated!"

There was no mistaking the voice or the face — it was that of Prophet Arthur!

Chapter 14
March on Megiddo

"A great job, Prophet Arthur! A great job. I thought I had dispensed with those two when I lasered that heliojet near Bethlehem."

Brother Bartholomew was speaking. Prophet Arthur smiled a smile of smug satisfaction.

Surrounded by guards both Faye and George looked dejected as they stood in what some referred to as the "Master's throne room."

It was some time since Faye and George had been in this spacious nerve control center of Brother Bartholomew's. Some changes had been made. In one section of the room was what appeared to be a mechanical monster, a frightening machine with a tall pillar as a base and a revolving circular platform above it, topped with what appeared to be some type of radar receiving device. The entire unit was covered with switches, buttons and screens and it stood some 30 feet high.

Brother Bartholomew noting George and Faye engrossed

"That's my Christ. It does everything I tell it to do."

in this large mysterious unit, spoke: "What fools you are. You pray to a God who does not hear you, not even in the Garden of Gethsemane!"

Pointing to the mechanical spy he boasted, "That's my Christ. It does everything I tell it to do. It follows my orders without question. I am God and Robo-X is my miracle worker

...keeps me advised on all the movements of my enemies... instantly relays defections within my rank."

Faye and George stared in disbelief. The computer and electronic gadgetry which once was supposed to have been a blessing was now a curse.

"And this time," Prophet Arthur proudly beamed, "this time Brother Bartholomew has great plans for you...plans from which you will not escape."

"Not my plans, Prophet Arthur, your plans," BB replied. "After all it was your idea originally and you should get the credit for it. Tell them what great destiny awaits them!"

"Very well, sir," Bishop Arthur continued. "You two prayed so fervently at the Garden of Gethsemane where this fabled Jesus was supposed to have spent his last night. And yet your prayers were not answered. Perhaps you did not pray hard enough...or, perhaps...at the wrong location? Perhaps you should have been praying at that heretical GARDEN TOMB where your Jesus was supposedly raised from the dead."

"Excellent idea! Excellent!" added Brother Bartholomew. "And what better way to pray, Prophet Arthur, what better way to pray!"

"Yes," Prophet Arthur continued, "what better way to pray than by kneeling, kneeling at the Garden Tomb...and what more comfortable way to kneel and enter into Christ's Kingdom quickly...than to kneel at a dual GUILLOTINE, set up right at the Garden Tomb!"

"Excellent! Excellent! Prophet Arthur you are indeed a wise man!" Brother Bartholomew commended.

"There's more, sir. We have electronically set our release mechanisms so that both heads will roll at the same time... in unison! And for your convenience, we'll place your bodies in the Garden Tomb...just in case your Master should come."

Faye's heart sank. Her eyelids dropped. George was furious and was ready to unleash a tongue lashing at both Prophet Arthur and Brother Bartholomew. Just as he was ready to speak before these confirmed monsters of iniquity the words of Scripture came to his mind...

"He was oppressed, and he was afflicted,
yet he opened not his mouth: he is brought
as a lamb to the slaughter, and as a sheep
before her shearers is dumb, so he openeth
not his mouth."

(Isaiah 53:7)

And George said nothing.

They were told that the execution day would be tomorrow. This would give BB sufficient time to summon a large crowd, and put on a great show.

Quickly they were led to an elevator which went down into a shaft that seemed endless, hundreds of feet below the Mount of Olives.

Faye spoke first. The room was cold and damp. There was no light except for the little light that seeped through the peep hole in their door.

"Daddy, I've been thinking..." and with that she burst into tears.

"Why are you crying, Faye? This is no time to cry. We must have faith. Paul was imprisoned just like we are...in Rome...and yet he asked Timothy to bring him the parchments...God's Word, that he might feed upon them. We still have that little Bible, Faye. It's in my pocket. Do you want me to read to you?"

"No, Dad, it wouldn't do any good. There's no way I can go to Heaven now. All this time I've been running, hiding with you, not realizing that you can go to Heaven...but not I. Never, daddy, never!" Faye screamed hysterically.

"I don't understand, Faye. Why do you say that?"

With tears running down her face and in a choked, half crying voice she sobbed, "LOOK AT MY FOREHEAD, DADDY! LOOK AT MY FOREHEAD! DO YOU SEE THE MARK? EVERYONE CAN SEE IT. 6...6...6 EVEN GOD

CAN SEE IT! MARKED FOREVER FOR DESTRUC-
TION."

George placed his arm around Faye, gently put her head
on his shoulder as he had done many times when she was a
little girl. At first he didn't know what to say...but he spoke:
"Faye, remember when you were just a little girl, 8 years
old, you tripped and fell in the school playground. There was
a slight scratch on your forehead. Do you remember what
you did?"

"Yes, Dad, I came running home after school crying my
heart out saying, 'I'll have a scar for life. I'll be an ugly lady.
No one will love me.'"

"That's right, Faye, but remember how I reassured you
that God would heal that wound. And within a few weeks it
disappeared."

"I know daddy, you're trying to be kind and understanding, but it won't work. That was a physical scar. This is a
spiritual scar. By taking the Mark 666 I am marked as one
rejecting Christ, giving my allegiance to antichrist."

"Symbolically, yes, but it was done under coercion and
somehow I feel this Mark will disappear. You had rejected
antichrist. You were forcibly led to the communion table and
against your will branded with his evil brand. I cannot understand all of God's Word...but I accept it. Since our initial
escape on the Sea House I've had much time to concentrate
on the Word of God. And there's one verse I remember in
Romans 11:33. It goes something like this:

> O the depth of the riches both of the wisdom
> and knowledge of God! how unsearchable are
> His judgments, and His ways past finding out!

And somehow, I believe, however we end our life here on
this earth, God will understand the circumstances under
which you received The Mark...for He is all-seeing and all-
knowing. And in His infinite mercy He will provide the
answer."

After a time of Bible reading and prayer they again began

to talk. Faye asked, "How did this Mark idea come about in the first place?"

"The Mark is not an original idea, Faye," George replied trying to comfort her. "Other ruling powers have adopted a Mark in their day. Nazi Germany had its *swastika;* the Soviet Union its *hammer and sickle.* Both were universally recognized. I've done a little research on this. In Daniel 7:4 we are told that Babylon was symbolized by God in a vision given to Daniel as a lion with eagle's wings. The Medo-Persian empire was portrayed by a bear's rising up with three ribs between its teeth in Daniel 7:5. And in Daniel 7:6 the Graeco-Macedonia influence was pictured as a four-headed leopard with wings. Royal families and dynasties even had their own marks.

In the late 1960's and early 1970's a common Mark was the Broken Cross or Peace Symbol, as some called it. It was first used as a peace symbol by marchers in England, led by Lord Bertrand Russell in the late 1940's. It was developed by superimposing the *semaphore code signs* for N and D and stood for nuclear disarmament. As far back as the Middle Ages this symbol was a common symbol used by godless forces with the cross reversed and broken."

"Is the word MARK actually in the Bible?" Faye questioned. "Yes, it occurs eight times in the Bible. And all are found in the book of Revelation and all pertain to antichrist. The word comes from the Greek *charagma.* It means etching or stamp such as a badge of servitude."

Brother Bartholomew was busy making great plans for the Garden Tomb execution site. "Everything must work like clockwork," he warned Prophet Arthur.

If BB were aware of what was occuring in the Space Exploration department his mind would have been on more important things. Dr. Curter who had become a liaison officer to Brother Bartholomew was summoned to the Space Exploration briefing room. The news was not good. Quickly he raced to Brother Bartholomew's office, and dashed in apolo-

getically. "Why so flustered, Curter?" Brother Bartholomew
questioned. "I'm afraid I have some bad news, sir. The tidal
drag of the moon is slowing the earth's rotation. Recent
nuclear explosions combined with air pollutants have caused
some sort of cosmic chaos. The moon's rotational period is
now matching that of the earth and this is eliminating the
tidal drag."

"What does all this mean, Curter?" Brother Bartholomew
asked.

"Simply this. The *sun* is continuing to exert tidal pull,
further slowing down the earth. The sun also may cause the
moon to reverse direction and move closer to the earth until
the moon is torn apart at a distance of 10,000 miles. Earthquakes, enormous tides will result...but even more cata-
strophic, the expansion of the sun in its dying throes will
cast off an intense heat...a heat so intense that it might kill
everything on earth."

"When will this occur?" Prophet Arthur asked.

"Our Space Exploration laboratory was not prepared for such an ineventuality and therefore their research of this area of phenomenon was not conducted until just a few days ago."

"What are you trying to say, Curter, speak up and stop this mumbo jumbo!"

Curter stammered, "What I am trying to say, sir, is that this catastrophe could strike at any moment!"

Frantically, Brother Bartholomew began pushing buttons, flipping switches shouting into his control console to alert all units to prepare for a catastrophe of the sun, urging everyone to take cover.

And even as he spoke it appeared as though the axis of the earth was turning, the sun coming closer. The oppressive heat closed in like a suffocating blanket.

The scene was beyond description. The hot rays of sun broke through the polluted screen of dust and grime that had so long covered the earth and these rays seemed to lick up this barrier like a flame licking up particles of chipped wood. It came searing, hotter, and hotter, and hotter. Screaming, agonizing screaming even penetrated the deep shaft where Faye and George were imprisoned. Those who but for a moment glanced up at this holocaust of horror were instantly and permanently blinded.

> And the fourth angel poured out his vial upon the sun; and power was given unto him to scorch men with fire.
> And men were scorched with great heat, and blasphemed the name of God, which hath power over these plagues: and they repented not to give him glory. (Revelation 16:8-9)

And then as suddenly as the oppressive heat and brilliant light of the sun had appeared... it just as suddenly disappeared! And the earth was plunged into a terrifying DARKNESS.

Dr. Curter was a genius. And

> And the fifth angel poured out his vial upon the seat of the beast; and his kingdom was full of darkness; and they gnawed their tongues for pain.
> And blasphemed the God of heaven because of their pains and their sores, and repented not of their deeds. (Revelation 16:10-11)

having great scientific insight, he was prepared against any

The earth was plunged into a terrifying DARKNESS.

problem he thought might occur. Patiently he had obeyed
every command of Brother Bartholomew. He was among the
first to have The Mark 666 imprinted on his forehead. But
as the years passed, his closeness to this power brought some
revelations...revelations that Dr. Curter felt were chinks of
weakness in the character of this man who would be God.
God was supposed to do good, Dr. Curter reasoned. But this
man was a mixture of good and evil and now leaned heavily
to doing simply everything evil.

Dr. Curter realized he had already taken his position with
Brother Bartholomew. There was no backing out now. But
in his last days the least he could do was to contribute some
good to humanity...even if it would cost him his life. Perhaps
in so doing, he reasoned, he might gain the peace of knowing
that he had caused Brother Bartholomew also to pay and
suffer. Bring BB to grief...he who had grieved millions. That
was it!

He made up his mind. He would have his vengeance. He
would help Faye and George escape.

Faye and George were praying. It was pitch black. George, in his prayer was quoting II Corinthians 4:6...."For God, who commanded the light to shine out of darkness..."

The sound of the elevator descending interrupted them. They looked up. In the pitchblackness of the surroundings, they heard the elevator door open. And coming towards them...a thin ray of light!

As the light came closer they heard a voice: "Don't be afraid, it's me!"

"Dr. Curter," Faye shrieked in fear.

"Quiet," Dr. Curter urged. "I am not your enemy. I am come as your friend. I have watched your testimony through these years. There's not much I can do, but I can set you free. Your Lord will have to do the rest. A short time ago Brother Bartholomew gave me my own private heliojet...as a reward. It's waiting up above. It won't be missed for an hour. Tell me where you want to go in Palestine. It can take you anywhere in Palestine and be back within the hour. No one will know it. I'll program the control mechanism to fly you there automatically."

"Praise God," George replied.

"Take us to GIHON!"

"Why Gihon?" Dr. Curter questioned. "That's right outside the inner city walls of Jerusalem. It's just a dried up spring. I thought you would want to get farther away from this place than that."

"But as you wish, George, but I can't go with you. The heliojet will land you on the spot, then it will take off again and return here to the Mount of Olives all within the necessary hour. It won't be missed."

Brother Bartholomew was listening to a geophysical report from aides in his office. Things had quieted down to a point where he could proceed with his planning.

And the sixth angel poured out his vial upon the great river Euphrates; and the water thereof was dried up, that the way of the kings of the east might be prepared. (Revelation 16:12)

The aide was speaking: "Sir, something unusual is occurring. The intense heat from the sun has caused vast destruction. Fortunately its course has been changed to give us temporary relief. But reports indicated that the river Euphrates is drying up."

"Why is this so drastic?" Brother Bartholomew demanded.

"For as long as we can trace," the aide continued, "the Euphrates River has been a formidable barrier to East-West transportation and communication. The River is nearly 1800 miles long, a thousand feet to a mile wide at some points, and it is as deep as 57 feet at the average depth. While modern day weaponry can cross this with ease, nevertheless, it has been a subtle dividing line. I know the Bible is a fabled book but Dr. Curter pointed out to me Isaiah 11:15. It's quite prophetic sir...

> 'And the Lord shall utterly destroy the tongue of
> the Egyptian sea; and with his mighty wind shall
> he shake his hand over the river, that is, the
> Euphrates, and shall smite it in the seven streams,
> and make men go over dryshod.'

This drying up of the River, the Euphrates, may be just the sign to encourage China or Russia to begin another invasion."

Brother Bartholomew gazed at the aide and spoke sharply, "Nonsense, you've been reading too many fairy tales. Get me Dr. Curter!"

Within moments Dr. Curter arrived.

"Curter, what have you been babbling about? Have you also outlived your usefulness? Should I set up 3 guillotines for tomorrow? What a picture that would make—the 3 Wise Men!" With that he flipped a switch to light up a video screen. "Let's look in on our God-fearing duet down below. Perhaps I'll send you down to keep them company."

The screen was lit. Brother Bartholomew looked at it in shock. The picture showed an empty room!

He turned to Dr. Curter enraged...about to speak. Just

then Prophet Arthur rushed in with a video communique.

"Brother Bartholomew. There's trouble in the South. The Egyptian-African coalition of nations is on the march. Their war cry is 'TO THE SEA WITH BROTHER BARTHOLO-MEW...FORCE HIM TO THE SEA!'"

Another aide rushed in, "Brother Bartholomew, the armies from the North are marching down from Russia. They are headed towards Jerusalem!"

Brother Bartholomew was visibly moved. "From the South, from the North. It's a pincer movement. Those traitors. Like a clever mousetrap they hope to close in on us and snap us into oblivion. But they are not wise enough. Once and for all, we'll demolish them. Prophet Arthur launch MIRV on our scheduled contingency battle plan."

The aide shuddered. MIRV, the Multiple Independently-targeted Re-entry Vehicle, had devastating nuclear power. No nation had dared to use it before. Even though countries went to war, this was one international treaty they always had respected.

Prophet Arthur pushed the ignite button. The sequence began. There was no reversing now. It was too late. Soft, silent whistles were heard. All knew what it was. The MIRV's had been launched. Soon they would take their deadly toll.

But some of the invading forces had already reached Jerusalem. The city was being invaded. The prophecy of Zechariah 12:2,3 was becoming a reality.

> "Behold, I will make Jerusalem a cup of
> trembling unto all the people round about,
> when they shall be in the siege both against
> Judah and against Jerusalem.
>
> And in that day will I make Jerusalem a burdensome
> stone for all people: all that burden themselves
> with it shall be cut in pieces, though all
> the people of the earth be gathered together
> against it."

The MIRV's did their deadly work and Brother Bartholomew beamed at their amazing ability to change the enemy's mind. It was easy to force Egypt and her coalition from the South and the Russian coalition from the North to come to terms. Brother Bartholomew even convinced them that they should not be fighting each other, but should merge together to fight an even greater enemy...those who believe they are Kings from the East...the Chinese!

Leader Chou was infuriated. His hopes for victory over the dynasty of Brother Bartholomew were crushed. He had cleverly encouraged the Egyptian and Russian coalitions to fight in a pincer movement to wipe out the United States of Europe's stronghold in the Middle East. Then, their energies spent, Leader Chou had planned to rush in with his hordes of soldiers and quickly overtake the two victors and make them subservient to China and his leadership. He would have become the Leader of the World.

But the humiliating defeat by Russia and Egypt washed out those dreams. "Why didn't they win?" he gasped. "Those traitors marched to defeat...But...If they couldn't do the job, I must march in myself and once and for all conquer the world. The yellow hordes of China will wipe the white man from the face of the earth. We are in the majority anyway. It would be an easy accomplishment," Leader Chou believed.

He had a plan...a clever plan that would bring his armies marching down from Turkey, in an armada of inconspicuous sailing ships across the Mediterranean to Haifa. This would not start as an obvious attack. This would be a Chinese Trojan Horse!

The heliojet had landed them safely. Under the cover of darkness it had deposited them at the place called GIHON. George took Faye's hand and slowly they descended the 32 steps to the spring called the Virgin's Spring. While it was still dark, they could yet feel that the spring bed was dry. But in a few feet they were soon wading in cold water. Faye stumbled on the stony floor. She removed what was left of her sandals. Both Faye and George, parched from going so

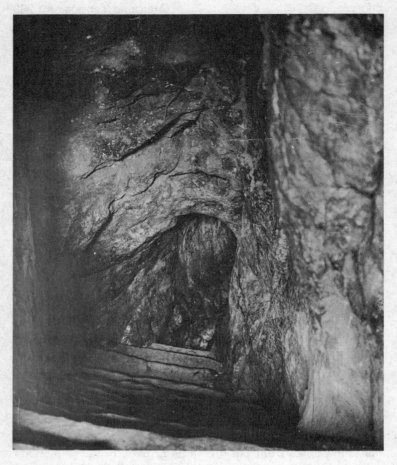

long with so little water, knelt in the cool spring and drank slowly and thankfully.

George spoke first.

"Faye, perhaps we should stay right here, just for a little while. I somehow feel the Lord wants us to be still and not move anymore."

"How did this tunnel come about, Dad?"

"This is called Hezekiah's tunnel," George replied. "This is a water shaft dug in solid rock. It's described in II Kings 20:20. It was constructed by King Hezekiah's engineers when the Jerusalem water supply was threatened by the approach of Sennacherib's army in 701 B.C. He built what is called by some the 'Siloam tunnel' to convey water from Gihon, where we are now, to the new upper pool of Siloam."

Suddenly the stillness was broken by the amplified sound of Brother Bartholomew...carrying his voice over the many Video lampposts that covered the city. His voice was loud and ominously clear...

For they are the spirits of devils, working miracles which go forth unto the kings of the earth and of the whole world, to gather them to the battle of that great day of God Almighty. (Revelation 16:14)

ALL ELEMENTS OF THE ARMY. EMERGENCY. REPORT TO DIVISION HEADQUARTERS. PREPARE TO MARCH ON MEGIDDO!

Chapter 15

Search for Tomorrow

MEGIDDO!

A dreaded name.

Megiddo, a city situated on the Great Road, which linked Gaza and Damascus, and controlling the principal pass through the Carmel Range, connecting the coastal plain and the Plain of Esdraelon. Megiddo was important because of its domination of the intersection of two vitally important trade and military routes. One of the best recorded and most interesting military operations of ancient times took place at Megiddo when Thutmose III defeated an Asiatic coalition headed by the King of Kadesh. The importance of this area is reflected in the statement of the Egyptian king that the capture of Megiddo was the capture of a thousand towns.

"Har Megiddon" in the Hebrew; the "Mountain of Megiddo." At the foot of this mountain lie the Valley of Jezreel and the Plain of Esdraelon...the entire valley-plain region being together called, ARMAGEDDON! This was the scene of many decisive battles.

Here in this valley-plain region Gideon defeated Midian (Judges 6:33). Here Saul met death at the hands of the Philistines (I Samuel 31). In 1918 the then Allied forces under General Allenby entered northern Palestine through the Megiddo Pass to wrest it from Turkish forces. Subsequently he was named Viscount Allenby of Megiddo.

The sailing sloops went undetected as they entered the Haifa harbor. Brother Bartholomew's men were too preoccupied with the other fronts of attack which the Chinese had already started.

The world had never witnessed such a vast array of men and arms. The mass destruction leveled by the MIRV's had convinced Brother Bartholomew that to insure the survival of his own army this war with China would have to be fought with conventional weaponry.

Brother Bartholomew was kept busy directing the plan for conquest from his war operations office atop the Mount of Olives.

Prophet Arthur looked at him amazed as he entered with a report and found Brother Bartholomew poring over a Bible.

"A Bible? The world is falling apart! Why are you reading the Bible?" Prophet Arthur asked.

"This fabled book has some good object lessons in it...and some good plans for ambushes are in the Book of Joshua. It's excellent for the geography of this land. Who knows, the clue to once and for all defeating the Chinese might be right within its pages?"

Prophet Arthur began to give the information which he had just received, "I have word that soon the Chinese army will be near Mount Tabor. Our generals say that even though it is only 1843 feet high, if captured it would make a good command post for our enemy. They surprised us at Haifa. Innocent looking sloop sailing ships came into harbor. Our men thought them nothing but old sailing vessels. But on command, their holds opened, landing platforms extended down to the ground and a large array of tanks overran

Haifa leaving a wake of dead in their path. They, too are headed for Megiddo."

"Are you sure of that information?" Brother Bartholomew questioned.

"Yes," Prophet Arthur replied, "Our videoscopes confirm this."

"Good! That may be their biggest mistake. In Judges 5, the army of Sisera with 900 chariots moved near the entrance to the Esdraelon Plain to attack Israel. In the meantime a storm caused the Qishon River to overflow its banks, turning the fields into a quagmire. The chariots became hopelessly stuck in the mud...and the Israelites won an overwhelming victory!"

"But it is not raining, Brother Bartholomew, and no rain is predicted." Prophet Arthur revealed.

"Prophet Arthur, how long have you been close to me and yet still not realize that I control the heavens and the earth? It will be a simple matter to send rain over the Plain of Esdraelon and, in fact, to restrict the deluge to that area and to that area alone!"

Hezekiah's tunnel was a welcome relief from the unbearable heat of the last few hours. Faye and George had proceeded further into the tunnel to escape the hot air.

At some places it was necessary for them to crawl on their hands and knees, sometimes flat on their stomachs. The tunnel seemed full of twists and turns.

"How long is this tunnel?" Faye questioned.

"In a straight line it would be some 750 feet but this tunnel does not follow a straight line...but rather a circuitous route and it's over 1700 feet in length."

"Where does it lead to, Dad?"

"It goes through the High Rock, the Ophel, to the reservoir called the Pool of Siloam. This is the same pool to which Jesus sent the blind man with the command 'Go, wash in the pool of Siloam.' That was in John 9:7. The blind man went in, washed, and came out seeing!"

Turning another very sharp corner suddenly a streak of light broke through. Far in the distance they could see an opening. Faye was bruised and weary. The long days of running were catching up with her. She was exhausted.

"Let's rest here just a moment, Dad," she begged.

"Good idea, Faye. And with this little light, we can sit down and give thanks to God for bringing us safely this far."

"What is happening outside, Dad? The shouting, the screaming, the noise of explosives? Does the Bible give any clues to what is happening?"

George took the well-worn Bible from his coat pocket. "Yes, Faye, the Bible tells us much about His plan for tomorrow. Like many we were fools thinking Revelation and portions of Daniel and Jeremiah and Zechariah were just imaginations of men long ago. Even many clergymen passed these truths off as mere symbolism, and not as events which would actually come true. Yet God's prophecies have all been accurate up to this point. There is no reason to doubt that the rest of His Word will not prove accurate as well. Let's look at God's Timetable."

Turning the pages, he continued, "The Fourth Vial, the scorching sun as revealed in Revelation 16:8-9 and the sudden darkness which is the Fifth Vial described in Revelation 16: 10-11 have already occurred. With the March to Megiddo now occurring, we must assume that the drying of the Euphrates River in the Sixth Vial judgment has come to pass, too. This would bring us up to the present time when the Armies of the East and the Armies of Brother Bartholomew, Antichrist, meet at Armageddon. And if I remember a very vivid statement on that is found in Joel 3:9-11...

> 'Proclaim ye this among the Gentiles; Prepare war, wake up the mighty men, let all the men of war draw near;
> let them come up;
> Beat your plowshares into swords, and your

pruninghooks into spears: let the weak say,
I am strong.

Assemble yourselves, and come, all ye heathen, and
gather yourselves together round about: thither
cause thy mighty ones to come down, O Lord.'

This truly presents the scene that is now taking place."

"You know what I wish, Dad? I wish I could be up in
Heaven looking down on this battle. Wouldn't it be wonderful! But what about those Israelites who bear the seal of
God, the 144,000. Where are they??

"God will deliver them. He says so in His word. And also Gentiles like us who have accepted Christ as our Messiah will be safe — safe with Christ whether we live or die. And after this judgment, at Armageddon Christ will come down with His armies from Heaven to slay the wicked and redeem the saved. We'll meet Helen and Sue and Tommy and Bill and Tom Malone. It won't be long now, Faye. What a grand and glorious reunion that will be!"

And I looked, and lo, a Lamb stood on the mount Sion, and with him an hundred forty and four thousand, having his Father's name written in their foreheads. (Revelation 14:1)

After this I beheld, and, lo, a great multitude, which no man could number, of all nations, and kindreds, and people, and tongues, stood before the throne, and before the Lamb, clothed with white robes, and palms in their hands:
...These are they which came out of great tribulation, and have washed their robes, and made them white in the blood of the Lamb. (Revelation 7:9, 14)

"Oh, Dad," Faye cried, "it's going to be so wonderful...so wonderful. If only God would remove the Mark from my head. I would be so ashamed to face him hearing the mark of antichrist!"

"God will do it Faye, I am sure God will do it."

Brother Bartholomew stood on a hill looking down over the Plain of Esdraelon. Before him the mightest armies in the world were massing...and slowly approaching the point of contact.

An ominous cloud of dust seemed to hang heavy over the miles and miles of flat plain. The noise of approaching armies

The Plain of Esdraelon...ARMAGEDDON!

thundered and echoed against the hills.

Leader Chou who claimed via radio to have with him some 200 million troops assembled felt confident of victory as his heliojet soared above his advancing tank columns. Almost 15,000 tanks were proceeding across the hot desert floor.

Brother Bartholomew smiling, as though he had the situation well in hand, stood watching the mass of millions at the point of confrontation. With him Prophet Arthur, hands on hips, watched as though he were to see a dream come true.

Suddenly Brother Bartholomew raised his arm, and removed the protective cap from the ruby laser ring.

Through the din of tanks and armor he shouted to Prophet Arthur, "Now you will see the heavens themselves empty every drop of rain on the Plain of Esdraelon. Then Leader Chou will be like putty in my hands."

Just as he finished speaking, the very heavens opened, like a scroll being rolled back. What appeared to be a mysterious cloud formation from high in the sky was descending.

Brother Bartholomew knew his Scriptures well. And the sign in the sky revealed to him that the Army of the Lord was descending. This was no time to be fighting the Chinese.

> And I saw heaven opened, and behold a white horse: and he that sat upon him was called Faithful and True, and in righteousness he doth judge and make war. (Revelation 19:11) *

Quickly by picturephone he contacted Leader Chou who was in his heliojet. The heliojet of Leader Chou soon landed bearing a white flag of truce. It then picked up Brother Bartholomew and Prophet Arthur, and whisked them away to the Mount of Olives!

Atop the mountain headquarters both Leader Chou and Brother Bartholomew hastily signed an agreement. Prophet Arthur called in Defense Strategy Command and together they mapped a plan of attack against the armies of God.

Bishop Arthur anxiously spoke to Leader Chou. "We must work together. With your 200 million army combined with my millions not even God will withstand our assault. We will win the victory. They raised their glasses in a diabolical toast to victory. Then quickly Brother Bartholomew issued orders to the armies in the field to prepare for the onslaught that was to follow.

Faye and George rested, and then decided to continue again what seemed an endless crawling and walking through the tunnel of King Hezekiah towards its termination point at the top of the hill.

Like two happy children finally reaching the top of a verdant green hill...they literally ran the last few feet and fell on the ground gazing up at the sky.

After a few minutes, Faye jumped up. Weary and bruised she saw a pool of water.

"There it is, Dad...there it is...THE POOL OF SILOAM!" Without hesitation she jumped in the pool, and swam in the cool refreshing waters. It was as though she had found an oasis after walking in a parched, sun-baked desert. The sparkling clear waters seemed to give her new life.

As quickly as she dove in she emerged, happy and laughing.

George looked at her stunned.

"Dad," her face looked suddenly worried, "what's the matter? Why are you staring at me like that?"

"Your face, Faye, your face," he shouted as he jumped up and pointed hysterically happy.

"What's wrong with my face, Daddy, what's wrong with my face?"

"The Mark, Faye, The Mark is GONE. DISAPPEARED. The 666 has DISAPPEARED! It's not there!"

Faye cried tears of joy as they ran into each other's arms with Faye shouting, "God answered my prayer, Daddy... God has answered my prayer!"

"Faye," George replied, "Scriptures had made it very plain to me that accepting The Mark was an unpardonable sin. Yet I believed God would provide an answer. And now I remember Tom telling us that he used a fade-out temporary dye on his forehead. It's funny how things come back. It was Bishop Arthur who told me a long time ago that no one can be privileged to wear The Mark unless they desire it voluntarily. So now it is clear. Brother Bartholomew, in his sinister planning, used a temporary fade-out Mark on you. And when you plunged into the Pool of Siloam it washed away!"

Faye beamed with happiness. "And you know Dad, one thing puzzles me...Brother Bartholomew issued plaques to everyone with the inscription PRAYER CHANGES THINGS. But you said the plaque in his office was THINGS CHANGE PRAYER. Why the difference?"

"That almost slipped my mind, Faye. Isn't it odd how these relatively insignificant things all fall together. Let's see...THINGS - that's 6 letters...CHANGE...that's 6 letters and PRAYER...why that, too, is 6 letters! If only we had known then..."

On the Plains of Esdraelon the armies had received their orders. Quickly they merged as one.

Who were they fighting? There was mass confusion. Here they were one moment ready to tear each other apart...the next moment joining forces against what seemed to be an invisible force.

Suddenly all eyes focused on the sky. What appeared to be a mysterious white cloud way off in the distance was now becoming clearly visible.

It seemed unbelievable. Men everywhere were rubbing their eyes...for they believed that what they saw must be some hallucination...a mirage because of the desert heat.

There in front was a Rider, a magnificent, stately, Kingly rider...a rider on a WHITE HORSE and armies of people were following him; they too on white horses.

> His eyes were as a flame of fire, and on his head were many crowns; and He had a name written, that no man knew, but He himself.
>
> And He was clothed with a vesture dipped in blood: and His name is called The Word of God.
>
> And the armies which were in heaven followed Him upon white horses, clothed in fine linen, white and clean.
>
> And out of his mouth goeth a sharp sword, that with it he should smite the nations: and he shall rule them with a rod of iron: and he treadeth the winepress of the fierceness and wrath of Almighty God.
>
> And he hath on his vesture and on his thigh a name written, KING OF KINGS, AND LORD OF LORDS.

(Revelation 19:12-16)

There was a loud thunder. Then silence. Brother Bartholomew and Leader Chou fell to their knees along with Prophet Arthur. From their vantage point atop the Mount of Olives they could see the entire Plain of Esdraelon on their life-size video screen.

Suddenly there was a loud voice speaking...a voice never before heard by mortal man. The voice of God!

Soon their eyes were directed to the Mount of Olives.

And the entire army of men, multiple millions, fell to the ground dead, as one. THE BATTLE WAS OVER.

Circling overhead it seemed like all the birds of earth were gathered. And as if by command, they swooped down on the inert bodies, gorging themselves with the flesh of men.

Then the greatest earthquake man has ever known suddenly erupted. Cities of all nations around the world collapsed. Giant hailstones, weighing as much as 100 pounds each, fell in an avalanche of death.

> And the remnant were slain with the sword of him that sat upon the horse, which sword proceeded out of his mouth: and all the fowls were filled with their flesh. (Revelation 19:21)

> And the seventh angel poured out his vial into the air; and there came a great voice out of the temple of heaven, from the throne, saying, It is done.
> And there were voices, and thunders, and lightnings; and there was a great earthquake, such as was not since men were upon the earth, so mighty an earthquake, and so great.
> And the great city was divided into three parts, and the cities of the nations fell: and great Babylon came in remembrance before God, to give unto her the cup of the wine of the fierceness of his wrath.

And every island fled away, and the mountains were not found.
And there fell upon men a great hail out of heaven, every stone about the weight of a talent (100 pounds): and men blasphemed God because of the plague of hail; for the plague thereof was exceeding great. (Revelation 16:17-21)

From their vantage point at the Pool of Siloam Faye and George could see the entire action. They were stunned as the reality of all their hopes began to formulate into victory.

Ahead of them a yawning chasm opened. Fire and smoke gushed forth as the earth opened. Almighty God on His White Horse summoned an angel. With him the angel brought a large key and a ghastly chain.

Soon their eyes were directed to the Mount of Olives. Coming from the fortress on top of the Mount were two defeated and humbled figures.. Brother Bartholomew (antichrist) and Prophet Arthur (the false prophet). The angel led them to the awesome chasm. Bound in chains they were thrown into what appeared to be a bottomless pit.

And the beast was taken, and with him the false prophet that wrought miracle before him, with which he deceived them that had received the mark of the beast, and them that worshipped his image. These both were cast alive into a lake of fire burning with brimstone. (Revelation 19:20)

The Lord was off his White Horse now. And his feet were coming to rest on the Mount of Olives. Just as his feet touched the hallowed Mount it split in two, leaving a great valley through the center, with springs of water gushing out of the earth in two directions, part towards the Mediterranean, and part toward the Dead Sea. With the water came many bodies...among them that of Leader Chou.

And His feet shall stand in that day upon the mount of Olives, which is before Jerusalem on the east, and the mount of Olives shall cleave in the midst thereof toward the east and toward the west, and there shall be a very great valley; and half of the mountain shall remove toward the north, and half of it toward the south.
And it shall be in that day, that living waters shall go out from Jerusalem; half of them toward the former sea (Dead Sea), and half of them toward the hinder sea (Mediterranean Sea): in summer and in winter shall it be. (Zechariah 14:4, 8)

Both Faye and George were crying...crying tears of joy at what they saw. And as they looked up God's Army on white horses, clothed in fine linen, white and clean were coming into view. There through the moisture of their tears...there they could see HELEN, little SUE, TOMMY, BILL and TOM MALONE, waving and singing praises to God.

Faye and George held hands, tears streaming down their face...looking up at that wonderful sight...their choking, tearful voices sang in unison...

> It's not the first mile
>   That's so important.
> It's the last mile
>   When day is done.
>
> Then we'll see Jesus
>   In all His splendor
> And He will have for us
>   The Crown we've won.

It was going to be a grand reunion. Their search for tomorrow had ended.

There in front was a Rider, a magnificent, stately, Kingly rider...a rider on a WHITE HORSE and armies of people were following Him; they too on white horses.

What Will You Do With Jesus?

You have just read 666.

It may seem just too fantastic to be true. While it is written in novel form the facts of the RAPTURE (when believing Christians meet Christ in the air)...the Tribulation Period and its judgments...these facts are true! You can find them in the book of Revelation and in other places in the Bible.

Take any Bible...the King James Version, the new revised versions, even the Duoay Version. Those who do not accept the New Testament will find these same prophecies substantially made in the Old Testament book of Daniel.

The main question however is this:

WHAT WILL YOU DO WITH JESUS?

Will you state that He never existed?

Will you simply say He was a good man who did good things?

Will you say His message is not relevant to our enlightened age?

Would you buy a car without first finding out the facts relevant to that car?

Would you invest money in a venture without first finding out details of that organization?

Would you get married without first finding out more about the individual with whom you pledge your entire life?

Your answer would probably be NO to each of these three questions.

Then WHAT ABOUT JESUS? WHAT ABOUT HEAVEN? WHAT ABOUT HELL? WHAT ABOUT ETERNAL LIFE? WHAT ABOUT ETERNAL DAMNATION? WHAT ABOUT YOUR FUTURE AND THAT OF YOUR CHILDREN?

First, I am sure you will agree that your life here on earth will not go on and on. Any funeral director can attest to that fact. Any nurse or doctor can tell you that physical life on this earth someday ceases for each of us.

Second, if you have examined world conditions very carefully, you will admit that the world is certainly not getting better and better. Scientists even acknowledge the fact that the next 30 years will give us more complex problems in population growth, in famine, in crime, and in war.

Third, money (or the lack of it) will not cure your ills nor the ills of the world. Even if the wealth were spread out more evenly it would not resolve the problems. In actuality the spread of wealth worldwide on an even basis would make almost all Americans far poorer than they are now.

Fourth, if you look at it honestly, the permissive use of drugs and sexual freedom from the moral code will not build a better world.

Then what can you do?

Well, you can simply choose to ignore Christ and the Scriptures...go on living your life, doing the best you know how to meet your problems, work and provide an income for your family, set aside a nest egg for retirement...

But THEN WHAT?

What happens when it comes time for you to depart from this earth?

Then WHAT WILL YOU DO WITH JESUS?

It takes NO DECISION on your part to go to Hell!

It does take a DECISION on your part, however, to go to Heaven!

> He that believeth on Him is not condemned:
> but he that believeth not is condemned already,
> because he hath not believed in the name of the
> only begotten Son of God. (John 3:18)

Here are five basic observations in the Bible of which you should be aware:

1. ALL SIN

> For all have sinned, and come short of the glory of God. (Romans 3:23)

2. ALL LOVED

> For God so loved the world, that He gave His only begotten Son, that whosoever believeth in Him should not perish, but have everlasting life (John 3:16)

3. ALL RAISED

> Marvel not at this: for the hour is coming, in which all that are in the graves shall hear his voice,
>
> And shall come forth; they that have done good, unto the resurrection of life; and they that have done evil, unto the resurrection of damnation. (John 5:28,29)

4. ALL JUDGED

> ...we shall all stand before the judgment seat of Christ. (Romans 14:10)
>
> And I saw the dead, small and great, stand before God; and the books were opened....(Revelation 20:12)

5. ALL BOW

> ...at the name of Jesus every knee should bow... (Philippians 2:10)

Right now, in simple faith, you can have the wonderful assurance of eternal life.

Ask yourself, honestly, the question....

WHAT WILL I DO WITH JESUS?

Will you accept Jesus Christ as your personal Saviour and Lord or will you reject Him?

This you must decide yourself. No one else can decide that for you. The basis of your decision should be made on God's Word—the Bible.

God tells us the following:

"...him that cometh to me I will in no wise cast out. (37)
Verily, verily (truly) I say unto you, He that believeth on me (Christ) *hath* everlasting life" (47)—(John 6: 37, 47).

He also is a righteous God and a God of indignation to those who reject Him....

"...he that believeth not is condemned already, because he hath not believed in the name of the only begotten Son of God"—(John 3:18).

"And whosoever was not found written in the book of life was cast into the lake of fire"—(Revelation 20:15).

YOUR MOST IMPORTANT
DECISION IN LIFE

Because sin entered the world and because God hates sin, God sent His Son Jesus Christ to die on the cross to pay the price for your sins and mine.

If you place your trust in Him, God will freely forgive you of your sins.

"For by grace are ye saved through faith; and that not of yourselves: it is the gift of God: (8)
Not of works, lest any man should boast" (9)— (Ephesians 2:8, 9).

"...He that heareth my word, and believeth on Him that sent me, *hath* everlasting life, and shall not come into condemnation: but is passed from death unto life" —(John 5:24).

What about you? Have you accepted Christ as your personal Saviour?

Do you realize that right now you can know the reality of this new life in Christ Jesus. Right now you can dispel the doubt that is in your mind concerning your future and that of your loved ones. Right now you can ask Christ to come into your heart. And right now you can be assured of eternal life in heaven.

All of your riches here on earth—all of your financial security—all of your material wealth, your houses, your land will crumble into nothingness in a few years.

And as God has told us:

"As it is appointed unto men once to die, but after this the judgment: (27)
So Christ was once offered to bear the sins of many; and unto them that look for Him shall He appear the second time without sin unto salvation" (28)— (Hebrews 9:27, 28).

Are you willing to sacrifice an eternity with Christ in Heaven for a few years of questionable material gain that will lead to death and destruction? If you do not accept Christ as your personal Saviour, you have only yourself to blame for the consequences.

Or would you right now, as you are reading these very words of this book, like to know without a shadow of a doubt that you are on the road to Heaven—that death is not the end of life but actually the climactic beginning of the most wonderful existence that will ever be—a life with the Lord Jesus Christ and with your friends, your relatives, and your loved ones who have accepted Christ as their Saviour.

It's not a difficult thing to do. So many religions and so many people have tried to make the simple Gospel message

of Christ complex. You can not work your way into heaven—
heaven is the gift of God to those who believe in Jesus Christ.

No matter how great your works—no matter how kind you
are—no matter how philanthropic you are—it means nothing
in the sight of God, because in the sight of God, your riches
are as filthy rags.

"...all our righteousnesses are as filthy rags..."—
(Isaiah 64:6).

Christ expects you to come as you are, a sinner, recognizing your need of a Saviour, the Lord Jesus Christ.

Understanding this, why not bow your head right now
and give this simple prayer of faith to the Lord.

Say it in your own words. It does not have to be a beautiful
oratorical prayer—simply a prayer of humble contrition.

1000

By
Salem
Kirban

Published by SALEM KIRBAN, Inc., Kent Road, Huntingdon
Valley, Pennsylvania, 19006. Copyright © 1973 by Salem Kirban.
Printed in the United States of America. All rights reserved, including the right to reproduce this book or portions thereof in any
form.

ISBN 0-912582-09-X
Library of Congress Catalog Card No. 72-97136

CAST OF CHARACTERS

RESURRECTED BELIEVERS

Helen Omega: Wife of George Omega. Helen, with her two children, were caught up in the Rapture prior to the Tribulation Period.

Sue & Tommy Omega: Children of George and Helen Omega.

Tom Malone: Was Presidential Secretary to Brother Bartholomew in the Tribulation Period. Because of his Christian testimony, however, Brother Bartholomew snuffed out his life with a death ray from a laser gun.

Bill Sanders: Husband of Faye Sanders. Bill was the first person to die by guillotine in the Tribulation Period because of his Christian testimony.

LIVING BELIEVERS who went through the Tribulation Period

George Omega: Husband of Helen Omega. TV news commentator.

Faye Sanders: Wife of Bill Sanders and daughter of George & Helen Omega. Faye, experienced the trials of the Tribulation Period along with her father, George Omega.

Terry Malone: Wife of Tom Malone. She went through deep trials in the Tribulation Period.

Sylvia Epstein: Wife of Abel Epstein.

OTHER CHARACTERS

Brother Bartholomew: Antichrist. Powerful world leader in the Tribulation Period.

Dr. Curter: Scientist. He, amid the Tribulation Period, had preserved Brother Bartholomew's body in a deep freeze cyro-capsule and eventually rejuvenated him.

Abel Epstein: Husband of Sylvia Epstein. Inventor of the Ruby Laser.

Walter Brinks: Executive in World Television Network.

Harry Sutherland: Vice-President of World Television Network.

Carole Sutherland: Wife of Harry Sutherland.

Phil Sutherland: Nephew of Harry Sutherland.

Esther Sanders: Daughter of Bill and Faye Sanders.

Bart Malone: Son of Tom and Terry Malone.

CONTENTS

ACKNOWLEDGMENTS

To **Dr. Gary G. Cohen,** Professor of Greek and New Testament at Biblical School of Theology, Hatfield, Pennsylvania, who carefully checked the final manuscript and supplied many helpful suggestions which have been incorporated in this book.

To **Frank Nofer,** artist, who skillfully designed the front cover.

To **Dick Miller,** artist, who captured many of the events in this book in illustration form.

To **Robert Krauss,** who coordinated all the art work and designed the charts.

To **Doreen Frick,** who devoted many hours to proofreading the text.

To **Batsch Company,** for excellent craftsmanship in setting the type.

To **Walter W. Slotilock,** Chapel Hill Litho, for making many of the negatives necessary for printing.

To **Dickinson Brothers, Inc.,** for printing with all possible speed and quality.

To **Diane Kirban,** H. Armstrong Roberts and many other photographers who pooled their resources so that we may have photos that convey the message of this book.

All Scriptures verses used, unless otherwise identified, are from the King James Version of the Bible.

The New American Standard Bible (ASV) By Permission of The Lockman Foundation.

The Amplified New Testament By Permission of The Lockman Foundation.

The Amplified Old Testament, Part 1, Copyright © 1962 by Zondervan Publishing House. Used by Permission.

The Amplified Old Testament, Part 2, Copyright © 1964 by Zondervan Publishing House. Used by Permission.

FORWARD

Salem Kirban's latest book, **1000**, comes to the public as one of the freshest pieces of thinking in the field of Bible prophecy seen in the last few years. It is a work about the future Millennial Age—about which there are so few books in print.

All pre-millennialists should welcome this volume because they, too, believe that: (a) there will yet be a literal one thousand year reign of peace and harmony upon the earth; and (b) this reign will only begin when Christ Himself inaugurates it at His Second Coming. Thus this book should find a welcome because we believe that the above, which are incorporated into the very warp and woof of Mr. Kirban's book, are the clear teachings of the Bible, which is the very Word of God.

A word of caution, however, should be given to the Bible scholar who reads this book. The purpose of this book is to acquaint the reader with the MAJOR TEACHINGS of the Bible concerning this coming Millennial 1000 Year Age. This purpose is achieved through the vehicle of a story whose details are a made-up fiction BUILT UPON BIBLE TRUTH. One simply must not allow himself to toss the whole book aside with its Bible truth simply because here or there he discovers that on SOME DETAIL another Bible scholar or writer has suggested a different interpretation than found herein.

To that one who seeks after the Biblical truth concerning the Millennium, let him open his Bible to Revelation chapter 20 and Isaiah chapter 11. There he will read of the glory and peace of this coming wonderful era, and he will see that it will be 1000 years in length and that Satan will be then bound "that he should deceive the nations no more till the thousand years should be fulfilled" (Revelation 20:3). Then let him turn to Zechariah 14:16-21, Isaiah 65:20, and to Revelation 20:7-9 and he will learn that there will be imperfections and sin (though held down) even during this Golden Age as new unredeemed children are born into the millennial world. Finally, let the reader pass from Revelation chapter 20 to chapter 21, and realize that the Millennial 1000 Years are the gateway to that perfect eternity with Christ our Messiah for which we all long. It is upon these great truths that this fictional work is built.

Lastly, let us say that Mr. Kirban's scenes of judgment should cause each of us to examine ourselves. The fright and grief that they portray are certainly true to the Biblical picture...just as is the abundant joy painted by Mr. Kirban upon the faces of those who know and love Christ throughout this and then the coming age. This is surely a book to read, a book to cause us to examine ourselves, and a book to give to others.

Gary G. Cohen, Th.D.
Professor of New Testament
Biblical School of Theology
April, 1973   Hatfield, Pennsylvania

WHY I WROTE THIS BOOK

Ever since I wrote the book **666,** a novel on the Tribulation Period, I felt compelled to finish writing on God's complete panorama of prophecy.

The logical follow-up would be a book on the 1000 year Millennial Age since this period comes after the 7 year Tribulation Period.

And that's what troubled me! The little research I had done through the years on the Millennium convinced me...that while it was a period of unsurpassed blessings...there was not much available detail on this in Scriptures that could fill a novel.

I had accepted Christ as my personal Saviour at 8 years of age at Montrose Bible Conference in Montrose, Pennsylvania.

As I recalled the many, many years I sat under Bible teaching and preaching, I could not recall ever hearing a message on the Millennium. I am sure that there have been messages given on this portion of Bible truth, but my impression is that they are few and far between.

This amazed me.

The Millennium...a period where believers will spend 1000 years! And yet very little is said about it from our pulpits.

This, in part, convinced me that perhaps there wasn't much to say about the Millennium.

But my heart would not give me an inner peace. The Lord was telling me to write a book on the 1000 years. And I knew I would not have peace until I did so.

I began to personally search the Scriptures...reading all available books on the subject...checking and cross-checking.

This would not be an easy book to write. It would be like building a house. I would have to map out a very extensive blueprint of what the Millennium is, its blessings, its government, its activities, and its participants.

Hours and hours of research were finally condensed into 11 pages of framework.

Finally I was ready to write the book. I felt the form of a novel would best explain all the details Scripture tells us about this 1000 year Millennium Period.

This would not be a novel in the ordinary sense of the word. Events and characters would have to be plausable...and the sequence of events and the events themselves must dovetail into what God tells us about the Millennium. This took careful weaving of the fabric of the story line.

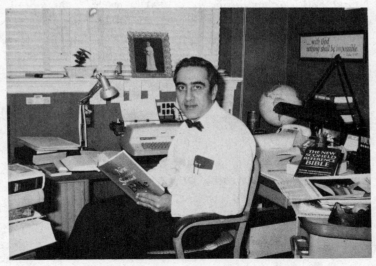

Author finishing last chapter of book **1000.**

The book has ten chapters. Actually, the research and the building of an 11-page framework took more time than the writing of the book!

Before I began each chapter I asked the Lord for guidance, clarity of mind and fluidity of thought. He answered my prayers.

Following the pattern of **666,** I believed it very important that Bible references be included right in the paragraphs to which they pertain.

While this is a novel, and the characters are fictitious, it is important to remember that the framework of the book is anchored in biblical FACT.

There WILL BE a 1000 year Millennium Period.

There WILL BE a Judgment, just prior to this period, of the Nation Israel.

There WILL BE a Judgment also of the Gentiles.

There WILL BE great social and economic changes.

Satan WILL BE bound in the bottomless pit during this 1000 years and then be released at the end of this period for a brief time.

God WILL reign during this 1000 years in a Theocratic government whose headquarters will be in Jerusalem!

May I suggest you read THE SEQUENCE OF EVENTS (on succeeding pages) which gives you a bird's-eye view of the entire Millennial Age on which the book **1000** was based.

May I make one more suggestion.

The book **1000** was NOT written to entertain. Undoubtedly many who read this book will consider it an interesting science-fiction story. IT IS NOT!

This book deals with LIFE and DEATH.

Your life...or your death!

You have a life span of only some 70 years here on earth.

You have a life span of an eternity...after death...

either resurrected with Christ
to spend an eternity in Heaven

or

resurrected to meet Christ as your Judge
at the Great White Throne Judgment
and condemned
    to spend an eternity in the Lake of Fire!
(Revelation 20:11-15)

Where should your priorities lie? With this present life or making sure of your final destination in a life where you will spend all of eternity!

In the presence of eternity, the mountains are as transient as the clouds.

It was Daniel Defoe who wrote back in 1701:

Wherever God erects a house of prayer,
The Devil always builds a chapel there;
And 'twill be found, upon examination,
The latter has the largest congregation.

Before you read **1000**...determine to read it as though you are actually playing a part in this Millennium Period.

After reading the book, if you find your own beliefs (or lack of them) places you in the congregation of the damned...then chapter 10 can be the most important chapter in your life. And it can point you to life.

My prayer is that you might choose life!

That's why I wrote this book!

Salem Kirban
Huntingdon Valley, Pennsylvania
April, 1973

THE COMING SEQUENCE OF EVENTS
in GOD'S PROPHETIC TIMETABLE

The sequence of events, according to God's Word, the Bible, appears to be as follows:

RAPTURE, including the FIRST RESURRECTION

This can occur at any time. Believing Christians (both dead and alive) will "in the twinkling of an eye" rise up to meet Christ in the air. Read 1 Thessalonians 4:13-17 and Revelation 20.

TRIBULATION

This will be a period of 7 years, following the Rapture, of phenomenal world trial and suffering. It is at this time that Antichrist will reign over a federation of 10 nations which quite possibly could include the United States. See Daniel 9:27 and Matthew 24:21.

*BATTLE of ARMAGEDDON

This will occur at the end of the 7 year Tribulation Period when the Lord Jesus Christ comes down from Heaven and wipes out the combined armies of more than 200 million men. The blood bath covers over 185 miles of Israel. See Revelation 14:20, and 19:11-21.

(While there is a 7 year period of Tribulation on earth... believers, who have already been raptured into heaven, will stand before their Lord to receive crowns and rewards. Their sins have already been paid for at the cross. See 2 Corinthians 5:10. This is called the **JUDGMENT SEAT OF CHRIST**).

*JUDGMENT of the NATION ISRAEL

Before the 1000 year Millennium begins all **living** Israel will be regathered in Palestine (Ezekiel 20:35). The unbelievers will be cut off (Ezekiel 20:37) and cast into Hades, and eventually into the Lake of Fire (Matthew 25:30). The believers, those who have accepted Jesus Christ as Messiah and Lord, will be taken into the Millennium (Ezekiel 20:40-44).

*JUDGMENT of the GENTILES

Before the 1000 year Millennium but after the Judgment of the Nation Israel...all **living** Gentiles who have survived the Tribulation Period will be regathered in Jerusalem (Joel 3:2; Zechariah 14:4). The unbelievers will be cast into Hades, and eventually into the Lake of Fire (Matthew 25: 41). The believers, those who have accepted Jesus Christ as Saviour and Lord, will live on earth for the Millennium Period (Matthew 25:34).

*RESURRECTION of the TRIBULATION SAINTS

Those who have accepted Christ during the Tribulation Period will be raised from the dead by the close of the Tribulation's 7 years as part of the First Resurrection (Daniel 12:1-2 and Revelation 20).

*DISPOSITION OF EVIL ONES

During this same period...at the end of the Tribulation... Antichrist and the False Prophet are thrown into the Lake of Fire (Revelation 19:20).

Satan is bound in the bottomless pit for 1000 years (Revelation 20:1-3).

*MILLENNIUM (1000 Years) **REIGN OF CHRIST**

This is a period when all the believers of all the ages reign with Christ. Those previously resurrected in the Rapture and those saints who died in the Tribulation and were *resurrected*...will reign with Christ in the Millennial Age as **Resurrected believers.** They will be given positions of responsibility in the Millennial Kingdom (Matthew 19:28, Luke 19:12-27).

The saved of Israel will again be in a position of prominence (Isaiah 49:22-23). They will be given positions of leadership (Isaiah 61:5-6). Gentiles and Jews alike who are still *living* at the close of the Battle of Armageddon, and who are permitted to enter the Millennial Kingdom, are known as **Living Believers.** These were not raptured (they were not believers at the time of the Rapture), nor did they die in the Tribulation period (they survived). They are still in their human unresurrected bodies.

During the Millennium these **Living Believers** will still be able to reproduce children. Children born of these Living Believers will still be born with a sin nature. And for them, salvation is still required. They must individually make a decision whether to accept Jesus Christ as Saviour and Lord...or to deny Him (Ezekiel 36:37-38; Jeremiah 30:19-20).

*THE FINAL REBELLION

At the end of the 1000 year Millennium Period, Satan will have a brief and last opportunity to deceive people. You must remember that many will be born during the Millennial Period. Millions will follow Satan. This vast number of people will completely encircle the Living Believers within Jerusalem in a state of siege.

When this occurs, God brings fire down from Heaven killing the millions of Satan's army (Revelation 20).

*GREAT WHITE THRONE JUDGMENT

This is when the unsaved, non-believers, of all of the ages are resurrected and are judged before God. These are condemned forever to the Lake of Fire. Both living (from the Millennium) and dead **unsaved** are judged here. Those previously dead, up to this point, have already been in hell in torment, awaiting this Final Judgment Day (Revelation 20:11-15).

EARTH BURNS UP

To purify this earth, so tainted with the scars of sin, God sets it afire with a fervent heat. See 2 Peter 3:7,10.

The NEW HEAVENS and the NEW EARTH

All Christians finally reach the ultimate in glory reigning forever with Christ in a new heaven and a new earth (Revelation 21).

*Those time periods preceded by an asterisk (*) are the area that the novel **1000** covers. If you give special attention to these portions of God's Plan for tomorrow, you will understand the book **1000** much better.

Chapter 1 of the book **1000** begins with the final stages of the BATTLE OF ARMAGEDDON.

(Anyone interested in a detailed examination of why these events are placed in this order, etc., may refer to J. Dwight Pentecost's large reference book, *Things to Come;* Grand Rapids: Zondervan Publishing Co., 1958. See pages 370-546.)

THE PROMISED LAND

Fulfilling God's promise to Abraham (Genesis 15:18), this is the area the Jews will occupy in the 1000 year Millennial reign of Christ.

Present area of Israel including occupied territories

The Promised Land

Copyright © 1973 by Salem Kirban

Persian Gulf

KUWAIT

Euphrates River

IRAQ

850 miles

Hamath (Numbers 13:21)

200 miles

350 miles

SYRIA

Damascus

Sea of Galilee

Amman

Dead Sea

River of Egypt (El Arish)

LEBANON

Beirut

ISRAEL

Jerusalem

JORDAN

Elath

Gulf of Aqaba

SAUDI ARABIA

CYPRUS

Mediterranean Sea

KADESH BARNEA

SINAI

Suez Canal

Cairo

Suez

Gulf of Suez

Red Sea

U.A.R. (Egypt)

IN EXPLANATION

While this book...**1000**
deals with the conflicts
    just prior to the Millennium
    and in the Millennium itself,
Believers
    (those who have accepted Christ as
    Lord and Saviour)
should realize that for them it will be 1000 years of almost perfect happiness and contentment.

WHAT AN INHERITANCE!

All of the wonderful things which man has vainly sought in his own strength, without God, will at last be poured out in the Kingdom of His Son during the 1000 year MILLENNIUM.

    With Satan imprisoned during this time (Revelation 20:1-7) . . . the Millennium Period will be one of

  1. PEACE
    Because there will be no war, nations will not have to devote a great part of their budget to war materials. There will be an economic prosperity such as never before has been experienced.

                               (Isaiah 11:6-9)

    Perhaps the most well-known verse in relation to this is: "And He shall judge between the nations, and shall decide (disputes) for many people; and they shall beat their swords into plowshares, and their spears into pruning hooks; nation shall not lift up sword against nation, neither shall they learn war any more."

                        (Isaiah 2:4 Amplified Bible)

Many political leaders use this verse referring to the goals of this present world. However, this verse refers to the coming MILLENNIUM 1000 YEAR AGE . . . not to this present age.

2. HAPPINESS
This will be the fulfillment of happiness because there will be no more war nor will there be the multitude of sorrows now present to man on this earth.

(Revelation 20:3; Isaiah 11:6-9)

"Therefore with joy will you draw water from the wells of salvation."

(Isaiah 12:3 Amplified Bible)

3. LONG LIFE AND HEALTH
Here in the 1000 year Millennial Period both sickness and death will be well nigh removed. Death will not be banished completely, however, during this period. Open sin may cause some to die because the Millennial Period, while filled with multiple blessings is still not the end of God's final judgments.

(Isaiah 65:20)

Keep these things in mind, however:
A. The DEFORMED will be HEALED
"And in that day shall the deaf hear the words of the book, and out of obscurity and gloom and darkness the eyes of the blind shall see."

(Isaiah 29:18 Amplified Bible; also read Isaiah 35:5,6)

B. SICKNESS will be REMOVED
"And no inhabitant will say, I am sick. . . ."

(Isaiah 33:24 Amplified Bible)

C. SEXUAL REPRODUCTION will EXIST
Those saints who live through the Tribulation Period and enter the 1000 MILLENNIUM in their natural bodies will be able to have children throughout this 1000 year age. In fact the population of the earth will once again become great.

But it must be kept in mind that those who are born DURING the 1000 year Millennial Age will have a sin nature and it WILL be necessary for them to accept Christ if they are to participate in the final and continuing eternity that begins after this 1000 year period.

Here are two more verses to help you understand this wonderful blessing:

"Out of them shall come songs of thanksgiving and the voices of those who make merry. And I will multiply them, and they shall not be few; I will also glorify them, and they shall not be small."

"Their children too shall be as in former times. . . ."
(Jeremiah 30:19,20 Amplified Bible)

4. PROSPERITY

The Millennium Period will be one of unequalled prosperity. There will be such an abundance that there will be no want.

Perhaps the most familiar verse . . . and one we hear quoted as only beginning to come to pass today . . . is the verse below, which actually refers to the 1000 year MILLENNIUM PERIOD:

"The wilderness and the dry land shall be glad, the desert shall rejoice and blossom as the rose and the autumn crocus.

It shall blossom abundantly, and rejoice even with joy and singing; the glory of Lebanon shall be given to it, the excellency of Mount Carmel and the plain of Sharon. . . ."
(Isaiah 35:1,2 Amplified Bible)

Think about this for a moment!

Here will be a desert that will have all the *glory of Lebanon* given to it! The glory of Lebanon is found in the strength and stateliness of its cedars. *The excellency of Carmel and Sharon,* which consisted of corn and cattle, will likewise then characterize this transformed desert!

5. A JOY IN LABOR

Under the direction of Christ there will be a perfect economic system in which people will work in complete joy and desire to provide the necessities of life.

"They shall build houses and inhabit them, and they shall plant vineyards and eat the fruit of them . . . My chosen and elect shall long make use of and enjoy the work of their hands."
(Isaiah 65:21,22 Amplified Bible)

6. LANGUAGE WILL BE PURE

In this blessed period language will not be used for taking God's name in vain or for other wrong purposes. Lips will glorify and praise God. Perhaps the language of the earth will at this time be unified.

"For then I will give to the people a clear and pure speech from pure lips . . ."

(Zephaniah 3:9 Amplified Bible)

7. GOD WILL BE PRESENT
This will be a time when we can fellowship with God and enjoy His manifested presence in a special way.

"My tabernacle or dwelling place also shall be with them; and I will be their God. . . ."

"The abode of God is with men, and He will live among them, and they shall be His people and God shall personally be with them and be their God."

(Ezekiel 37:27, Revelation 21:3 Amplified Bible)

While much of this book. . .**1000**, deals with the conflicts of the early days immediately following the Tribulation, the reader should remember that the vast majority of the time of the Millennium (hundreds of years) will be filled with an abundance of prosperity, happiness and international goodwill.

There will be virtually no sickness, no poverty, no death. The limited exceptions are incorporated in this book. . .**1000**.

The greatest battle this world will ever experience and the largest casualty rate in history will occur at the end of the 1000 Millennium Period when Satan is loosed for a brief period of time.

With this background information in mind you should be able to read the novel **1000** with greater understanding.

Salem Kirban

3 DECISIVE WARS

War	Participants	Occurs	Reason for War	Outcome	Scripture References
1	Russia and Allies (Arab nations, Iran, Germany) vs. Israel	Before or during first 3½ years of Tribulation Period (This could happen at any time!)	Russia desires Israel's vast mineral wealth.	God will intervene and through an earthquake in Israel plus rain and hail, the Russian army will be wiped out. It will take the Israelites 7 years to collect the debris. It will also take them 7 months to bury the dead!	Ezekiel 38:1–39:16
2 Battle of Armageddon	Armies from All Nations vs. God at Jerusalem	At End of 7 year Tribulation Period	Flushed with power Antichrist will defy God, seek to destroy the 144,000 witnessing Jews and Jerusalem.	The Lord Jesus Christ comes down from heaven and wipes out the combined armies of more than 200 million men. The blood bath covers over 185 miles of Israel and is "even unto the horse bridles." (Revelation 14:20) Antichrist and the False Prophet are cast alive into the Lake of Fire. (Revelation 19:20) Satan is bound in the bottomless pit for 1000 years. (Revelation 20:1-3)	Joel 3:9, 12 Zechariah 14:1-4 Revelation 16:13-16 Revelation 19:11-21 Ezekiel 39:17-29
3 The Final Rebellion	Satan vs. God	At End of 1000 year Millennium Period	God allows Satan one more opportunity on earth to preach his deceiving message.	Satan will be successful in deceiving vast multitudes (out of those born during the millennial period) to turn away from Christ. This horde of perhaps millions of people will completely circle the Believers in Jerusalem in a state of siege. When this occurs, God brings FIRE down from Heaven killing the millions in Satan's army. Satan is then cast into the Lake of Fire, where the False Prophet and Antichrist are, and they will be tormented day and night for ever and ever.	Revelation 20:7-10

Copyright © 1972, Salem Kirban, Huntingdon Valley, Penna., U.S.A.

Chapter 1

THE GREAT REUNION

What he saw seemed like a dream. Could it be true? Or would he suddenly wake up into reality?

After struggling through seven long years for survival...against what seemed to be incredible odds...victory seemed impossible.

And George Omega was crying. Imagine, he a grown man...crying.

But George Omega could not hold back the tears.

A hardened newspaperman who had witnessed and reported on many tragedies...a man who had seen death first hand...had related stories of man's inhumanity to man...had come to accept both the joys and the tragedies as "matter of fact." As anchorman for the World Television Network...he had once been respected...but these last seven years he was hunted. And the hunter was Brother Bartholomew, President of the United States of Europe.

Now it was all over. No more running.

Suddenly the reality of it all hit him...like a blast of cold air refreshing a steamy desert.

And he cried!

With tears streaming down his rugged face...he turned to Faye Sanders, his daughter...

"Faye, it's over. It's over. Praise God...every promise of the Bible IS true!"

"Daddy, you're crying. And I'm so happy, too. Daddy, the King is here...and NOTHING WILL EVER BE THE SAME AGAIN!"

I remembered the many times I had arrived home by plane and searched the crowds for my wife, Helen.

> And it shall be said in that day, Lo, this is our God; we have waited for Him, and He will save us: this is the Lord; we have waited for Him, we will be glad and rejoice in His salvation.
> (Isaiah 25:9)

And she was never there. I had never understood the Rapture. The sea of faces brought me quickly to reality. It was then that I had realized that not only Helen but also our two children, Sue and Tommy, no longer lived on earth. I feared that this separation would be eternal. And that would be a long time.

How often I had remembered quoting from *Antony and Cleopatra* the familiar line:

"Eternity was in our lips and eyes."

And Helen would burst into tears...hold me tightly (as though in the mere holding she could snatch me from an eternity of separation).

I'll never forget the look of love in her eyes as she would softly quote a poem she had written which she called her "poem of love."

Even now I could still hear her voice:

> Eternity is not a moment's tears
> For those who turn away
> Eternity is endless years
> A night with no more day!

Helen knew me better than I knew myself. And somehow I guess she knew that I would never make it at the Rapture. I got the feeling that she was preparing me for what was ahead. And each time she came to that second verse, she would clutch me close to her, look up into my eyes, softly kiss me, and as the tears came tumbling down her cheeks, repeat:

> Eternity is not a moment's love
> For those who seek His light
> Eternity is Heaven above
> A day with no more night!

I was so overcome with emotion...I whispered these last lines into Faye's ear.

"Think of it, Faye, it's here...a day with no more night."

I was referring to the fact that soon Helen and our family and Bill Sanders, Faye's husband, would all be together again.

Little did I realize the significance of that statement.

And that's why I was crying!

The heavens had opened. Suddenly the dark clouds disappeared. It was like taking off on a rainy, gloomy day and suddenly breaking through the cloud barrier into brilliant sunlight.

Our days of stumbling in darkness, in defeat, in despair were over. Suddenly it was as though over the entire earth a heavenly light had been switched on. Darkness had simply disappeared ...vanished. Everything was light.

Faye and I searched the sea of faces coming down from the Heavens. I can remember the first time I saw man actually land on the moon. It just seemed unbelievable.

And this scene was even more unbelievable. There...actually coming down from the Heavens was Jesus Christ...actually riding on a white horse...and there riding with Him were the troops of Heaven. It was a scene of joy for Faye and me...but the very countenance of Christ was one of judgment.

...justice is far from us, and righteousness does not overtake us; We hope for light, but behold, darkness; For brightness, but we walk in gloom.

We grope along the wall like blind men, We grope like those who have no eyes; We stumble at midday as in the twilight, Among those who are vigorous we are like dead men.

(Isaiah 59:9-10 ASV)

For it will be a unique day which is known to the Lord, neither day nor night; but it will come about that at evening time there will be light.

(Zechariah 14:7 ASV)

There...actually coming down from the Heavens was Jesus Christ...and riding with Him were the troops of Heaven.

It was then that I caught a familiar face. After years of searching the crowds at airports ...now in the sky, I could see Helen, Sue, Tommy and Bill... and even Tom Malone who had saved my life a short time ago... at the expense of his.

Faye was jumping up and down for joy. "Daddy, look there's Bill! And look, over there, it's little Sue with Tommy. But, Daddy, they're no longer small. What happened? Why they've grown up!"

"Faye, there's a lot we don't know right now...but soon it will all be made clear. I haven't seen them for years...and yet we recognize them. Faye, I'm so happy."

> And I saw heaven opened, and behold a white horse; and He that sat upon him was called Faithful and True, and in righteousness He doth judge and make war.
>
> His eyes were as a flame of fire, and on His head were many crowns; and He had a name written that no man knew, but He Himself.
>
> And He was clothed with a vesture dipped in blood: and His name is called The Word of God.
>
> And the armies which were in heaven followed Him upon white horses, clothed in fine linen, white and clean.
>
> And out of His mouth goeth a sharp sword, that with it He should smite the nations: and He shall rule them with a rod of iron: and He treadeth the winepress of the fierceness and wrath of Almighty God.
>
> (Revelation 19:11-15)

"Daddy, how will I talk to them? Will their bodies be like mine? Will they recognize us? Will we be married? Will Bill still be my husband?"

"Faye, easy now, I'm just as confused as you. I could kick myself for not reading up on Bible prophecy. And now, I just don't have the answers. Come to think of it, I can remember Helen saying she had never heard anyone preach on the Millennium."

"Millennium? What's that Daddy?"

"Millennium means *1000 years,* Faye. That's one thing I remember. After the 7 years of Tribulation...which we just went through...comes this 1000 years."

"But why wouldn't anyone preach about it, Daddy?"

"Oh, I suppose some ministers have...but Helen never heard a message on it. I remember in those Last Days before Helen was raptured...the few times I did go to church...seems to me the big theme was love. I got the feeling they believed love would cure everything. Their hypocrisy sickened me...they spent more money on building large churches and selling everyone on bigger and bigger congregations...so much so they never had time to pray for little Mrs. Smith who was sick...or old Mr. Jones...that is, unless he had money."

"Did Mom ever mention hearing anything about the future age?"

"Yes, Faye, she attended a church where prophecy was preached quite regularly...so much so that the man was labeled a sensationalist. But I don't recall her saying that even he preached on the Millennium."

"Guess he just couldn't understand it, Daddy."

"Guess not, I know I don't. But we know it's real, Faye... because it's here...RIGHT NOW!"

* * *

Sylvia Caraway had tasted of every luxury. She had considered herself fortunate. "Marry a rich Jewish man," her mother told her, "they treat their wives well, and life will be a bed of roses."

For a while it proved more than that...it was a bed of orchids.

And Sylvia loved every minute of it...or at least she thought so.

Sylvia had grown up in the tenement row houses of Brooklyn. Poverty—she had plenty of it. Everday was potato soup. She got her greatest childhood thrills by joining her friends in smashing school windows, jamming typewriter keys, and setting schools on fire. One day she read where the city of New York spent $1 million just replacing school windows. It thrilled her to know she had a part in this carnage.

At the age of 14 she had experienced every known thrill. And from that day on she set her sights on marrying a millionaire.

Then one day she met Abel...and she knew that this was her man.

Abel Epstein had a corner on the teen magazines and record

publishing business. Everything his hand touched seemed to turn to gold.

When they were married in Palm Springs...Abel gave her a $25,000 Rolls-Royce. Nothing was too good for her. "Sylvia," he would say, "your bed of orchids is made possible by the teenage bubblegum set."

Abel gave her a $25,000 Rolls-Royce. Nothing was too good for her.

Then he would go on to explain how he and others made millions on record promotions. He told me that in 1971 the Osmond Brothers, David Cassidy, the Jackson Five and a couple others collected royalties on more than $60 million worth of nonrecord merchandise alone...shirts, posters and the like.

But this was too easy for Abel...and soon he was tinkering in experiments with light. That's how he got involved in the Laser Beam market.

"Sylvia," he said one day, "I always did like the impossible and I think I've latched on to a moneymaker."

I'll never forget, Sylvia recalled to herself, the day Abel finally came up with a winner—the Laser Ring.

Somehow I was frightened when one day we were visited by

Brother Bartholomew. Why was he so interested in this discovery? Why did he make Abel feel so important...important enough to offer him a post in government.

That's all Abel needed.

"Sylvia, I've reached the top. For once in my life, I'm really important."

I questioned that.

"Important for what, Abel, because your new invention can kill masses quickly? Have you so easily forgotten your own people and what Hitler did to them in Germany?"

"Don't talk foolish, Sylvia. We're living in an enlightened age. Brother Bartholomew assures me this Laser Ring will be used in the pursuit of peace."

Somehow, I couldn't believe him. But once Abel made up his mind...no one changed it. He gave me plenty of money. So why worry? For me the life to live would be continuous luxury. But somehow, worry I did.

Within a short time we flew to Jerusalem. "That's where all the action is," Abel kept telling me. And action there was. It was to change my life.

It was there I came across a book that at first appeared to me to be science-fiction.

It told about the Tribulation Period of 7 years...about a rising man of peace who would become a man of terror. Then it all came back to me. My early childhood years...church... those Sundays when I put off accepting Christ as my Saviour. Then my life had more than ever become filled with sin and greed.

But there in Jerusalem amid those awful tribulation period years, I at last repented and turned to Christ as my Saviour. The glow of the world had suddenly lost its luster. For the first time in my life I found real abiding peace, and the riches that surrounded me seemed like filthy rags. **But we are all as an unclean thing, and all our righteousnesses are as filthy rags; and we all do fade as a leaf; and our iniquities, like the wind, have taken us away.   (Isaiah 64:6)**

I wanted to tell my new-found discovery to someone but I knew Abel would laugh in my face. I can still hear him now, "Don't

tell me Sylvia's got religion.
Your religion is in your mink coat, your Rolls-Royce, your jet-set friends, your houseful of servants...come on baby... don't spoil it for us...live it up."

Whatever I would say would simply fall on deaf ears. And each time I did try to witness to him of the tragedy that would befall him...he would laugh all the harder.

"Sylvia, you've got some imagination. You ought to write a novel. Who ever heard of God coming down from the sky...and on a horse at that...and all those so-called Christians that died ...riding on white horses. What a laugh. Why 99% of those people never rode a horse in their life...let alone riding a horse some 10,000 feet in the air. Won't that be a sight!"

I knew it was useless. It would have been easier fabricating a lie...something really out in left field.

"Hell? Sylvia there is no hell and no heaven. Hell is here on earth. I worked hard for my money. That's heaven. And let me cut you off without one red cent. And you'll find that's hell!"

That was the final straw. Tears came to my eyes. Abel had been so thoroughly brainwashed. He was already believing a lie! It was like a cancer that was eating within him. And nothing I could say would change his mind.

Do you know what it is to stumble across some good news ...and have no one to share it with? That's how I felt. Abel wouldn't listen, and his friends were equally as deaf to the impending tragedy.

And for this cause God shall send them strong delusion, that they should believe a lie.
(2 Thessalonians 2:11)

That's when I thought of Terry Malone. She knew what suffering was all about. Her husband Tom had been Presidential Secretary to Brother Bartholomew. And it was Abel's cruel invention, the Ruby Laser, that had snuffed out Tom's life a short time ago...a death ray directed from the sinister hand of Brother Bartholomew.

But Terry had acted strangely lately. Up until a few days ago she was always telling me about Christ. In whispered tones she often urged me to decide now for Christ...unravelling the panorama of events that was to happen. And while I found her story fantastic, her warmth and dedication impressed me. I knew I could turn to her in a time of stress.

But now, it appeared as though a shadow had crossed her path. And when I rushed to tell her the good news...that Terry Malone's Saviour was my Saviour, too...there was a veiled happiness on her face.

I knew that since Tom's death she had been on Brother Bartholomew's social calendar. Rumors had it that BB (as we called him) had made a secret visit to her home when Tom ran off with George Omega and his daughter, Faye Sanders. That's when Tom was blasted into eternity by the Ruby Laser.

"Terry," I said, "I thought you'd be the happiest person in the world when I told you the good news that I'm in Christ now ...I have no more fears...why even my desire for easy living and wealth are gone...I wouldn't even mind scrubbing floors. Terry, when you hear me say that...you know it's for real."

Terry in a half-hearted smile replied: "I am glad, Sylvia, very glad. It's just that...oh, never mind...you would never understand. Please forgive me."

Suddenly the sky lit up. Such brightness I had never seen. I knew something was about to happen.

And my only regret was that Terry was not sharing in that joy.

* * *

Abel Epstein had reached the top. Right there at Megiddo he was helping Brother Bartholomew in the movement of armies on that vast plain.

"I think we have those Chinese licked, sir. It's just hard to tell, the clouds are obstructing my view."

A grin of smug satisfaction wreathed his face as he thought, "Wait till I tell Sylvia how we licked that Chinese Army of 200 million men...me and BB. Bet I'll become Presidential Adviser after this."

"Sir," Epstein directed his comments to Brother Bartholomew, "looks like Israel is going to be ours. Reports indicate that Jerusalem has just about had it!"

"Glad to hear that Abel. With Jerusalem falling, the whole world will be ours. This puts you in line for a promotion, too. Now the world will know who to believe in. Those Bible prophets swayed too many of our people. We'll set them straight."

Nothing could have made Abel happier. In his record selling days he was known as a wheeler and dealer. He knew all the angles. He prided himself in the fact that he could "sell refrigerators in Alaska." In no way would he miss out on this victory. And, if Sylvia, was right and there was a Heaven and Hell...

For thus saith the Lord of hosts; After the glory hath He sent me unto the nations which spoiled you: for he that toucheth you toucheth the apple of His eye.

(Zechariah 2:8)

And in that day will I make Jerusalem a burdensome stone for all people: all that burden themselves with it shall be cut in pieces, though all the people of the earth be gathered together against it.

And it shall come to pass in that day, that I will seek to destroy all the nations that come against Jerusalem.

(Zechariah 12:3,9)

he'd deal himself right into Heaven too.

Suddenly it seemed as if the world stood still.

The heavens opened.

He gasped in amazement as he looked into the sky. There were those horses...with riders. The leader appeared to have eyes of penetrating fire.

Reports were jamming Brother Bartholomew's control tower of operations.

"Our armored cavalrymen are going blind, sir. They appear disoriented."

"Get the officers to keep them in check," BB bellowed.

"Can't sir, even the officers seem berserk...like they're going mad. Advise instructions. I can't control the army any longer but ...."

In that day, says the Lord, I will smite every horse [of the armies that contend against Jerusalem] with terror and panic, and his rider with madness; and I will open My eyes and regard with favor the house of Judah, and will smite every horse of the opposing nations with blindness.

(Zechariah 12:4 Amplified Bible)

Abel Epstein quickly turned on all orbiting TV stations. The entire wall in front of him was a panel of pictures. The carnage of death that filled the screens was unbelievable!

With that came sudden silence as though his sentence had been cut short even before completion.

Abel Epstein quickly turned on all orbiting TV stations. The entire wall in front of him was a panel of pictures...each showing a portion of the plains that lie before them.

> Now this will be the plague with which the Lord will strike all the peoples who have gone to war against Jerusalem; their flesh will rot while they stand on their feet, and their eyes will rot in their sockets, and their tongue will rot in their mouth.
> (Zechariah 14:12 ASV)

The carnage of death that filled the screens was unbelievable... and everywhere there appeared to be thousands of blind soldiers being trampled on by stampeding men, vehicles, and horses.

Suddenly a staggering light pierced the sanctity of BB's control center.

> And he shall plant the tabernacles of his palace between the seas in the glorious holy mountain; yet he shall come to his end, and none shall help him.
> (Daniel 11:45)

Abel Epstein blinked his eyes... turned around...but Brother Bartholomew had vanished!

* * *

To Faye and George it was like having a box seat at the Inauguration of a President.

Standing on the Mount of Olives they had witnessed the flash of light that suddenly struck in the direction of Megiddo. At that time they did not realize that Brother Bartholomew had quickly met his end and was now in the Lake of Fire.

Both Faye and George knew that reunion with their loved ones would soon be accomplished.

> And the beast [Antichrist] was taken, and with him the false prophet that wrought miracles before him, with which he deceived them that had received the mark of the beast, and them that worshipped his image. These both were cast alive into a lake of fire burning with brimstone. (Revelation 19:20)

"Daddy, what will it be like? Will I be able to touch mom and talk to her? Will I be able to kiss Bill...just like when we first met?"

Then the reality of all those years struck home. All they had yearned for was about to happen.

Would it be too much for them?

It was a time when they should be filled with joy...yet, there was some apprehension.

"I just don't know, Faye, I just don't know. Helen, Sue and Tommy and Bill and even Tom Malone will have new bodies. We do know that. They will be real bodies of flesh and bones. But they will be resurrected bodies...like a glorious continuation of our present bodies."

"But I just don't understand," Faye interrupted.

"I know it's hard honey, but you understand the caterpillar, don't you? Remember when you used to catch one when you were small. I would find you a jar and punch a couple holes in the lid. You put in a few twigs and some leaves. Then one day, what happened?"

"The caterpillar disappeared! I mean it went into a cocoon it had spun for itself."

"That's right, Faye...a cocoon ...like a casket. If you had opened it, it would appear lifeless and without much form. But then, remember the day you ran downstairs from the bedroom shouting for me to come up. And when we looked...there in that bottle was a beautiful butterfly with brilliant wings. Did we keep it in the bottle?"

> ...some will say, "How are the dead raised? And with what kind of body do they come?"
>
> You fool! That which you sow does not come to life unless it dies;
>
> And that which you sow, you do not sow the body which is to be, but a bare grain, perhaps of wheat or of something else.
>
> But God gives it a body just as He wished, and to each of the seeds a body of its own.
>
> (1 Corinthians 15:35-38 ASV)

"No, dad, we let it fly out in the open skies and in the sunshine."

"Faye, I think that was one of God's object lessons to us on how our resurrected bodies will come forth in new beauty. We don't understand it. But we know it is a reality."

"Will we have the same habits, Daddy? And what about Bill. Will he still be his same old stubborn self?"

"No, Faye, when we meet them everything will change. You will see."

> So also is the resurrection of the dead. It is sown in corruption; it is raised in incorruption.
>
> It is sown a natural body; it is raised a spiritual body. There is a natural body, and there is a spiritual body.
>
> (1 Corinthians 15:42,44)

"Will they be able to walk through doors like Jesus did when He met the disciples after His resurrection?"

It is sown in dishonour; it is raised in glory: it is sown in weakness; it is raised in power. (1 Corinthians 15:43)

"We soon will see, Faye. After all if we can accept x-rays and radio waves that penetrate bodies and walls...why should it be any more difficult to accept the fact that resurrected bodies can do the same or more. In Christ we will be liberated from physical and earthly restraints."

"It seems fantastic Dad. Won't it be great to see Mom and Bill and everyone. It's been so long. And we can recognize them, can't we, Dad?"

For if we believe that Jesus died and rose again, even so them also which sleep in Jesus will God bring with Him. (1 Thessalonians 4:14)

"Of course, honey, Moses and Elijah were recognized on the Mount of Transfiguration. The risen Lord was known to His disciples and to Mary at the tomb."

Just then, a swoosh of air seemed to engulf them.

Faye and George looked around.

There, next to them, on the Mount of Olives was Helen, Sue, Tommy, and Faye's husband, Bill Sanders.

Faye and George were overwhelmed with joy. Bill still had his dimples. Sue and Tommy were mature young adults. There were no more tears of separation as Helen whispered tenderly into George's ear, "Sweetheart, I missed you at the Rapture...but it's all over now...and we're together again."

For Bill and Faye it was a tender moment. Bill, who just a short time ago had died under

...He took Peter and John and James, and went up into a mountain to pray... And, behold, there talked with Him two men, which were Moses and Elijah.... (Luke 9:28,30)
* * *
And as they thus spake, Jesus Himself stood in the midst of them... and He said... Behold my hands and my feet, that it is I myself: handle me, and see; for a spirit hath not flesh and bones, as ye see me have. (Luke 34:36,39)
* * *
Jesus saith unto her, Woman, why seekest thou? whom seekest thou? She, supposing Him to be the gardener, saith unto Him, Sir, if thou have borne Him hence, tell me where thou hast laid Him, and I will take Him away.

Jesus saith unto her, Mary. She turned herself, and saith unto Him, Rabboni; which is to say, Master. (John 20:15-16)

the blade of a guillotine, was now in Faye's arms...perfect and whole in a completed resurrected body. It was a great reunion!

* * *

Just a few feet away Sylvia placed her arm about Terry Malone. And then witnessing the phenomenon in the sky... suddenly released her grip. Within a moment Tom Malone was there...beaming as he whirled Terry in his arms.

And for Terry Malone the great reunion was filled with happiness, but beyond the outer joy Sylvia sensed a heart burdened with tears!

Chapter 2

SORROW at SINAI

Abel Epstein was both bewildered and furious. Where had Brother Bartholomew disappeared? And what a time to leave!

Every phone in the control center was ringing. And each one he answered brought messages of utter confusion and calamity.

"Get us help, get us help. Mayday! Mayday! Some unseen force is wiping out our entire army!"

Abel Epstein, in an attempt to remain calm replied, "Pull back your forces 3 miles and let's reappraise the situation. Brother Bartholomew is not here. He's probably on his way out to the front."

"Negative, sir, he is not here...and we have no forces to pull back. Just the Lieutenant and I remain from our entire regiment."

Epstein angrily slammed down the phone.

For the first time in his life fear suddenly gripped him. Cold sweat poured out over his massive body. He jerked the Jerusalem contact phone from the wall and bellowed, "Get me Dr. Curter."

Dr. Curter was beginning to have doubts about the whole Megiddo expedition as he sat in his laboratory atop Mt. Herzl. From here looking northeast he could see the Mount of Olives.

Picking up his binoculars he scanned the horizon as suddenly the whole area was flooded with brilliant sunlight. Unusual, he thought. Something is happening.

It was only when he spotted Bill Sanders embracing his wife Faye that Dr. Curter lost his composure. His face turned ashen white. How could this be. He had personally witnessed the guillotine execution of Sanders. Could it be a dream?

The jangling phone brought him to his senses.

"Hello, this is Dr. Curter."

"Curter, this is Epstein at Megiddo Control Center. Everyone's gone mad here. Utter chaos. I'm boarding a helicopter. Will be there in 10 minutes. Stay where you are. I have a plan."

"A plan for what?" Dr. Curter was about to ask. But before he could, Epstein had hung up.

As Epstein boarded Brother Bartholomew's helicopter he instructed the pilot to circle the Megiddo plains.

What he saw was unbelievable.

What was once a plain now seemed like a quagmire. Here in the heat of the desert...the dry 105° heat...where in the world did the water come from?

He picked up the radio phone and after several tries finally reached a ground commander.

"What's happening down there? Where's the red mud coming from?"

"It's not mud, sir."

The voice seemed weak.

"Speak up," Epstein demanded.

"I have no strength sir. All around me are bodies...horses and men...and blood...blood... blood. It's...It's like a sea of blood. I can't speak sir...my tongue...I caaaan't...."

And the wine press was trodden outside the city, and blood came out from the wine press, [reaching] as high as horses' bridles, for a distance of one thousand and six hundred stadia [about 200 hundred miles].

(Revelation 14:20 Amplified Bible)

Then it dawned on him. Was what Sylvia had told him finally coming true? No, he couldn't believe such fantastic tales. There

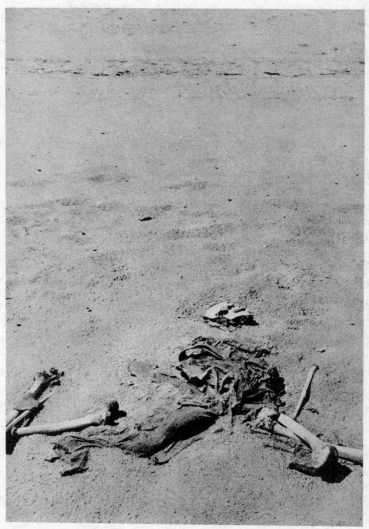

Epstein instructed the pilot to circle the Megiddo plains. What he saw was unbelievable.

had to be an explanation to all of this. The sudden earthquakes ...falling stars...they must have been a chain reaction from the air pollutants. That's it. It can't be God...whoever he is or wherever he is.

The pilot turned to him.

"Sir, if I didn't know better I would say that battlefield looks like a sea of blood...and it looks like it covers miles and miles of the Plain of Esdraelon."

"Nonsense, head this crate for Jerusalem and let's get to Mt. Herzl as quickly as possible."

As Helicopter 1 approached Jerusalem, Epstein's heart sank in despair. He had not been a good Jew but he did remember his early years in Hebrew school... seven years of learning, reading the Talmud.

> For, behold, the Lord will come with fire, and with His chariots like a whirlwind, to render His anger with fury, and His rebuke with flames of fire.
>
> For by fire and by His sword will the Lord plead with all flesh: and the slain of the Lord shall be many.
>
> (Isaiah 66:15-16)

He hadn't remembered much. But in the Talmud, Gemarah Kiddushim 496 was a phrase of beauty he had remembered. It was so poetic and so true. As though in prayer he bowed his head and softly repeated it...

> Ten parts of beauty were allotted the world at large:
> out of these Jerusalem assumed nine measures
> and the rest of the world but one...
> Ten parts of suffering were visited upon the world —
> nine for Jerusalem and one for the world.

If there was any tenderness in Epstein's heart...this was the moment. But instead of an awakening towards the Messiah...as he saw the destruction...he became more bitter.

If there is a God, he thought, why did He allow this suffering ...this tragedy to "His" Jerusalem?

"Then he remembered that verse in Psalms...Psalm 137:5-6... and in derision he quoted it:

If I forget you, O Jerusalem,
May my right hand forget her skill
May my tongue cleave to the roof of my mouth,
If I do not remember you,
If I do not exalt Jerusalem
    Above my chief joy.

In his bitterness he thought...the Hebrew school did me some good after all...he remembered that verse. To him it proved that God was not on the scene. For Jerusalem lay waste. The world was upside down.

Abel Epstein, who had come from selling records, to creating a laser ring, was not through yet! He was smarter than God... whoever he was. He, Epstein, would find a way out of this mess. Then he would live it up again!

The sudden descent of the helicopter engine brought him back to reality.

Flying over the Hebrew University the helicopter started its landing pattern onto Mount Herzl.

There was the Hill of Remembrance, on the ridge, dedicated to the six million European Jews killed by the Nazis in World War 2. The sight brought more bitterness to Epstein's heart. "Hitler was a saint compared to Brother Bartholomew," he thought, "why there must be at least 200 million dead out there at Megiddo!"

The helicopter landed atop Mount Herzl. Here Theodore Herzl was buried, the man who was first fired by the vision of a Jewish statehood and launched the movement. In 1949, forty-five years after his death, the body of Dr. Herzl had been brought in state from Vienna to Jerusalem.

The place seemed deserted.

Epstein quickly raced up the marble steps...each step echoing throughout the vast structure. It seemed eerie.

Running down a familiar hall, he came to Dr. Curter's office... swung open the door...and gasped in amazement and fright.

Epstein angrily grabbed a book and hurled it at the bird.

There in the chair was Dr. Curter. He looked alive. But the glassy stare of his eyes revealed differently. What eyes were left. There, perched on his head was a huge bird, gorging his belly as he pecked at Curter's eyes and took chunks from his swollen tongue.

Epstein angrily grabbed a book and hurled it at the bird. The sharp crack was heard throughout the hall as the book squarely hit Dr. Curter's head. His body slid awkwardly off the chair and sprawled on the floor. As other birds quickly flew in at the smell of open flesh...Epstein ran hysterically from the room and down to the waiting helicopter.

> And I saw an angel standing in the sun; and he cried with a loud voice, saying to all the fowls that fly in the midst of heaven, Come and gather yourselves together unto the supper of the great God;
> That ye may eat the flesh of kings, and the flesh of captains, and the flesh of mighty men, and the flesh of horses, and of them that sit on them, and the flesh of all men, both free and bond, both small and great.
> Revelation 19:17-18

* * *

Sylvia was noticeably worried. Standing there on the Mount of Olives with Terry she could sense something was wrong. Terry should have been overjoyed at this reunion. And she was...but.

Suddenly Sylvia realized in her concern for others and her witnessing this glorious reunion...she had forgotten about herself and Abel.

It was like hitting her with a ton of bricks. "Dear Jesus," she whispered to herself, "I want to be near you...and I want Abel to come to know you as Saviour and Lord."

Funny, she thought. She had thought of Abel as her lucky charm, her security blanket, her ace in the hole. After she married him she never wanted for money, perfume, or furs. Everywhere she went, she went first class. "Baby," he told her, "now that you've married me...you're going to travel first class!"

And first class she went. It was a cold, convenient love. There was never any warmth. Abel was all business in everything he did. He never even took time to eat properly or spend time with her. She was revolted by the way he gulped down a chicken sandwich and a soft drink...then dashed off to another business deal. When she complained, he would reply, "Make up your mind, baby, do you want me or money. You can't have them both."

And for a while, she was glad to settle for the money.

She attended all the social balls in New York. She thought nothing of spending $150 for a ticket to the Diamond Ball at the Plaza and dancing for hours to the bands of Meyer Davis and Peter Duchin.

She remembered even bidding for the Velazquez portrait at Wildenstein Gallery and seemed quite relieved when she was outbid by the final bid of $5.54 million!

Her greatest thrill, or so she thought, was when Abel sent her off on a worldwide cruise aboard the S.S. France. Her cabin cost $99,340 and she remembered filling her cigarette box in her suite with 500 crisp dollar bills for small tips.

And every August, without fail, she would head up to Saratoga Springs, New York for the Saratoga auction of yearling race horses.

But now, all the dazzle of money and society seemed to crumble into emptiness.

It's funny, she thought. Money can't buy happiness. Money couldn't win the war. Money couldn't bring peace. And when you die, money can not buy back one more minute of time.

A rich man's wealth is his strong city, And like a high wall in his own imagination. (Proverbs 18:11 ASV)

The only thing that was real was her Saviour. Now, more than ever before, the reality of her salvation in Christ became apparent. And she clung to the precious promises she had learned as a child. But her heart ached. Why, oh why, didn't she learn more of these truths then. There it was...the entire blueprint of tomorrow laid out for her in the Bible. And she had squandered her time on charlatans and personal gain. The agony of regret seemed more than she could bear. The events around her were happening too fast. She could not think straight. She was like a little baby...helpless...waiting to be led.

Suddenly, a noise distracted her. Abel came bounding through the door. His face was ashen white.

She had never seen him this way. He looked pitiful. She felt so sorry for him. She wanted to hold him in her arms.

She had never felt like this before. Abel was always the master of his ship. But now it seemed like Abel's ship was without a rudder.

"Sylvia, grab your bags and hurry. We've got to get out of here!"

"Why, honey. Where can we go?"

"This place is a holocaust. Megiddo is one vast burial ground ...dead all over...sickening blood like a miry swamp. You should have seen it. I was lucky to get out alive. Even Dr. Curter is dead! Stop wasting time, Sylvia...let's get moving. There's a Concorde jet at Lod airport. I've given orders to hold the flight till we get there. We're flying to New York!"

"Abel, sit down and let's reappraise the situation. Don't you see there's nothing either of us can do. The King has arrived. Terry told me about it. It's all written in the Book of Revelation and it's actually coming true."

"Sylvia, stop listening to those fairy tales. Besides I don't accept the New Testament."

"I know that Abel, but the same prophecies are written in Daniel, Isaiah, Zechariah and Joel as well. You've witnessed the Battle of Armageddon. Tell me, where is Brother Bartholomew?"

"How did you know he disappeared?"

"I didn't, Abel, but if he did, he was Antichrist, and he's been cast into the Lake of Fire."

"Now I know you're having hallucinations, Sylvia. We've got to get out of here."

"Honey, listen to me...there's no time to lose. Let's get down on our knees now. Ask the Lord Jesus Christ to come into your heart. Accept Him as your Saviour...please darling."

> And he shall plant the tabernacles of his palace between the seas in the glorious holy mountain; yet he shall come to his end, and none shall help him.
> (Daniel 11:45)

Darling...funny, she had rarely called Abel darling. She slipped her arm about his waist. He seemed like a frightened boy now. For the first time in her life she felt a deep passionate love

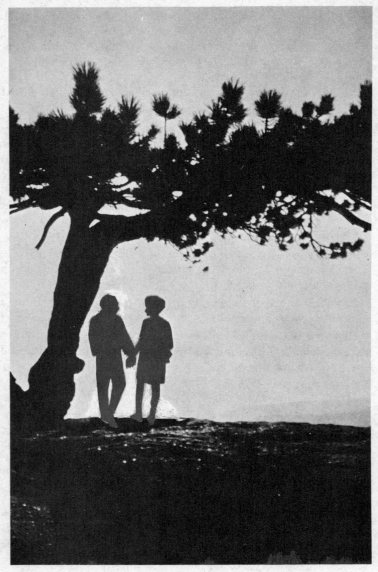

For the first time in her life she felt a deep passionate love for him. Abel, the cold, cool, millionaire now needed an understanding love.

for him. Abel, the cold, cool, millionaire now needed an understanding love. She quietly tried to open the Word of God to him...as much as she could remember...she told him that his Messiah, his Redeemer had come...and soon for those who would not believe, would come an unbelievable and irreversible judgment. For a moment she thought he was on the verge of believing...his eyes moistened. Gently she brushed away a tear. He was about to speak.

A loud explosion outside their window jolted him to reality.

Cursing, he threw her down to the floor.

"Sylvia, you can have your heartless God. I've got my money in New York. And that's where I'm going. I'll buy my way into your Heaven...if there is one!"

The sleek Concorde supersonic airliner...all $35 million of it...was about to start its engines on the Lod airport runway when Abel Epstein rushed up to the gates. He was quickly waved on.

He settled back in the soft, cushioned seats and ordered a cocktail from the stewardess. Abel Epstein had done it again. He'd show this God a lesson or two.

The stewardess came back. "Sorry, sir, we have no liquor anymore. All aircraft have been taken over by other personnel. Would you care for a glass of milk or a soft drink?"

Abel was furious and was about to vent his fury on the helpless stewardess. But he had second thoughts when he looked at her hand.

She was carrying a Bible.

He pushed his seat back into

And again I say unto you, It is easier for a camel to go through the eye of a needle, than for a rich man to enter into the kingdom of God.

(Matthew 19:24)

[God] who hath saved us... not according to our works... but according to His own purpose and grace.

(2 Timothy 1:9)

For by grace are ye saved through faith; and that not of yourselves; it is the gift of God: Not of works, lest any man should boast.

(Ephesians 2:9)

And when Simon saw that through laying on of the apostles' hands the Holy Ghost was given, he offered them money,

Saying, Give me also this power, that on whomsoever I lay hands, he may receive the Holy Ghost.

But Peter said unto him, Thy money perish with thee, because thou hast thought that the gift of God may be purchased with money.

(Acts 8:18-20)

the reclining position and closed his eyes. Soon, he thought, I will be in New York with 10 million other sensible people and things will be back to normal. It was all a bad dream, he comforted himself...a bad dream.

The Concorde Jet took off for the some 6000 mile journey. His face curled into a smile. He would be in New York in about 3 hours! Sylvia could quote all the verses she wanted to...but he wouldn't be there to hear them. She ought to read Proverbs 19:13. That was one verse he often quoted to her: "...a nagging wife annoys like constant dripping."

If Abel Epstein knew that this very moment his financial adviser, George Henderson, was winging his way to Jerusalem he would have lost every sense of security.

His slumber would not be for long. He was to find in New York an unforgettable picture of tragedy and terror.

He could stand no more surprises. But this one would be the biggest!

* * *

Sylvia looked into the mirror. Her hair was a mess. The tears had etched a path down her face. Yet she was no longer concerned about external beauty.

"Abel, dear Abel, why didn't you listen to me. Oh, God, please dear God, save him. I'll do anything for you. Just please save him."

It was some time later she finally found George and Faye with Terry Malone.

Between choking tears she poured out her story to them.

As she looked into their faces, she knew they understood... understood, perhaps too well.

"Sylvia, have you ever heard of Kadesh-Barnea?"

"No, George, why?"

"Well, just before Helen, Bill and Tom left us, they said they were accompanying the Redeemer to Ain Quedeirat."

"What's that?" Sylvia inquired.

"Ain Quedeirat is the Wilderness of Paran, known in Bible days as Kadesh-Barnea. It is in the area called the Arabah which means desert or plain. This is in the Sinai Peninsula. It is a desolate and nearly empty land. It has been the route for many armies. In this area Moses received the Ten Commandments. The Jews wandered here for 40 years.

The Sinai Peninsula itself is 260 miles long and 150 miles wide between the Gulf of Suez and Gulf of Aqaba. If you remember your Bible story, this was the site

> And I will bring you into the wilderness of the people, and there will I plead with you face to face.
>
> (Ezekiel 20:35)

of the famous 'Grasshopper Retreat.' It was in Numbers, chapter 13, where God instructed Moses...I forget the rest."

"I know, Dad," Faye chimed in, "God told Moses to take one leader from each tribe and send spies into the land of Canaan. And 40 days later they came back to the wilderness of Paran at Kadesh. Caleb told the group to go up and possess the land... but they said, 'We felt like grasshoppers before them, they were so tall.' I remember Mom telling me that story."

"That's right, Faye, and they all cried to go back to Egypt. And that's when judgment fell."

"What's that have to do with what's happening now?" Sylvia pleadingly inquired.

Mount Nebo, from which Moses viewed the Promised Land.

Just then a messenger ran up to George Omega.

"You're wanted on the phone, sir. You may take it on the phone in the Intercontinental Hotel lobby. It's a transatlantic call, sir."

George picked up the phone. It was his boss at World Television network.

"Get over to Kadesh-Barnea," he screamed. "Some religious fanatics here have told me something's about to happen there."

"When did you get religion, Walter Brinks?"

"I didn't. Don't be stupid...but these characters have been hitting some predictions right on the button...as though they've been reading it in a book...all planned ahead. It's uncanny! And I want a scoop. They tell me the next big event is some kind of a judgment of the nation Israel. And its going to take place in Kadesh-Barnea...some forsaken place in the Sinai Peninsula. Their Redeemer is going to make a personal appearance."

KADESH - BARNEA
(And Its Environs)

"You mean the Messiah, Jesus Christ?"

"Call Him what you want, Omega...but think of the ratings. We'll outpull the old Johnny Carson show. It'll be the scoop of the century. Get a couple mobile TV units there at the King David Hotel and high tail it down to this Kadesh place. As soon as you get there, I want you on the air. We'll telecast via orbiting satellite. I've cleared everything."

George related the entire conversation to Faye, Terry and Sylvia. And much against his will he let them accompany him to Kadesh-Barnea.

Their race against time seemed useless. For when they arrived at Kadesh-Barnea all was still. Occasionally a band of Bedouins with a troop of camels would pass, and one would hear his rhythmic Arabic voice prodding the camels on.

"I wonder if Moses knew then that the sons of his sons would wander here still contending with a Pharaoh?" George mused.

* * *

Whatever was happening, Abel Epstein didn't like it. Suddenly it seemed like an invisible army was rounding up everyone of Jewish extraction...assigning them to ships in the harbor.

Epstein had gathered all his negotiable money and joined the others. Some were singing a song, "How the Oppressor has ceased!" It didn't make sense. Some

> ...thou shalt take up this proverb against the king of Babylon, and say, How hath the oppressor ceased! The golden city ceased!
> (Isaiah 14:4)

seemed hilariously happy. Others like Epstein were confused and sad. Where in the world was this ship going? Who in the world ever heard of this Kadesh place?

It didn't matter. He was tired of running. He fell asleep comforted by a money belt bulging with cash.

> Who are these that fly as a cloud, and as the doves to their windows?
> Surely the isles shall wait for me, and the ships of many lands first, to bring the sons of Israel home again from far away, their silver and their gold with them, unto the name of the Lord thy God, and to the Holy One of Israel, because He hath glorified thee.
> (Isaiah 60:8-9)

* * *

From George Omega's specially built TV booth he had a panorama picture of the action at Kadesh-Barnea. Soon the "ON" light would signal time for his telecast. How he wished he knew more about Bible prophecy. Outside of a few externals he had no idea what was about to happen.

Suddenly from nowhere, it seemed, Helen was by his side.

"But darling, where did you come from and how could you? The doors are closed and we're 50 feet high."

"Honey, you must remember I have been resurrected in Christ. Resurrected believers are not constrained by physical barriers. Besides you'll need help in this telecast."

With that the signal to broadcast lit up.

"This is George Omega reporting to you from Kadesh-Barnea, which is right outside of Israel, to the east. They say nothing is new under the sun. But what we are about to see today will not only be new, but to some, unbelievable. I understand the Redeemer...Christ, the Messiah, will actually be here. This will be His first appearance on television and certainly His first appearance on earth since the resurrection. It will be an historic occasion...yet one edged with much tragedy and also triumph. With me by my side is my wife, Helen."

"Helen is different...that is she was taken up in the Rapture... now she has a new resurrected body. It appears to look just like ours. I recognize her. Yet it is a perfect body, free from the ailments and the aging that still plague us."

"She is living in a new dimension without the restraints of time and space. Yet the marvelous thing about this is that I can communicate with her and she is still, and more so, my attractive Helen."

"You may ask how can I tell a resurrected believer from a living believer? Actually, it's very easy. Helen, as all resurrected believers, has an inner glow of perfection and somehow, don't ask me how, her entire silhouette is edged in a luminous glow."

It is sown a natural body; it is raised a spiritual body. There is a natural body, and there is a spiritual body.

For our conversation [citizenship] is in heaven: from whence also we look for the Saviour, the Lord Jesus Christ:

Who shall change our vile body, that it may be fashioned like unto His glorious body, according to the working whereby He is able even to subdue all things unto Himself.
(1 Corinthians 15:44)
(Philippians 3:20-21)

"Helen, I am sure you can fill in the details of this occasion."

Helen, realizing far more the awe of this event, gently touched George's hand in understanding.

"I don't know how to begin," she started, "for what we are about to see here is not pleasant. The Millennium of 1000 years is soon to begin and what we will witness is often called the JUDGMENT OF THE NATION ISRAEL".

"God's chosen people are now back in Israel to stay. Their long years of wandering are over. Their Messiah, and ours, will never again hide His face from His people."

"What we are about to see here is the Judgment of Israel in fulfillment of Ezekiel 20:33-38 which tells us:

...it shall come to pass, when all these things are come upon thee, the blessing and the curse, which I have set before thee, and thou shalt call them to mind among all the nations, whither the Lord thy God hath driven thee,

And shalt return unto the Lord thy God, and shalt obey His voice according to all that I command thee this day, thou and thy children, with all thine heart, and with all thy soul;

'...I shall be king over you. And I shall bring you out from the peoples and gather you from the lands where you are scattered...

And I shall bring you into the wilderness of the peoples, and there I shall enter into judgment with you face to face.

As I entered into judgment with your fathers in the wilderness of the land of Egypt, so I will enter into judgment with you...

And I shall make you pass under the rod, and I shall bring you into the bond of the covenant;

And I shall purge from you the rebels and those who transgress against Me...they will not enter the land of Israel. Thus you will know that I am the Lord.'"

Helen turned to continue but Sylvia's tears broke the silence.

"Not my Abel, not my precious Abel...God can't be that cruel!" she sobbed.

Startled, George Omega grabbed the microphone. "I'm sorry for that interruption, and yet God's judgments are sure. Sylvia is one of our best friends, yet her husband failed to accept the Redeemer as King."

Sylvia frustrated and angry dashed to the elevator that quickly whisked her to the ground level.

She could never forget what she saw. All over the plain were what appeared to be millions of people,

That THEN the Lord thy God will turn thy captivity, [restore your fortunes] and have compassion upon thee, and will return and gather thee from all the nations whither the Lord thy God hath scattered thee.

If any of thine be driven out unto the outmost parts of heaven, from thence will the Lord thy God gather thee, and from thence will he fetch thee:

And the Lord thy God will bring thee into the land which thy fathers possessed, and thou shalt possess it; and He will do thee good, and multiply thee above thy fathers.

And the Lord thy God will cleanse thine heart, and the heart of thy seed, to love the Lord thy God with all thine heart, and with all thy soul, that thou mayest live.

(Deuteronomy 30:1-6)

...Thus saith the Lord God; Behold, I will take the children of Israel from among the heathen, whither they be gone, and will gather them on every side, and bring them into their own land:

And I will make them one nation in the land upon the mountains of Israel; and one king shall be king to them all: and they shall be no more two nations, neither shall they be divided into two kingdoms any more at all;

And David my servant shall be king over them; and they all shall have one shepherd: they shall also walk in my judgments, and observe my statutes, and do them.

And they shall dwell in the land that I have given unto Jacob my servant, wherein your lined in formation according to their final residence. Quickly she ran to the New York line. Almost instantly she spotted Abel.

Breaking through the barriers, it seemed with superhuman effort, she grabbed Abel's arm and pulled him away from the crowd. Hysterically she half carried him to an open place directly in front of the TV cameras.

fathers have dwelt; and they shall dwell therein, even they, and their children, and their children's children for ever: and my servant David shall be their prince for ever.
(Ezekiel 37:21-22,24-25,28)

And I will plant them upon their land, and they shall no more be pulled up out of their land which I have given them, saith the Lord thy God.
(Amos 9:15)

There in splendor beyond words was a Throne. Her eyes so filled with tears, she looked up at the person on the Throne. Though her vision blurred, no one had to tell her. Little Sylvia Epstein was face to face with her Saviour.

She knew what she must do. Tearing the buttons from Abel's shirt she yanked the money belt from around his waist. Abel seemed in a trance, like a little boy, starry eyed and speechless.

She flung the belt at the foot of the Throne.

In an impassioned plea she cried: "Here, Abel, give your all... all your money...I love him, Lord. He doesn't deserve to die. He always gave to the United Jewish Appeal. He even bought Israeli bonds...Look at this money. There must be a million dollars... Abel, give it to the Lord for the rebuilding of Israel...Oh, Abel, repent."

And even as she hysterically spoke she saw no sign of repentance in Abel's stony face. Fear, yes; repentance, no. Her head bowed. It was too late!

Her Redeemer looked down. It was a look of both compassion and of judgment. The voice of what sounded like an angel then came from the side of the throne and thundered across the plains:

Why should I fear in days of adversity,
When the iniquity of my foes surrounds me,
Even those who trust in their wealth,
And boast in the abundance of their riches
No man can by any means redeem his brother,

She flung the money belt at the foot of the Throne. In an impassioned plea she cried: "...I love him, Lord. He doesn't deserve to die."

Or give to God a ransom for him —
For the redemption of his soul is costly...
For he sees that even wise men die...
And leave their wealth to others.
This is the way of those who are foolish
As sheep they are appointed for the realm of the dead
And their form shall be for Sheol to consume. [1]

The One upon the throne then waved His arm. George Omega continued the telecast, saying,

"Two men are escorting Abel Epstein to a judgment platform whose ceiling is one that appears to be luminous rod. There are two runways extending out, as one passes through...almost like separating sheep. Epstein is now under the rod...."

"George", Helen added, "if I may interrupt. This is the final fulfillment of the Old Testament Scripture from Malachi 3:2-5. Let me read it to our audience:

'...who can endure the day of His coming? And who can stand when He appears? For He is like a refiner's fire and like fullers' soap (bleaching the dirtiest garments).

He will sit as a...purifier of silver, and He will purify the Levites (the ministers of God). At that time my punishments will be quick and certain.'"

"This is exactly what we are seeing here."

"Yes, Helen, Abel Epstein is now being led away and off of the platform. The swinging door to life and freedom on the right has closed. The only possible route now is the runway to the left. This leads to a transportation column of what appears to be an endless chain of busses. It's hard to describe. Epstein seems meek and unresponsive as though all life has suddenly left him."

"What we have witnessed here is sorrow at Sinai!"

Amid the tears, Faye whispered something into Terry's ear.

Those few words she uttered took but a few seconds, but they were going to have their effect for 1000 years!

[1] Psalm 49:5-15

Chapter 3

VALLEY OF TEARS

This was a time when George Omega should be happy but recent events troubled him.

The scene he had witnessed where suddenly some 8 million Jews were separated like sheep and goats...left an indelible impression on him. For from his early days on television there were many among these whom he could recall as his real friends.

They lifted him out of a poverty pocket TV announcing occupation, to one of prominence in New York on a major network.

And George Omega couldn't forget this kindness and concern.

Helen sensed this as he sat rather dejectedly in his Jerusalem apartment overlooking the Valley of Kidron.

George chose this location for his living quarters because he had often stayed here in his search for the identity of Brother Bartholomew. He came to love the site. And on his own he had prepared a TV documentary on the importance of this valley throughout history.

"David's City," as he liked to call Jerusalem, was bounded by two valleys. The valley most visible today is the Valley of Kidron. It lies on the extreme east. On the extreme south and west was the Valley of Hinnom.

Between the Kidron Valley east of the city and the Hinnom Valley on the south and west, there was a smaller central valley. Gradually, through the years, this central valley became filled

The Kidron Valley in Jerusalem.

with debris and its level rose, so that now it seems like an ordinary street in the Old City, leaving no division between ancient eastern and western ridges.

It was here that Christ and His disciples about 30 A.D. crossed the Kidron valley to the Mount of Olives to Gethsemane. But many years before this, David crossed the Kidron in his escape from his rebellious son, Absalom.

> And all the country wept with a loud voice, and all the people passed over: the king himself passed over the brook Kidron, and all the people passed over, toward the way of the wilderness.
> (2 Samuel 15:23)

Through the Kidron valley occasionally there ran a seasonal torrent, the Brook Kidron. This, however, was dry much of the time even in a rainy year. Asa, third king of Judah (964-923 B.C.),

> And also Maachah his mother, even her he removed from being queen, because she had made an idol in a grove; and Asa destroyed her idol, and burnt it by the brook Kidron.
> (1 Kings 15:13)

a godly King deposed his wicked grandmother, a daughter of Absalom, and burned her idol at this Brook Kidron.

And in the old 1967 6-Day War the Israeli Army crossed the ancient Valley of Kidron and ascended the Mount of Olives in their final act of victory.

George spoke, so moved by recent events, as though he was addressing a television audience...although gathered around him were only his loved ones...his wife, Helen, Sue, Tommy, Bill and Faye Sanders, Tom and Terry Malone and Sylvia.

"This is Jerusalem..." He paused to mask the tears in his voice.

"Jerusalem...a recorded history of over 4000 years...perched high amid the Judean hills...the city of David...the city of Solomon's Temple...the city of Isaiah and Jeremiah, giant prophets."

"Jerusalem...a city where every stone, ages old or recent, represents a drop in time...."

And then with a twinge of bitterness in his voice, George

> Nevertheless for David's sake did the Lord his God give him a lamp in Jerusalem, to set up his son after him, and to establish Jerusalem:
> Because David did that which was right in the eyes of the Lord, and turned not aside from any thing that he commended him all the days of his life, save only in the matter of Uriah the Hittite.
> (1 Kings 15:4-5)

continued...

"Jerusalem...is first and foremost a city of war, taken, lost, retaken nearly 50 times within the last 3000 years. Ironic, isn't it, from childhood we've been told to pray for the peace of Jerusalem. What peace? All I've seen here in the last few days is intense sorrow and suffering."

> Pray for the peace of Jerusalem: they shall prosper that love thee.
> (Psalm 122:6)

George still had the scene at Sinai deeply etched in his mind, and what he felt to be the unfairness of it all, was finally beginning to surface.

He continued: "Jerusalem...a city of peace. Why God Himself referred to its habitants as men of Sodom and Gomorrah."

> Except the Lord of hosts had left unto us a very small remnant, we should have been as Sodom, and we should have been like unto Gomorrah.
> Hear the word of the Lord, ye rulers of Sodom; give ear unto the law of our God, ye people of Gomorrah.
> (Isaiah 1:9-10)

Helen interrupted: "George, Jerusalem is the city of righteousness. In Isaiah 1:21-26 we have a completed picture. We can't just look at the past, but in God's overall design. Let me read it to you:

> How the faithful city has become a harlot,
> She who was full of justice!
> Righteousness once lodged in her...
> Your silver has become dross...
>
> Therefore the Lord God of hosts,
> The Mighty One of Israel declares,
> I will be relieved of My adversaries,
> And avenge Myself on My foes.
>
> I will also turn My hand against you,
> And will smelt away your dross as with lye,
> And will remove all your alloy.
>
> Then I will restore your judges as the first,
> And your counselors as at the beginning;
> After that you will be called the city of righteousness,
> A faithful city."

There were tears now in Helen's eyes as she continued:

"George, don't you see? Our Messiah is a refiner burning off the worthless to prepare us for an eternity of perfect peace and rest. These so-called friends...in your eyes...the eyes of a mere human may appear to be lasting and worthwhile. But God looks at them through the microscope of His perfectness. We may not understand His ways but we know His ways are the best."

> O the depth of the riches both of the wisdom and knowledge of God! How unsearchable are His judgments, and His ways past finding out!
>
> (Romans 11:33)

"George, if you could see beyond today...into God's eternal tomorrow, and if you could project the actions of your friends in tomorrow's eternity in Heaven then you would know that God's ways are always best."

> Surely, you will be ashamed of the oaks which you have desired, And you will be embarrassed at the gardens which you have chosen.
>
> For you will be like an oak whose leaf fades away, Or as a garden that has no water.
>
> And the strong man will become tinder, His work also a spark. Thus they shall both burn together, And there will be none to quench them.
>
> (Isaiah 1:29-31 ASV)

Tommy, George's son, spoke: "Dad, look at me, your own son. Remember the time I broke my leg in football. Despite all the doctors did one leg was shorter than the other. I walked with a limp. Now look at me. No limp. Perfect. I wore glasses. Now look at me. No glasses. Perfect."

"And Dad," Sue chimed in, "remember when you last saw me. I was just a little child. But now I'm a full grown young woman. Remember at birth when you discovered I only had 3 fingers on each hand. Now look at me, Dad...look at my hands!"

With that she thrust her hands in front of her.

George, startled, looked closely. There were two beautiful hands...complete.

At the moment Helen thought she was getting through, Sylvia suddenly burst into tears.

"It's alright for you to be so happy...like you belong to an exclusive club. But what about me? What about my Abel? Suppose you had seen your husband literally dragged from New York out to that forsaken desert and judged like some criminal?

And without even a chance to say goodbye...hustled off to..." her voice trailed.

The air was tense.

"To where?" Sylvia screamed. "To where, Helen? Tell me WHERE?"

As a living believer, Helen would never have been able to contain herself. Most likely she would have broken down and cried. But now, in her new body as a resurrected believer, perfect in Christ, an inner glow provided peace and understanding.

"Sylvia, we must face reality. Abel rejected His Messiah as Lord, and because he did not accept His Lord's free offer of pardon by accepting Jesus as his Saviour he had to stand in judgment for his sins. He will be cast into the Lake of Fire."

"How can God do this?" Sylvia cried convulsively. "How can a God of love condemn a man like my Abel to an eternity of suffering? Does He have no heart?"

...cast...the unprofitable servant into outer darkness: there shall be weeping and gnashing of teeth.

(Matthew 25:30)

"That's just it, Sylvia. God is a God of love...He told us in 1 John 2:15,17:

Do not love the world, nor the things in the world.
If any man love the world, the love of the Father
is not in him.

And the world is passing away, and also its lusts;
but the one who does the will of God abides forever."

"God so loved the world, He gave His own son, Jesus Christ to redeem the world. You remember reading that in John 3:16. And verse 17 tells us that

...God did not send the Son into the world to
judge the world; but that the world should be
saved through Him."

"How can a God of love condemn someone to Hell?" Helen continued. "God doesn't condemn anyone to an eternity in the Lake of Fire. God provided a way out. If we don't choose to accept His way...we cannot blame God. It was there...the way of escape."

Tom Malone interrupted. "You see, Sylvia, God provided an atonement, a sacrifice since time immemorial. All man had to do was accept it. It's as simple as that."

"But I tried to tell Abel to repent and to give the Messiah all his money. You saw me throw it on the ground," Sylvia reminded him.

For God sent not His Son into the world to condemn the world; but that the world through Him might be saved.

He that believeth on Him is not condemned: but he that believeth not is condemned already, because he hath not believed in the name of the only begotten Son of God.

(John 3:17-18)

Tom continued: "Sylvia in Proverbs 14:12 we were told

There is a way which seems right to a man.
But its end is the way of death."

By this time Sylvia was sobbing hysterically. Sue went over, placed her arms around her shoulders trying to comfort her. But it was to no avail.

Helen felt she must continue: "Sylvia, God provided a way and He is a God of love. But when man chooses not to follow that way and rejects His sacrifice...God then becomes also a God of judgment. It was not a loving God who condemned Abel to hell. It was Abel who condemned himself because he would not accept the atonement provided by God through His son, Christ Jesus. And in Hebrew 2:3 we are told,

"How shall we escape if we neglect so great salvation?"

"I'm sorry, Sylvia, but you just have to face reality."

Sylvia's body shook with sobs.

George looked pale and worried.

Faye gripped Bill's hand. Somehow this whole scene was too much for her emotionally. Was the room too hot? Suddenly everything seemed to be spinning. Bill, Tom and Terry Malone ...everyone just became a sea of faces wrapped in a transparent gauze. Faye got up from her chair in an attempt to get some fresh air.

But her feet were like the wobbly legs of a marionette...and the strings wouldn't move.

Faye collapsed and lay still on the floor!

As George Omega stared at Faye, now resting on the couch, his mind wandered back a few years to Walter Brinks...a man who habitually took cat-naps on his huge office couch. Walter Brinks had been a self-made man. He believed in stepping on people. He often remarked to George Omega, "Georgie, boy... you want to know how to climb the ladder to success? The ladder to success is built on a mass of broken bodies. The more bodies you pile up...the higher up on the ladder you get. Learn to use people...step on them until you get to the top. Then you're king of the realm. That's when you've got power. And no one... I mean NO ONE can take it away from you!"

For a while it appeared that Walter Brinks was right. His theory had quickly landed him a top executive job at World Television Network. He was gruff but somehow George liked him. But whenever he gave George an overseas assignment he hounded him for scoops. In a way, Walter Brinks was fearless, too. George had seen him walk into the center of riots to get an

George remembered those last few years...the long food lines... the impossible taxes...the fight for job openings.

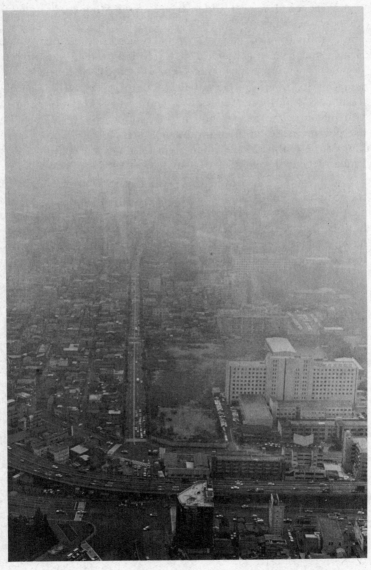

For many days no city in the United States had seen the sun...a pall of grey death hovered over most of the world.

on-the-spot interview...while police and rioters were still exchanging gunfire. Walter even carried his own gas mask. He was not one to let a little tear gas interrupt his news scoops. Often George watched him laugh hilariously as he repeated the story of how all the reporters ran from scenes of disturbances rubbing their eyes...while "little old gas-masked me got right into the center of things."

George remembered those last few years. Each year the riots became more and more intense. They were measured in terms of casualties on both sides...soldiers, police, and civilians. Any little thing touched off a riot...the inability of some to get hospital treatment, the long food lines...the impossible taxes...the fight for job openings.

There were just so many people on earth that jobs became scarce. Schools, as known in the late 1970's, were a thing of the past. Industries had set up specialized learning centers. Young people seemed like men from outer space with computers plugged into their heads. George remembered calling these changes to the attention of Walter Brinks.

"George," Brinks replied, "you're just old fashioned, I'm afraid. This is progress, man...real progress. Think how far we've advanced in the last 30 years. We can control population growth through vaccination. We can control riots by infiltrating water systems of troubled cities with a pacifying drug. We can control human behavior. And one day we will be able to control our environment."

Brinks admitted that controlling the environment still was a problem. For many days no city in the United States had seen the sun. For the last few years a pall of grey death hovered over most of the world. Pollutants had so affected the minds of people that they did things they normally would not do.

"Mentally disturbed by the lead poisoning and oxygen deficiencies in the air—it's no wonder some of our population is acting erratically, George...but times will get better. I can feel it in my bones."

George had not been so sure. And often he had talked to his boss about the events of the Rapture. But each time Brinks would wave him off with a laugh.

"George," he said jokingly, "if God ever comes down and judges us Gentiles, you can bet I'll be the first one on the spot to televise the occasion." And then reflecting on the possibility, he continued, "Think of the commercial time we could sell. We could sell one minute for a quarter of a million dollars. Look at me, George. One day I'll be President of this network."

An office boy interrupted Walter Brinks, waking him from his reflective thought.

"Sir, something unusual's happening in the halls. There's talk of an armada of ships in the harbor...there's...there's...."

"Stop stammering boy...out with it."

"People have suddenly lost their ability to control themselves sir. I saw it with my own eyes. Men and women...looking just like you and I...except they have a luminous type of glow outlining their body...they came in and soon people just started following them...as though they were directed by some unseen force."

"What did they say?" Brinks demanded.

"I heard one of them say the ships were headed for the Middle East and that a judgment of Gentiles was to take place...whatever that means...in some old Bible-type name they called the Valley of Jehos...something."

Walter Brinks made it his business to know everything... including the Bible...although he didn't believe in it.

Almost with devilish joy he shouted, "Valley of Jehoshaphat! What a story! Old George must have been right after all. Judgment of the Gentiles. Now I remember it. Quick, get my limousine. I'm headed for Kennedy International Airport!"

"And on your way out, tell my secretary to get me George Omega in Jerusalem. Use our orbiting satellite phone system. It's quicker."

In a few minutes, George was on the phone:

"George, I've got good news for you. Looks like we're going to have to drop those soap operas for a few days. Big things are happening. Your Judgment of Gentiles is coming up. What a show that will be. But boy will those housewives howl when they see we've taken General Hospital off the air. I'm lining up advertisers for this Special. We'll shoot it from every angle. George, I want you to give me background copy coverage. Sweep the dust off that Bible, George and fill in the details. I want plenty of interviews. And get some of those who are sentenced to death on the tube. Wow...what a scoop! What a day ...what a day. Move...George...move. Remember...George... first those condemned to death...then interview anyone else you want. Money's no object. Offer a cool million to start for exclusive TV rights. That will impress them."

George was dejected. First, Sylvia's outburst, then his own misgivings about the coming Millennium...and now all Walter Brinks could think about was a scoop.

...Why doth this generation seek after a sign?...

Having eyes, see ye not? and having ears, hear ye not? and do ye not remember?

(Mark 8:12,18)

He had not yet gotten over the heartsick scene at Kadesh-Barnea where millions of Jews were divided in the judgment of the nation Israel.

Now would he be forced to witness another judgment...that of the Gentiles. Physically he felt he could not hold up...but Brinks had a forceful way about him. One didn't say "No" to Walter Brinks.

From his Mount of Olives apartment George was just a stone's throw away from his television control center.

Just a few days before great changes had occurred in this area. Christ, the Redeemer King had burst through the sky with His army. Helen, Sue, Tommy and Bill Sanders and Tom Malone were in this army. It was a happy occasion...yet tragic.

As the King's feet touched the Mount of Olives...the entire mountain split apart...right in the middle from east to west. It created a huge valley.

George recalled televising this story after it occurred. Brinks was proud of this scoop. He used a split screen. And as George

And His feet shall stand in that day upon the Mount of Olives, which lies before Jerusalem on the east, and the Mount of Olives shall be split in two from the east to the west by a very great valley; and half of the mountain shall remove toward the north, and half of it toward the south.

(Zechariah 14:4 Amplified Bible)

Walter Brinks had the TV cameras pan across the New York sky-line even as the earthquake was occurring.

recounted the events and showed how half of the Mount of Olives was to the North and the other half to the South...Brinks showed the destruction of New York City with the flashes of lightening...the booming thunder and the hailstones that weighed nearly 100 pounds.

It was almost with a sense of pride and accomplishment that he had the cameras pan across the New York skyline to show how the earthquake had split the city into three parts.

It seemed like ages ago...although it had only been a few days ago. George was overwhelmed at the sudden speed of events...as though he were flying in a jet plane, 1000 miles per hour ...covering so much territory in so short a time...he just could not fathom its significance. The poles of time were whizzing by so fast ...it all became a blur.

Helen sensed this, motioned to George, and then she began the description of the events.

> And there were voices, and thunders, and lightnings; and there was a great earthquake, such as was not since men were upon the earth, so mighty an earthquake, and so great.
>
> And the great city was divided into three parts, and the cities of the nations fell: and great Babylon came in remembrance before God, to give unto her the cup of the wine of the fierceness of His wrath...
>
> And there fell upon men a great hail out of heaven, every stone about the weight of a talent [nearly 100 pounds]: and men blasphemed God because of the plague of the hail; for the plague thereof was exceeding great.
> (Revelation 16:18-19, 21)

"George Omega and I are situated at a crest overlooking the Valley of Jehoshaphat. Up till this time it has been known as the Valley of Kidron. But our King and Redeemer has given it a new name...the Valley of Jehoshaphat."

"And quite a significant name it is. For Jehoshaphat means, 'Jehovah judges.' And we are about to witness just that. Jesus Christ, the Redeemer will become Jesus Christ, the Judge."

"From here one can see Jerusalem's East Gate, the Golden Gate, closed for hundreds of years...but now open. This scene

> Then said the Lord unto me; This gate shall be shut, it shall not be opened, and no man shall enter in by it; because the Lord, the God of Israel, hath entered in by it, therefore it shall be shut.
>
> It is for the prince; the prince, he shall sit in it to eat bread before the Lord; he shall enter by the way of the porch of that gate, and shall go out by the way of the same.
> (Ezekiel 44:2-3)

Garden Tomb

CALVARY &
GOLGOTHA

PALESTINE ARCHAEOLOGICAL
MUSEUM

ST POLYEUCHT
MOSAIC

POST
OFFICE

TOWER OF
THE STORK

BUS
STATION

HEROD'S
GATE

Saladin Street

ENTRANCE TO
SOLOMON'S QUARRIES

Suleiman Road

Es-Sa Adich Road

DAMASCUS
GATE

BATH OF
VIRGIN MARY ST

POOL OF
BETHESDA

MOSLEM
QUARTER

CHURCH OF
ST ANNE

ST STEPHEN'S
GATE

NOTRE DAME
DE FRANCE

CHRISTIAN
QUARTER

FRANCISCAN CONVENT
OF FLAGELLATION

CHURCH OF
ST EUTHYMIUS

SOBORS DE SION
PRETORIUM

ECCE HOMO

TO
MOUNT OF
OLIVES

TERRA
SANCTA

OUR LADY
OF THE SPASM

SCARP OF
ANTONIA

HARAM ES-SHERIF

NEW
GATE

COPTIC
PATRIARCHATE

MOSLEM
WAQF

GOLDEN
GATE

ST SAVIOUR
CHURCH

KANKAH
MOSQUE

CHURCH OF THE
HOLY SEPULCHRE

PLACE OF
CONSUL

MOSLEM
CEMETERY

COLLEGE
DES FRERES

HOSPICE
ALEXANDRE

DOME OF
THE ROCK

GREEK ORTHODOX
PATRIARCHATE

CASA
NOVA

OMAR
MOSQUE

CHURCH OF
THE REDEEMER

LATIN
PATRIARCHATE

POOL OF
HEZEKIAH

MURISTAN

CHURCH OF
ST JOHN
PRODROMOS

KHAN ES
SULTAN

KALIDI
LIBRARY

TOMB OF
APSALOM

David Street

WAILING
WALL

TOMB OF
ZACHARIAH

JAFFA GATE

ST MARK'S
CHURCH

JEWISH
QUARTER

AQSA
MOSQUE

CITADEL

CHURCH OF
ST THOMAS

HURVA
SYNAGOGUE

ARMENIAN
GARDENS

ARMENIAN
QUARTER

DUNG
GATE

EXCAVATIONS

ST JAMES'
CATHEDRAL

HOUSE OF
ANNAS

Omar Bel El-Khatab St

MOUNT
OPHEL

GIHON FOUNTAIN

ZION GATE

ARMENIAN
PALACE OF CAIAPHAS

TOMB OF
PHARAOH'S
DAUGHTER

DORMITION
ABBEY

HEZEKIAH'S
TUNNEL

CENACLE

ST PETER
GALLICANTUS

POOL OF
SILOAM

SILOAM
VILLAGE

MOUNT SION

CONVENT OF
ST ONUPHRIUS

N

VALLEY   OF   HINNOM   (GEHENNA)

FIELD OF BLOOD
(HACELDAMA)

CRUSADER
CHARNEL-HOUSE

0   200 metres
0   200 yards

TO HEBRON
BETHLEHEM

THE OLD CITY OF
JERUSALEM
in the 1970's

looks so impressive from below, from the Valley of Jehoshaphat... but that open gate will serve as a picture of regret for those who failed to claim the promise of redemption. To the right, and far below in the valley is the village of Silwan. This you may recall was the Bible city of Siloam."

"Directly in front of us are several great tombs...the most noticeable is the tomb of Absalom, David's third son. David, incidentally, is soon to become Regent of Jerusalem. You may recall that Absalom was a most handsome man. Once a year he would get a haircut. His cut hair weighed all of 3 pounds."

"Absalom had great designs on King David's throne and, in fact, proclaimed himself King. His selfish greed ended in his own death when his hair became caught in the branches of an oak tree, and his murderers caught him."

"In that last battle, 20,000 men died."

George interrupted. "The Mount of Olives is no longer what it once was, as it appeared in previous centuries, a lonely place where one would wander and meditate. Today, if one were to name it after the objects most conspicuous on its slopes, it should be called the Mount of Hotels.

"Below us is a scene I find most difficult to describe...a huge sea of a mass of faces...an open area where the Judge sits upon a throne...made from materials I fail to recognize. A luminous glow permeates the spot. I don't know what to say. I just don't...."

But in all Israel there was none to be so much praised as Absalom for his beauty: from the sole of his foot even to the crown of his head there was no blemish in him.

And when he cut the hair of his head he weighed it (for at each year's end he cut it, because its weight was a burden to him) and it weighed 200 shekels by the king's weight.
(2 Samuel 14:25-26 Amplified Bible)

Then said Joab, I may not tarry thus with thee. And he took three spears in his hand, and thrust them through the heart of Absalom, while he was yet alive in the midst of the oak.
(2 Samuel 18:14)

And the people of Israel were defeated there before the servants of David, and the slaughter there that day was great, 20,000 men.
(2 Samuel 18:7)

Tom Malone stepped in to fill the gap. "George Omega is a young Christian, a Living Believer. Perhaps, I, a Resurrected Believer, can give a more complete account of what you are witnessing on your television screens."

"This is the Judgment of the Gentiles. As Scriptures indicate, it is taking place immediately after the Judgment of the Nation Israel. What we will see are Living Gentiles...not Resurrected Gentiles...who will be judged on the basis of whether they have or have not accepted Christ as Saviour and King. The die has already been cast. It is now too late to change their decision. For those eventually destined to the Lake of Fire...this is a regret they will take with them throughout all of eternity."

"This is a judgment of individuals...not of nations as a whole. Rulers will be judged on the basis of wrongs committed. And their subjects will be judged on whether they obeyed and followed God or men."

> Then Peter and the other apostles answered and said, We ought to obey God rather than men.
>
> (Acts 5:29)

"May I repeat, this is a judgment of the Living Gentiles...not the dead. The Great White Throne Judgment will not take place until *after* the 1000 year Millennium. At that time godless leaders, who are presently dead, such as Chairman Mao, Adolph Hitler, Alexei Kosygin and others, will be resurrected and face the final judgment. This is found in Revelation, chapter 20, verses 12 and 15."

"Now, let's go down to the Valley floor to give you a first hand account. George Omega should be there by now. Come in, George."

"This is George Omega...the press of the crowds is unbelievable. The wailing and crying are hard to imagine. If I could rename this place I believe I would call it the Valley of Regret. For here, shortly, for these all of future life will be determined within a few seconds...what many termed a Bible fantasy is suddenly becoming a horrifying reality. Just a moment...the judgment is about to begin."

"A young woman stands before the Redeemer King. She wants to speak and yet words just don't come out. It's like waiting a lifetime to say a poignant speech and then when that moment arrives...one becomes speechless. She fails to look up. Her head is bowed...as though in prayer. Her hand clutches a well-worn Bible. The Redeemer King is about to speak. Let's listen."

> Come, you who are blessed of My Father,
> inherit the kingdom prepared for you
> from the foundation of the world.

"May I step in a moment, George?" Tom Malone inquired. "This is a familiar verse of Scripture taken right from the New Testament book of Matthew, chapter 25, verse 34."

"Thank you, Tom for that background information. And now another steps forth. I can't believe it. It's my own boss. Why it's Walter Brinks. Walter! Walter! What are you doing here?"

"I don't understand it. There is no response. His eyes stare blankly in space as though some unseen power has suddenly made him powerless. He walks toward the Redeemer King but the face has suddenly changed. It's uncanny. It's not a face of kind redemption...but suddenly it appears as the face of a stern judge. He's speaking. He's speaking. I've never seen such an abrupt change of personality.

> Depart from Me, accursed one, into the eternal
> fire which has been prepared for the devil and
> his angels."[1]

George felt weak and horrified.

"Oh no! Oh, this can't be. They can't. He's my boss. My best friend! Where are they taking him?"

...these will go away into eternal punishment[2]

"What about that girl? Is she going there, too?"

...but the righteous into eternal life.[3]

The events and the horror of the day were too much for George Omega. He could not watch anymore. It was all over.

What he longed for...1000 years of happiness...so far had been days of disaster and heart-rending tragedy.

He met Faye and Bill and Helen back at the apartment.

[1] Matthew 25:41   [2] Matthew 25:46   [3] Matthew 25:46

Faye was crying as Bill put his arms around her.

That action of love triggered a violent outburst.

"Get away from me, Bill. Look at you...holier than thou...I'm going to have your baby in 7 months...but you're no longer my husband. You're a Resurrected Believer," she said, with a lifting sneer to the tone of her voice.

"And what am I?...a peon on earth. I can look at you. I can even touch you. But I can't love you! I can't love you! Am I going to bring a child in a world like this. All Daddy and I have seen these past few days are terrible judgments. The crying and screaming are driving me crazy. Is that all this new age knows is judgments! Where's the love?"

"A baby!" Bill shouted. "Honey, I'm so happy!"

But George Omega, both surprised at the announcement and shocked, had other thoughts.

Somehow he felt that a worse thing was yet to come.

Little did those in that room realize how true that would be!

Chapter 4

JOURNEY TO JERUSALEM

With Walter Brinks gone, George Omega was quickly summoned to New York. Terry Malone and Sylvia Epstein accompanied him.

He dreaded the flight...because he wanted to remain in Jerusalem where all the action was occurring.

But World Television Network was in a state of chaos. And an urgent transatlantic call made it mandatory that he return to headquarters.

How would the place look, he wondered. All the familiar faces he once knew...would they be gone...would some still be there? Harry Sutherland, one of the vice-presidents at the Network had briefed him via phone...but the conversation was not long.

Harry Sutherland...funny...George thought...never dreamed he was a Christian. He was so quiet...never talked to me about the Bible.

Guess I'll be in for a few surprises, George thought, as the Concorde jet crossed the continent of Europe.

Soon the seat belt sign was turned on and George knew that the answers to many of his questions would be forthcoming shortly.

The pilot was on the intercom.

"Good evening, ladies and gentlemen. Or should I say, good day. We are experiencing some unusual occurrences. In our normal flight schedule this would be evening since we will be landing in New York at 7:30 PM. We are presently 500 miles out at sea and already in our landing pattern. But as you can see, it is not evening. For the past few days a rather surprising phenomena has faced us. We seem to have a perpetual day. Even the moon is reflecting much more light."

"Scientists and agriculturists have told us if such a condition continues it will revolutionize the farm belts throughout the world resulting in increased productivity."

> Moreover the light of the moon shall be as the light of the sun, and the light of the sun shall be sevenfold, as the light of seven days, in the day that the Lord bindeth up the breach of His people, and healeth the stroke of their wound.
>
> (Isaiah 30:26)

Sylvia, who had majored in Ecology in college, also worked for the United States government in Environmental Protection.

"George," she said, "do you realize what is happening? With increased productivity and land reclamation...famine will be abolished. Everyone will have enough to eat. Why even wars could cease. Last year alone 15 million people died of hunger. Apparently the blessings of the Millennium are already starting."

"Sylvia, if that's true," Terry interrupted, "if the Millennium is really starting, won't that mean that there will be other changes taking place on the earth, too? What about the smog and air pollution that has been choking New York City where all private autos were banned last year...where oxygen units were placed in telephone booths throughout the city? Will this change?"

Just then the pilot continued on the intercom: "A bulletin has just been received. I am sure many of you are aware of the tremendous pollution problems we have been faced with not only in America but also throughout the world. Within a radius of 35 miles of Los Angeles alone there are 45 incorporated cities. Within a 60-mile radius of downtown Los Angeles live 12.6 million persons who, up until the recent auto ban, drove 6.9 million cars. Los Angeles was known as the most motorized cluster of human beings in the world. And New York City was not far behind. One in 4 deaths in New York are linked to pollution. This pall of death was reaching frightening proportions because our 7-mile umbrella ceiling that envelopes our entire earth was trapping us. Pollutants, rising in the air, hit this barrier and then came right back down."

"Our whole earth system has become so clogged we were rapidly coming to a standstill. Recent weather reports have indicated some amazing changes. We have just received these announcements. Normally our landing into Kennedy International has to be made solely on instruments, even in daylight ...visibility being less than 1 mile."

"Meteorologists tell us violent updrafts of air in the past few days have apparently created a new atmosphere...like someone opening the door of a smoke-filled room and a draft of air suddenly filling the room expelling the polluted climate. They report it was like lifting the lid off of a pressurized container. Upon release there was a 'whoosh,' and the earth looked like a new baby...no more wrinkled skin of aging."

"What that all comes down to is this...from what can be gathered there is no more 7 mile ceiling enveloping the earth system. All the pollutants in the air have been released into outer space. The air system is bright and clear. All systems are go. Our landing will be a visual approach...and even at 7:30 PM...in BRIGHT DAYLIGHT. What else can I say but PRAISE GOD!"

Everyone on the plane clapped and cheered.

"Unbelievable," George shouted. "Simply unbelievable!"

"Sylvia," Terry exclaimed, "Normally on happy occasions... or when a plane is delayed in takeoff...the pilot orders a round of free drinks for everyone...but now, it's like living a clean life...free of sin. Everyone is so happy...no need for bars or for smoking sections. I've got to pinch myself. I can't believe it's true."

Terry was going to say more but a sudden feeling of faintness caused her to grip her seat and recline to retain her composure.

In every disaster...the looters were there first.

They were even robbing the dead.

The scene at the New York office of World Television Network was hectic. It was like picking up the pieces after a disaster. One of George's first jobs was finding out who was left. Harry Sutherland asked him to call a meeting of all personnel. World Television had employed 1400 people. It was going to be a difficult task. Phone lines were down, rubble filled the streets... many buildings were no longer standing.

"What in the world has happened, Harry?" George exclaimed.

"We've had a severe earthquake here...a few days ago. Many thousands were killed. Who knows, perhaps a million. Fortunately we foresaw the crowded conditions of Manhattan and built ourselves a new, low, one-story headquarters outside the city. Our old building is nothing but a pile of rock. Just a few cracks in the wall here, however. Not serious."

"How did you maintain any order and get things moving again?"

"At first, it seemed impossible. Amazing, in the midst of crisis... the New York labor unions were fighting as to who would remove the rubble, squabbles and strikes erupted over 'hazardous and overtime pay.' Undertakers were demanding cash in advance for funerals and grave diggers were picketing funeral parlors because many of the bodies were buried in a common grave...thus cutting out a major part of their income."

> And there were voices, and thunders, and lightnings; and there was a great earthquake, such as was not since men were upon the earth, so mighty an earthquake, and so great.
>
> And the great city was divided into three parts, and the cities of the nations fell: the great Babylon came in remembrance before God, to give unto her the cup of the wine of the fierceness of his wrath.
>
> **(Revelation 16:18-19)**

"I can't believe it, Harry!"

"There was much more. The looting was unbelievable. Where all the people came from I don't know...but they drove in like hordes from as far away as Akron, Ohio and Greenville, North Carolina. Some even came down from Canada. Before rescuers could begin their work...the looters were there robbing the dead. In fact...do you remember the Canadian seal episode where seals were clubbed to death and then skinned?"

"Yes, I recall."

"Remember, that many seals did not die from the blows... but were simply stunned. And money-hungry hunters skinned them alive. What I saw a few days ago, I could never believe. I still get nauseated thinking of it. And I know it's true because I witnessed it myself. Some people were lying under a pile of rubble. What I thought were rescuers were feverishly lifting the rocks. This was on Wall Street. When they reached the bodies which appeared dead...they methodically went through their pockets pulling out their wallets, ripping off their wrist watches. A few started to move. I ran over to stop them...but one burly fellow pinned my arms back while his friends did the dirty work. And this, you will not believe. One man they called 'pliers Joe' pulled a pair of pliers from his pocket...they looked like a dental tool. He yanked open this one man's mouth, secured the plier to a gold tooth and pulled."

"George, the man was not dead, the earthquake had simply stunned him...and the pulling of his tooth brought him to his senses screaming hysterically...and trying to get up. Before I could do anything 'pliers Joe' grabbed a hammer from his pocket and brought it crashing down on the poor man's skull. They stripped him of every last cent he had...and went on to the next pile of bodies."

"Harry, I find that hard to believe. Can man actually be that cruel to his fellow man?"

"Such inhumanity is not hard to believe, George. It's been going on for many years. Don't you remember way back in December, 1972, as an example, when that Eastern Air Lines jet crashed in the Everglades? Over 90 were killed. Who were the first people on the scene in the muck and in that eerie darkness? The LOOTERS. And rescue teams said they were methodically robbing the dead...taking watches and wallets. Remember the rescue team report, '...what can you do? We were trying to help the survivors and get them out of there.'"

"I do recall that, Harry. In fact, one Coast Guardsman, a personal friend of mine told me, 'I don't know how people like that get here so fast.'"

"But tell me, Harry, with all these difficulties...strikes, crime, etc., how has so much order and restoration been achieved?"

"That's what got me digging into Isaiah, Zechariah and Revelation. I was never much of a Christian...as far as witnessing to others. That's why you may have been surprised to see me left. When the earthquake struck, I knew something was happening...went straight to the Bible. Odd, isn't it...for years it gathered dust on my shelf...a good thing to have around for weddings and funerals...a status symbol. Then suddenly, I would have fought off ten men to get hold of a Bible. What was an object of little importance, overnight became my most treasured possession. As I studied hour after hour...I knew that what had occurred was the Battle of Armageddon and soon the Millennium would be ushered in. That meant judgments, first for the Jew and the nation Israel and then for the Gentile."

"I reasoned to myself, if the Bible hit Armageddon on the button for accuracy...then everything else would also fall into place *exactly* as Scriptures said it would. And it has! Shortly after this chaos here, what appeared like an army of men arrived both on ships and space ships!"

"You mean they used our space shuttles, Harry?"

"Yes, just about every means of transportation. You know our advanced delta-winged space shuttles reach an altitude of 25 miles and a speed of 2800 miles per hour *less than two minutes after lift-off.*"

"Who were these men?"

"I later found out they were Resurrected Believers...in fact I recognized some...they worked in our office...died in the early 1970's. Bodies looked like ours...but all physical defects were gone...they never seemed to tire...like superhuman... angel-like. Their silhouette was outlined in a luminous glow. That's the way you could spot them. Walls, ordinary hazards of traffic didn't affect them. And through some unseen power, of God, I am sure, they were able to corral first all living Jews ...and a few days later all Gentiles. I know you couldn't see me in that sea of faces in the Valley of Jehoshaphat but I was there ...and then just as quickly, shuttled back.

"It's like a new world. No more confusion. All of the trouble-makers are now gone. Everyone is working day and (I was al-most going to say night)...no more bickering and in a few days we will be back to normal."

"But I've talked enough, George, I understand there is going to be a big meeting in Jerusalem and after you get things in order here, I'd like you to go back to cover it."

"Sir," a secretary interrupted, "telephone for Mr. Omega."

"Excuse me, Harry, I'll take it in my office."

An old familiar chorus crossed George's mind, and he started singing it as he walked to his office...

> One thousand years with Christ the Son;
> One thousand years and they've just begun;
> One thousand years, what wedded bliss!
> One thousand years, what joy is this!

"Hello, this is George Omega."

"George, come over to the apartment, quick. It's Terry, she's sick, dreadfully sick!"

"What's wrong, Sylvia? She seemed alright on the plane."

"Can't talk now, George. Please hurry."

* * *

Terry looked like a little child tucked in among the clean white hospital covers. Her pale face seemed to blend in with the pillow. Her long silken blonde hair was disheveled. There was no doubt about it. Terry was a sick girl.

George had no time to ask questions when he arrived at the apartment. Foremost in his mind was rushing her to the hospital.

"Terry," he said, "I've been so busy, I haven't had a chance to call Tom. I'll call him now."

Suddenly Terry's eyes opened. "No, oh, no, please George, please don't call Tom now. You'll only worry him...and me. Please, George."

"But Terry, you're sick...Terry, what do you feel is wrong with you?"

"Nothing, George, nothing, it's probably something I ate on the plane. Suddenly I felt woozy and weak."

Dr. Leyton walked in with his nurse.

"Mr. Omega, would you mind sitting in the waiting room a few minutes while we give Mrs. Malone an initial examination. It won't take long. I'll be out shortly to inform you of my findings."

A thousand and one things raced into George's mind as he sat in the waiting room. There was so much to do...another flight back to Jerusalem...and now Terry added to the complications. George had left Sylvia at the house, much to her reluctance, requesting she pack for their flight back to Jerusalem.

Just then Sylvia popped in.

"Sylvia, what on earth are you doing here? Why aren't you packing?"

"George, I'm the fastest packer this side of Madison Avenue. I'm worried about Terry. She isn't her usual self. You know, I think she's..."

Dr. Leyton interrupted the conversation.

"Mr. Omega, where is Mrs. Malone's husband?"

"He's in Jerusalem, Doctor. He is a Resurrected Believer, of course."

"Oh, that may complicate things. When did Mr. Malone die?"

"A little over two months ago, sir. Don't you remember? He was the first to die by guillotine right on a church lawn by Brother Bartholomew."

"A little over two months ago? I'm glad to hear that. I am sure Mr. Malone will be very happy."

"Why, Doctor?"

"Well, he is going to become a father. Terry Malone is pregnant...in her third month."

"I don't believe it," Sylvia stammered joyously. "I don't believe it. Tom will be thrilled. Wow. Think of it, George...first Faye is having a baby and now Terry. That's a double blessing!"

"Let's hope so, Sylvia. Let's pray that both Faye and Terry go full term."

"Mr. Omega...you're a newspaperman but apparently not up on your news. That shouldn't be any problem now...that is, Terry going full term. She's had some initial difficulty that normally would require two weeks of complete bed rest. But in this new Millennial Age our medical techniques have been completely revolutionized."

"In the past, in spite of all man's progress in the science of medicine and surgery, we were still living in a world of suffering and death. Rides past endless miles of homes, hospitals and sanitariums made us aware of this fact."

"Our accident ward and emergency room are just about going out of business. Disease and illness as we know it is already slowing down, we believe, soon to minimal."

And the inhabitant shall not say, I am sick....
(Isaiah 33:24)

No longer will there be in it an infant who lives but a few days, Or an old man who does not live out his days; For the youth will die at the age of one hundred And the one who does not reach the age of one hundred Shall be thought accursed.
(Isaiah 65:20 ASV)

"Never before have I seen so many crutches brought back to this hospital in spite of the recent earthquake devastation we have witnessed. My own nephew who has been deaf and dumb since birth can now hear and speak."

"You will recall in the 60's through the 1980's we relied heavily on antibiotics and chemical derivatives for healing. But in the last few days our swing back

Then the eyes of the blind shall be opened, and the ears of the deaf shall be unstopped.

Then the lame man leap as an hart, and the tongue of the dumb sing: for in the wilderness shall

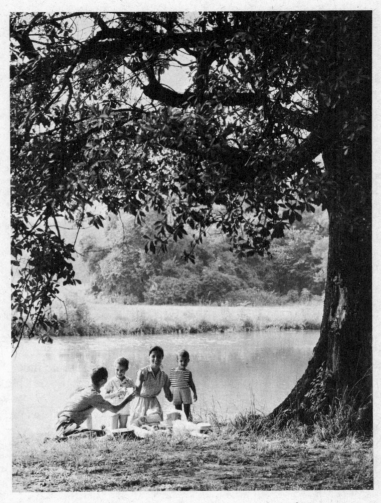

Think of it, LEAVES, both in crushed and whole form, are providing amazing and quick healing!

to the simple things and our lack of these drugs...has forced us to turn back to herbs...old fashion

waters break out, and streams in the desert.

(Isaiah 35:5-6)

remedies. In the past they had some limited success. But now we are finding such ordinary things as leaves...think of it, LEAVES, both in crushed and whole form, are providing amazing and quick healing. There is actually power in a simple leaf! God's power!"

"That's what we have prescribed for Mrs. Malone. By the morning she'll be as good as new and can accompany you to Jerusalem."

It was a wonderful reunion at Lod airport in Jerusalem. Tom had not been told of the problems that occurred in New York

And by the river on its bank, on one side and on the other, will grow all kinds of trees for food. Their leaves will not wither, and their fruit will not fail. They will bear every month because their water flows from the sanctuary, and their fruit will be for food and their leaves for healing.

(Ezekiel 47:12 ASV)

nor that Terry was going to have a baby. George, after much thought, felt it better that Terry break the news in her own way upon their return.

What was this new world going to be like? George asked himself. For years he had been dealing with Brother Bartholomew. He knew what that world of tribulation was like. Bartholomew's ruling with an iron fist, crushing those who failed to toe the line.

1000 years...the Millennium...somewhere along the line he was told the Millennial Kingdom would be a *theocracy*. He should know the full impact of that word...theocracy...he mused. Exactly what does that mean?

He pulled a book from his bookshelf...the dictionary. Let me see, R, S, T...Ta...Te...Th...here it is, THEOCRACY. Slowly, he read:

THEOCRACY

1. a form of government in which God or a deity is recognized as the supreme civil ruler.
2. a system of government by priests claiming a divine commission.
3. a state under such a form of government.

George wanted to investigate further. He glanced through THINGS TO COME by J. Dwight Pentecost and quite by accident came to page 502. There was a Scripture reference to the theocratic kingdom in the Millennium. It was found in Isaiah 40:10,

> Behold the Lord God will come with might,
> With His arm ruling for Him...

He checked other translations. What did that mean? "...His arm ruling for Him...?

And there he found it...

He will rule with awesome strength.

All of his pent-up joy suddenly burst like a balloon. George Omega sunk dejectedly in his chair.

Helen came in to remind him of his appointment in the Temple Court to meet David, Regent of Palestine.

"Why are you troubled, George?"

"Helen, do you realize this Millennial government is a theocracy?"

"Of course I do."

"Do you know what a theocracy is...God will rule with a rod of iron. Is that any different than the seven tortuous years I've been through with Brother Bartholomew? Helen, I don't know...I'm beginning to have my doubts."

"Honey, it's only natural for you to have this reaction. But a theocracy isn't new. A true theocracy was established at the time of creation. God was recognized as sovereign. Part of this sovereignty that belonged to God was delegated to man, who was to rule over the earth in a form of intermediary authority. In that theocracy Adam derived his authority from God."

> Thou shalt break them with a rod of iron; thou shalt dash them in pieces like a potter's vessel.
>
> Be wise now therefore, O ye kings: be instructed, ye judges of the earth.
>
> Serve the Lord with fear, and rejoice with trembling.
>
> Kiss the Son, lest he be angry and ye perish from the way, when His wrath is kindled but a little. Blessed are all they that put their trust in Him.
>
> (Psalm 2:9-12)

"Why can't it be a Republic, where legislative, executive and judicial power is lodged in the people? This would be more democratic? Surely God in this Millennial Age will be a God of love and of grace. With all the unsaved gone...why can't a democratic form of government work perfectly?"

"George, it's true those who have not accepted Christ as Saviour have already been sent to Hades. And at the end of the 1000 years they will go to the Lake of Fire. But you must remember that there are still millions of Living Believers here on earth. Some are married. Other Living Believers will marry. Their conjugal relationships will still enable them to have children...even though such relationships cannot occur with Resurrected Believers. From this union will come children. Earth's population is going to soar."

"Will these babies automatically be Christians without sin?" George asked Helen.

"That's just it, honey," she replied, "you must keep in mind that all those who will be born of Living Believers during this 1000 year Millennial Age will have a sin nature. It will be necessary for them to accept Christ as Saviour and Lord if they are to participate in the final and continuing eternity that begins after the Millennium."

...out of them shall proceed thanksgiving and the voice of them that make merry: and I will multiply them, and they shall not be few; I will also glorify them, and they shall not be small.

Their children also shall be as aforetime, and their congregation shall be established before me, and I will punish all that oppress them.

(Jeremiah 30:19-20)

"But what's that all have to do with a Theocracy and a Republic?"

"Our ways are not God's ways. If a theocracy did not exist, positions of leadership could go to unredeemed men and women. God has already given human rule its chance, and it failed miserably. This no doubt is one reason God through Christ will

Incline your ear, and come unto me: hear, and your soul shall live; and I will make an everlasting covenant with you, even the sure mercies of David.

Behold, I have given him for a witness to the people, a leader and commander to the people.

(Isaiah 55:3-4)

rule with awesome strength. This is one reason why David is Regent of all of Palestine."

"Remember all the talk about a one world system many years ago. It would never work under the government of sinful men. Now we will see a true world government...a unified government...ruled and governed by our King Redeemer. And Israel will no longer be divided."

And I will make them one nation in the land upon the mountains of Israel; and one king shall be king to them all: and they shall be no more two nations, neither shall they be divided into two kingdoms any more at all...

And the heathen shall know that I the Lord do sanctify Israel when my sanctuary shall be in the midst of them for evermore. (Ezekiel 37:22,28)

Tom Malone kissed the tears from Terry's cheeks.

"Terry, this should be the happiest day of your life. We're going to have a baby. Won't it be something if you and Faye have your baby on the same day."

"It could happen, honey," Terry sobbed.

"Suppose Faye has a boy and we have a girl...and one day they get married. Wouldn't it be a wonderful plan? Bill and I...even though we are Resurrected Believers...will through our children be able to complete a union of love. Honey, don't cry. George told me all about it. You won't lose the baby. Everything will work out great...you'll see."

"Everything will work out great." Those words seemed to unbalance Terry into uncontrollable sobs.

Tom gently placed her on the couch, and tucked her under a blanket. He then kissed her tear stained cheeks.

"I know you're tired honey. The strain's been too much for you. Sylvia will stay with you while you get some much needed rest."

Terry dropped off to sleep with the words, "Everything will work out great" ringing in her ears. Softly she prayed, "I hope so, I hope so."

Chapter 5

LIFE IN THE LEAF

To George Omega, everyday brought a new surprise. George discovered that his new boss at World Television Network was a Living Believer. If anything, he would have believed that Harry's wife, Carole, would have been. In all the rushing of the past few days he forgot to ask about Carole. Carole was on a 21-day Holy Land tour just before everything broke loose.

Come to think of it, he did recall Harry trying to track her down a couple days ago.

In a few minutes George would be on worldwide satellite TV beaming his Special Event newscast back to the United States. So much had changed in the alignment of the nations and in the topography of the world that he knew he would need help. That's why he asked Bill Sanders and Tom Malone along. As Resurrected Believers they would have a thorough grasp of the situation.

Walking to the Temple area he automatically looked for the familiar Dome of the Rock and the more recently built Temple around it, which had been Brother Bartholomew's masterpiece. This eight-sided building, surmounted by a beautifully proportioned dome covered with shiny gold-toned aluminum, had been a sight to behold. He remembered the eight arcades, known as scales or balances, where Moslems believed on Judgment Day a giant set of these balances would be here to weigh the merits of each one.

But the Dome of the Rock and Brother Bartholomew's newer Temple were both gone. An earthquake at the time of the Battle of Armageddon had disintegrated them both.

The Temple area was now a vast court. Construction had already begun on the building of a most elaborate Temple. Construction methods had improved so greatly in the past 30 years that it was anticipated this Temple would be completed within a few short months.

What would it be like to meet David? he mused. Would he be like one of us?

Then he brought me to the nave and measured the side pillars; six cubits wide on each side was the width of the side pillar...

And He said to me, "Son of man, this is the place of My throne and the place of the soles of My feet, where I will dwell among the sons of Israel forever. And the house of Israel will not again defile My holy name, neither they nor their kings, by their harlotry and by the corpses of their king when they die...

This is the law of the house: its entire area on the top of the mountain all around shall be most holy. Behold, this is the law of the house.

(Ezekiel 41:1; 43:7,12 ASV)

Quickly George, Bill and Tom mounted the stairs leading to the TV telecasting tower.

No sooner had they seated themselves when George's phone rang.

An agitated voice could be heard on the other end.

"George, this is Harry Sutherland. You'll be going on in two minutes. But I need your help. I can't locate Carole. I guess you knew that we hadn't been too close lately. That was one of the reasons I sent her on that Holy Land tour...thought she could get closer to what it's all about. But my personal life hasn't been without fault, either. In all our married life, not once did I talk to her about her need of God. Once I started to but she hit me where it hurts when she replied, 'Don't tell me about your God with all the running around you do!' But I need her now...more than ever before. I've tried every available avenue... I can't even reach the tour guide in East Jerusalem. He was headquartered in the St. George Hotel. George, I'm desperate. She has to be somewhere. I'm going out of my mind!"

"I'll get busy on it right away, Harry...but my ready light is on now. Be in touch, soon."

George turned to face the TV camera and he began his commentary.

"Hello, this is George Omega, once more coming from the heart of Jerusalem. Jerusalem where for years Israel has asked *'Ma ihieh hassof?'* What will be the end? Jerusalem, with a recorded history of some 4000 years...has been more familiar to more people for a longer period of time than any other place on earth. This is the city of David, who unified the land and proclaimed Jerusalem the capital in the tenth century B.C. This is the city of Solomon's Temple. This is the city of Isaiah and Jeremiah."

"Throughout the centuries of their dispersion, in whatever far corner of the earth they found themselves, the Jews prayed for their return to Zion. Archaeologists and historians have long wondered why Jerusalem should have been established where it was. It enjoyed none of the physical features which favored advancement and prosperity, such as were enjoyed by other important cities in the world. It stood at the head of no great river. It overlooked no great harbor. It commanded no great highway. It possessed no mineral riches. It was off the main trade routes. Yet over it multiple thousands have been slaughtered throughout the centuries. It has been burned and pillaged, wrecked and razed but always to grow again from its own rubble. No other city has so profoundly touched the lives and laws of men. Hundreds of millions who have never seen Jerusalem honor it in thought and in prayer."

"An interesting sidelight for our viewers," Tom interrupted, "while Jerusalem has never stood at the head of a great river... recent events have changed that. As many of you know a stream now runs beneath the Temple area. Right in this area the water is up to one's ankles and just some 5000 feet from here it's impossible to walk across. There are many trees now growing on

Then he brought me back to the door of the house; and behold, water was flowing from under the threshold of the house toward the east, for the house faced east. And the water was flowing down from under, from the right side of the house, from south of the altar.

Now when I had returned, behold, on the bank of the river there were very many trees on the one side and on the other.

both sides of this river. What did you find in the Dead Sea area, Bill?"

"Tom, it's really amazing! This river flows east through the desert into the Jordan Valley and the Dead Sea. In fact the Dead Sea is no longer dead. Many of you who have travelled here remember that the Dead Sea has the earth's lowest surface, 1300 feet below sea level. The salt concentration reached 25%, four times that of ocean water. The magnesium bromide prevented the growth of organic life, and the heat was extreme. In this area God's destruction of Sodom took place."

"But the waters here now are no longer salty. They are fresh and pure. This is a fisherman's paradise because fish abound in this sea! There are all kinds of fish here...and all kinds of fruit trees grow along the river banks. We have been told that the leaves will never turn brown and fall!"

"An unusual phenomena, Bill," Tom added, "is that the fruit trees will bear a new crop every month — without fail! These waters flowing from the Temple area have most unusual characteristics...a special blessing of life from God. And the leaves of these trees have already been used for healing. My own wife, Terry, has benefited from this new spiritual medicine."

"An interesting thought," George remarked, "is that in direct contrast to this, the marshes and swamps in the area do not contain fresh water but continue

Then he said to me, "These waters go out toward the eastern region and go down into the Arabah [the valley of the Jordan]; then they go toward the sea, being made to flow into the sea, and the waters of the [Dead] sea become fresh.

And it will come about that every living creature which swarms in every place where the river goes, will live. And there will be very many fish, for these waters go there, and the others become fresh, so everything will live where the river goes.
(Ezekiel 47:1,7-9 ASV)

And it will come about that fishermen will stand beside it; from Eingedi to Eneglaim there will be a place for the spreading of nets. Their fish will be according to their kinds, like the fish of the Mediterranean Sea, very many.
(Ezekiel 47:10 ASV)

And by the river on its bank... will grow all kinds of trees for food... and their leaves for healing.
(Ezekiel 47:12 ASV)

The Dead Sea is no longer dead. The familiar salt towers have all disappeared!

salty. I wonder if this is a picture of this Millennium Period...that while peace and happiness will prevail in this near-perfect time... we will still be witnessing some conflict."

"Bill, fill our viewers in on the nature of this new Kingdom and on Jerusalem's part in this."

"Thank you, George. As I am sure you know, the world government now is a theocracy. The theocratic rule will center in Jerusalem. This is the center of our Millennial earth. As our television cameras pan the skyline, let's get a shot of the entire area from our blimp overhead. Jerusalem is already much bigger than it ever was before in history. But the city will even be enlarged far beyond its present dimensions. It will never again be destroyed."

"Everyone is now able to come to Jerusalem. There is no need for passports...nor for that matter, innoculations. No baggage inspection. No body frisking. You will find this city completely accessible. Quite a contrast, isn't it from the world of the 1970's and 1980's."

"And, of course, Jerusalem is now the world's center of worship."

George, thought for a moment, then spoke. "Bill, do you know something that all of us Living

But its swamps and marshes will not become fresh; they will be left for salt.
(Ezekiel 47:11 ASV)

...in the last days... the mountain of the Lord's house shall be established in the top of the mountains, and shall be exalted above the hills; and all nations shall flow into it.

And many people shall go and say, Come ye, and let us go up to the mountain of the Lord, to the house of the God of Jacob; and He will teach us in His paths: for out of Zion shall go forth the law and the word of the Lord from Jerusalem.

And He shall judge among the nations, and shall rebuke many people: and they shall beat their swords into plowshares, and their spears into pruning hooks; nation shall not lift up sword against nation, neither shall they learn war any more.
(Isaiah 2:2-4)

All the land will be changed into a plain from Geba [the northern border of Judah] to Rimmon south of Jerusalem; but Jerusalem will rise and remain on its site from Benjamin's gate as far as the place of the First Gate to the Corner Gate, and from the Tower of Hananel to the king's wine presses.

And people will live in it, and there will be no more curse, for Jerusalem will dwell in security.
(Zechariah 14:10-11 ASV)

And an highway shall be there, and a way, and it shall be called The way of holiness; the unclean shall not pass over it;

Believers have taken for granted ...and perhaps didn't realize? And yet it is a major change...so major, some of us failed to recognize it. In fact, I'm amazed, simply amazed. This is a tremendous boon to those of us who are in the television industry... and radio!"

> but it shall be for those: the wayfaring men, though fools, shall not err therein.
>
> No lion shall be there, nor any ravenous beast shall go up thereon, it shall not be found there; but the redeemed shall walk there.
>
> (Isaiah 35:8-9)

"What's that, George?" Bill inquired.

"Our languages. We can suddenly understand each other! No more English, French, Spanish, or Russian. A few moments ago I was speaking to some Italians and a couple Israelis and we each understood each other. It never dawned on me that I would need an interpreter."

"That's true, George," Tom added, "you see, so many changes have occurred so rapidly in the past few weeks it's difficult for us to comprehend them all. What we are witnessing is a unified language. Every obstacle to human understanding and international accord has been taken away.

"Think what this will do for world trade...with these barriers removed!"

> For then will I turn to the people a pure language, that they may all call upon the name of the Lord, to serve Him with one consent.
>
> (Zephaniah 3:9)

"Right, Tom, but let's describe the scene before us," George continued. "This Temple area is being greatly enlarged as the worship center of the world. Just a moment...David, Regent over all of Palestine, has just made his entrance. Let's go down to the rostrum."

Suddenly everything became quiet. Here was David. George felt shivers run up and down his back. As a Resurrected Believer he had the same glow about him as Helen, Bill and Tom. But his regal robes quickly identified his royal status. Could this be the David born in 1040 B.C., George thought to himself ...the little David that slew Goliath, the Philistine, with a few pebbles; the David who Saul tried to slay; the David who committed adultery with Bath-sheba and murdered her husband to conceal his crime...?

His thoughts were interrupted by David, speaking:

> The Lord is my rock and my fortress and my deliverer;
> For the waves of death encompassed me;
> The torrents of destruction overwhelmed me;
> The cords of Sheol surrounded me;
>> I cried to my God;
>> And from His temple He heard my voice [1]

> And I will make an everlasting covenant with you,
> According to the faithful mercies shown to David.
> Behold, I have made him a witness to the peoples,
>> A leader and commander for the peoples. [2]
> Strangers shall no longer make Israel their slaves.

> But they shall serve the Lord their God, and
> David their king, whom I will raise up for them. [3]

David then went into the body of his message:

"In this Millennium Period, our Redeemer King, our Messiah, Jesus Christ, will receive worship. He will not engage in acts of worship. As your Regent the Lord has chosen me to lead in worship. There will be memorial sacrifices...memorials of that perfect sacrifice made by the One typified by all sacrifice, the Lamb of God, that taketh away the sin of the world."

"As you know, those born in this Millennium Period are born in sin. Salvation is still necessary for them to gain access to the coming New Heavens and New Earth. The memorial sacrifice will *not* be a means of salvation. Salvation will wholly be based on the value of the death of Christ and will be appropriated by faith alone even as Abraham appropriated God's promise and was justified.

> And without faith it is impossible to please Him, for he who comes to God must believe that He is, and that He is a rewarder of those that seek Him. [4]

> For what does the Scripture say? And Abraham believed God, and it was credited to his account as righteousness. [5]

---

[1] 2 Samuel 22:2, 5-7   [3] Jeremiah 30:9   [5] Romans 4:3, quoting Genesis 15:6
[2] Isaiah 55:3-4   [4] Hebrews 11:6

This Worship Center when completed will be a spacious square, 34 miles each way and containing about 1160 square miles. This area will be the center of all divine government and worship and will be readily accessible to all."

George Omega requested permission to address Regent David: "Sir, can you tell us a little about the Temple?"

Regent David replied:

"The Temple will be in an area 8⅓ miles long and 6⅔ miles wide...as written in Ezekiel 48:8.

The Redeemer King has appointed me Regent over all of Palestine...ministering under the authority of Jesus Christ, the King. It will be my duty to divide the land allotted to us.

What you may not realize is that now, for the first time ISRAEL will possess ALL the land promised to Abraham in Genesis 15:18-21."

"We have noticed some changes occurring, sir...what will these land changes mean?"

The topography of the land will soon be altered. Mountainous terrain will soon all disappear.

David again spoke, saying,

"The topography of the land, its features, have been greatly altered. Mountainous terrain has all but disappeared. A great fertile plain has come into existence.

Even as prophesied in Isaiah 35:7 and 51:3 there will be renewed fertility.

And rain...there will be an abundance of rain.[1]

Rain will become a blessing...and its withholding will be a penalty for those who refuse to honor God.[2]

Land will be reconstructed throughout the world because of the ravages of the period of tribulation.[3]

And Palestine will be redistributed among the 12 tribes of Israel within the next few days.[4]

ISRAEL IS ONCE AGAIN REUNITED AS A NATION!

In those days the house of Judah will walk with the house of Israel, and they will come together from the land of the north to the land that I gave your fathers as an inheritance."

"This is George Omega, bringing to a close our special telecast from Jerusalem. Regent David closed his short message to those assembled in the Temple area with a quotation from the Old Testament, Jeremiah 3:18. Its significance — Israel is back in their land...united...the fulfillment of prophecy...to the letter!"

"If I may add just a word, George, so that our viewers will understand the make-up of this new government?"

"Go right ahead, Tom."

"David is Regent over Palestine in this 1000 year Millennium Period. But he will have nobles and governors reigning under him. These subordinate rulers, working under David, will exercise the theocratic power and

And their leader shall be one of them, And their ruler shall come forth from their midst; And I will bring him near, and he shall approach Me....

(Jeremiah 30:21 ASV)

Behold a king will reign righteously, And princes will rule justly.

(Isaiah 32:1 ASV)

---

[1] Isaiah 30:23
[2] Zechariah 14:17
[3] Isaiah 61:4-5; Ezekiel 36:33-35
[4] Ezekiel 48:1-29

administer the government. But it must also be kept in mind that there will be also lesser authorities who will rule as well. Quite a description of this is found in Luke 19:12-18. Many of them will rule over a block of 15 cities throughout Israel, being responsible to the head of the tribe, who, in turn will be responsible to David. And, of course, Regent David is responsible to the Redeemer King Himself. These appointments have been made to certain Resurrected Believers as a reward for their previous faithfulness during their earthly lives."

"One other thing...we will soon be witnessing the appointment of many judges. This reign is universal, covering the entire earth. This same subdivided authority will be found in the United States, in Australia, in Africa... everywhere. So you see, we finally have a unified world government...but one under the authority of our Lord and Saviour."

> And I will restore thy judges as at the first, and thy counsellors as at the beginning: afterward thou shalt be called, The city of righteousness, the faithful city.
>
> (Isaiah 1:26)

> And there was given Him dominion, and glory, and a kingdom, that all people, nations, and languages, should serve Him: His dominion is an everlasting dominion, which shall not pass away, and His kingdom that which shall not be destroyed.
>
> And the kingdom and dominion, and the greatness of the kingdom under the whole heaven, shall be given to the people of the saints of the most High, whose kingdom is an everlasting kingdom, and all dominions shall serve and obey Him.
>
> (Daniel 7:14,27)

* * *

It had been an exciting day and George looked forward to going home to his apartment to see Helen, Sue and Tommy. Upon arriving he found Sylvia there as well as Faye and Terry.

For a period that was supposed to be happy, Sylvia and Terry never seemed to reflect it.

"George!" Sylvia exclaimed, "I just came back from the Judge's office on Nablus Road. I asked him what happened to Carole Sutherland in the judgment of the Gentiles in the Valley of Jehoshaphat. George, George...she's been sent to Hades. She never made it, George. She never made it! What will we tell Harry?"

George whitened. A feeling of revolt stirred within him. It hadn't all been settled...this Millennium. Somehow George felt that the turmoil within him would one day explode. He could not control his anger as he spoke.

"Why Carole? Why did God have to do this to Carole? She seemed so good. She attended church even more than Harry. Why not Harry? I never knew Harry was a Christian...but Carole ...she always spoke religious...counted out her tithe every Sunday...observed Lent...everything. She lived the life!"

Helen started to speak, but Sue interrupted.

"Daddy, Christ saved us not according to our works but by His grace. Don't you remember Ephesians 2:8-9...*By grace are ye saved through faith.* That's the key word, Daddy, FAITH. It is the GIFT of God. That's another key word, Daddy, **GIFT.** It's not something we can achieve on our own by money or by doing good deeds or by living a good life. To spend an eternity with God in heaven means we must accept His GIFT. Verse 9 tells us it is NOT OF WORKS. So many people fail to understand such a simple verse. Its simplicity becomes a stumbling stone for them. We must accept reality. They were wrong, those who used to claim that every religion is good and that no matter what road you travelled you would get to Heaven. This was FALSE. It simply was not true. Nowhere in the Bible was such a statement ever made. In fact Matthew 7:13-14 says just the opposite:

> Enter in at the narrow gate;
>> for wide is the gate,
>> and broad is the way
>> that leadeth to destruction,
>> and many there be who go in that way;
> Because narrow is the gate,
>> and hard is the way,
>> which leadeth unto life
>> and few there be that find it.

But many people don't bother to read the Scriptures. They go on making up their own ideas of what the Bible says. Then when judgment comes...oh, do they cry and plead...but it's too late ...too late, Daddy!"

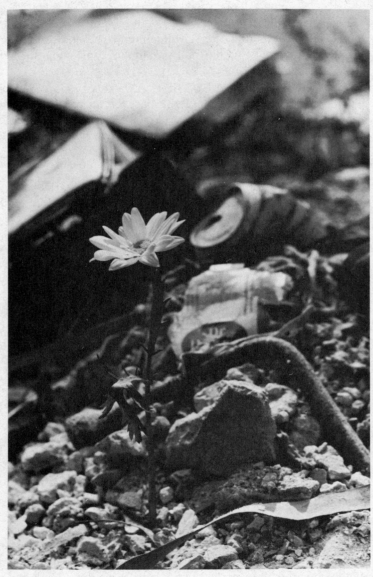

No more trash problems. The slum areas had disappeared.

Helen tried to soften Sue's comments: "George, you are now seeing first hand the reality of judgment. And it hurts. I can understand. But how often has there been sorrow in Heaven... God gave His Son on Calvary to redeem man...but man remained so engulfed in a race for material gains...that he ignored the gift; and by so ignoring God's free gift of life, he remained condemned in his sins. That's what Carole did!"

* * *

It wasn't easy for George to pick up the phone and call Harry Sutherland. How could he break the news? If it happened in the 1970's and Carole had died in some accident...at least George could comfort Harry with the wishful thought that she was in Heaven and soon he would see her there.

But this was not the 1970's...nor the 1980's.

And he could offer Harry no hope. It was beyond that. All he could say was that Carole was judged at the Valley of Jehoshaphat...and while in the milling multitude of millions... Harry passed through the right gate, Carole was ushered through the left gate and escorted by a cordon of guards to Hades to await eternal punishment in the Lake of Fire.

And that's exactly what he told Harry when the phone connection was finally established.

But all Harry could reply as though hypnotized in horror was: "No hope...no hope...for an eternity...oh my...no hope!"

* * *

The months passed quickly. In that time George had flown several times back to New York. It was a new city. No more air pollution. No more trash problems. No more abandoned cars. No more crime. The slum areas had disappeared and there was no more art for art's sake or scientific energies wasted on improving liquor qualities. All that which was once foolishly spent had suddenly been turned for world improvement. What many

...In the day that I shall have cleansed you from all your iniquities I will also cause you to dwell in the cities, and the wastes shall be builded.
(Ezekiel 36:33)

Behold, the days come, saith the Lord, that the plowman shall overtake the reaper, and

Presidents had aspired for...a "Great Society"...was now a reality.

Even wars had been eliminated.

No wonder such progress could take place. George remembered how in the 1970's the United States budget was some $250 billion. Of this, $78 billion was spent for defense and even $1 billion for flood relief. This was no longer necessary. No wars... no need for a defense budget nor arms. No hazards such as floods, fires, auto accidents...no need for relief budgets. Psalm 91 was at last a reality.

the treader of grapes him that soweth seed; and the mountains shall drop sweet wine, and all the hills shall be dissolved.
(Amos 9:13)

And I will cut off the chariot from Ephraim, And the horse from Jerusalem; And the bow of war will be cut off. And He will speak peace to the nations; And His dominion will be from sea to sea, And from the River to the ends of the earth.
(Zechariah 9:10 ASV)

They shall not hurt nor destroy in all my holy mountain: for the earth shall be full of the knowledge of the LORD, as the waters cover the sea.
(Isaiah 11:9)

Billions of dollars were no longer needed to run the United States Government. When a semblance of peace came in January, 1973 in Vietnam, Dr. Henry Kissinger had a staff of over 100 people. In 3 years time, from 1969 to 1972 the cost of running the White House doubled from $31 million to $71 million.

And working under the President at that time were 2.8 million people, drawing some $32 billion a year in salaries — *double* that of 10 years earlier in 1962!

The nation was in a Trillion dollar economy and yet it had empty pockets!

In fact, in the early 1970's, social welfare spending of all kinds by all levels of government in the U.S. topped $160 billion... and more than half of all the money American taxpayers paid went for that purpose.

But that was all in the past. These billions of dollars would no longer be wasted in man's

And they shall build houses, and inhabit them; and they shall plant vinyards, and eat the fruit of them.

They shall not build, and another inhabit; they shall not plant, and another eat: for as the days of a tree are the days of my people, and mine elect shall long enjoy the work of their hands.

puny efforts to erect a great society.

The 1000 year Millennium Age had changed all that. No more social welfare was needed. No

They shall not labour in vain, nor bring forth for trouble; for they are the seed of the blessed of the Lord, and their offspring with them.

(Isaiah 65:21-23)

more government control was needed. No more peace envoys flitting back and forth from Hanoi to Paris and from Washington to Paris.

Monies once foolishly wasted were now being directed towards a perfect industrialized society under the direct guidance of the Redeemer King. Everyone was able to work now. And everyone's needs could be met. We were living in an age of economic prosperity.

* * *

Faye suddenly awoke. She felt a strange stirring within her. It was the 9th month of her pregnancy...yet the pains normally accompanying an impending birth were not there. She was not worried. She remembered her doctor told her to drink Chamomile tea every night in her ninth month. How she treasured the promise of Ezekiel 47:12...

...their leaves for healing.

These leaves from the river bank off the fruit trees...growing where once there was a Dead Sea...now were eliminating the pain of childbirth.

Long ago in England the true chamomile was recognized by its flower and its important healing blue oil. It blossomed from May to October and the leaves were dried for tea. The tea was an aid to digestion and had a soothing, cleansing, anti-spasmodic effect. And now God had perfected this leaf for healing.

And although the pains were not there...she knew it was time to go to the hospital. She was alone at the time. George had gone over to check on Terry and Sylvia about an upcoming telecast.

Faye quickly picked up the phone, dialing Terry's apartment.

"George, oh I'm so glad to hear your voice. Can you come over, quick. I'm going to have my baby."

"Hold on," George gasped, "Terry is also going to have her's."

She's in labor. I'll get in the car and be right over. Keep calm, Faye, honey, keep calm. I'll be there quickly!"

It was like a family reunion in the hospital.

Bill beamed at Faye. He was so proud of her. And Faye was like a breath of springtime...holding her treasured possession ...a baby girl.

"What shall we name her, honey?" Bill asked.

"I would like to name her, Esther. I believe great things are in store for her, Bill. She won't become Queen of Persia, but I believe God will use her in a mighty way."

* * *

Tom Malone sat on Terry's bed. Terry was beaming. It was one of the few times Tom had seen her so radiant.

But why shouldn't she be. In her arms was a cuddly boy. Doctors had been afraid for a moment that the child was to be born blind...but a healing leaf applied to his eyelids at birth brought immediate sight.

"What will we name him, darling?" Tom asked as he kissed her gently.

"Let's call him, Bart."

"Fine, a short version of Bartimaeus...the blind man healed by Jesus as he went out from Jericho on His way to Jerusalem... wonderful...so true to our own experience! Fine, we'll call him Bart!"

Esther and Bart.

What did the future hold for them?

The Millennium was to be 1000 years of peace!

But for Esther and Bart it would also be filled with trials and tragedy.

Chapter 6

MARRIAGE at MEGIDDO

Bart Malone had reached his 48th birthday. And the Malones, the Omegas, and the Sanders decided to throw a surprise party ...not only for Bart but also for Esther Sanders.

Terry was concerned for Bart. While setting up the decorations she questioned George.

"I don't understand Bart lately, George. In just a few days his whole attitude towards life appears to have changed. I thought your offer of having him help you at World Television Network would be a tremendous outlet for his talents. I may be prejudiced, I know, but I've never met anyone like Bart, who is so discerning and so capable of handling many jobs."

"Terry, Bart took to the task like a fish to water. He loves television and is an excellent researcher. He shows a particular interest in the events of the Tribulation Period. It seems as if he's asked me a thousand questions on our experiences during that time. I thought he was coming along fine. I guess that's why I took him to the Temple area the other day for an open court hearing. But even I was surprised...and I must admit, a little dismayed."

"What happened, George? You never told me."

"A man was brought to Regent David who was caught short-weighing groceries in his store and pumping his meats with water to gain more profits. It seemed rather ridiculous since food is so much in abundance, and there is want of nothing. But there's always someone who wants to make more. I guess the real reason for his arrest was his threat to kill the lady who exposed his manipulations."

"What's this have to do with Bart?"

"Bart and I covered the judging of this case. Bart and I both thought this would be a routine case. It was the first case on the docket for Jerusalem that morning. That's the only reason we found it worthwhile to be there with our TV cameras. We assumed a slap on the wrist by the judge, a warning, would be the crux of the whole thing."

"Was it?" Terry anxiously inquired.

"No, that's just it. The judge heard the case with Regent David. Regent David then simply said...

All those plotting evil will be killed.
He will strike the earth with the rod of His mouth,
And with the breath of His lips He will slay the wicked. [1]

And with that the poor rascal was literally blown to bits as though a laser beam had struck him. Poof...vanished!"

"Then what happened?"

"I tried to report it matter-of-factly but I'm sure Bart sensed the shock in my voice at so swift a judgment. Later, as we drove back to the studio, Bart let me have it...

'I don't understand this, Mr. Omega. This is supposed to be the Millennium...where there's peace and love. You told me that Brother Bartholomew used the laser ring to exercise his power over man. Frankly I can't see any difference here. This man didn't kill anyone. Sure, he tried to make a few extra dollars. Why couldn't he have been detained or put on a special work force. And if God is so omnipotent and perfect, what happened to His perfect work? You know sir, I think someone is being sold a bill of goods!'

And I saw an angel come down from heaven, having the key to the bottomless pit and a great chain in his hand.

And he laid hold on the dragon, that old serpent which is the Devil, and Satan, and bound him a thousand years,

And cast him into the bottomless pit, and shut him up, and set a seal upon him, that he should deceive the nations no more, till the thousand years should be fulfilled: and after that he must be loosed a little season.

(Revelation 20:1-3)

[1] Isaiah 29:20 and 11:4.

I tried to explain to Bart that even in the Millennium there will be some who will rebel even though Satan has been bound for these 1000 years in the Bottomless Pit. But you know, Bart has a mind of his own. And nothing I could say would satisfy him."

"I'm sorry, George, so sorry. Let's pray for Bart, that he will see the foolishness of his ways. I'm sure Esther will have an influence on him. They've been seeing a lot of each other lately. They're so young...only 48 and already I've overheard them talking about marriage."

* * *

It was a real family reunion. The Resurrected Believers who were present included Helen Omega, Sue and Tommy, along with Bill Sanders and Tom Malone. The Living Believers included George Omega, Faye Sanders, Terry Malone, Sylvia Epstein, and Harry and Phil Sutherland, who had both flown in from New York.

Phil Sutherland was Harry's nephew, a tall, handsome mustached man, with wavy, jet black hair. He had recently been promoted to a Vice-Presidential slot at World Television Network's New York main office. He was 45, a millennial child, young, up and coming, and on the move. Everyone, especially the ladies, loved him.

When Bart and Esther walked in holding hands...everyone shouted "SURPRISE" and it was a real surprise. Blushingly they went around kissing each one and whispering a thank you.

Harry broke the ice: "Well you youngsters have finally reached 48. You know, back in our days we thought 48 was middle age. But everything is different in this Millennial Age. Why you're just teenagers! How does it feel to be grown up?"

No longer will there be in it an infant who lives but a few days, Or an old man who does not live out his days; For the youth will die at the age of one hundred And the one who does not reach the age of one hundred Shall be brought accursed [a rebellious sinner].

(Isaiah 65:20 ASV)

"Great, Harry, just great," Bart replied.

The spread was unbelievable. All kinds of foods and fruits

that would tempt the most sluggish appetite. Oranges as big as grapefruit, seedless, easy to peel and succulently sweet... lemons a rosy pink, larger than pre-millennial oranges. Not bitter, not sweet...a hollow bamboo shoot thrust into the lemon served as a straw. It took the place of soft drinks. One lemon producing a full glass of juice...juice "so heavenly" as George often remarked, that "It's the drink of Resurrected Believers!" It was a real thirst quencher.

Faye was talking to Terry, "I've never had so much fun. No more weight watching...no more counting calories. It's like heaven here. We can eat anything. Joy, oh what perfect joy!"

> Thou shalt multiply the nation, Thou shalt increase their gladness; They will be glad in Thy presence As with the gladness of harvest, As men rejoice when they divide the spoil.
>
> (Isaiah 9:3 ASV)

Terry's face turned from a smile to sudden concern as she noticed Bart and Esther huddled in a corner talking excitedly.

Esther, like a gift from Heaven, her body so beautifully proportioned, had long hair shimmering in golden tresses over her shoulders. Terry sensed not just an outward beauty...but an inner beauty. Esther was soft-spoken almost to the point of retiring, yet firm in her convictions and in her testimony for God. There was no compromising with Esther. And though she was aware of her desirability among men...she had more than once told Bart she believed in the purity of marriage.

Bart, young and aggressive, found this hard to understand. And in light of what he believed was unfair judgment at the Temple area, his sense of balance was becoming unhinged.

Bart almost embarrassingly held Esther tightly in his arms. He hoped the relative darkness of the corner near the drapes would hide his actions and muffle the sounds of agitated conversation.

"Esther, honey, I love you. I need you. I can't go on living this way. Life is just becoming too complicated. We've been dating now for 10 years...ever since we've been 38. Let's get married."

"Bart, I love you, too. But there's so much to consider...Mom and Mrs. Malone and Uncle George and Daddy. Have you asked your father?"

"What communication can my father and I have? He's a resurrected believer!"

"That doesn't mean anything, Bart, you can talk to him."

"Esther, are you so blind that you can't see the hurt in my mother's eyes? Sure she can talk to him...but that's all!"

"But...Bart..." Esther tried to continue realizing that a real gulf did exist between Living and Resurrected Believers...a gulf that would not be totally resolved until after the Millennial Period.

"Honey, five years ago, I gave you an engagement ring. I don't think it's unreasonable to get married now...even next month...please darling, please. Things are just falling apart with me. If I don't have you, I don't know what will happen. You should have been at the Temple area when that judgment took place. I'm concerned, Esther, concerned...and I just can't go it alone anymore. I need you, Esther. I need you!"

For the first time in her life Esther saw Bart cry. Tears etched their way down his rugged face. He tried to hold them back... but they welled up in his eyes and like a burst dam, suddenly overflowing. At first Bart pretended they weren't there as he buried his face in her lap. Esther, understandingly, took out her favorite orchid handkerchief which Bart had given her on their first date, and gently wiped away the tears.

She kissed the lobe of his ear and whispered, "Everything will be alright, Bart...please don't cry...I will marry you...next month ...and you can announce that right now!"

Bart beamed as he kissed Esther. No other words were spoken. That kiss expressed what words could never tell.

Bart, partially to regain his composure and stop the flow of tears walked over to young Phil Sutherland, the bright and aggressive tall nephew of Harry Sutherland. Bart wanted to change the subject...anything to halt the moisture in his eyes. Then, too, now that marriage was just around the corner, he wanted to firm up his job with Phil who had just recently been named as a new Vice President at World Television Net-

"Everything will be alright, Bart...I will marry you."

work. After all, Bart thought, as a husband, I'm going to have added responsibilities.

Phil was glad to get to know him. Doubts also had been creeping into Phil's mind about the whole Millennium Period, and from some of the remarks he overheard Bart make, Phil sensed he would find a sympathizer in Bart.

"Mr. Sutherland, sir, I hope to get married soon and, well, I just wondered. You know Mr. Omega has been using me in the area of research for his telecasts. Do you think it will be permanent, sir? Will I have a chance to travel and see world activities first hand?"

"Tell me, Bart," Phil Sutherland asked, in what appeared to be a change of the subject, "what did you think of the Judgment at the Temple area the other day?"

"Frankly speaking sir, I was very upset. Well, I just thought it to be unfair. I felt that the judgment was very harsh. It got me to thinking, sir...."

This was the answer Phil Sutherland had hoped to hear. At last someone was thinking like himself.

"Bart, don't worry, there's a permanent job for you at World Television Network. Both George Omega and my uncle Harry have been telling me of your unusual depth in news coverage and of your recent research on Brother Bartholomew."

"Yes, sir, he must have been a very fascinating man. Don't misunderstand me...not that I admire him...but to have gained so much power in so short a time. I feel as though I actually knew him. Crazy thought, I know."

"Not so crazy as one would imagine. Often in researching an individual as extensively as you have...one almost gets to know him...almost to know him as one's own father. And in this knowing, we sometimes can understand a man's actions and why he did the things he did."

"I guess you're right, Mr. Sutherland," and then, seeking to dismiss the subject, "but, sir, I feel like I'm sitting on top of the world...ready to get married. I'd like to spend my honeymoon in New York City. I've never been there...and I've read so much about it. First, we'll get married right here in Jerusalem, of course."

"Of course, Bart, in Jerusalem," Phil interrupted. "But may I make a suggestion about that?"

"Sure, sir, sure." A blush came over Bart's face, as he realized how quickly he was making a hit with his new boss...and yet Phil's thinking and his seemed to run in the same patterns and he felt sudden kinship.

Phil, beckoned him closer, so he could talk in a whisper, unheard by anyone.

"Bart, a thought just occurred to me. Jerusalem has been so much in the news these past 50-odd years...and your wedding is going to be an important event. I just hate to see it overshadowed by some judgment or other that may occur on the same day...demanding TV coverage."

"Yes, Mr. Sutherland."

"Phil will be fine, Bart. Just call me Phil."

"Fine, Phil."

With this Phil Sutherland continued to reveal his new thoughts to Bart, saying, "What area in Palestine, besides Jerusalem has real news significance...digging back in past history? You've done plenty of research...what area do you think, Bart?"

"I'm not sure, Phil."

"You were just talking of Brother Bartholomew. Where were his achievements climaxed?"

"Megiddo, at the Battle of Armageddon...the Plain of Esdraelon."

"Precisely...and what better place to hold your wedding than at Megiddo!"

"But why there?"

"Just this...Megiddo has long been remembered for its evil. Now, you and Esther, will unite in marriage there...each having one parent who is a Resurrected Believer and one parent who is a Living Believer. It will be a TV triumph...like the old soap operas...a triumph over injustice.

We can promote it as the MARRIAGE AT MEGIDDO. It will be the culmination of all things good!"

"Excellent idea, Phil...never thought of it that way. Boy, will Esther be thrilled!"

"May I make a suggestion, Bart...why not let Esther announce your impending marriage and you then announce the location. It will be a doubleheader surprise."

About five minutes later Phil Sutherland stood before everyone waving his arms. His voice assumed a pretended formality as he said, "May we have your attention, everyone...Bart Malone and Esther Sanders have a couple of announcements."

Esther stood sheepishly in front of the whole family gathering. Everyone was quiet. She smiled as she prepared to speak...

"Bart asked me to make an announcement...and then he'll make an announcement that even I don't know. As you know Bart and I have been engaged for 5 years. Now we believe it is the Lord's will that we be married...within the month. And we're so happy!"

Shouts of joy and congratulations filled the room. Sylvia, between the tears kissed Esther and said, "I'm so happy, I'm crying." And soon Esther was surrounded by Faye and Terry Malone who, in turn, then hugged Bart.

Bart hushed the audience and stood next to Esther, his arm

tightly around her waist...he then gently kissed her on the fore-head and began his speech.

"I hope you are ready for another surprise. We were thinking of getting married in Jerusalem. In fact, that's what Esther and I had talked about. But I have a surprise for all of you...including Esther. It may strike you as unusual at first...but I am sure it will be a blessing for all of us. Phil Sutherland gave me the idea. And I think it's great."

"Quit holding us in suspense," George interjected. "Where's the wedding going to be held?"

Bart straightened up, put on his biggest smile and continued: "The wedding will take place in MEGIDDO. Think of it...a MARRIAGE AT MEGIDDO!"

Bart's attention was suddenly drawn to his mother. It was as though something he had said had suddenly enveloped her in tragedy.

She let out a small "ohhh" and collapsed in the arms of Faye Sanders.

Why did mother have to be so emotional, he thought. What was to be a happy occasion had quickly changed its focus.

And Bart was disturbed.

* * *

To get Bart's mind off the impending marriage and to give Esther time to get ready for this event, Harry Sutherland, his nephew Phil—the new V.P.—and George Omega all got together and decided that Bart should join Phil and George in a news expedition to Egypt.

"Why Egypt?" Bart inquired.

"Egypt is stirring," Phil replied.

"And when anyone stirs...we're there." George continued. "You see the rulers of Egypt are disenchanted with the theocratic type of government emanating from Jerusalem. Some of the old bitterness of Arab-Israeli conflict still lingers. Some say it initially

But thou, Bethlehem Ephratah, though thou be little among the thousands of Judah, yet out of thee shall He come forth unto Me that is to be ruler in Israel; whose goings forth have been from of old, from everlasting.

(Micah 5:2)

was triggered by the shooting down of the Libyan passenger jet by the Israeli's in February, 1973 killing over 100 people and the subsequent Black September reprisal in Sudan of two U.S. diplomats. We don't know if this is simply talk in the wind or whether we will see some sort of uprising. This trip will give you a good time for research...in case some conflict arises."

Bart remarked, "Everyone knows that Christ in the Millennium has been given absolute power to govern."

"Not only that," Phil interjected, "but Gentiles as well as Israelis must submit to the authority of Christ. This may be hard for some to accept...this theocratic authority. And I suppose, most difficult for those in Egypt and other Arabic countries ...who now see the promises going in the direction of the nation of Israel; particularly Palestine's enlarged territory!"

> **All the ends of the world shall remember and turn unto the Lord: and all the kindreds of the nations shall worship before thee.**
>
> **For the kingdom is the Lord's: and He is the governor among the nations.**
>
> **(Psalm 22:27-28)**

* * *

Cairo was resplendent in color when the trio of Phil, George, and Bart arrived. It no longer experienced the Khamsin...the wind that lays a tapestry of sand and dust across the skyline.

This was the Millennial Earth and Cairo was a part of it. Cairo had been a city of much suffering through 2000 years. No more were women carrying incredible cargoes on their heads. Produce and other forms of commerce were abundant. Both Cairo University and the once-Islamic Al Azhar were now engaged in practical training that would equip its young men and women for productive work in this enlightened age.

Cairo...once in the dregs of poverty...was finally, in reality the "Garden of the world"...a name the historian Ibn Khaldun had called it in the 14th century.

The familiar Sphinx and the Pyramids were still being repaired from the damage which they sustained during the Tribulation earthquakes. There was a friendliness everywhere in the streets...joyful reunions as men greeted relatives with *"Ya habibi, ya habibi"* — My sweetheart, my sweetheart. More

No more were women carrying incredible cargoes on their heads.

shouting followed: *"Souma, Souma,"* and *"Ya qalbi"* — My heart.

The Arabs were a warm-hearted, friendly people. Too often they had been misunderstood in the 1960's to 1980's. What many did not realize is that it takes a lot to make an Arab angry. Often this tenderness is interpreted as cowardice.

George Omega laughingly remarked: "I recall reading about Dr. Youssef Idris' strategy for defeating Israel in the 1970's."

"Idris had said,

> 'We'll get all 34 million Egyptians together and march them to the Suez Canal. On a given signal, when we are face-to-face with the enemy, all 34 million of us will smile. Are you aware of how disarming it would be to look on 34 million smiling Egyptians?'"

"Dr. Idris had a point, didn't he?" George chuckled.

Bart was particularly impressed with the rich oriental rugs... the hammered copper plates...the ornate brass trays...and the deeply satisfying Turkish coffee.

Soon they arrived at Abdin Palace, in the center of Cairo. It was from here where Abdel Nasser and Anwar Sadat once ruled their country. But all that was yesterday. What seemed important then...was now merely a memory...no longer of any significance...the trials...the struggles...the tribulations...all forgotten; surpassed by the over flowing light of the Millennial years.

Hassan Ahmed was now Governor of Egypt. He had high aspirations upon his appointment. The Palace was beautiful. The walls were heavy with masterpieces of art. The sparkle of crystal was everywhere. One of the baths even had walls of salmon-colored alabaster.

While this was the Millennial Age...none of the customs and traditions which were genuinely Arabic had changed...yet, with an old Arabic word thrown in periodically for flavor, all spoke the universal language. This in itself broke down barriers of difference.

As George Omega interviewed Governor Ahmed, it was ap-

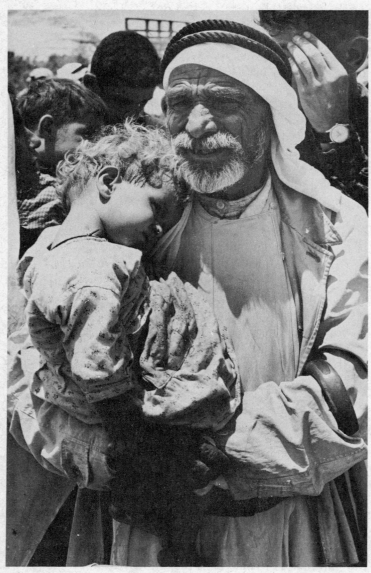

The Arabs were a warm hearted, friendly people. Too often they had been misunderstood in the 1960's to 1980's.

parent to Bart that all chose their words carefully.

"Sir, I understand that there have been some rumors, some rumblings about, shall I say, 'being under the yoke of Israel.' Are these old hatreds still evident?"

"How should I answer you...yes or no? This is the Millennial Age. We strive for perfection. We are blessed with full knowledge.

> And all thy children shall be taught of the LORD; and great shall be the peace of thy children.
> (Isaiah 54:13)

There is no comparison in this Age with the tragedies of the Tribulation Period. What a difference! The curse has been removed...as promised in Isaiah, chapter 11, verses 6 to 9, the wolf and the lamb lie down together. Quite a picture of Israel and her Arab cousins, wouldn't you say?"

"Egypt, Syria, Jordan and our brothers in Lebanon, who have had many injustices...have now seen justice take effect. But there are still problems. And to those of us who lived during those

> He will not be disheartened or crushed, Until He has established justice in the earth; And the coastlands will wait expectantly for His law.
> (Isaiah 42:4 ASV)

Tribulation years...some cannot forget so easily. Our children born since then ask questions. They want answers. Sometimes our answers do not satisfy them. They all do not understand this new theocracy. Some of them do not have this same love and devotion for God that we have. Some even want to go back to 622 A.D. and revive Mohammed. Some still search for Mecca. Some still climb to a small cave among the rocks of Mount Hira to spend days in fasting and meditation."

Then, holding up a poster, as if to bolster his argument, Ahmed continued.

IT IS HE [ALLAH] WHO HAS SENT...
AN APOSTLE FROM AMONG THEMSELVES...

"Look at this! We are finding these throughout the city of Cairo."

"What does it mean?" Harry questioned.

"It reads like this:

IT IS HE [ALLAH] WHO HAS SENT
AN APOSTLE FROM AMONG THEMSELVES.

"How will this problem be resolved?" George Omega queried.

"I fear for trouble," Ahmed hesitatingly replied. "That's why it is hard for me to give you straight answers. An early Arabic poem perhaps capsules the devil-may-care attitude of these who rebel. It goes:

With the sword I will wash my shame away,
Let God's doom bring on me what it may!

Yes, I fear trouble. I don't know what Regent David will do, and I myself don't know what to do."

The interview ended. Bart had been greatly impressed. Somehow inside he admired the rebellious attitude that was erupting. He tried to ask himself why. But he could come up with no answers.

The trio of George Omega, Phil Sutherland, and Bart were quiet on their way home. Phil mentioned that perhaps some were getting tired of such quick judgments in Jerusalem. Perhaps, he thought outloud...a harsh theocracy...in spite of its many benefits was not quite the answer.

It was then that Bart spoke... much to the amazement of everyone.

> In that day there will be inscribed on the bells of the horses, "HOLY TO THE LORD." And the cooking pots in the Lord's house will be like the bowls before the altar.
>
> And every cooking pot in Jerusalem and in Judah will be holy to the Lord of hosts; and all who sacrifice will come and take of them and boil in them. And there will be no longer a Canaanite [grasping traders] in the house of the Lord of hosts in that day.
>
> **(Zechariah 14:20-21 ASV)**

"I think you're right, Phil. People are getting tired of having religion stuffed down their throat. Even the bells on the horses have written on them 'These are Holy Property.' And if that isn't enough...even the trash cans in the Temple area are as holy as the bowls at the altar. That's just going too far!"

* * *

What was once a sprawling kibbutz was now a beautiful plain

dotted with occasional homes and abundant farm land. The communal farms of yesterday were gone. The kibbutzim, perhaps necessary in their time, tended to break the family unity, and they disappeared in the late 1980's. No longer did the dreaded *sharav*...that mass of oven-hot air...plague the area. And the readiness of Nehemiah 4:17.

> ...every one with one of his hands
> wrought in the work,
> and with the other
> hand held a weapon.

was no longer necessary in this Millennial Age.

This was the area of Megiddo...once linking Gaza and Damascus and controlling the principal pass through the Carmel range, connecting the coastal plain and the Plain of Esdraelon.

It was here by the waters of Megiddo (Judges 5:19) that Israelite forces under Deborah and Barak annihilated the army of Sisera. It was here that Josiah, the last righteous king of Judah ...before the disintegration of the southern kingdom 586 B.C.... was hit by Egyptian archers and soon died (2 Kings 23:29-30).

And this area...scene of the world's most bitter battle...the Battle of Armageddon...was to become the site of a holy union in marriage.

* * *

Esther Sanders—daughter of Faye and Bill Sanders, granddaughter of George Omega—was a vision of ethereal beauty in her flowing wedding gown. The fingertip veil of illusion made her a vision of loveliness. The gown was floor length of white velvet, with Venice lace trim. It was fashioned with a high neckline and bishop sleeves. Her flowers were red and white carnations with white rosebuds on a white Bible with white ribbon streamers.

George Omega brought the commentary via World Television Network. It was most difficult for him...for this was his family. He recalled the struggle for life itself when not too many years ago his own daughter, Faye, and her husband, Bill, sought to escape the ever-seeking grasp of Brother Bartholomew...the tragedy when Bill met his death on BB's guillotine. Those

"Here on the Plain of Esdraelon...where once millions fought in a battle against the Lord...here you have just witnessed a MARRIAGE AT MEGIDDO!"

memories...so vivid and so real...those events seemed so important then...but God had softened those memories...and transformed them into blessings in this Millennial Age. But somehow, it was difficult for George to choke back the tears. Now...some 50 years later...Faye's daughter and Terry's son were getting married. He thought within himself of an old poem,

> The stately ship is seen no more
> The fragile skiff attains the shore
> And while the great and wise decay
> And all their trophies pass away
> Those found in Christ, in peace sublime
> Still float above the wrecks of Time.

He glanced down at Terry Malone, the groom's mother. This should be her happiest day. And yet he sensed a twinge of sadness...something he just couldn't put his finger on.

George ended his television coverage: "Here, on the Plain of Esdraelon...where once millions fought in a battle against the Lord...here now, where once Armageddon was a word of terror and of judgment...here is love, here is marriage, here is beauty in our Redeemer King. You have just witnessed a MARRIAGE AT MEGIDDO!"

Terry thought to herself...George, I pray you're not wrong ...but I feel we will yet witness a terror beyond our wildest beliefs. She bowed her head..."Please let it not be Esther and Bart...please,...please!"

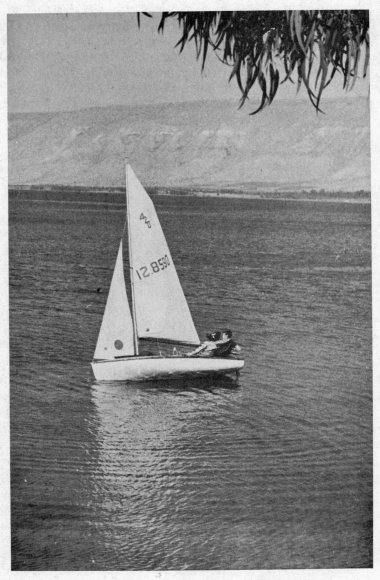

Their small boat rocked very slowly in the middle of the Sea of Galilee. It was easy to see Bart was in love...All the heartaches... the misunderstandings...Terry's tears at Megiddo were a thing of the past, Esther thought.

Chapter 7

TO LICK THE DUST

Esther had persuaded Bart not to choose New York as their honeymoon site...but rather Galilee.

It was to be their last moment of real happiness...although neither suspected what was ahead.

Bart, who prided himself on his ability to recall events of history, fascinated Esther with his almost photographic memory.

Their small boat rocked very slowly in the middle of the Sea of Galilee. The warmth of the sun...the gentle breezes made a perfect setting for their honeymoon.

No longer was the Sea a polluted waste as it had become in the 1970's. It was again the crystal clear...and this time...quiet Sea that was so evident in the days of Christ's ministry prior to His crucifixion.

It was easy to see that Bart was in love. He stretched out on the boat and laid his head upon Esther's lap. Playfully she ran her finger up and down his nose, around his ears...and when he talked too much...across his lips...sealing it with a kiss.

All the heartaches...the misunderstandings...Terry's tears at Megiddo, were a thing of the past, Esther thought. Bart and I are married now. We're both Christians...at least I know that I am and I am almost certain that Bart is. Nothing can come between us. Ahead of us is continual happiness.

Bart broke the silence: "Honey there's an old Jewish sage who said:

> Jehovah hath created seven seas
> but the Sea of Galilee is His delight.

That man knew what he was talking about."

For Bart and Esther...this was a honeymoon to be remembered. To them there was no fairer sight in all Israel than the view from the Sea of Galilee...with its waters of sapphire blue. Bart reminded Esther that this lake had at one time been called the Sea of Kinneret because it was shaped like a *kinnor* (harp).

Bart continued, "Josephus, concerning this region, said,"

> ...its nature is wonderful as well as its beauty;
> its soil is so fruitful that all sorts of trees can
> grow upon it."

"And the Talmud of old said that the fruit here ripens as fast as deer can run and that one could eat a hundred pieces of it and still wish for more."

"Hush, you walking encyclopedia, this is no time for a history lesson. This is a time for sweet words of gentle love."

For the rest of the afternoon, for Bart and Esther, those gentle words of love came easy.

* * *

For both of them the honeymoon ended too quickly. As they entered Jerusalem there appeared to be great confusion. The native Jews were being almost mobbed by anxious men and women visitors from all over the world. It was as though these tourists were hanging onto the coat sleeves of the citizens of Jerusalem.

"What's going on, honey?" Esther asked.

Bart went over and talked to a bystander and then returned.

"The people of Israel are the VIP's of the Millennium Period. Suddenly they've been transformed from a curse to a blessing. Once prisoners of hope...they are

As for you also, because of the blood of My covenant with you, I have set your prisoners free from the waterless pit.

Return to the stronghold, O

now the object of God's fulfilled promises."

"This is their October festival, I was told. In the old days it was one of mourning. Now it's one of joy. And everyone throughout the world sends representatives to come and worship at the Temple. The Jews are the 'apple of His eye' now and, in my opinion, it becomes a status symbol to enter the Temple with a Jew. That's why you see so many hanging onto their arms."

> prisoners who have the hope; This very day I am declaring that I will restore double to you.
> (Zechariah 9:11-12 ASV)
>
> Thus saith the Lord of hosts; In those days it shall come to pass, that ten men shall take hold out of all languages of the nations, even shall take hold of the skirt [garment] of him that is a Jew, saying, We will go with you: for we have heard that God is with you.
> (Zechariah 8:23)

Esther could sense a well of bitterness springing up in Bart's heart and silently she prayed. She knew that the nation Israel had suffered much through the centuries...and she knew that this Millennial Age was one in which the people of Israel would rightfully receive the promises God had long ago made to them through their forefather Abraham.

> And I will make of thee a great nation, and I will bless thee, and make thy name great; and thou shalt be a blessing:
> And I will bless them that bless thee, and curse him that curseth thee: and in thee shall all families of the earth be blessed.
> (Genesis 12:2-3)

Somehow, just somehow, she would have to wash away the well of anger in Bart's heart with a double portion of love.

Bart was seated in Phil Sutherland's office in New York. Phil had called George Omega in Jerusalem and said that he needed Bart. Something had come up and Bart was great on research. "It will get Bart's feet wet in this industry," Phil assured a doubting Omega. George had been reluctant to have Bart travel so quickly after his honeymoon.

Phil Sutherland seemed to have changed in the past few months. Bart got the impression that he was no longer the dedicated believer which he had at first appeared to be. Bart hesitatingly questioned him about this.

"Bart," Sutherland leaned back on his chair slowly, as though thinking of how best to express his feelings...

"Bart, I must admit there was once a time when I did not love the memory of my Aunt Carole, Harry's wife. But then, one day, I read her old diary and suddenly I realized that she was a precious jewel. Then when I asked Uncle Harry, he, with tears, told me of that day at the Valley of Jehoshaphat...that day when God condemned my aunt whom I never saw to an eternity in..." his voice trailed off in bitterness.

"And the Jews...sure I can appreciate their suffering...but I've suffered, too...the Arabs have also suffered. I've read about

"I've seen their miserable refugee camps after the 6-Day War."

their miserable refugee camps after the 6-Day War. And I've also seen the rich, haughty self-righteous Jew in Manhattan... with his maids, his butlers, his chauffeurs. I've seen one hypocrite step on the lives of my friends...who were believers...just so he could reach the top of the heap...over their dead bodies. Then he went around sanctimoniously 'preaching Christ.'"

"But, Mr. Sutherland, Phil," Bart interrupted, "doesn't forgiveness and turning the other cheek enter into this?"

"Turning the other cheek?" Sutherland let out a sarcastic laugh. "I've turned a hundred cheeks...but when I learned that my own aunt was sent to Hades...that was it! Look Bart, suppose you woke up one day and found that Esther had been sent to the Lake of Fire...not for a day...not for a year...forever. Understand that...forever! Slowly suffering FOREVER. AND THERE WAS NOTHING...no, NOTHING YOU COULD DO ABOUT IT!"

Bart Malone whitened.

"Bart, let me show you what's in store for those of the nation Israel. Pick up that Bible there. Turn to Isaiah, chapter 61. Now read aloud verses 5 and 6."

Bart began to read:

> And strangers will stand and pasture your flocks,
> And foreigners will be your farmers and your
>   vinedressers.
>
> But you will be called the priests of the Lord;
> You will be spoken of as ministers of our God.
> And will eat the wealth of nations,
> And in their riches you will boast."

"Hear that, Bart, one of these days World Television Network may be taken over by the nation Israel. And you, you'll be out tending cattle somewhere in the Plain of Esdraelon...not for your benefit...but for theirs!"

Phil Sutherland could see that the point was just about hitting home. Bart Malone would make a good partner in his future plans. But he had to make sure.

"Another verse, Bart. Read Isaiah 49:22-23!"

Bart continued reading:

> Thus says the Lord God.
> Behold I will lift up My hand to the nations,
> And set up My standard to the peoples;
> And they will bring your sons in *their* bosom,
> And your daughters will be carried on *their* shoulders.
>
> And kings will be your guardians,
> And their princesses your nurses.

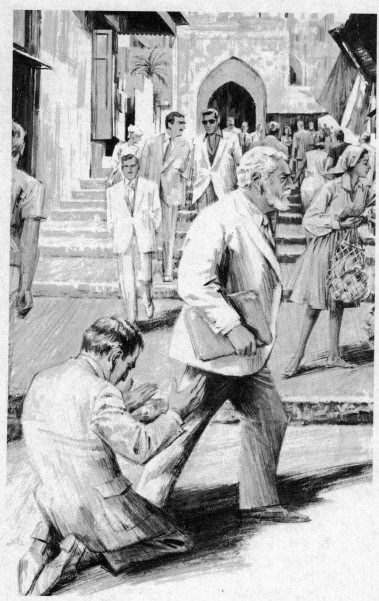

"They will bow down to you with their faces to the earth, And lick the dust of your feet."

They will bow down to you with their faces to the earth,
And lick the dust of your feet;

There was more, but Bart could go no further. He knew now
the life ahead would not be easy. And he and Phil Sutherland
were going to change it!

For the Resurrected Believers, such as Tom Malone, Bill
Sanders, Helen, Sue and Tommy Omega, the Millennium was
not a time of testing. They had already been through their testing years prior to the inception of the Millennium...and they
had seen themselves as sinners and turned in faith to Christ for
forgiveness. Now they were righteous and completely fulfilled
in Christ.

And although they were having a part in the millennium, they
were on the earth, in a sense, as co-rulers with Christ, having
duties to perform which they did eagerly. They loved the
theocratic government and they cooperated with everything
without resentment.

It was natural for them to approve of all that Regent David
and the others did, because their eyes were looking (as it were)
from the top of the Master Weaver's pattern...seeing the design
in all its perfectness.

While underneath, George Omega, Faye Sanders, Terry Malone, Bart and Esther Malone, Sylvia Epstein and Harry and
Phil Sutherland were seeing the apparent mismatch of tangled
threads that to them spelled disorder, and in some created
jealousy and dissent.

How often Tom Malone wished that for one brief moment
he could show his loved ones the other side. Yet each time he
approached Terry and quoted such familiar verses as:

...we know that all things work together for good
    to them that love God,
    to them who are the called
    according to His purpose. [1]
There hath no temptation taken you
    but such as is common to man;
    but God is faithful,
    who will not permit you to be tempted
    above that ye are able,

---

[1] Romans 8:28

"Tom, darling, I'm sorry, I'm so sorry...oh Tom, I need you so
much...forgive me...I'm sorry."

> but will, with the temptation,
>   also make a way to escape,
>   that ye may be able to bear it. [1]

...these verses appeared to have no effect on Terry. Then Tom would always add:

> In everything give thanks;
>   for this is the will of God in Christ Jesus
>   concerning you. [2]

"It's easy for you to quote verses," Terry shouted...as though Tom was hard of hearing.

"You can give thanks in everything...because everything's going your way. You have no problems. You're resurrected. You have it made. It's I that have the problems. I've got to face the everyday life. I've got to wipe away Esther's tears...try and straighten out Bart's misgivings about the Millennium. And I have no one to turn to. You're no longer a husband to me. You resurrected believers with that holy glow about you. And those Jews running around with the Gentiles doing all the dirty work... Do you call this justice? In some ways, everything is so perfect here it's driving me crazy. Every place I turn I see holy trash cans or holy dishes. Why even the smoke is holy anymore! And everyone hanging on the coattails of Jews as they flock to the Temple—as though each Jew was the President of the United States or something. I can't go on like this. I can't go on. I've counselled and counselled with Bart and Esther. Esther is so sweet...so understanding...but Bart...it's like suddenly he has been born of the devil!"

Suddenly the horror of her words hit her in the pit of the stomach as though all the morning sicknesses of all her pregnancy had come at one time. She felt weak and completely drained. She burst into uncontrollable sobs repeating over and over again...

"Tom, darling, I'm sorry, I'm so sorry...oh Tom, I need you so much...forgive me...I'm sorry."

As they prayed Tom knew that it was all in God's perfect hands now. And Tom could see the orderly pattern of His plan.

---

[1] 1 Corinthians 10:13.   [2] 1 Thessalonians 5:18.

He could also see the underneath...and he knew some tangled threads would provide even greater sorrow before perfect peace ever came to those he loved so dearly.

* * *

Abdin Palace in Cairo was a scene of much activity. Phil Sutherland, George Omega and Bart Malone had flown there to televise what was to be an impending news event.

Hassan Ahmed, Governor of Egypt, briefed the trio on the problem. Old hatreds were arising among many of the youth born during the Millennium, Ahmed related. Some of the rebel Egyptians were exercising great influence now in the government...and they resented what they believed was preferential treatment of Jews in this Millennial Age.

Once a year a pilgrimage was to take place to Jerusalem. They objected to the fact that all edicts and all laws came out of Jerusalem. And to pay homage, by sending bowing delegations yearly to Jerusalem...this was too much.

The rebels sought to have a dual center of worship...one in Jerusalem, but one also in Cairo.

They ran through the streets of Cairo whipping up its residents in a frenzy shouting:

"Do you want to lick the dust off the feet of the Jew? If you don't, then join us in our protest march to Jerusalem. Stand up for your rights!"

> And many people shall go and say, Come ye, and let us go up to the mountain of the LORD, to the house of the God of Jacob; and He will teach us of His ways, and we will walk in His paths; for out of Zion shall go forth the law, and the word of the LORD from Jerusalem.
> (Isaiah 2:3)

Ahmed threw his hands up in the air: "What can I do? I am only the Governor. I cannot fight all these people. I'm afraid we're headed for trouble. All these years Egypt has been blessed with prosperity. Our lands have never been so fertile...our crops have never been so productive. The rains have watered our deserts. Now they blossom with every kind of fruit and vegetable. Whenever the season became dry...God, as though He was watching us every day, sent forth the refreshing rain. Now, I don't know what will happen...but what can I do?"

Phil Sutherland smelled trouble...and a good story...so he

and George and Bart flew back to Jerusalem to cover what was sure to be a conflict of important magnitude.

* * *

Never had Phil Sutherland seen so many people in the Temple area. The spacious central square was filled. Everyone sensed something important was about to occur.

The word had gotten out that Egypt was going to refuse to worship the Redeemer King. Part of its leadership had made a decision to formally protest...even though most of the people of Egypt did not concur with the action of this segment of their leaders.

Hassan Ahmed looked out of place. Yet he felt that he had to follow through. He had only to turn around to meet the angry stares of his rebel government. There was no backing out. At last he knew how Pilate felt in that judgment hall...knowing that what he was about to do was wrong...but yet, too weak to take any other stand.

Ahmed eloquently made his plea to Regent David.

Regent David began to speak:

> You are saying that Egypt, filled with all the
> blessings given by your Redeemer King...Egypt
> is refusing to bow down in worship?
>
> Do you realize the import of your decision? That
> such a decision is high treason against God
> and the penalty is swift?

Ahmed spoke quietly:

"Yes, my gracious Regent. My leaders have made this decision. This year, we will not enter the Temple to make our sacrifice of memorial. This is the decision of Egypt."

Suddenly all eyes focused on the Temple. It was a massive structure. Pillars on each side of the porch appeared to be 100 feet high. The doorway was some 43 feet wide. [1]

Facing us was the doorway to the east. The inner wall's eastern entrance was closed six days of the week...but open on the Sabbath.

---

[1] A complete description of the Millennial Age TEMPLE can be found by reading Ezekiel, chapters 40 through 48.

Suddenly a glorious light appeared from the east. Noise ceased as an overpowering presence was felt.

George Omega was telecasting some color descriptions when this unusual phenomena appeared. He began to shout...

"There is nothing wrong with your television set. What we are hearing is almost like the roar of rushing waters...the entire landscape in Jerusalem is lighting up as never before.

And without any given signal... suddenly everyone is burying their face in the dust of this Temple area. I have never witnessed anything like this before. Hassan Ahmed and his rebel leaders appear like helpless waifs in a violent storm. All color has been drained from their faces. They are the only ones standing...standing in amazement and in confusion. Listen...I think Regent David is about to speak..."

> And behold the glory of God of Israel came from the way of the east: and His voice was like a noise of many waters: and the earth shined with His glory.
> (Ezekiel 43:2)

AND IT WILL BE
THAT WHICHEVER OF THE FAMILIES OF THE

EARTH DOES NOT GO UP TO JERUSALEM TO
WORSHIP THE KING,
THE LORD OF HOSTS,
    THERE WILL BE NO RAIN ON THEM.

AND IF THE FAMILY OF EGYPT DOES NOT GO
UP OR ENTER,
    THEN NO RAIN WILL FALL ON THEM;

IT WILL BE THE PLAGUE WITH WHICH THE
LORD SMITES THE NATIONS
WHO DO NOT GO UP TO CELEBRATE THE
FEAST OF TABERNACLES. [1]

Suddenly a burst of even more brilliant light shot out from the eastern entrance and Hassan Ahmed and his delegation vanished. It had been as though a laser beam had brought

---

[1] Zechariah 14:17-19.

sudden destruction on them. Where they stood was now an empty courtyard! [1]

* * *

It was a trying day and George, Phil and Bart hurried back to the apartment to wash off the dust of the day and to get ready for dinner.

Terry and Faye were busy in the kitchen. Both decided they would cook Bart and Esther's favorite dishes.

Both had spent much time in Beirut and Baalbek. They had roamed hand in hand through the mountains of Marj Uyun and through the Cedars of Lebanon. They called this their "Little Bible Land." For while it had been in the middle of much conflict in past history, it was now blessed with God's special outpouring on its fertile lands.

Bart and Esther loved the food of the Lebanese. And often, they longed for those succulent dishes.

Esther had taught her mother how to make *kibbeh*. Esther taught her and Terry both how to combine the lamb meat with *burghul* — crushed wheat.

"Where did you find this dish, Esther?" Terry asked.

"Bart and I were in Zahle in Lebanon. If you ever want to eat great *kibbeh*...the finest is made and served in the restaurants of Zahle!"

"Here, Mom, you pound the wheat and lamb for a while... then just knead it and season it."

After the initial work was done, Bart came in, lifted up some of the raw mixture with his fingers and plunged it into his mouth.

"Bart, you're eating that RAW!" Terry shrieked.

"It's ok Mom, we've often eaten it raw. It's called *kibbeh nieheh* when raw."

Faye ground the chick peas, added olive oil and a few other ingredients for another appetizer dish Esther called *hommus*.

The wrapped grape leaves, the fried eggplant, the shish kabob ...all made that night a memorable evening...a lull before the storm.

---
[1] Isaiah 11:3-4; Numbers 16:19-35.

Bart had become increasingly restless over the recent events. The people of Egypt were suffering because of a lack of rain. Phil Sutherland had purposely sent Bart to cover these events for World Television Network.

> No longer will there be in it an infant who lives but a few days, Or an old man who does not live out his days; For the youth will die at the age of one hundred And the one who does not reach the age of one hundred Shall be thought accursed.
>
> **(Isaiah 65:20 ASV)**

Bart never could erase that one picture of an Indian, who had migrated to Egypt, carrying his dead wife...emaciated. He had never looked hunger in the face before. He had never seen anyone die because they did not have enough to eat. Now, everywhere he turned...he witnessed the tragedy and the stench of famine...God's judgment.

And this was just one more event that boiled the cauldron of bitterness within him. He was afraid soon that this cauldron would boil over!

Bart reported back to Phil Sutherland at his Jerusalem office.

"Mr. Sutherland, Phil, from your own reading and study do you think that the tribulation period could have been as bad as this? Was the battle of Armageddon as tragic?"

"Bart, down the centuries many warriors of many nations passed back and forth upon the stage of Esdraelon. George Adam Smith in his classic *Historical Geography of the Holy Land,* published way back in 1894, wrote:

The elephants and engines of Antiochus,
  the litters of Cleopatra and her ladies,
the Romans who come and plant their camps
  and stamp their mighty names forever on the soil...
Pompey, Mark Antony, Vespasian and Titus,
  pass at the head of their legions,
And the men of Gaililee sally forth upon them
  from the same nooks in the hills of Naphtali
  from which their forefathers broke with Barak
  upon the chariots of Canaan...
...then the ensigns of Christendom came.
Crusading castles rise...

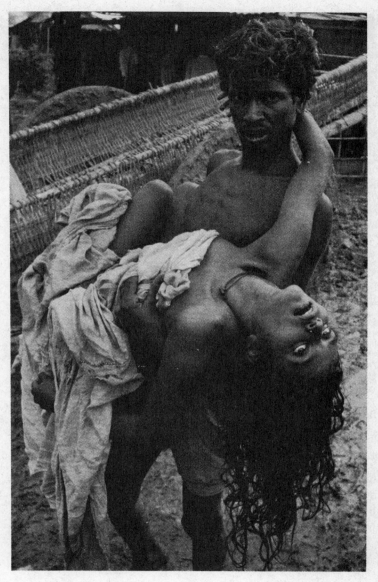

He had never looked hunger in the face before. Bart never could erase that one picture of an Indian, who had migrated to Egypt, carrying his dead wife.

Once more by Bethshan the Arabs break the line
    of the Christian defence
    and Saladin spreads his camp
    where Israel saw those of the Midian and the
        Philistine...
Esdraelon is closed to the arms of the West
till in 1799 Napoleon
    with his monstrous ambition of an Empire
    on the Euphrates,
    breaks into it by Megiddo,
    and in three months again,
    from the same fatal stage,
    falls back
    upon the first great retreat of his career.

"It was through Megiddo Pass that General Allenby's Australian cavalry came thundering into the valley in 1918 to break the back of the Turkish line."

Sutherland continued, "Over and over again through thousands of years, blood has flowed in battle for the possession of this strategic point of Megiddo. But the bloodiest was the Battle of Armageddon, Bart. Over 200 million were killed by the hand of the Lord. The blood bath covered over 185 miles!" [1]

Phil Sutherland could see anger suddenly flow into Bart's face...like a tide coming in on a peaceful beach...soon to erupt into a violent storm.

"Phil, you will never catch me licking the dust from off the feet of a Jew, even if it is Regent David! I may be confused... but I won't be confused for long. I'm going to do some research and I'll come up with an answer. Why should we Gentiles have to go bowing into Israeli Jerusalem? There must be another way. There's just got to be another way!"

Phil Sutherland's lips curled in a half smile. There must be another way, he thought, and he was going to help Bart Malone find it.

It was to be a way that would end in a destiny neither Phil nor Bart would have thought possible!

---

[1] Revelation 14:20; 19:19-21.

Chapter 8

THE SECRET at SODOM

Over 900 years had passed since Bart and Esther were united in marriage. It seemed like yesterday.

Age knew no limits in this Millennial Kingdom and they had the physical appearance and stamina of persons 25 years of age in the pre-millennial earth. Disease had been abolished and the tragedy of old age did not exist.

No labor strikes, no struggle to make ends meet...the normal problems and tensions of the 20th Century were not prevalent during this 1000 years.

And the inhabitant shall not say, I am sick: the people that dwell therein shall be forgiven their iniquity.
(Isaiah 33:24)

No longer will there be in it an infant who lives but a few days, Or an old man who does not live out his days; For the youth will die at the age of one hundred And the one who does not reach the age of one hundred Shall be thought accursed.
(Isaiah 65:20 ASV)

Through the hundreds of years since their wedding Esther noted a growing restlessness in Bart. In spite of a perfect kingdom ruled by the Redeemer King and Regent David, there was continually an atmosphere of uneasiness that surrounded her husband.

She was worried about his years of association with Phil Sutherland.

Esther, Terry, Sylvia and Faye were having a coffee break before taking a leisurely walk through the Garden of Gethsemane. This familiar site was still in Jerusalem and the trio

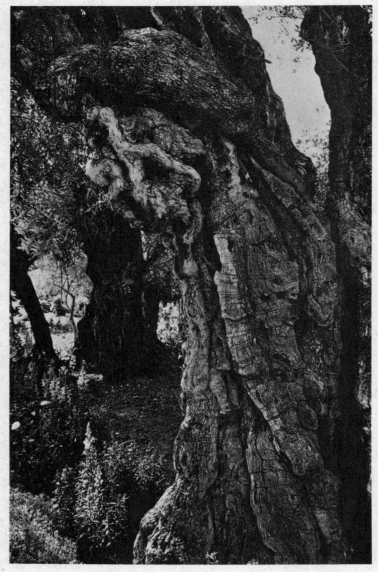

Terry was happy the Garden of Gethsemane was empty. They could be alone.

often found this place a quiet respite when tensions mounted.

"Esther, has Bart said anything to you lately about his upcoming trip to Sodom?" Terry questioned.

"Just offhand he mentioned he was going there with Phil Sutherland and Dad. Why?"

Sylvia put her arm around Terry. "Come on, Esther and Terry, let's go to the Garden and pray. God knows all about our problems. We'll solve nothing rehashing Bart's sudden change in attitude. Only prayer can change things."

Terry was happy that the Garden of Gethsemane was empty for once. They could be alone.

Tears came to Faye Sanders' eyes.

"Mom, why are you crying?" Esther asked.

"Honey, this place brings back precious memories."

"You mean when Christ prayed here before His crucifixion?"

"Yes, but also when Dad and I were running for our lives...

almost 1000 years ago...running from Brother Bartholomew. We knelt to pray. We thought we were all alone and free at last. But in the shadows of the Garden was Prophet Arthur, the False Prophet of the Tribulation Period. It was the beginning of a trail of tears for us...but God gave us the victory."

"Mom, Satan is now bound in the bottomless pit. Where is it?"

"Honey, we do not know. Perhaps it is the Black Hole in the sky that troubled scientists in the 1970's...a vast void that appears to have no end."

Sylvia, a completed Jew, loved to question Faye Sanders.

"Faye, just exactly who is Satan?"

And I saw an angel come down from heaven, having the key of the bottomless pit and a great chain in his hand,

And he laid hold on the dragon, that old serpent, which is the Devil, and Satan, and bound him a thousand years,

And cast him into the bottomless pit, and shut him up, and set a seal upon him, that he should deceive the nations no more, till the thousand years should be fulfilled: and after that he must be loosed a little season.

(Revelation 20:1-3)

"Satan is a fallen spirit, and an imitator...not an originator. He imitates completely the pattern and program of God. This is how he has fooled so many people. So successful was he originally that he fooled one-third of the angels of heaven into following him!"

> And his tail [Satan's] swept away a third of the stars of heaven, and through them to the earth. And the dragon [Satan] stood before the woman who was about to give birth, so that when she gave birth he might devour her child.
> (Revelation 12:4 ASV)

"That was his original rebellion. Do you realize that Satan was not only one of the wisest of the created beings but also one of the most beautiful. Ezekiel 28:13 describes his beauty...

> You were in Eden, the garden of God;
> Every precious stone was your covering:
> The ruby, the topaz, and the diamond;
> The beryl, the onyx, and the jasper;
> The sapphire, garnet, chrysolite;
> And the gold, the workmanship of your settings and
>   sockets
> Was in you.
> On the day that you were created
> They were prepared."

"You mean to tell me Satan had all that...and he still was not satisfied!" Sylvia exclaimed. "I remember when my Abel bought me my mink coat. Wow, I thought that was seventh heaven!"

"No Sylvia, Satan was not satisfied. You see, God gave Satan ...as He gives us...a capacity to choose. Satan could have chosen this complete perfectness, but he chose to depart from it. Just as you and I have had that choice...and as those in the Judgment of the nation Israel and the Judgment of the Gentiles have had that choice. Remember, even one-third of the angels at one time chose to follow Satan."

"Faye," Terry interjected, "I remember back in my old Sunday school days our teacher outlined Satan's sins. If I can recall ...Satan's biggest words were I WILL!"

"That's right, Terry. There were five 'I will' statements by Satan. They are found in the Old Testament book of Isaiah, chapter 14, verse 13:

"I WILL ASCEND TO HEAVEN"
Satan wanted to abide there *as* God!
"I WILL RAISE MY THRONE ABOVE THE STARS
OF GOD"
He wanted to usurp God's authority.
"I WILL SIT ON THE MOUNT OF ASSEMBLY
IN THE RECESSES OF THE NORTH"
Here Satan was expressing his desire to control
all the affairs of the universe!
"I WILL ASCEND ABOVE THE HEIGHTS OF THE
CLOUDS"
Satan's glory was a *reflected* glory. His brilliance
came from God's Light. But Satan wanted a
greater glory than God's.

"I WILL MAKE MYSELF LIKE THE MOST HIGH"

"Can you imagine the sinful folly of that last statement? Satan
was the wisest of God's beings. He was the most powerful. He
could go from one end of the universe to another. But the fact
that he was not omniscient (all knowing); he was not omnipotent
(all powerful); and he was not omnipresent (present everywhere
at the same time)...these facts built up in him a rebellious pride."

"Mom, Satan wasn't called Satan at that time, was he?"

"No, honey, before his fall his name was Lucifer. That means
'the light bearer' or 'the brilliant one.' It was an appropriate
name then. And I recall reading somewhere in Scriptures that
one day...in fact, one day soon, he will return as an imitation
light bearer and fool many."

"Was Brother Bartholomew one of his followers?" Sylvia
asked anxiously.

"Yes, Sylvia, Brother Bartholomew was the most powerful
and cruelest man of the pre-millennial age...a man indwelt of
Satan. And his influence will soon be felt again."

Terry began to weep. Faye wondered what she had said to
suddenly reduce Terry to tears. Somehow Sylvia seemed to
understand what it was all about. She put her arm around
Terry's shoulder and motioned to Faye to pray.

It has been a dusty trip to Sodom...but reports of some unusual occurrences had sent Phil Sutherland, George Omega and Bart Malone there in a hurry.

Phil had sensed that the mood of the people was changing.

"George, I've just completed a trip around the world. And I'm telling you that people are just fed up...all of this authority that comes right out of Jerusalem has them stirred. They want localized authority and power. They've had it...this 'under the thumb' pressure is too much. And those drastic judgments by a God you can't see...without benefit of a fair trial. It's discrimination in its highest form. Israel is getting everything and we're their servants. The lid's about to blow off. I can sense it."

"Phil, are you sure?" George questioned. "I haven't heard any rumblings, any protests."

"Of course not, they'd be crazy to protest. You see what happens. Poof...instant death. I tell you...it's all building up inside them. It'll be an avalanche of protest once the time is right. Then I dare that man on the throne to try and instantly wipe out millions. That's when He will sit and listen."

George was amazed at Phil Sutherland's growing bitterness. Yet Phil had never really acted like a steadfast believer. And this combined with his remorse over his aunt Carole who had been committed to Hades...all added up.

George turned to Bart.

Chronicles
NEWS OF THE PAST

VOL. I, NO. 8

SODOM AND GOMORRAH WIPED OUT IN WORST DISASTER SINCE FLOOD

Burning Sulphur, Violent Blasts, Flames Shooting Up to the Sky...

HYKSOS TAKE EGYPTIAN CAPITAL

Mysterious Blaze-Quake Sweeps Valley of Siddim

(Chronicles News Service)

HEBRON, 11 Nisan.— Nature's four basic elements — earth, fire, wind, and water — combined today to bring terror and death to the twin-cities of Sodom and Gomorrah, in the worst catastrophe the world has seen since the Great Flood.

The disaster, a deadly combination of storm, earthquake, fire and flood, struck with a suddenness that provided no opportunity for escape. All the inhabitants of the two cities are believed to have been killed.

LOT SAVED!

Advancing Waters Threaten Zoar

"Bart, what has your research turned up on Sodom and these recent activities?"

"Well, Sodom goes way back into history...about 2000 B.C. when the Bible declared that it was destroyed and became part of what was known prior to the Millennium, as the Dead Sea. There were 5 cities in this southern portion of the Dead Sea area...Sodom, Gomorrah, Admah, Zeboiim and Zoar.[1] These were the 'cities of the plain.'"

"This area, prior to Sodom's demise, was very fertile," Bart continued.

"Four Mesopotamian kings under Chedorlaomer considered it worthwhile to make war on these five cities. They captured Lot. But Abraham rescued his brother's son. The wickedness of Sodom and Gomorrah caused God to destroy them." [2]

"What have your recent findings shown?" Phil inquired.

"Just this. People in the settlement near what was once Sodom...that's in the area of Neot ha-Kikar...have reported some strange sights...an unusual man."

"What was unusual about him?" George asked.

"Unusual in that he is surrounded by an aura of light. Some here have called him an angel of light...a second Messiah. We've had other reports of his appearance. Time and distance don't seem to trouble him. First I got a report of his appearance in Santiago...a day later in Tokyo...another day in Nairobi...the next day in Anchorage...and at another time in Chicago."

George and Phil took this in thoughtfully, then George asked, "What's so unusual about that...with the speed of our passenger planes...that's not impossible!"

Bart responded quickly. "True, but how do you explain this? His activities appear to be increasing. Just yesterday we received reports he was in 5 different heavily populated cities throughout the world...all 3000 to 5000 miles apart!"

"And what's amazing is this...people who feel they have ailments of one kind or another report instant healings. People who were afraid to gripe before about theocratic rulership are finding that he's giving them a sympathetic ear...promising

[1] Genesis 14:2; Deuteronomy 29:23; Genesis 13:12.
[2] Genesis 14:1-12; 19:24-26.

"...Sodom goes way back into history...about 2000 B.C. when the Bible declared that it was destroyed and became part of the Dead Sea."

them that at the end of this time period...things will *really* be perfect...and that everyone will have a say in government. And they won't have to work, either. That's what they like to hear."

"But his big promise is this...no more annual pilgrimages to Jerusalem...and no more special favoritism to the Jews. They'll be treated like everyone else."

"I'm for that," Phil chimed in.

"But that's not all. Here's the turning point! You know how the lack of rain has turned Egypt into a famine area? Well, guess what?"

"What?" Phil anxiously asked.

Bart's face could not conceal his excitement as he shouted, "IT'S POURING CATS AND DOGS in EGYPT! And this man did it. He was there and he made it rain!"

"What's his name?" George questioned.

"The people are starting to call him, **PRINCE OF LIGHT!**"

"He must be an imposter," George cautioned.

"You're wrong, George," Phil replied. "If he were an imposter, he would have been killed instantly by God. These activities have been going on for some time ...now this rain. It's a miracle. THIS MUST BE THE TRUE GOD...this Redeemer King we've been worshipping for the past 1000 years...he is the imposter. Let's clear the network and give full coverage to the PRINCE OF LIGHT. I want him followed every step of the way."

And when the thousand years are expired, Satan shall be loosed out of his prison,

And shall go out to deceive the nations which are in the four quarters of the earth, Gog and Magog, to gather them together to battle: the number of whom is as the sand of the sea.

(Revelation 20:7-8)

"I've already called New York, sir, and suggested that. I knew that's what you would want," Bart replied.

"But," cautioned Phil, "Let me ask that we wait here. I've been told THE PRINCE OF LIGHT will be making a special appearance here...right at Sodom."

"If that's so...have the girls join us. They'll want to see this miracle worker, too."

Bart called Faye, Esther, Terry and Sylvia...filled them in on the background, and told them to drive to Sodom as quickly as possible.

* * *

Abel Epstein was no longer a proud man. He was in Hades... the unseen world...awaiting the Great White Throne Judgment.

How often he had kidded Sylvia when Sylvia tried to tell him about her Christ.

"Sylvia," he would say, "so I'll go to Hell...at least I'll meet all my friends there. We'll be so busy drinking, we won't have any time for regrets."

Yet, never before had Abel felt so helpless and so hopeless. Money had been his servant before. He could have anything he wanted. When he was sick...he summoned the best doctors... when he was restless, he hired an entire plane to fly him to Acapulco. He loved the warmth of light. His apartment was bathed in walls of luminescent light...and he could turn to any imaginable hue at the flip of a switch. "A hue for every mood," he used to boast to Sylvia.

Now, he had no idea where he was. The terror of complete darkness was punishment enough. Dark...dark...midnight dark ...pitch dark...eerie dark...a darkness so black that it conjured countless images of fright in his mind.

Instinctively, he would reach for a switch...hoping that all of this was a dream from which he would soon awake...a cruel dream.

But there was no switch. He found himself grappling helplessly in the air, reaching frantically...for a switch nowhere to be found.

The reality struck him time and time again. There was no switch. There would never be a switch. There was no light. There would never be any light. Just total and complete darkness.

How often he tried to talk and communicate with others. He would open his mouth but nothing seemed to come out. Was their sound coming out? He mouthed the words carefully...enunciating clearly. Then in frenzy...he shouted until his throat became hoarse...and yet no sound...and no reply.

Was Hades so big that the human voice found no reflecting wall to bounce back the sound?

He could not even hear himself. It was like talking in a vacuum.

First NO LIGHT
then NO SOUND

What else could there be?

He REMEMBERED and for a while this consoled him. He remembered *The Wall Street Journal*. It was in June, 1972 when he had first read about the Black Holes in space. Time Tunnels...that's what they called them. There were mysterious signals coming from these deep recesses of space. These signals were picked up by Explorer 42. He recalled that the computers related that the signals came from an object in our galaxy that was many thousands of billions of miles from earth. And what amazed the researchers was that this unknown object seemed to have a diameter *smaller* than that of the earth. Yet the energy it was producing made it 1000 times more powerful than the sun. Bewildered scientists named it Cygnus X-1. Some even believed it to be a time tunnel. [1]

What could this be? Abel searched his mind without any solution. Was this heaven? Would it become the Lake of Fire? He knew enough Bible to know that the Lake of Fire would become his next and final destination.

And death and hell were cast into the lake of fire. This is the second death [the lake of fire]. (Revelation 20:14)

Or was Cygnus X-1 where he was right now...Hades?

Then, suddenly, his thoughts came back to Sylvia. He had taken her for granted. Women were to be used...that was his motto. He had cruelly taunted her about the bevy of beauties he had on a string, while Sylvia quietly went on praying for him. She wasn't perfect, he knew that. She loved money and the things it could buy. But the last few months she had suddenly changed

And if thy hand offend thee, cut it off: it is better for thee to enter into life maimed, than having two hands to go into hell,

[1] The Wall Street Journal, June 16, 1972.

No Light
No Sound
A Memory

...and he loved her...oh, how he loved her. If only he could hold her in his arms...just once...and kiss her and tell her he loved her.

into the fire that never shall be quenched:

Where their worm dieth not, and the fire is not quenched.
(Mark 9:43-44)

The darkness seemed to carry a cloak of dampness that enveloped Abel Epstein. He cried but there were no sobs. The tears that normally would come...just never came. It was a hollow cry.

Suddenly he realized Hades had played a cruel trick on him. For not only now, but throughout eternity he would be plagued constantly with the torment of a MEMORY.

The picture the world had conjured up of the devil with a pitchfork constantly prodding everyone...this would be a relief, he thought to himself.

Facing him was a penalty far more unfathomable...

NO LIGHT
NO SOUND
A MEMORY

* * *

By the time Faye, Esther, Terry and Sylvia reached the area of Sodom they found Phil Sutherland, George and Bart engaged in a very agitated conversation.

Something was wrong, the women could sense that.

Bart briefed the girls on what had transpired. The ladies were visibly shaken by what they heard.

Faye rushed to George...like a child suddenly seeking security from her father.

"Dad, can't you see what is happening? Satan has been loosed. We knew that this would occur at the end of the Millennium. And now that it's here...why aren't we recognizing it for what it is? Daddy, do something...don't let Phil and Bart get involved in this fantasy!"

It was a highly emotional scene. Faye was in tears. Sylvia, Esther and Terry look bewildered...and for the first time... frightened.

"It's not Satan," Bart blared out. "Can't you see we've been living under a rod-of-iron rule long enough. We've had it! Then when God finally comes around...we fail to recognize him as God. How foolish can we be?"

Esther clutched Bart tightly...not knowing what to believe... not willing to let him go. The world was falling apart around her ...and she felt helpless. Bart had changed during the hundreds of years of their marriage. Somehow now he was a more determined man. The judgments in Jerusalem troubled him. Lately he got to kicking the trash cans in the city sneeringly calling them, "Holy trash cans...you're no more holy than the trash I throw in them."

"Bart, honey, my mom and your mom went through so much. They lived in the Tribulation Period. They witnessed the terror and tragedy. Antichrist was far more severe in his judgments when you consider that he was a tyrant without righteousness. But now our Redeemer King has saved us from all of this...our every need has been supplied. There's been no more old age... no more sickness...no more poverty...."

She had said a wrong word...poverty. It struck a cord of responsiveness in Bart.

"Poverty? No more? Did you see the thousands in Egypt when they had no rain? Did you see the helpless babies crying until they could cry no more?...bellies bloated from famine? Well, I did. And who brought them rain...WHO? I'll tell you who...THE PRINCE OF LIGHT himself...HE BROUGHT THEM RAIN! That's what I call compassion. That's what I call love. That's what I call understanding...not a God who sends his edicts through David to administer. What makes David so self-righteous and above sin. Ask him about a cute, little Bath-sheba. Does he still look out the window from his high and mighty home? Every telephone pole in Jerusalem should be plastered with the Bible pages of Second Samuel, chapter 11."

Terry was hysterical. "Bart...that's enough...that's enough. STOP! STOP! I CAN'T STAND IT! I CAN'T TAKE ANY-MORE! What's happening to us?"

Sylvia was also disturbed at Bart's sudden outburst. She thought that she would nip his beliefs in the bud by her question:

"Bart, what makes you so sure THE PRINCE OF LIGHT is God and not an imitation?"

Bart, now haughty and proud, realizing that he was winning his point poured out something he had not wanted to reveal... at least not yet.

"I haven't told Phil Sutherland or Mr. Omega this...because I didn't feel it was time. But now that you've asked...I'll tell you. I myself may not even understand the full import of it yet."

"The other day as I was walking alone in Jerusalem I was suddenly made aware of an unusual light coming in my direction. I looked up. There he was, THE PRINCE OF LIGHT! He was so beautiful. Never before...never, have I seen anyone so beautiful...as though every stitch of cloth on him was a shimmering, sparkling diamond...reflecting a light whose brilliance and beauty...well, it was just beyond description.

"What happened?"

"Well, he placed his hands on my head as though giving me a blessing and then said something I could not understand. He did not call me Bart or my full name, Bartimaeus. He said:

SON OF BARTHOLOMEW
IN THEE
WILL MY NEW KINGDOM RISE

"And in that moment, I knew I was annointed of God...but why, Bartholomew?"

Terry let out a piercing scream...rushed to Bart and fell, clutching his feet, sobbing uncontrollably.

Sylvia's face was ashen. "Bart, you fool. Terry went through a living death for you in the Tribulation Period. When your father, Tom, escaped with George and Faye...Brother Bartholomew promised Terry full pardon for Tom whenever they found him. But on ONE CONDITION. That condition was that Terry become his wife!"

"DO YOU UNDERSTAND THAT, Bart...HIS WIFE! Terry would do anything to save Tom. That's how much she loved him. In Brother Bartholomew's secret chambers she went through the wedding ceremony. Can you imagine the torture your mother was going through? CAN YOU IMAGINE?"

SON OF BARTHOLOMEW...
IN THEE WILL MY NEW KINGDOM RISE

"She never told anyone. I was Terry's closest friend in those days. And the irony of it was that...it was my Abel's ruby laser invention that Brother Bartholomew used to snuff out Tom's life instantly."

"That's why Terry told me alone, and only me, her secret."

Terry, half rising, her face bathed in tears, held up her hand helplessly, "NO, SYLVIA, NO, SYLVIA, please, please...." And then she lapsed into unconsciousness in a tangled heap at Bart's feet.

"It has to be told, Terry. I'm sorry. It's just gone too far. It has to be told."

"What has to be told?" Bart asked angrily because Sylvia was destroying all he hoped to build up by his recent revelation.

"This, Bart," Sylvia replied.

"YOUR NAME IS NOT BART. AND IT IS NOT BARTI-MAEUS EITHER. YOUR NAME IS *BARTHOLOMEW!* That's why Terry called you Bart...for short and let everyone believe it was short for Bartimaeus."

"I don't understand," Esther quivered.

"Let me put it in plain language. BART...is NOT Tom's son. *BART'S FATHER WAS NONE OTHER THAN BROTHER BARTHOLOMEW!"*

There was no more hiding the truth now. BART, who had been born in those first days of the millennium, *after* the great judgments of Israel and of the Gentiles, was the son of the man who had been the ANTICHRIST!

The secret had been revealed...at Sodom!

Chapter 9

POINT OF NO RETURN

George Omega had never seen Phil Sutherland so happy in the almost 1000 years they had worked together.

Phil had cleared the networks of World Television for a special announcement.

In a rather unusual procedure Phil advised the regular news commentator that he himself would make the announcement.

The studio had an air of excitement. The rumor had it that Phil had a special guest who would appear with him.

All but required personnel were kept out of Studio 1. Even George and Bart had to watch the proceedings on a monitor in another room.

Phil began his telecast:

Ladies and Gentlemen:
We stand at a momentous time in history.
Perhaps no greater event can surpass what
will soon occur!

And to prepare you for the last opportunity
for humanity, it gives me great pleasure
to introduce...for the first time anywhere...
on television...our Redeemer
THE PRINCE OF LIGHT!

Looking at the screen in unbelief George could see that some form entered Studio 1, but it was hard to distinguish the characteristics. The light emanating from his body surrounded him in a halo which cast an eerie glow.

He began speaking...

VENGEANCE IS MINE
 I WILL REPAY
YOU HAVE OFTEN READ IN YOUR SCRIPTURES

FOR YET IN A VERY LITTLE WHILE,
HE WHO IS COMING WILL COME.

REMEMBER THE FORMER DAYS,
WHEN AFTER BEING ENLIGHTENED
YOU ENDURED A GREAT CONFLICT OF
*   SUFFERINGS*

HOW MUCH SEVERER PUNISHMENT DO YOU
THINK HE WILL DESERVE WHO HAS TRAMPLED
UNDER FOOT THE SON OF GOD...

IT IS TIME FOR NATIONS TO ESTABLISH THEIR OWN GOVERNMENT AND TO OVERTHROW HE WHO WOULD CALL HIMSELF The Messiah!

THIS MESSIAH HAS GIVEN ISRAEL A SUPERIOR POSITION OF AUTHORITY AND THEOCRATIC RULE FILLED WITH UNJUST ACTION.

HOW LONG WILL GENTILES BE TENDERS OF CATTLE AND SLAVES TO THIS SO-CALLED SUPERIOR RACE?

BEHOLD I HAVE COME TO DO THY WILL!

AND THE VOICE OF MY PEOPLE HAS TOLD ME THE TIME FOR VENGEANCE HAS COME!

WITH ONE HEART AND ONE VOICE LET US MARCH ON JERUSALEM.

AND WHEN THE BATTLE IS WON, WITH JUSTICE FOR ALL, LET US BEGIN A NEW HEAVEN AND A NEW EARTH IN PEACE AND EQUALITY.

As quickly as it began...the TV special was over and Phil Sutherland began giving the background commentary and a call for action.

Bart turned to George: "George, this is the real thing. Did you hear all those Scripture Verses THE PRINCE OF LIGHT quoted from the tenth chapter of Hebrews?"

George looked dismayed. "Bart, just because someone quotes Scripture, that doesn't make him a Believer...let alone the Messiah. Even Satan can quote Bible verses!"

> And Moses and Aaron went in unto Pharaoh, and they did so as the Lord had commanded: and Aaron cast down his rod before Pharaoh, and before servants, and it became a serpent.
>
> Then Pharaoh also called the wise men and the sorcerers: now the magicians of Egypt, they also did in like manner with their enchantments [secret arts].
>
> (Exodus 7:10-11)

But there was no talking to Bart. George had spent hours trying to explain what was happening but Bart seemed gripped by an unknown power.

When Bart arrived home in Jerusalem, he found Esther in tears. Never had he seen her so emotional. As soon as he came in the door Esther got down on her knees, grabbed Bart around the legs and pleaded with him.

"Bart, please turn back before it's too late. Can't you see what you're doing to our marriage? You're turning your back on God in order to accept an imposter...that's all this PRINCE OF LIGHT is...an imposter. Bart, sit down with me and let's read the Scriptures."

Bart had a mind of his own...but one last time, he would go through the motions just to please Esther.

Esther opened her Bible.

"Look, Bart, the PRINCE OF LIGHT is none other than Satan himself. From the moment of his downfall, Satan has set himself in opposition to God. To unfallen man in the garden of Eden, he appeared in the guise of a serpent.[1] He was behind the universal corruption and consequent judgment of Noah's day.[2] He tempted David to number Israel.[3] Then there was the murder of the Hebrew babies in the time of Moses.[4] Some of these actions on the part of Satan were an attempt to blot out the line through which the Redeemer was to come."

Bart looked on unimpressed.

Esther continued: "In the time of wicked Queen Athaliah, an attempt was made to destroy the whole of the royal house. It was only through the intervention of his aunt, Jehoshabeath, and the fidelity of Jehoida, the priest, that the sole survivor, the young King Josiah, was preserved...thus continuing the royal messianic line.[5] And look what happened when the Messiah was born. Satan sought to destroy the children of Bethlehem through Herod.[6]

> And his tail swept away a third of the stars of heaven and threw them to the earth. And the dragon stood before the woman who was about to give birth, so that when she gave birth he might devour her child.   (Revelation 12:4)

"Satan tempted our Lord when He was about to enter His public ministry. In fact, Satan personally took over in this temptation from the pinnacle of the Temple.[7] Then Satan entered into Judas Iscariot, hoping at last to achieve his purpose.[8]

"In fact, in what appeared to be Satan's greatest victory, at Calvary, the Christ of God turned defeat into victory. He undid the works of the devil,[9] annulled his power,[10] and defeated him who had the power of death."

"If all this were true," responded Bart, "then Satan would have no power now. He would be a helpless and defeated weakling. Therefore our PRINCE OF LIGHT is not Satan. He is our Redeemer and God. And this one you call Redeemer King is losing his power. He must be Satan!" Bart spoke firmly in his belief.

"No, Bart, you're wrong. You are twisting the Scriptures. Despite Satan's fall after the Battle of Armageddon he is still the ruler of the air. He's been bound

> ...ye walked according to the course of this world, according to the prince of the power of the air [Satan], the spirit that now worketh in the children of disobedience.   (Ephesians 2:2)

---

[1] Genesis 3:4-7.
[2] Genesis 6.
[3] 1 Chronicles 21:1.
[4] Exodus 1:16.
[5] 2 Chronicles 22:10-12.
[6] Matthew 2:16.
[7] Matthew 4:1-10.
[8] Luke 22:3.
[9] 1 John 3:8.
[10] Hebrews 2:14.

in the bottomless pit these 1000 years by God. Now God has released him for a season."

"How can you believe such nonsense, Esther? Now tell me, why would God bind Satan for 1000 years and then let him go? Why doesn't He let Brother Bartholomew go, and Prophet Arthur, the two you have labelled as the Antichrist and his False Prophet? You've told me they're in the Lake of Fire forever. Yet they were only tools of this person you call Satan. If God were going to let anyone go...He'd let these two go. He certainly wouldn't let the chief criminal on the loose again. Don't you understand, Brother Bartholomew is my father. And I'll do anything to make sure he gets to Heaven. And the PRINCE OF LIGHT promised me this would be his first action after we overtake the government of Jerusalem."

"Don't you understand," Esther pleaded, "the millennium is not the final and perfect state of this world's history. It's the last of a long series of Divine periods during which man in the flesh is being given opportunity to turn from his sin to God. It is also in some ways the severest test of all, because it is a condition of privilege higher than man ever enjoyed before! What I'm trying to say is that this is the final test of fallen humanity under the most ideal circumstances!"

"Esther, I've had enough. There's just too much work to do. You're so religious you just can't see the light when it finally hits you. Your mother and Sylvia have been feeding you a bunch of fairy tales. You..."

The ringing of the phone cut the conversation short.

"It's Phil Sutherland. He wants me to get out to the Plain of Esdraelon on the double. The armies of the world are assembling there for their invasion of Jerusalem. Now look, Esther, get out of this place. Fly to New York with your mother, Sylvia, and my mom. Your dad is already there. I'll meet you there when it's all over. Don't just stand there...move!"

"Bart, what are you doing? Are you out of your mind? You're a pawn in this Prince of Darkness' wicked game. Bart, don't you see I love you. I love you, Bart! I love you! Don't go, Bart. Please don't go. If you go...I may never, never see you again. Oh

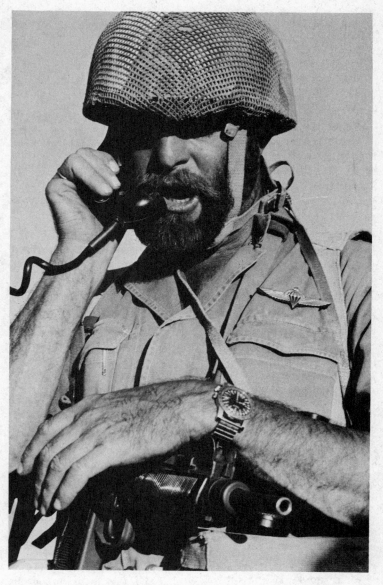

"Armies of the world are assembling there for their invasion of Jerusalem."

...Bart...puleeese...puleeese, darling...Bart. BART! STOP! STOP!...STOP!"

* * *

This was to be the PRINCE OF LIGHT'S triumphant hour. On World Television Network he had issued the call for volunteers to join his Victory Army. Even he was surprised at the response. When asked the count, Phil Sutherland replied, "It's just impossible...why the number appears as great as the sand of the seashore! This is a real success!"

And when the thousand years are expired, Satan shall be loosed out of his prison,

And shall go out to deceive the nations which are in the four quarters of the earth, Gog and Magog, to gather them together to battle: the number of whom is as the sand of the sea.

(Revelation 20:7-8)

Even after living in 1000 years of prosperity, wealth, without sickness and very little death...an abundance of everything... the PRINCE OF LIGHT was still able to accomplish the raising of an army **as numerous as the sand of the sea.**

Bart was inwardly happy when he heard this. Soon victory would be here and his father would be reunited with him. What a reunion! The invasion of Jerusalem would be accomplished in a matter of moments.

* * *

Esther, Faye, Terry and Sylvia were down on their knees praying in Esther's apartment. Their hearts were heavy with sorrow. Esther was heartbroken...her prayer broken by uncontrollable sobs.

Suddenly the whole sky appeared emblazoned in a red fury. It looked like fire was shooting out of the heavens beamed at selective targets on earth. Explosions rocked the foundation of their home.

Then as quickly as it came...it disappeared. And there was silence. Utter and complete silence. It seemed as though the world suddenly stood still.

Faye and Terry knew it was all over. God's judgment had come down on the onrushing army at

And they went up on the breadth of the earth, and compassed the camp of the saints the outskirts of Jerusalem. She knew that all of the rebels had been wiped out by fire from Heaven.

about, and the beloved city [Jerusalem]: and fire came down from God out of heaven, and devoured them.
(Revelation 20:9)

There was no need to tell Esther. Sylvia could see the agony of this truth etched out on her face. Millions of people suddenly consumed by fire. It seemed unbelievable. But she knew it was true.

Esther, put on a light sweater and decided to go out for a walk. She left unnoticed as Faye, Terry and Sylvia were on their knees in prayer.

Esther walked through the Inner City, pausing briefly at Golgotha.

She walked through the Inner City, pausing briefly at Golgotha, then down Jaffa Road, past Ben Yehuda...then outside of the city limits. The warmth of the sun gave her an inner peace. She was walking...walking but not knowing where.

The events of the past whirled through her mind and she began talking, not realizing she was talking outloud. So stunned was she from recent experiences that she failed to realize each question she posed was being answered.

"What will happen to my Bart? Where is he?"

The span of God's patience is ended. He has waited long for sinners to repent and accept His grace.

Bart will appear at the Great White Throne judgment.

AND I SAW A GREAT WHITE THRONE, AND HIM THAT SAT UPON IT. [1]

IT IS A FEARFUL THING TO FALL INTO THE HANDS OF THE LIVING GOD. [2]

"But he seemed good. He didn't mean to do what he did. He was deceived."

THERE IS NONE RIGHTEOUS, NO, NOT ONE. [3]

A MAN IS NOT JUSTIFIED BY THE WORKS OF THE LAW... [4]

ALL MAN'S RIGHTEOUSNESSES ARE AS A POLLUTED GARMENT. [5]

"But can't he change his mind now? Now that he is...now that he is standing before God...can't he change his mind? Now he must realize that the PRINCE OF LIGHT was Satan. I'm sure he does. Now he knows who is God!"

AT THE LAST JUDGMENT IT IS TOO LATE TO START BELIEVING.

THE BOOK OF LIFE WILL BE OPENED.

"And what will happen?"

IF ANYONE'S NAME WAS NOT FOUND WRITTEN IN THE BOOK OF LIFE, HE WAS THROWN INTO THE LAKE OF FIRE. [6]

"No, not my Bart. Not Bart. Please, not Bart!"

---

[1] Revelation 20:11.　　　[2] Hebrews 10:31.　　　[3] Romans 3:10.
[4] Galatians 2:16.　　　[5] Isaiah 64:6.　　　[6] Revelation 20:15.

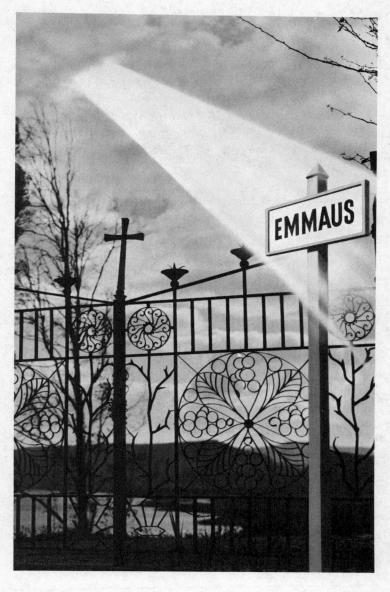

Esther fell to the ground...weeping. And as she looked up...a sign post came into view. She hadn't seen it before. On it... EMMAUS!

"Lake of Fire! What will happen to Bart there?"

IT IS A FIRE WHICH CANNOT BE QUENCHED. [1]
THERE SHALL BE WEEPING AND GNASHING OF TEETH. [2]
THERE IS NO PEACE TO THE WICKED. [3]
THE SMOKE OF THEIR TORMENT GOES UP FOREVER AND EVER; AND THEY HAVE NO REST DAY AND NIGHT. [4]

"I can never stand it...eternal separation from Bart. My whole life in Heaven will be one of eternal regret."

AND HE SHALL WIPE AWAY EVERY TEAR FROM
    THEIR EYES;
AND THERE SHALL NO LONGER BE ANY DEATH;
THERE SHALL NO LONGER BE ANY MOURNING,
    OR CRYING,
    OR PAIN:
THE FIRST THINGS HAVE PASSED AWAY. [5]

Esther must have walked about seven miles from Jerusalem. It suddenly dawned on her that she had been talking...and someone else was providing answers. When she realized this she stopped and there beside a lonely olive tree, instinctively she fell to the ground...weeping...and as she looked up...a sign post came into view. She hadn't seen it before.

On it...EMMAUS!
She ran all the way back to Jerusalem...burst into the room where Faye, Terry and Sylvia were praying.

Startled, the trio looked up, imagining that the heat of the day and the judgment of fire, had disoriented Esther.

---

[1] Mark 9:43, 45, 48.   [2] Matthew 25:46.   [3] Isaiah 57:21.
[4] Revelation 14:11.   [5] Revelation 21:4.

Esther shouted, "This earth will pass away...a New Heaven and a New Earth will appear...a New Jerusalem with no need of sun or moon...nor even a Temple!"

Faye wondered outloud: "If only Bill could be here. Somehow, I believe that he and Tom Malone and Helen, Sue and Tommy, are aware of all these events. Won't it be a grand reunion to be really back together again...no more separation...no more we with natural bodies and

And I saw a new heaven and a new earth: for the first heaven and the first earth were passed away; and there was no more sea...

And I saw no temple therein: for the Lord God Almighty and the Lamb are the temple of it.

And the city had no need of the sun, neither of the moon, to shine in it: for the glory of God did lighten it, and the Lamb is the light thereof.

(Revelation 21:1,22-23)

they with resurrected bodies. Soon all of us will have resurrected bodies!"

There was a tinge of regret in Terry's voice: "Yes, but our family will not be complete...with Bart not...." her voice trailed off.

Sylvia, still picturing Abel with his money belt having been thrown down at the feet of the Redeemer at Kadesh-Barnea understood Terry's regret.

* * *

George, rushing in from a flight from New York, interrupted their conversation.

"OK, everyone, let's hop in the car. You need a change in scenery. Let's take a ride towards Bethel."

When George started the trek...he suddenly realized that the change in scenery would not be a pleasant one.

The impact of the judgment of of fire was seen everywhere. Like the plagues of Egypt the judgment had been selective. Only certain homes were destroyed...with those, who had followed The Prince of Light, dead. Some whom George thought were fol-

And Moses stretched forth his rod toward heaven: and the Lord sent thunder and hail, and the fire ran along upon the ground; and the Lord rained hail upon the land of Egypt...

Only in the land of Goshen, where the children of Israel were, was there no hail.

(Exodus 9:23,26)

lowers of the Redeemer King to the end..some of his closest friends...were objects of judgment from the fire that emerged from Heaven. They, apparently, had been among those as numerous as the sands of the sea who had cast their lot with the false Messiah.

George wanted to turn the car back...but he realized that it was too late. Already the damage had been done. Perhaps, he thought, their actually seeing this disaster of death, might prove a blessing.

Soon it appeared they could go no farther. Groups of men were carting off bodies and traffic jams were building up.

George decided to turn around and go back home. Just then Esther screamed, "There's Bart. There's Phil!"

She jumped out of the car and ran to a pile of bodies. She saw two men lifting bodies tying their hands and feet with a cord.[1] She grabbed the arms of one of the men shouting, "STOP, STOP!! What are you doing? That's my husband. That's Bart! Oh, my poor, poor Bart...what have they done to you?"

She heard a familiar voice and looked up. The two men were Bill Sanders and Tom Malone.

Faye ran over to be with Esther, her daughter. Never had she seen her so distraught. The scene was too much for everyone. The judgment was too terrible for the eye to behold. Phil Sutherland, Bartholomew Malone...lying there dead!

Faye tenderly placed her arm about Esther, and spoke, "Esther, honey, God will make us to understand later concerning that which still troubles us about His judgments. It is impossible for us as living believers fully to understand all of God's dealings. He tells us...

> As the heavens are higher than the earth, so are My ways higher than your ways, and My thoughts than your thoughts."[2]

"I cannot understand God as Creator. His works are infinite. My eyes can scarcely fathom them, much less explain them. Nor do I understand God as Saviour. His love is inconceivable. His mercy toward us surpasses all our imagination. How then, can

---

[1] Matthew 22:13.   [2] Isaiah 55:9.

Esther saw two men lifting bodies. She grabbed the arms of one of the men shouting, "STOP, STOP!! That's my husband!"

I understand Him as Sovereign Judge! But the moment is soon coming, honey, when we shall know even as also we are known.[1] Then, what today seems bewildering in the plan of God will be made perfectly clear to us."

Esther looked up at her mother, somehow understanding. "Mom, 1000 years. I thought it would be a long time...but it was just a moment...a split second of eternity...how can anyone trade a few short years of sin to forfeit an eternity with our Saviour? What a reunion that will be...a reunion that will never end!"

Then Esther took one last look at Bart's lifeless body. No one will ever know the regret that swept through every fiber of her being.

As if to say goodbye, she held Bart's hand. From it dropped a crumpled note.

Dear Esther...my whole heart's
desire is to be forever with you.
Love,
Bart

"Poor, darling Bart," Esther cried..."Oh, Bart, how I wish a million times it could be true. But it can't be true...never, darling, never."

And Esther was right.

For Phil Sutherland...

For Abel Epstein...

For the millions who had made Satan their god throughout the ages...

And for Bartholomew Malone.

They had reached the point of NO RETURN!

---

[1] 1 Corinthians 13:12.

EPILOGUE

The long day of night has ended.

And the eternal day without night has begun.

Satan, after the Millennium, has been cast into the Lake of Fire to join Antichrist and the False Prophet forever (Revelation 20:10).

The unsaved dead, after the Millennium, are then raised from the dead in what commonly is referred to as the "second resurrection" (the first resurrection being when the believers were raised to life eternal with Christ) — (Revelation 20:5-14).

Then — the saddest verse of all:

And whosoever was not found written in the book of life was cast into the lake of fire.

(Revelation 20:15)

All the saints of all the ages are now resurrected believers living in their glorified bodies eternally with Christ.

For living believers, George Omega, Faye Sanders, Terry Malone, Harry Sutherland, Sylvia Epstein and Esther Sanders there is a glorious reunion with Helen Omega, Sue and Tommy Omega, Tom Malone and Bill Sanders (resurrected believers).

For George, Faye, Terry, Sylvia, Harry and Esther now take on a new glorified body as they enter the New Jerusalem.

Together they enjoy forever throughout all of eternity a life with

1. NO NIGHT
There will be night there. Christ will be the light that illumines that City (Revelation 21:25).

2. NO TEARS...NO DEATH

There will be no more tears in Heaven. There will be no more pain in Heaven. There will be no more sorrow, no crying in Heaven. There will be no more death in Heaven!

...God shall wipe away all tears from their eyes; and there shall be no more death, neither sorrow, nor crying, neither shall there by any more pain: FOR THE FORMER THINGS ARE PASSED AWAY. (Revelation 21:4)

3. NO MORE SEPARATION

All the saints of all the ages will be there. No more will friends have to part again. No more will the Malones and the Omegas and Sanders have tearful farewells. No more disagreements. No more misunderstandings with our loved ones! Together they will rejoice in everlasting joy and companionship.

The 1000 years of Millennium were just a pause on the vast panorama of eternity.

And if you could look ahead, into the window of heaven, you would see George and Helen Omega, Bill and Faye Sanders and a host of their friends rejoicing in the eternal joys that will be theirs forever.

And for Esther...whose husband, Bart, will spend an eternity in the Lake of Fire...there is equal joy in the New Heavens and the New Earth...for "...the former things shall not be remembered or come to mind" (Isaiah 65:17).

> The false and empty shadows
> The life of sin, are past —
> God gives me mine inheritance,
> The land of life at last.
> 'Tis finished — all is finished —
> Their fight with death and sin!
> Fling open wide the golden gates,
> And let the victors in.

Chapter 10

THE CHOICE

You have just read *1000*.

Remember, in the introduction to this book, I said that undoubtedly many who read it will consider it an interesting science-fiction story.

IT IS NOT!

This book deals with LIFE and DEATH.

Your life...or your death!

While the book *1000* was written in novel format the facts of the 1000 year MILLENNIUM PERIOD and the judgments ...are true!

You will recall throughout the book are numerous Scripture references directing you to the Bible for specific events and judgments.

Now, you must face up to a CHOICE.

And the main question is this:

WHAT WILL YOU DO WITH JESUS?

Will you state that He never existed?

Will you simply say that He was a good man who did good things...like many other good men?

Will you say His message is not relevant to our enlightened age?

Your decision should not be based on what your friends or

relatives say or do not say...or on your own private concept of heaven or hell. These really, in the final analysis, *do not matter!*

What is important...and what will govern your tomorrow in ETERNITY...is WHAT DOES THE BIBLE SAY? In light of God's standards, set forth in the Bible, your final destiny will be determined.

You can, as many do, simply choose to ignore Christ and the Scriptures...go on living your life, doing the best you know how to meet your problems, work to provide an income for your family, set aside a nest egg for retirement...

But THEN WHAT?

What happens when it comes time for you to depart from this earth?

Then WHAT WILL YOU DO WITH JESUS?

It takes NO DECISION on your part to go to Hell!

It **does** take a DECISION on your part, however, to go to Heaven!

> He that believeth on Him is not condemned:
> but he that believeth not is condemned already,
> because he hath not believed in the name of the
> only begotten Son of God. (John 3:18)

Whether you are Jew or Gentile, here are five basic observations in the Bible of which you should be aware:

1. ALL SINNED

   For all have sinned, and come short of the glory of God. (Romans 3:23)

2. ALL LOVED

   For God so loved the world, that He gave His only begotten Son, that whosoever believeth in Him should not perish, but have everlasting life (John 3:16)

3. ALL RAISED

   Marvel not at this: for the hour is coming, in which all that are in the graves shall hear his voice.

   And shall come forth; they that have done good, unto the resurrection of life; and they that have done evil, unto the resurrection of damnation. (John 5:28,29)

" . . . and another book was opened,
which is the book of life:
and the dead were judged out of those things
which were written in the books.
. . . and whosoever was not found written in the
book of life was cast into the lake of fire."

Revelation 20:12, 15

4. ALL JUDGED

> ...we shall all stand before the judgment seat of Christ.
> (Romans 14:10)

> And I saw the dead, small and great, stand before God;
> and the books were opened...(Revelation 20:12)

5. ALL SHALL BOW

> ...at the name of Jesus every knee should bow... (Philippians 2:10)

Right now, in simple faith, you can have the wonderful assurance of eternal life.

Ask yourself, honestly, the question....

WHAT WILL I DO WITH JESUS?

Will you accept Jesus Christ as your personal Saviour and Lord or will you reject Him?

This you must decide yourself. No one else can decide that for you. The basis of your decision should be made on God's Word—the Bible.

Jesus tells us the following:

> "...him that cometh to me I will in no wise cast out...

> Verily, verily I say unto you, He that believeth on me hath everlasting life"—(John 6:37,47).

He also is a righteous God and a God of indignation to those who reject Him....

> "...he that believeth not is condemned already, because he hath not believed in the name of the only begotten Son of God"—(John 3:18).

> "And whosoever was not found written in the book of life was cast into the lake of fire"—(Revelation 20:15).

YOUR MOST IMPORTANT
DECISION IN LIFE

Because sin entered the world and because God hates sin, God sent His Son Jesus Christ to die on the cross to pay the price for your sins and mine.

If you place your trust in Him, God will freely forgive you of your sins.

> "For by grace are ye saved through faith; and that not of yourselves: it is the gift of God:
>
> Not of works, lest any man should boast"—(Ephesians 2:8,9).
>
> "...He that heareth my word, and believeth on Him that sent me, *hath* everlasting life, and shall not come into condemnation: but is passed from death unto life." (John 5:24)

What about you? Have you accepted Christ as your personal Saviour?

Do you realize that right now you can know the reality of this new life in Christ Jesus. Right now you can dispel the doubt that is in your mind concerning your future. Right now you can ask Christ to come into your heart. And right now you can be assured of eternal life in heaven.

All of your riches here on earth—all of your financial security—all of your material wealth, your houses, your land will crumble into nothingness in a few years.

And as God has told us:

> "As it is appointed unto men once to die, but after this the judgement:
>
> So Christ was once offered to bear the sins of many: and unto them that look for Him shall He appear the second time without sin unto salvation." (Hebrews 9:27,28)

Are you willing to sacrifice an eternity with Christ in Heaven for a few years of questionable material gain that will lead to death and destruction? If you do not accept Christ as your personal Saviour, you have only yourself to blame for the consequences.

Or would you right now, as you are reading these very words of this book, like to know without a shadow of a doubt that you are on the road to Heaven—that death is not the end of life but actually the climactic beginning of the most wonderful existence that will ever be—a life with the Lord Jesus Christ and with your friends, your relatives, and your loved ones who have accepted Christ as their Saviour.

It's not a difficult thing to do. So many religions and so many people have tried to make the simple Gospel message of Christ complex. You cannot work your way into heaven—*heaven is the gift of God to those who have their sins forgiven by trusting in Jesus Christ as the one who bore their sin.*

No matter how great your works—no matter how kind you are—no matter how philanthropic you are—it means nothing in the sight of God, because in the sight of God, your riches are as filthy rags.

"...all our righteousnesses are as filthy rags...."

(Isaiah 64:6)

Christ expects you to come as you are, a sinner, recognizing your need of a Saviour, the Lord Jesus Christ.

Understanding this, why not bow your head right now and give this simple prayer of faith to the Lord.

Say it in your own words. It does not have to be a beautiful oratorical prayer—simply a prayer of humble contrition.

My Personal Decision for CHRIST

"Lord Jesus, I know that I'm a sinner and that I cannot save myself by good works. I believe that you died for me and that you shed your blood for my sins. I believe that you rose again from the dead. And now I am receiving you as my personal Saviour, my Lord, my only hope of salvation. I know that I'm a sinner and deserve to go to Hell. I know that I cannot save myself. Lord, be merciful to me, a sinner, and save me according to the promise of Your Word. I want Christ to come into my heart now to be my Saviour, Lord and Master."

Signed. . . . .

Date. . . . .

If you have signed the above, having just taken Christ as your personal Saviour and Lord...I would like to rejoice with you in your new found faith.

Write to me...Salem Kirban, Kent Road, Huntingdon Valley, Penna. 19006...and I'll send you a little booklet to help you start living your new life in Christ.

JUDGMENT DAYS

REWARD JUDGMENTS FOR BELIEVERS

"and I will dwell in the house of the Lord for ever." (Psalm 23:6)

INCORRUPTIBLE CROWN (Victor's Crown)
". . . every man that striveth for the mastery is temperate in all things . . . they do it to obtain a corruptible crown; we an INCORRUPTIBLE." (I Corinthians 9:25)

CROWN OF REJOICING (Soul Winner's Crown)
". . . what is our hope . . . or crown of rejoicing? Are not even ye in the presence of our Lord Jesus Christ at His coming? For ye are our glory and joy." (I Thessalonians 2:19, 20)

CROWN OF RIGHTEOUSNESS
"Henceforth there is laid up for me a crown of righteousness, which the Lord, the righteous judge, shall give me at that day: and not to me only, but unto all them also that love His appearing." (II Timothy 4:8)

CROWN OF GLORY (Crown for Service)
"Feed the flock of God which is among you . . . (be) examples to the flock . . . And when the chief Shepherd shall appear, ye shall receive a crown of glory that fadeth not away." (I Peter 5:2-4)

CROWN OF LIFE (Martyr's Crown)
". . . the devil shall cast some of you into prison, that ye may be tried . . . be thou faithful unto death, and I will give thee a crown of life." (Revelation 2:10)

"Every man's work shall be made manifest . . . because it shall be revealed by fire . . . if any man's work abide . . . he shall receive a reward . . . if any man's work shall be burned, he shall suffer loss: but he himself shall be saved; yet so as by fire." (I Corinthians 3:13-15)

WOOD
HAY
STUBBLE

GOLD	
SILVER	PRECIOUS STONES

RAPTURE
BELIEVERS meet CHRIST in the air

1000 YEAR MILLENNIUM

JUDGMENT OF UNBELIEVERS

BOOK OF LIFE

THE BOOKS OPENED

"And whosoever was not found written in the book of life was cast into the Lake of Fire." (Rev. 20:15)

". . . the tares are the children of the wicked one: The enemy that sowed them is the devil; the harvest is the end of the world; and the reapers are the angels. As therefore the tares are gathered and burned in the fire; so shall it be in the end of this world." (Matthew 13:38-40)

LAKE OF FIRE

Use this ORDER FORM to order additional copies of

666/1000
by Salem Kirban

You will want to give **666/1000** to your loved ones and friends.

An excellent book to give to those who want to know how their world is changing and how to prepare for their future . . . for the next 10 years . . . and for an eternity!

PRICES

1 copy: $5.95

3 copies: $15 (You save $2.85)
5 copies: $23 (You save $6.75)

ORDER FORM

To:
SALEM KIRBAN, Inc.
Kent Road
Huntingdon Valley, Penna. 19006 U.S.A.

Enclosed find $_____ for _____ copies
of **666/1000** by Salem Kirban

*I will pay UPS for small delivery charge.

Name_____
     Mr./Mrs./Miss   (Please PRINT)

Street_____

City_____

State_____Zip Code_____

*If your local Christian bookstore cannot supply you . . . you may order direct. To insure safe arrival, books will be shipped via United Parcel Service. **(1)** You will pay UPS for small delivery charge. **(2)** For actual cost of books, send check direct to:
SALEM KIRBAN, Inc., 2117 Kent Rd., Huntingdon Valley, Pa. 19006 U.S.A.

SECRET ORGANIZATIONS ACTIVE TODAY
invading even the Church and Sunday School are part of

SATAN'S ANGELS EXPOSED!
by Salem Kirban

$4.95
ILLUSTRATED

AT LAST! SATAN'S STRATEGY REVEALED!

Most people are unaware that Satan's subtle deception has now infiltrated the Christian church. Many imagine Satan as a grotesque individual with horns. But Satan, who before his fall was an angel of light, now cleverly deceives even those who are born again by his "imitation holiness."

SATAN'S ANGELS EXPOSED reveals how Satan is using an army of Judas Iscariots to undermine believers through "Christian" music, through false healers, through powerful religious groups that reach millions with a polluted, watered-down doctrine.

This "Angel of Light" as the Great Imitator is the "prince of this world" and his successes in the Church and in high political places are exposed ... clearly, concisely. Protect your children and those you love. You need to know the facts!

From Baal worship

To Witchcraft

To Satan worship

And Now Even Infiltrating The Unsuspecting Church!

Satan's Symbols Explained

How to recognize doctrines of demons!

SPECIAL SECTION Reveals

How secret organizations, whose threads of terror reach back centuries ago, are carefully weaving their power plot to control the world for Satan. Illustrated chapters reveal the behind-the-scenes manipulation of:
The Illuminati, The Golden Dawn, and **Druid Witchcraft.**

Plus! Exposing the strange rise of political and economic power of:
The Bilderbergers, The Trilateral Commission, and the **Bancor Plan** for a universal money system!

SATAN'S ANGELS EXPOSED!   **$4.95**

If you enjoyed 666/1000, you will want . . .

666
Pictorial Format

by
Salem Kirban

Now! The book *666* has been transformed into a FULL COLOR Pictorial Format. Excellent for young and old alike.

Same size as other books, except each page is in **Pictorial Format**. Last chapter is a Decision Chapter pointing the reader to Christ.

Quantity Prices
Single copy: $2.95
 3 copies: $7.85 *(Save $1)*
 7 copies: 17.50 *(Save $3.15)*
12 copies: 27.50 *(Save $8.50)*
Check must accompany order

*If your local Christian bookstore cannot supply you . . . you may order direct. To insure safe arrival, books will be shipped via United Parcel Service. **(1)** You will pay UPS for small delivery charge. **(2)** For actual cost of books, send check direct to:
SALEM KIRBAN, Inc.
2117 Kent Road
Huntingdon Valley, Penna. 19006
U.S.A.

ORDER FORM

THE RESURRECTIONS

Heaven

Resurrection and Ascension of Christ into Heaven
(Matthew 27:52-53 tells of others who were resurrected after Christ—these were the wave-sheaf of the harvest to come. Leviticus 23:10-11.)

Acts 1:1-11
Matthew 27:50-53

Paradise

Believers who have died before the Rapture. Present in a celestial, spiritual body.*

"And Jesus said unto him, Verily I say unto thee, Today shalt thou be with me in paradise." Luke 23:43

"We are confident, I say, and willing rather to be absent from the body, and to be present with the Lord." 2 Corinthians 5:8

Believers meet with Christ in the air 1 Thessalonians 4:16

"...the dead in Christ shall rise First..."

"Then we which are alive and remain shall be caught up together with them in the clouds to meet the Lord in the air..." 1 Thessalonians 4:16-17

Judgment Seat of Christ

"For we must all appear before the judgment seat of Christ...." 2 Corinthians 5:10
Believers now in New Bodies Philippians 3:20-21

Marriage of the Lamb Revelation 19:7-9

Christ Returns to Earth with His Saints
1 Thessalonians 3:13; Zechariah 14:4

Resurrection of Tribulation Saints
Daniel 12:1-2

Great White Throne

"And whosoever was not found written in the Book of Life was cast into the Lake of Fire." Revelation 20:15

Unbelievers cast into Lake of Fire eternally

Resurrection of the Dead Unbelievers
Revelation 20:11-13; Jude 6

"And I saw the dead, small and great, stand before God; and the books were opened; and another book was opened, which is the book of life; and the dead were judged out of those things which were written in the books, according to their works.
And the sea gave up the dead which were in it; and death and hell delivered up the dead which were in them: and they were judged every man according to their works." Revelation 20:12-13

| About A.D. 30 | This Present Age | A.D.? Rapture | Seven Year Tribulation Period | | 1000 Year Millennial Age | Great White Throne |

About A.D. 30 — This Present Age — A.D.? Rapture — Seven Year Tribulation Period — Mount of Olives Armageddon — 1000 Year Millennial Age — With Satan Antichrist and False Prophet

*Physical body remains in grave awaiting Rapture

A NEW STANDARD
of EXCELLENCE!

NOW! AT LAST! A BIBLE WITH 2000 PAGES OF HELPS TO MEET EVERY NEED IN YOUR LIFE!

Salem Kirban's
REFERENCE BIBLE
KING JAMES VERSION

Now, the world's best **seller** will become the best **read** in your home! Salem Kirban has taken the beloved King James Version and added 2000 pages of crystal-clear Commentary. Here are 10 reasons why many acclaim that this Bible is the first really new Bible since the 1909 Scofield. Over 500 photos and charts **Full Color.** Only 1¾" thick. Handy to carry to church!

10 EXCLUSIVE Features NO OTHER BIBLE HAS!

1. Commentary on Every Page
Unlocks Guidelines for Living

Salem Kirban
In his clear, descriptive style, Salem Kirban's Commentary Notes appear on **over** 1000 of the Bible text pages. He is the author of over 35 books!

Gary G. Cohen
Dr. Cohen clearly explains the 100 most difficult Bible passages. Dr. Cohen is Executive Vice President of Clearwater Christian College.

Charles Haddon Spurgeon
The most famous preacher of the 19th century. His devotional Commentary *(written during his greatest trials)* are on over 300 pages.

2. Promise Verses In Margin
When you need faith and courage . . . often the Promise Verses in the Bible are hard to find because these gems lie buried in the text. We have highlighted these Promise Verses in yellow (in the text) and **also** repeated the same verse in the MARGIN of the same page. Now, by leafing through your Bible, you can each day

Sample Page — Actual Page Size: 6" x 9"

select a Promise To Live By! See sample page in this column.

3. Time Period Symbols
The Bible is confusing to many because they do not realize that the text refers to 3 basic Time Periods (past, present and future). Within these 3 Time Periods are at least 15 **further** Time Divisions. In the margin of each page of The Salem Kirban REFERENCE BIBLE, the Time Symbol Picture helps you identify the correct Time Period . . . making God's promises so much richer to you and to your loved ones.

Scattering of Israel

Current World

Continual Promise

Rapture

Armageddon

Judgment Seat of Christ

Marriage of the Lamb

Judgment of Nation Israel

4. Rare, Old Bible Etchings

Unusual etchings of Bible scenes designed by craftsmen over 100 years ago. Enjoy the same etchings your great grandparents found joy and comfort in!

5. Full Color Holy Land Photographs

Vivid photographs taken by Salem Kirban reveal the beauty of the Promised Land as it is **right now** . . . today!

6. Full Color Charts on Future Events

Over 50 Charts including the 21 Tribulation Judgments, Three Coming Decisive Wars, The Three Heavens, The Resurrections. A few are picture below in reduced size.

Time Period Views of The Prophets
The prophets had a twofold ministry. They exposed the sins of their own time. They also revealed the future (as God revealed it to them).

When reading the Books written by the 16 prophets (Isaiah through Malachi) this Chart will help you understand the scope of time periods referred to by the prophet.

© Copyright 1979 by Salem Kirban

© Copyright 1979 by Salem Kirban

© Copyright 1979 by Salem Kirban

7. 380 Page Commentary on The Book of REVELATION

The last book in the Bible, **Revelation,** deals with future events and is the most difficult book for many to understand. We have Visualized the book by **1** placing only 2 verses on each page **2** writing a clear Commentary **3** including an explanatory illustration **4** tying the verses in to current events and **5** by a red arrow, pointing to the proper Time Period!

8. Major Doctrines Explained

There are at least 28 major Doctrines in the Bible. These DOCTRINES are explained in Commentary units marked with this Symbol placed next to identifying verse!

9. Major Attributes Explained

There are 17 Attributes *(or characteristics)* that identify God! Each ATTRIBUTE is explained in Commentary units marked with this Symbol placed next to identifying verse!

10. Extra NEW TESTAMENT Commentary

As an added bonus, you will discover **100 added pages** of special New Testament Commentary. All in FULL COLOR. Includes many Charts, Maps and Graphs!

SALEM KIRBAN BOOKS

Salem Kirban is both a news analyst and a recognized authority on Bible prophecy. This unusual combination enables him to foresee trends in economic patterns, in lifestyle, in world power struggles, and in impending disasters! Salem Kirban is the author of over 35 best-selling books!

CHARTS ON REVELATION
by Salem Kirban $4.95

An excellent teaching aid when studying Bible prophecy. Newly designed crystal clear charts make future events easier to understand. Full color charts on the Rapture, Tribulation Period, Millennium and New Heavens and New Earth! **Includes** God's Promises to Arab and Jew!

COUNTDOWN TO RAPTURE
by Salem Kirban $4.95

How close are we to the midnight hour? Where will it all end? Are we headed for complete chaos? Salem Kirban covers **11** critical areas of change. He also projects a Time Clock showing how close we are in the final Countdown To Rapture. Filled with photos and charts!

GUIDE TO SURVIVAL
by Salem Kirban $4.95

This is Salem Kirban's first book. It sells as well today as when first published in 1968. This new edition has been completely updated and revised. **Almost 300 pages.** This book tells how the world will END. Over 50 photos and Bible prophecy CHARTS!

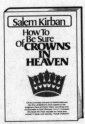

HOW TO BE SURE
OF CROWNS IN HEAVEN
by Salem Kirban $4.95

Believers must appear before the Judgment Seat of Christ (2 Corinthians 5:10). Here their entire life will be reviewed before God (Romans 14:12). This exciting new book by Salem Kirban shows how you can be **sure** of receiving Crowns in Heaven. Must reading!

HOW TO LIVE ABOVE AND BEYOND YOUR CIRCUMSTANCES
by Salem Kirban $4.95

At last! Here are practical answers to perplexing problems that face Christians everyday. Answers to almost 50 questions that face young people, those who are married and those in the Golden Years of life. Full color! Over 100 photos!

LEBANON . . . A HARVEST OF LOVE
by Layyah A. Barakat
Photo Commentary by Salem Kirban $3.95

This unforgettable true story of how a barefoot girl from Lebanon overcame insurmountable odds to reach her people for Christ. A classic missionary story of trials, testings and final triumph! Full color photographs!

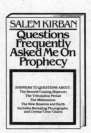

QUESTIONS FREQUENTLY ASKED ME ON PROPHECY
by Salem Kirban $4.95

This new updated version of a popular best-seller will answer those difficult questions many people sidestep. Answers clearly given to questions on Bible prophecy. Includes revealing photographs and crystal clear charts. **Plus added features!**

REVELATION VISUALIZED
by Gary G. Cohen
and Salem Kirban $12.75

Enlarged and updated. Excellent for teaching or studying Revelation. Only two verses to a page. Balance of page is explanatory commentary plus charts and photographs. Full Color! **Each verse has Red Arrow pointing to specific Time Period!**

THE RISE OF ANTICHRIST
by Salem Kirban $4.95

While the church sleeps . . . the advance forces of Antichrist have already arrived! Over 20 chapters include: *The Day They Reshape Man, The Plan To Control the Human Mind, The Day They Transplant Memories* . . . plus much more. Filled with PHOTOS!

SALEM KIRBAN, Inc., Kent Rd., Huntingdon Valley, Pa. **19006**

SALEM KIRBAN HEALTH BOOKS

Salem Kirban has spoken on Bible Prophecy in over 300 churches. Many times people, who were obviously ill, came to him asking for prayer. It was then Salem realized that he should write a few books on the Biblical approach to sound nutritional health!

HOW JUICES RESTORE HEALTH NATURALLY
by Salem Kirban $4.95

Salem Kirban reveals how he found the Fountain of Youth **at age 50!** He tells his own experiences of how juices eliminated fatigue . . . gave him new vitality . . . a new lease on life. **Fourteen** different juice combinations illustrated in **FULL COLOR!**

HOW TO EAT YOUR WAY BACK TO VIBRANT HEALTH
by Salem Kirban $3.95

Includes **147** different health restoring meals plus a special **3-Day Turn Around Diet!** Answers given to many questions people often ask about what foods to eat, how to have Reserve Energy, how to turn your marriage into a honeymoon!

HOW TO KEEP HEALTHY AND HAPPY BY FASTING
by Salem Kirban $2.95

A best-selling book on Fasting that approaches the subject Biblically! Discover the secret of how fasting relieves tension, helps you sleep better, restores your energy level eliminating fatigue. Plus much more! Filled with photographs!

THE GETTING BACK TO NATURE DIET
by Salem Kirban $3.95

Salem Kirban's best and most complete book on Health. Revealed at last! Nature's Secrets for keeping you well! **Only found in this book** . . . the most comprehensive Food Charts showing both **HIGH Stress** and **Low Stress** foods. Excellent!

SALEM KIRBAN, Inc., Kent Rd., Huntingdon Valley, Pa. 19006

ORDER FORM   SALEM KIRBAN Books

Quantity	Description	Price	Total
_____	Charts On Revelation	$ 4.95	_____
_____	Countdown To Rapture	4.95	_____
_____	Guide To Survival	4.95	_____
_____	How To Be Sure Of Crowns In Heaven	4.95	_____
_____	How To Live Above Your Circumstances	4.95	_____
_____	Lebanon . . . A Harvest Of Love	3.95	_____
_____	Questions Frequently Asked Me On Prophecy	4.95	_____
_____	Revelation Visualized (September, 1980)	12.75	_____
_____	Satan's Angels Exposed	4.95	_____
_____	Satan's Mark Exposed	4.95	_____
_____	Satan's Music Exposed	4.95	_____
_____	666/1000	5.95	_____
_____	666 PICTORIAL FORMAT	2.95	_____
_____	The Rise Of Antichrist	4.95	_____
_____	Armstrong's Church Of God (Plain Truth)	4.95	_____
_____	Jehovah's Witnesses	4.95	_____
_____	Mormonism	4.95	_____
_____	Christian Science	4.95	_____
_____	How Juices Restore Health Naturally	4.95	_____
_____	How To Eat Your Way To Vibrant Health	3.95	_____
_____	How To Keep Healthy By Fasting	2.95	_____
_____	The Getting Back To Nature Diet	3.95	_____
_____	The Salem Kirban REFERENCE BIBLE	47.77	_____

Total for Books _____

Shipping & Handling _____

Total Enclosed $ _____

(We do NOT invoice. Check must accompany order, please.)

☐ Check enclosed.
☐ Master Charge
☐ VISA

When using Credit Card, show number in space below.

When Using Master Charge
Also Give Interbank
No. (Just above your
name on card)

| Card Ex-pires | Month | Year |

POSTAGE & HANDLING Use this easy chart to figure postage, shipping and handling charges. Send correct amount and avoid delay.

TOTAL FOR BOOKS	Up to 5.00	5.01-10.00	10.01-20.00	20.01-35.00	Over 35.00
DELIVERY CHARGE	1.50	2.00	2.50	2.95	NO CHARGE

FOR ADDITIONAL SAVINGS: Orders Over $35.00 Are Now Postage-Free!

SHIP TO_____

Mr./Mrs./Miss   (Please PRINT)

Address_____

City_____State_____ZIP_____

SALEM KIRBAN, Inc., Kent Road, Huntingdon Valley, Pa. 19006